PERCEPTION

The EVE Series
Book Three

A. L. Waddington

Cover Design by Greg Simanson
Edited by Carol Farabee

This is a work of fiction. Names, characters, places, brands, media, and incidents are either the product of the author's imagination or are used fictitiously. Any resemblance to similarly named places or to persons living or deceased is unintentional.

PRINT ISBN 978-1-948143-08-0
EPUB ISBN 978-1-948143-09-7

Library of Congress Control Number: 2018956558

ACKNOWLEDGMENTS

I would like to thank my amazingly talented team at Scarlett Publishing who, without them, none of this would be possible. Also, my phenomenal editor Carol Farabee, who makes my words dance and makes sure the little things don't fall through the cracks. And mostly, my husband, Eric, who keeps us in line, holds my hand when necessary, and smacks me back to reality when I get a little lost in my writing. I love you all for all you do!

Also, I would like to thank Joslyn, the human encyclopedia of useless information, for knowing just how I love my coffee and serving it up to me in an IV drip. Plus, Keifer for adding the squirrelly antics to Ethan and his friends. And Alyssa, for standing beside me, believing in my series and giving Elizabeth her kind nature. And for Heather and her late-night runs for coffee and gummy bears. I cannot thank you all enough for all your love, support, and belief in my EVE series. You brought my characters to life and gave them their unique personalities. Thank you for allowing me to live my dream!

For Heather Wade - Unrue: I cannot imagine ever having a better friend. You are an amazing person who always has a kind word, a lending hand and a belief in the goodness of all. I love you!

It seems like forever
Since you've been gone
But I will hold my head up
And I will not cry
Cause God must have meant
Us to say good-bye
Even though it tears me up inside
You know I'm still all right to smile
It does make me wonder
If you ever meant those words
You said to me
Sometimes I hate you
When I think about what you did to me
Then I remember your voice,
Your smile, your shy laugh
And pain overwhelms me again
You have taught me never
To trust or believe in something
That I cannot see or touch
Because to me
Our love was a reality
To you
It was just a passing fling
And now…
It's just a fading memory

--A. L. Waddington

Chapter One

Thursday, November 26, 2009, Thanksgiving Day

THE SUN WAS FIGHTING to break free of the clouds that insisted upon hanging around when I opened my eyes and jumped out of bed. I rushed over to the bay window and threw the curtains aside. Fear and doubt ripped at my heart the moment my eyes rested on Jackson's house across the street. It appeared as dark and empty as it had for the last several days.

I slumped into the cushions feeling confused and lonely. I was sure he would have come back. I knew we had worked things out in our *other* life. I closed my eyes and rested my head against the cold glass. I could still feel the warmth of his arms around me as we stood in my father's study *there*. The soft warm caress of his lips upon mine . . . *How can he not be here? I was so sure that he'd be waiting for me when I awoke. Perhaps he had decided that he only wanted me there? Maybe he thought I was too much trouble to deal with here because most of my family's reaction to us?*

"It's about time you got up, sleepy head," my sister Sidney said as she came bouncing into my room.

"What?" I hadn't realized she had returned home from Northwestern. "Oh, hey, Sid. When did you get home?"

"Late last night. How ya doin'?" She plopped down on the other side of the window seat.

"Good. How's school?" I didn't know what to say to her. We have never been like sisters.

"Same ol', same ol'," She shrugged. "Classes, exams, papers, cheerleading."

"Sounds fun." I turned back to gazing out the window at the empty house across the way.

"Dad said you were having a rough time of it lately," she said softly. "I'm sorry you and Jackson broke up. He seemed like a nice guy."

"He is."

"You know, Jocelyn, it's probably just as well 'cause there are tons of guys at college and I'm telling ya, you don't want to be married and tied down before you even have the chance to live."

She tried to smile but didn't pull it off so well.

"Sid, it's not over yet. We just had an argument. I'm sure we'll work it out." I wanted my voice to sound confident even though I was no longer feeling it myself.

"Why would you want to get married at eighteen?" She wrinkled up her forehead at me.

"You wouldn't understand."

"Guess you're right about that. I still have two years left of my undergrad work, let alone med-school. I can't imagine being stuck with a husband." She laughed. "Hell, I'm having trouble just juggling a boyfriend."

"You're getting serious with someone?" The mere thought was intriguing. Sidney always had boyfriends, but never anyone whom she would keep longer than she deemed necessary.

"Yeah," she grinned, her smile growing wide. "He's downstairs. I brought him home for the weekend to meet the family."

"You're brave."

"Yeah, but he's special." A look I'd never seen passed briefly over her eyes and then was gone.

"How so?" I asked curious as to what she deemed special.

"He's sweet, considerate, kind." She blushed. "He understands me, my goals and supports them rather than trying to deter me from my studies. Of course, he wants to be a doctor too, so we have a lot of the same classes. Which is nice because then we get to study together."

"Does he have a name?" I laughed at her giddiness.

"Oh yeah, his name is . . ." She wrinkled her nose. "Don't laugh; it's Landon Atticus Harrison."

"What?" I busted out laughing despite myself.

"I know!" she laughed and doubled over, burying her face in her lap for a moment. "It's awful, isn't it! I know . . ."

"Does his mother not like him?"

"I don't think she did." Sidney squirmed around. "I mean, his brother has a perfectly normal boring name—David William." She threw her arms up in despair. "Then she comes up with Landon Atticus!"

"Talk about child abuse."

"Really . . . well, she's an English teacher." She shrugged again.

"Sounds to me like she's read too many classics. Isn't Atticus the name of the father in *To Kill a Mockingbird*?"

"He told me that's where she got it from. Apparently, it's her favorite book. Thankfully, he's cute. Otherwise the poor man would never have stood a chance in this world." She stood up and walked back over to the door. "Anyway, get yourself cleaned up and come downstairs. I'm dying for you to meet him."

"All right." I got up myself. "I'll be down in a sec."

She disappeared behind the closed door and the room went silent. I turned back around for one final look out the window. Nothing had changed. I was glad Sidney was home. It had felt so good to laugh again, and I hoped that her presence would ease the tension that hung over the house. I even hoped that with her being here it might open the door between my mother and me. I gathered up my clothes and headed into the shower.

My brother, Ethan, and my father, Shane, were already watching the Macy's Thanksgiving Day parade with Sidney and Landon when I came downstairs. The two of them were cuddled together looking very sweet. I could tell even though he was seated that Landon was over six feet tall. He had broad shoulders, dirty blond hair, pale green eyes, and was clean-shaven. The two of them sitting there looked like the classic copy of Ken and Barbie.

After brief introductions, I curled up on the corner of the couch with my morning coffee. Everyone was lounging around in pajamas and stocking feet, barely conscious. It was only nine o'clock in the morning. I couldn't believe that my family was up this early on a holiday.

Landon and Sidney wandered back into the kitchen to refill their coffee when I heard her burst out laughing and return stumbling into the family room, "Hey Dad, you'll love this. Landon just asked how come the turkey isn't in the oven."

The three of us joined her laughter while Landon stood there looking foolish. "I'm sorry, Landon. We're honestly not laughing at you. It's just, well, my wife doesn't cook. Our Thanksgiving dinner is prepared by Kroger's. I'll pick it up about two."

"Oh," Landon stuttered.

"I told you my mom can't cook. It's better to let someone else prepare it. That way none of us gets food poisoning." Sidney returned to her spot on the opposite end of the couch and Landon slowly joined her.

"Where is Mom?" I looked over at my father.

"Asleep," he grinned. "You probably won't see her until noon. She didn't get home from the hospital until almost three this morning."

Ethan grumbled something I didn't quite hear before stuffing his face with another donut. He looked over at me and grinned. I gave him a questioning look, but he just shook his head and mouthed "later" at me. I shrugged and turned back towards the television. It was going to be a long day.

Looking around at my huddled family relaxing over our version of a holiday breakfast—a box of mixed Dunkin Donuts and coffee, the drastic differences between my two families slapped me in the face. Never once in my memory of anything *there*, had my family been so utterly informal. Lounging around dressed sloppily on a holiday and eating in front of the television was something I couldn't even fathom.

A holiday *there* consisted of dressing up, extended family, home cooked dishes and desserts, and all centered round a big dining room table. *Here*, I knew we'd be pulling out the TV trays and munching all day while watching football.

By noon I was bored to tears. No one had really moved in hours and the only thing that had changed was the channel on the television. I wished Jenna was home, but I knew she had gone with her parents to her grandparents' house in Indianapolis. She wouldn't be home until Sunday evening at the earliest. Plus, both Caitlyn and Hilary were busy with their own family's versions of Thanksgiving. I pulled the blanket off the back of the couch and wrapped it tightly around myself before drifting off into a lazy nap.

A commotion awoke me about half past one. I heard Ethan arguing with someone in the foyer to the point that Dad got up to investigate. Sidney and I looked at each other while I tried to make some sense of what was going on.

"Please, will you just tell her I am here?" I suddenly recognized Jackson's voice.

"Don't you think you've done enough? Leave her alone!" Ethan shouted.

I leapt to my feet and ran towards the front door as I heard my dad respond. "Ethan, that is not for you to decide. Don't be rude. I'm sorry, Jackson."

"Jackson!" I squealed and practically jumped into his arms. I wrapped my arms around his neck and kissed him repeatedly about his face. He laughed while both my brother and father stood there stunned and confused.

"Well, um . . . we'll leave you two alone. Come on, Ethan," Dad uttered and dragged my brother back into the family room.

"I see events are becoming clearer," Jackson laughed. "I was worried I might have to try and explain everything to you."

"Not necessary." I stood with my arms still draped over his shoulders. "I'm so glad you're here. What about your family?"

"They came with me," he smiled. "All of them."

"Alex and Phoebe?" He nodded. "Really?" I couldn't believe it. "They probably think we're insane," I laughed.

"No, just in a relationship," he chuckled. "Misunderstandings are bound to happen occasionally."

"So, they don't hate me?" I grimaced.

"Of course not." He leaned over and kissed me with hunger and desire.

"I'm sorry if I ruined everyone's Thanksgiving."

"Do not worry about it. Mother, Phoebe and my brother's wife, Leslie, are over there cooking up a storm. You didn't ruin anything. Dad just discovered a new roaster that can cook a turkey in a third of the time, so this gave him the excuse he needed to try it out."

"Well then, I'm glad everything worked out," I laughed.

"My parents wanted to invite your family over for a formal Thanksgiving dinner." Jackson kept his arms loosely around my waist. "A peace offering if you will."

"You're kidding?"

"No. Why?" He looked hurt.

"Because my family, with the exception of possibly my dad, probably isn't going to be too thrilled about us getting back together," I stated softly, raising my eyebrows at him.

"This could smooth some of that over." His optimism amazed me. Unfortunately, it also told me volumes about how little he really did know about my family *here*.

"I don't think it's a good idea," I said with hesitation.

"Will you please ask them . . . for me?" *How can I say no to that?*

"All right, but you have to come with me." I knew this was not going to be good. Jackson smiled and nodded. We walked hand in hand back into the family room.

Dad was back in his recliner, Ethan in the other, and even Landon had gotten into the game. The three of them looked comical screaming like idiots at the television.

Jackson and I stood silently off to the side waiting for a commercial break. I knew better than to interrupt a football game. I wasn't sure about Landon, but I knew my dad and Ethan would be none too pleased.

"Hey, Dad, can I talk to you for a sec?" I asked at the next commercial break.

"Sure, go ahead." He barely turned his head in our direction.

"No, um . . . in the kitchen." I wanted to get him alone.

My dad fully turned and noticed the two of us standing there. "Oh, okay." He got up and followed us.

The kitchen was vacant and silent, probably unlike almost all kitchens on this day. There were no steaming pots on the stove, turkey in the oven, or pies cooling on the counter. Only an empty box of donuts and coffee creamer adorned our counters. I could see the strange look on Jackson's face when he realized our lack of festivities.

"How you been, Jackson?"

"Good, sir, good. And you?"

"I'm doing all right. What can I do for you both?"

"My family is cooking up an enormous Thanksgiving feast and would really like it if you and your family would consider joining us."

My dad shifted his weight uncomfortably, considering the full ramifications of saying yes. I knew he would truly love a home cooked family Thanksgiving dinner like the ones his family had had before he married my mother.

"Please thank your family for the very considerate invitation. I would absolutely love to. However, I have some concerns about how both my son and my wife would react to the offer, and I am very concerned about how they would behave if they came," he rambled nervously.

Jackson smiled considerately. "I wunderstand. I know that there are still some ill feelings about the future of our relationship." He glanced in my direction and slipped his arm around my waist.

"Yet, my family and I were hoping that this would be a good opportunity for us all to get together, sit down and calmly discuss and finally put to rest any apprehensions."

"If it were only that easy," Dad chuckled. "As educated as my wife is, I am afraid that she forgot to take the course on interpersonal communications. She doesn't exactly handle confrontations with style and grace." Despite myself, I snickered at his words. "Please tell your parents I appreciate their invitation and apologize because I must decline. However, Jocelyn can go as long as she promises to bring me some leftovers and a piece of homemade pumpkin pie."

"Of course."

"Thanks, Daddy." I hugged him briefly before turning towards Jackson. "I need to get ready. You want to hang out here and wait?"

Jackson glanced over at the archway leading into the living room where Ethan was still watching the game and grinned slightly. "How about I return in an hour to escort you to dinner?"

"Okay." I leaned up and kissed him quickly on the cheek.

*   *   *

I stood in front on my closet, staring stupidly at my wardrobe.

"He's much better looking than I remembered from your birthday." Sidney's voice came from my doorway before she entered my room. She closed my door and sat down on the corner of my bed. She picked up one of my throw pillows and fumbled with it thoughtlessly. "I can see why you are so taken with him."

All I could do was smile over in her direction. My stomach was in knots and I was so nervous about seeing Jackson's extended family for the first time *here*. It was so bizarre for me to even consider how they appeared on this plane. My only images were those from *there* and thinking of them in modern attire was unimaginable to me.

"You do realize that marriage is not just a ring around your finger, Jocelyn. It's more like a noose around your neck."

I turned and gave her a dirty look.

"That's a pleasant way of looking at marriage."

"Seriously, look at our parents. You can't tell me they're happy?" The tone of her voice dropped.

"No, they're not. I know that. I live here," I admitted and joined her on my bed. "I think they've drifted apart over the years."

"Drifted apart?" she snorted. "That's a mild understatement. They have nothing in common. They don't spend any time together." Her matter-of-fact admission hit home hard.

"I know people grow and change over the years, but you have to grow and change together. You also must have some things in common that you can discuss and share. But, I believe it is essential that each have their own personal hobby or activity. Something that allows you to escape . . . relax and gives you peace after a long stressful day." She gave me a weird look. "You know what I mean, something simple like reading a book or writing in a journal or whatever. Something that is just for you."

"I suppose. I know Mom and Dad still golf together," she shrugged. "But I don't think that they like each other very much. It's more like they're together out of habit than love."

"I'd like to believe they still love each other."

"Maybe." She shrugged again. "Who knows anymore?" Sidney shook her head as if clearing her thoughts. "So, what are you going to wear?"

Dread settled back over me once more. "I don't know. What do you think?"

"For meeting his siblings for the first time? I'd go with something casual but classy."

"Such as?" My limited wardrobe contained no such items. I had very few reasons for dressing up and therefore, almost all my clothes were school casual.

"Hang on." She sprang from my bed and headed for the door. "I've got the perfect outfit." I chuckled to myself as I listened to her footsteps banging on the stairs leading to her third-floor bedroom.

Sidney's room was enormous, not only in size but in pure uniqueness. One corner was a curved column, there were wooden ceiling beams, and everything in the room screamed Sidney. My dad had remodeled the space that had once been Mimi and Eddie's quarters into a modern playground of sorts for her when we were young. I was always so jealous of her room, not only because of its sheer size, but because she had her own private luxury bathroom and walk-in closet.

Sidney bounced back into the room and handed the outfit to me. I glanced over the articles and wrinkled my forehead. We have always had such drastically different styles, and this was all her. "Will you trust me for once?" she laughed.

"All right, but if Jackson doesn't recognize me, it'll be your fault," I stated with skepticism.

I slipped off my robe and climbed into her tan slacks with dark brown pin stripes, a sheer cream colored loose flowing blouse with oversized ruffles along the cuffs and some that elongated down the front and around the neck, and a darker brown oversized sweater jacket with cream and blue specks embedded in it. I stood in front of the mirror staring at a reflection I didn't recognize.

"Stop kidding around, Jocelyn," she laughed. "I swear, your fashion sense is nonexistent." She walked up behind me and pulled the neck ruffle out from under the jacket and untied the knot of the sweater I'd tied in front of me. She spun me around and tied it around my back, hanging loosely so that I couldn't even tell it was tied.

"Sorry," I giggled and had to admit her small touches made a world of difference.

"Isn't this sweet . . . my two daughters playing dress-up. You two didn't even do this when you were young." Our mother, Amy, stood in my doorway watching us, but no smile crossed her lips. "Where are you planning on going, Jocelyn?" Immediately, my palms began to sweat.

"I was invited over to the Chandler's for Thanksgiving dinner," I replied in a low voice.

"I thought you were done with all that nonsense," she scowled.

"Mom . . . please, we were all invited. Dad just didn't think you'd want to go."

"And he's right. Why would I want to ruin my holiday with people who couldn't care less about my daughter's education and her future?" she said with a hateful tone.

"That's not true. If you'd listen to us for once . . ." I tried to explain, but she cut me off.

"Listen to you? I have listened to you." She walked slowly towards us in an almost menacing fashion that took me by surprise. "I have heard all about this wedding nonsense, this crap about being in love and meant to be together and happily ever after," she scoffed. "Let me tell you something my darling daughter, there is no such thing as happily ever after and when this little charade blows up in your face and you're left on your own to take care of yourself and your children, you'd better hope you can support all of you on your own before you and your kids end up as another welfare statistic."

Her words burned into my deepest fears. Even Sidney looked shock at our mother's words.

"Mom, Jackson would never . . ."

"You are so naïve. Do you have any idea how many single moms I see every day, bringing their children in for check-ups or whatever, who dropped out of school and can't get the poor bastard to pay child support? They all get stuck in meaningless dead-end jobs and living off the system. I hate to see you become one of them." She shook her head slightly before turning to leave the room.

"I won't. We'll prove you wrong," I taunted. "I'll finish my graduate degree, you wait and see. Jackson and I can do this with or without your support."

My mother paused at my door with her hand on the doorknob and her back still towards us. In a low voice, I distinctly heard her say, "No . . . you won't. You're not special enough."

Tears welled up in my eyes before I could even get angry. Mom closed the door behind her and within seconds, her own bedroom door slammed shut.

I sat down at my vanity and blotted my eyes. "Don't let her get to you." Sidney came over and placed her hands on my shoulders. "You don't want to go over to Jackson's all red eyed." She leaned in a little closer. "Besides, Jocelyn, you are the most stubborn person I have ever met in my entire life. I know that once you put your mind to it, you can accomplish anything if for no other reason than to prove everyone wrong. If you say you can do this, I know you can."

"Thanks, Sid," I squeaked.

She smiled brightly. "Now, let's get your hair and make-up done. Jackson will be here soon."

*   *   *

Jackson arrived on time and we left without incident. We walked slowly across the yards. I wanted to be in good spirits, but my mother's words kept ringing in my ears. I couldn't believe how cruel she could be when she put her mind to it. She had never spoken to me before with such malice and contempt. I hated to think that our relationship was beyond repair, but I was beginning to believe it was riding that line.

The chilly wind whipped around us, causing Jackson to place his arm protectively around me. He smiled over at me in such a way that it renewed my faith in our love for one another. At least I could take some comfort in knowing that there were still some individuals in this world . . . and my *other*, who believed I was special.

*   *   *

I snuggled down beneath my comforter with glorious thoughts running amuck in my brain. Phoebe and Alex were all that I remembered and more. It was odd in a strange sense to meet their *other* spouses *here* when in my memories of them they were married to Silas and Veronica.

Here they were married to Carson and Leslie—very sweet, funny, and thoughtful individuals but strangely, nothing like their counterparts. I spent a large portion of the afternoon and evening attempting to wrap my brain around their bizarre situations. It was just plain weird.

I spent the next several hours tossing and turning trying to understand how they managed their dual lives and dual relationships. I couldn't imagine being consciously aware of both planes and being married and intimate with two separate people who were so drastically different from one another.

I realized again just how truly lucky I was to have Jackson . . . someone whom I could travel through both my lives with, love, laugh with and stand beside me through both the good and the bad times. As rare as our gift supposedly was, it truly was a miracle that we managed to find each other in this crazy world.

The acknowledgement of that finally gave my mind the peace and solace I'd been searching for since I'd crawled into bed. I smiled softly to myself and drifted off into a dreamless sleep.

CHAPTER TWO

Saturday, November 30, 1878

WALKING AROUND in a daze would be an understatement based on how I was feeling. Things were full speed ahead once again for the wedding and my poor mother, Annabelle, and Jackson's mother, Emily, were now scrambling to make up the time they had lost while Jackson and I were separated. According to them, they had lost precious hours in finalizing the smallest details.

My mother was continually hounding me about my dress until finally Emily spoke up and reassured her that it was all taken care of and that it was going to be a surprise. I could tell by her face that my mother wasn't happy with it, but she choked it down and kept quiet. I think she was simply happy that the wedding was back on and didn't want anything to rock the boat.

Jackson and my brother, William, took off early in the morning under a cloud of suspicion. Even William's wife, Olivia, had no idea what the two of them were up to. The only thing they would tell us was that with the holidays and the wedding quickly approaching now was not the time to ask questions. I suppose there was a lot of that going around.

After breakfast I headed over to Jackson's sister's house. It was only a short walk from ours and the air was unusually warm and comfortable despite being gray and unpleasant looking out. The leaves had left the trees and the ground was littered in a vast array of colors. I casually strolled down the cobblestones, enjoying the sound of my feet on the rocks and the crunching of leaves beneath me.

Phoebe had invited me over Thursday after dinner to help her with some sewing she had fallen behind on. She said that she was so busy with the baby that she never got everything done that she intended to throughout the day.

Her house was much smaller than ours and her parents', but it was a beautiful starter home, as she called it.

Her husband, Silas, was a teacher at the grade school and made a respectable living. He truly loved working with the children and Phoebe had told me once that the satisfaction and enjoyment he got from work was well worth the pay grade. She said it made him a much more pleasant individual to live with than someone who hated their career.

I hadn't thought much of it when she'd said it in passing shortly after they were married but looking back I can't help but wonder if perhaps she was referring to Carson.

Phoebe answered the door with her eighteen-month-old son, Wallace, on her hip and a little smudged flour across her cheek. The little guy smiled broadly and reached out for me as soon as he saw me.

"Good morning, Phoebe." I lifted her son from her arms. "Busy morning?" I laughed.

"Good morning, Jocelyn," she sighed deeply, wiping her brow only to smear more flour across her forehead. "And yes, it has been a very busy morning. Please come in." She stood aside and closed the door behind me. I followed her into the kitchen as she rattled on, seemingly unaware of her surroundings. "Ever since this little guy decided to become mobile, I cannot seem to get anything accomplished. Katie has been a God-send. I do not know what I would do without her. She has been doing so much more than her normal chores because this little man," she leaned over and tickled the cherub-looking baby and making him laugh aloud, "believes that everything needs to be dumped out onto the floor."

"I am sure it is just a phase he is going through," I attempted to give her hope.

"I hope so. I don't know how my mother did it with three of us or how your mother managed with five. And four of them boys!" She sighed heavily. "This one is enough to make me insane." Phoebe began kneading the dough on the island block.

"It will get better," I assured her.

"Soon, I hope. Silas already wants another one and I am not sure if I do."

"Wallace does need a playmate."

"That's the same argument he uses, but of course he is not the one who has to get fat, give birth, and then stay home and take care of both children." She smirked and leaned over towards me and whispered, "I really miss my office sometimes *here*." Then she stopped short and her face went pale. "I'm so sorry. I know your barrier is coming down, but I'm not sure how much you know."

"Not to worry, I recall most things. Not all, but the gap is closing."

"Good. I remember how frustrating it was. I could not tell what was real or what was imaginary. I thought for sure I was losing my mind."

"I'm in touch with that emotion," I laughed.

We finished the bread and retired to the family room to work on her sewing. Little Wallace was down for his morning nap and Silas was in his office preparing his lessons for the upcoming week.

The warmth from the fire was just enough to take a bit of chill out of the air. I believe it was warmer outside than in although I did not say so aloud. We sat in silence for a short time while Phoebe recomposed herself.

She appeared tired and worn out. She looked nothing like her elegant, refined, professional business-minded self in the twenty-first century. It would be difficult to be a high-powered criminal attorney in Boston who was quick-witted, instinctively clever, and amazingly brilliant in the modern world and literally overnight switching to the role of a housewife, whose days revolved around diapers, baking, sewing, and cleaning. Then I realized that I too would soon be seated in her shoes and faced with the same prospects that she was trying to accept.

"May I ask you a question, Phoebe?"

"Of course," she smiled gently.

"How do you do it? The dual lives I mean. Isn't it difficult at best?" I inquired in a very low voice.

She looked around making sure we were alone before she answered, "Yes, sometimes very. Then at other times, *this life* is a nice break from the hectic schedule of my life *there. Here* I get the chance to really enjoy Wallace in a fashion that I would never be able to *there.* I could never imagine being a stay-at-home mother *there.* For some women, it's what they want out of life and that's wonderful for them. For you and me, well . . . we get the amazing opportunity to do both. We get to experience the best of both worlds in one lifetime. This gift or curse, whichever you believe it to be, gives us a rare opportunity to really have it all."

"And you really believe that?" I questioned with skepticism.

"You don't?" she raised her eyebrows.

"For me, yes, I do. However, I believe our situations are quite different."

"How so?"

"I will have the same husband on both planes," I whispered softly.

Phoebe's smile broadened. "Yes, that does make our situation different. But I believe I would rather be in my shoes than yours or my mother's where that is concerned," she giggled a little and quickly placed her hand over her mouth.

"Really? Why is that?"

"I have variety in my life. I get a complete break from each world except for Wallace, of course," she smiled. "You will be able to appreciate my words more once you have been married for a while."

"You do not consider that adultery?" I whispered.

"No." She looked astonished at my words. "How can you even ask that?"

"You have two husbands."

"Yes . . . and?"

"I am assuming you have a full marriage on both planes." I couldn't bring myself to spell it out any more clearly than I already was.

Phoebe laughed out loud at my question. "My goodness, Jocelyn, are you asking me if I have a sexual relationship with both of them?" she whispered with tears in her eyes from laughter.

I couldn't believe how blasé she was behaving about such a serious topic, "Yes, but I do not understand your sense of humor in all this."

"I am laughing because of your innocence and naivety of real life. I have to keep reminding myself that you are still young and have not had any other serious relationships other than my little brother. If you had then perhaps you would understand the way I perceive things."

"Perhaps, but is it not strange having two husbands? I mean, they are completely different from one another. They do not have any similar characteristics."

Phoebe looked around again as we heard footsteps in the kitchen. She held up her finger to hush me. "Excuse me just one moment." She rose from her seat and pretended to stoke the fire and gently called, "Ms. Katie, could you come here a moment please?"

Her housekeeper, Katie, arrived promptly wiping her hands on her apron, "Yes, ma'am?"

"Ms. Jocelyn and I are going to take a walk and get some fresh air. Would you mind keeping an ear out for Wallace?" Phoebe asked.

"Of course, and shall I go ahead and feed him if he wakes before your return?"

"Yes, please. We shall not be too long."

Katie curtsied and exited. We wrapped our shawls around our shoulders and put on our bonnets and headed out.

A short distance from the house, Phoebe looked over at me with a strange look on her face. "Jocelyn, I know my lifestyle appears odd to you, but perhaps you will understand my reasoning after you hear my explanation. Yes, Carson and Silas are completely different men apart from their height, eye and hair color."

I couldn't help but laugh a little. Her words slightly understated the drastic differences between the two men. "Yes, they are."

"You see, before this . . . *EVE* thing happened to me, I led a very conservative, proper life *here* and a very modern happy-go-lucky lifestyle *there,* to say the least. I was a bit of a wild child, as my parents called me, and I enjoyed life to the fullest. Then, when the barrier started coming down, I honestly thought it was flashbacks or something from partying too much. When I finally confessed what was happening to Alex, he and my parents explained to me the truth, and I did not exactly take it that well." She paused to take a deep breath of fresh air before she continued. "When I finally did adjust I made up my mind that I was going to make the most of my situation and have the best of both worlds if this is what I had to deal with. So, I buckled down with my studies and graduated college at the top of my class. Then I went on to law school. I wanted to have a high-powered career that made good money so that I would never have to worry about things financially. Once I had achieved that, it put me in a position that I could marry a man with a carefree spirit that I enjoyed spending time with, made me laugh, was my best friend. I wanted someone whom I loved and that would love me for who I was and couldn't care less about my money. For me, that was extremely important. And I found that with Carson. He is an incredible man and I love him dearly."

"But what about Silas?" I inquired.

"Silas is a wonderful man also and I love him just as much. I love them both equally yet differently. Silas is a serious man who is very passionate about life and his career. He has a firm yet gentle hand and is quieter spoken than Carson." She laughed again, and I joined her. "Silas is a respectable loving man who takes good care of me, loves me, and is a wonderful father."

"What about Wallace?"

"You mean who his real father and how do I plan on explaining all this to him someday?" she said, looking me directly in the eye.

"Well, yes. Who is his biological father?"

"Carson, I believe. I have never had him tested . . . obviously. But he seems to favor him more than Silas. Wouldn't you agree?"

"Yes, I believe so." I nodded my head slightly, still baffled by her strange lifestyle choices.

"I suppose I will explain it to him the way I have to you when it becomes necessary."

"And you believe it to be fair to him? I mean to have two fathers?"

"Would you believe it to be better for him to be without a father on one plane or the other?"

"It is not uncommon in 2009 for a career woman to be a single mom," I pointed out. "At least you would only have one husband." I immediately regretted the words as soon as I'd said them.

Phoebe stopped and looked at me, narrowing her eyes a bit. "Don't judge me. None of us asked for this curse and if there is nothing that I can do to fix it without hurting those I love dearly, then I will make the best of it the way I see fit for me. Imagine yourself in my position for one minute. Why should I have to be alone on one plane because I fell in love on the other and he cannot travel with me? Does that mean that my son should grow up without a father on one plane? With his barrier being completely up until late adolescence or early adulthood, he would always remember the feeling of never having a daddy. Is that fair to him? Could you honestly do that to your child if Jackson could not travel with you?"

"No," I whispered softly, thinking of the picture of our three beautiful children. "I know I couldn't."

"I know you may find my choices difficult to understand but I assure you, I love both Silas and Carson with all my heart. While I do appreciate what you are saying, you need to look at the bigger picture for everyone involved. Don't judge me for the decisions I made to make this lifestyle more bearable for me and my son. Alex and I both believe we have done what is right for us."

"I do understand looking at it from your perspective. And I honestly am not judging you for your choices. I just wanted to understand how you saw things."

"It was not a decision I made lightly, but it is one that I am happy with. On one plane I have a high-powered career and a nanny to help me with my son when necessary. I make an excellent living, am well respected within the community, and have a husband that I adore. *Here*, I have a beautiful home, a hardworking and loving husband, a housekeeper, and a peaceful life that gives me some solace after a hectic day in the *other* plane. It's a nice reprieve. Plus, I have a beautiful son that means the world to me in both." She shrugged with a big grin. "I am very happy with my choices and while they may not be right for everyone in our situation, they are right for me personally."

"Then that's all that matters."

She placed her hand on my arm and gave it a gentle squeeze. We turned the corner and walked a little while without saying a word. The noon sun was fighting to break through the clouds and we could feel some of its warmth. Several of our friends and acquaintances were out and about and greeted us with glad tidings. Their thoughtfulness still somewhat amazed me with its direct contrast to how individuals behaved in the twenty-first century. Courteousness was not the first thing that came to mind when passing a stranger on the streets of Chicago in modern times.

"Is that Ms. Maryanne over there staring at you?" Phoebe leaned over and whispered, breaking my train of thought.

"Yes." Maryanne was standing next to her father in front of the general store talking to Christina's father.

"If looks could kill . . ."

I couldn't help but giggle. "I know."

"She really needs to stop blaming everyone else for her break-up with Dimitri."

"I doubt she ever will because she will never admit that it was her sparkling personality that drove him away," I said.

"Yes, she is very sweet. Just like her mother from what I hear," she smirked.

"A carbon copy of her mother to be precise," I replied, but Phoebe stopped and grabbed my arm firmly with a weird look on her face.

"Jocelyn . . . do you realize what you just said?" Panic flooded her face.

"What?" I said, feeling confused.

Her eyes widened as she waited for me to realize what I'd said, but I was completely clueless. "What?" I asked again a little louder.

She pulled me closer to her and whispered in my ear, "Carbon copy!" She stepped back a little and tilted her head and widened her eyes at me again.

"Yeah . . . so?" I shrugged. "What?"

"Jocelyn, I know you are not that thick!"

"What in the world are you flipping out about?"

Phoebe grabbed my arm a little more gently so as not to draw any attention to us from onlookers and guided me over to a more isolated location by the post office, which was closed on Saturdays.

"First off, you cannot say *carbon copy*. It has not been invented yet! Secondly, you cannot say *flipping out* either. It's slang and ladies do not use slang!" she scolded.

Then it hit me. I finally understood what Jackson and his parents had been constantly warning me about: little slip-ups. And I hadn't even realized it. The words had literally rolled right off my tongue without me giving it a second thought.

"Oh, my goodness!" My hands flew up over my mouth. "I had not even realized . . ."

"I know." She put her hand on my shoulder in a comforting manner. "It's all right, but you have to be more careful. No one heard you . . . this time."

"I am so sorry, I . . ." I fumbled my words, feeling dumbfounded.

"It's all right, calm down. No harm was done." She laughed slightly.

"Come on, we need to get back home. Wallace should be awake soon if he's not already."

* * *

Jackson came over a little before three in the afternoon. I had been trying to focus on reading Jane Austen's *Sense and Sensibility*, but I couldn't concentrate on it and kept rereading the same paragraph. I was thrilled when he showed up and I happily tossed the book aside.

"Where have you been all day?" I rushed into his eager arms.

"Doing a little holiday shopping," he laughed, flashing me a brilliant smile. "Guess you missed me."

"Only a little," I teased and kissed him on the cheek.

"I would have been here sooner, but my sister stopped by with Wallace. She told me something rather interesting about your conversation this morning." He gave me a coy smile.

"Really? What did she say?" I wasn't sure if he was referring to my inquisition into her lifestyle or my slip-up.

"Only that I need to spend a little more time monitoring your vocabulary," he laughed.

"I had a minor slip this morning," I grinned and shrugged.

"Something about a *carbon copy* and *flipping out*," he whispered before laughing loudly.

"Oh, stop it!" I playfully slapped him on the arm. "It could have been much worse."

"True."

"I am sorry. I said it without thinking first. It was stupid."

"Yes, it was. But understandable."

"Perhaps, but I will need to be more careful. This is all so incredibly strange. I do not feel like myself much of the time. I know things that I shouldn't and have no clue of why or how I know them. It's the most bizarre feeling," I half complained.

"It will be that way for a while, I'm sorry to say. But you will have to be more cautious of your vocabulary until the barrier is completely dissolved."

"I feel as if I don't know what is real and what is not anymore. I cannot seem to differentiate reality from memory. It's frustrating to know things that are to come but not be able to explain how I know them." I looked over at Jackson with pleading eyes. "Does that make any sense?"

"To anyone who did not know better, no," he laughed and put his arm around me. "But to me, yes. It makes perfect sense."

*   *   *

My mind was a whirlwind of thought as I tried to settle down for the evening. Mimi was setting out my gown for tomorrow morning and I watched her carefully moving about my room. It was strange to think of not having her in my life every day. Not to have her as my voice of reason when I was set on being stubborn and bullheaded was unchartered territory.

Even when I was behaving my worst, Mimi was always there to bring me around and force me to see things from a different perspective. I always loved her for it later, but I hated it at the time.

She kissed me gently on the forehead and dimmed the oil lamp while Eddie put a couple logs on the fire before they both left me for the night. I rolled over and watched the moonlight dance amongst the trees displaying their beautiful waltz along my bedroom walls.

Part of my mind knew this was a familiar ritual for me in my *other* world as well except the shadows were larger because the trees just outside my windows were so much older *there* and shaped differently from being trimmed back against the house.

My mind was like a jigsaw puzzle with several essential pieces still missing to make it complete. Without those pieces, I felt like I couldn't rest with any real peace. There were still so many unanswered questions, things that flashed before me that I didn't recognize or understand.

Strange objects and weird things that made no sense haunted me nearly every waking hour.

In a vague attempt, I closed my eyes and tried to splice together everything I had seen and been told recently to picture what exactly my life was like in the twenty-first century.

It was hard to fathom how drastically different it really was. Thinking of having a family that was not closely bonded, gadgets that practically do any and everything for you, devices to talk to people anywhere at any time, choices, opinions, and actual freedom were more than my nineteenth century mind could comprehend.

I couldn't help but think about when the barrier was finally demolished; would combining such different worlds in one person even be possible? I knew the Chandlers dealt with it as commonplace, but somehow, I didn't know if I could ever be so graceful.

CHAPTER THREE

Saturday, November 28, 2009

EAR PIERCING SCREAMS soared through the blackened house in the early morning hours. I bolted upright dazed and confused. It took several more moments before it registered in my brain that I was no longer asleep and for once it wasn't me who was screaming.

Footsteps stormed the hall followed by a barrage of confused swearing in my father's sleepy voice. My door flung open startling me even further, "Jocelyn?"

"Dad?" My dad stood in my darkened doorway looking frazzled in his pajama bottoms, no shirt, bare feet. and open bathrobe.

"Ethan?" My dad shouted and disappeared down the hallway.

I leapt out of bed and followed. My dad threw open Ethan's door as I collided behind him to see what was going on. Ethan was sound asleep and snoring, completely oblivious to anything going on.

"What in the world is going on?" My mother stood in their bedroom doorway rubbing her eyes. Neither of us answered her.

Another scream rang through the halls sending cold chills down my spine. "Sidney!" I hollered and ran to the bell-way stairs.

The screaming hit new heights when I threw open her door and ran up the stairs with my dad clamoring behind me, muttering disbeliefs and disruptions. When I hit the landing, I grabbed a hold of the railing and came to an abrupt halt in stunned disbelief at what my eyes were witnessing. My dad ran into me unaware that I had stopped short, shoving me forward into the room.

Sidney was sitting upright in her bed, her eyes unfocused and screaming madly. Landon was kneeling in front of her with both his hands on her arms and shaking her wildly. "Sid! Wake up! Wake up! Sidney!" he repeated over and over.

My dad pushed past me to Sidney's bedside. "Sidney!" he practically shoved Landon out of the way. "Wake up!" he said, grabbing her.

Sidney was nonresponsive to either of their pleas. She just continued screaming blindly. I held onto the rail hoping in vain that my knees would not give out. In my blurred vision of the events unfolding before me, I could see myself in Sidney's place and William screaming and shaking me wildly. The image made the tiny hairs on the back of my neck stand on end.

My mom's frantic shove brought me back into reality as she flew by me. "What is going on?" she hollered over Sidney's constant screams.

"She won't wake up!" Dad yelled back.

"Smack her!" she yelled.

"I will not!" he hollered over his shoulder.

My mom pushed Dad out of the way and hesitantly smacked her Sidney across the face. Sidney's eyes immediately focused on our mom, but quickly became confused. She was drenched with perspiration and tears. She was breathing heavily and starring at us with silent tears rolling down her reddened cheeks. I don't believe I'd ever seen my sister in such a state.

My parents tried to recompose themselves and began to question Landon extensively. I quietly turned and crept back down the stairs. I paused in the hallway at the bottom of Sidney's stairwell and leaned against her doorframe. I could hear muffled cries and words coming from her room, but nothing was audible.

I glanced in the direction of Ethan's room, which was still silent. I have no idea how he managed to sleep through all that. It was so like him though.

Sidney's bizarre screaming nightmare hit so close to home it aroused every feeling of terror and uneasiness that I had experienced myself in both periods. I knew that I had never seen Sidney in my *other* world. *Is it possible that she could have inherited this curse too? Could she have another life somewhere other than where mine was? Could that kind of thing even happen?*

My mind raced with questions that I had absolutely no answers for. I listened for a few more minutes to the mumblings from above before I made my way back to my room. The alarm clock announced that it was only two thirty in the morning.

I pulled the curtain back and glanced at the house across the way. Everything stood dark and silent. I reached for my cell phone, wondering if perhaps Jackson had his phone beside him as he slept.

I picked up my phone and stared at his name on my screen curious as to what would happen if I woke him up in the middle of the night. *Does it affect his day in 1878? Did my being awake right now mean that I'm soulless there? Does my body collapse there when I am abruptly awoken in the middle of the night here and my soul returned to this body? How does all of this work?*

I thought perhaps Jackson may have some answers, but I really wanted to speak with Robert and Emily. They were more likely to have the answers I was seeking. Still, it was two thirty in the morning and I couldn't justify waking them up over something that might well be as simple as a nightmare.

I pushed the button and waited for Jackson to answer. I wasn't sure what repercussions our being awake may have, but I felt I had to talk to him before I started screaming myself.

"Hello," a sleepy voice finally answered.

"Jackson, I'm sorry I woke you."

"Are you all right? What happened?" My heart ached for the concern I heard in his voice.

"Don't worry, I'm fine. It's Sidney."

"Sidney?"

"Look Jackson, I need you to do me a favor. I know you and William used to sneak in and out of my house undetected. I really need you to do that now if you will. Please?" I felt terrible thinking of the consequences my selfishness might bring about.

"All right," I heard the hesitation in his voice.

"I'm sorry to ask, I know it's late, but this is important."

"I will be there in a moment."

"Oh, wait . . . Jackson?" I gushed.

"Yes?"

"Be careful, my parents are up and about."

Jackson chuckled softly. "Not to worry, they will never know I am there."

I tossed my cell back on my bed and stared back out the bay window, waiting to see Jackson run across the yards. I curled up in the window seat and leaned my head against the cold glass. Several minutes passed with no movement around my yard or Jackson's. *Maybe it's just taking him a few minutes to get dressed or perhaps he's misplaced his shoes. Yeah right*, I laughed to myself, *like that would ever happen.* Jackson and his family were notoriously neat and organized, so unlike my own family.

"See anything interesting?" The sound of his voice caused me to jump out of my skin.

"Oh, my goodness!" My hands leapt up to my chest. "You nearly scared me to death."

He laughed softly. "William and I are very talented." Jackson walked over and put his arms around me and kissed me gently.

"I should say so," I kissed him back.

"You never even saw me cross did you?" His smiled widened.

"No," I shook my head in disbelief. "I'm impressed." I kissed him again.

"So, what has got your house in an uproar?" He crossed over and sat down on my bed. I walked over and peeked out my door quietly. "Oh, do not worry, your parents are still upstairs with Sidney and Ethan is asleep. I checked," Jackson whispered.

I closed the door without a sound and breathed deeply. This was going to be a long night, I thought, crawling back up on my bed and under my comforter. I was freezing. I situated myself, pulling the blankets up around my neck and snuggling into Jackson's chest. *This is where I belong, either here or there, this is my home.*

"Better now?" His voice was warm and soft.

"Much." I smiled up into his eyes and held them for a moment before he leaned over and kissed my forehead.

"So . . . explain," He wrapped his arms tightly around me.

Jackson and I cuddled in the dark while I explained Sidney's ordeal and my concerns thereafter. I told him about my fears and the feelings that were aroused in me seeing her like that. I confided in him all my thoughts, apprehensions, doubts, and skepticisms about everything that was building up in me. He remained silent listening to me rant and rave in a calm but dramatic fashion.

"Now do you think I'm insane?" I sighed loudly and thought of how crazy he must believe me to be.

But he only squeezed me tighter against him, "Not at all." He kissed the top of my head again. "I believe you have every right to be concerned about your sister especially after all you have been through recently. And yes, there is a chance that Sidney inherited the same gene you did. Perhaps Ethan did as well, I do not know. But I do know that if Sidney did inherit *EVE* she is at the right age for the barrier to begin disintegrating naturally."

"What are the odds of her having it?"

"I wish I could tell you, but I have no clue."

"But what about the time period thing? I don't ever remember seeing Sidney or anyone to her likeness *there*, do you?"

"No."

"Is it possible that her time period differs from mine?" I looked up into his eyes pleading for answers.

"I suppose it is possible. Anything is possible. I wish there was more I could tell you. I wish I had some answers or facts, something that would make you feel better."

"Would your parents know?" I asked with hope.

"Maybe," he sighed heavily. "I would bet one of my grandmothers would know."

"Can you ask them?"

"Sure," he chuckled slightly. "Do you have a Ouija Board or we could hold a séance on the next full moon."

"Thanks, glad to know your sense of humor is still intact." I rolled my eyes, trying not to laugh out loud.

"I'm sorry. They both passed away a long time ago." He settled back down. "I do wish we could ask them. There are still so many things about all this that I don't understand. I'm afraid it can be quite frustrating in the bigger scope of things."

"I wish there was a way to get some real factual answers," I complained.

"I know. Maybe that is why most of us avoid asking them. Perhaps knowing the truth is more harmful than the not knowing." Jackson sighed deeply and was quiet for several minutes, lost in his own thoughts.

"Doesn't it bother you not knowing how many people have this . . . this *EVE* thing?" I leaned up and looked at his silhouette in the dark. His face appeared troubled in the dark shadows.

"It did in the beginning. I was just like you and questioned everything. Now I think I have just accepted my life . . . or lives, as they are. But I must admit I was so thrilled when I learned that you had inherited it as well. I was considering what your Uncle Monte did because I could not imagine loving anyone like I love you and I really didn't want to only spend half my life with you."

"You know, after talking with your sister I do understand her reasoning, but I don't believe it is something that I could do either. I couldn't fathom sharing my life with or loving anyone as much as I love you." He gave me a gentle squeeze but said nothing as I rested my head back against his chest.

I closed my eyes and listened to his heart's strong steady rhythm. It was like a lullaby luring me off to another time and place where we would still be by each other's side. The idea of our parallel existences still felt rather absurd, yet strangely

I was becoming more and more comfortable with the bizarre feelings, visions and moments of déjà vu that encompassed my life daily.

*   *   *

The blinding morning sun blazing though my window woke me shortly before noon. Jackson, of course, was long gone. I had no idea what time he left but it was comforting to know that he'd stayed until he was sure I was sound asleep. I rubbed my eyes and listened to the sounds of everyone moving around downstairs. I wondered how Sidney was doing considering her horrific slumber. I wondered if I should try and talk to her about it and see if she would give me any details behind what caused her to wake up screaming in the dead of night. I seriously doubted she would. If she was experiencing anything remotely close to what I had, there was no way she was going to admit anything.

After a hot shower I went downstairs in search of my morning coffee. My dad was at the kitchen table looking tired and reading the morning paper.

"Good morning," he muttered without looking up.

"Good morning. Where is everyone?" I inquired, pouring myself a fresh cup.

"At the store. They left about an hour ago." I sat down across from him and he finally lowered the paper. His eyes were dark and heavy.

"Did you get back to sleep after all that?"

"I wish. I don't know what she was dreaming about, but it clearly scared the life out of her. I've never seen her like that before." My dad shook his head slightly.

"Me neither. Did she ever tell you what it was about?" I casually inquired, sipping my coffee.

"No, she wouldn't talk about it. I asked several times and so did your mother, but she refused to say anything."

"That's strange."

"Yeah, well, she's stubborn, just like you," he muttered. "So, what are your plans for today?"

"I'm heading over to Jackson's."

"Of course," he mumbled from behind his paper. "Like I even needed to ask."

"Funny, Dad," I got up and put my mug in the sink. "I'll be home later."

"Have a good day," he hollered after me as I headed to the front door.

"You too," I yelled back, closing the door behind me.

Despite the bright sunrays beaming down upon me, the air was cold and tore straight through my clothes. I zipped my sweatshirt the rest of the way up and pulled the hood over my head to block the wind from echoing in my ears. I descended the steps slowly, absorbing the ambiance around me and considered briefly the vast difference the view from these steps looked between the times.

How wonderful and strange the passage of time affected all things in this world. It still amazed me, and I couldn't help but wonder if I would ever stop feeling in awe of it. I hoped not.

Jackson was reading by the fire when I arrived. He appeared well rested despite having spent half the night over at my house dealing with my hysterics. His dark tan shirt complemented him nicely and he looked as handsome as ever.

I paused in the archway of their family room and watched him silently for a few minutes, waiting for him to notice my presence. I still could not believe how fortunate I was to have him in my life. Not only was he unbelievably gorgeous, he was kind and sweet with a heart of gold. His minor flaws were only those that enhanced his character of being old fashioned in his beliefs and treatment of me.

Adjusting to the differences between my two worlds was so bizarre. It seemed to me that the only stable characters were Jackson and his family. Their behavior never wavered no matter which plane we were on. I, on the other hand, was drastically different from one place to the other.

Although that gap somehow seemed to be shortening with the passage of time the larger the holes in my consciousness became.

"Hello, beautiful." Jackson looked up and smiled. "How are you?" He got up and walked over to greet me properly.

His lips pressed against mine as his arms wrapped around me, pulling me closer to him. Instantly, heat soared through my body and butterflies danced around in stomach. I draped my arms around his neck and ran my fingers through the back of his curls.

Reluctantly, he pulled away and took a step back. "You have got to stop that." A devilish grin slid across his shapely lips.

"I could say I'm sorry, but I wouldn't mean it." I smirked back while he took my hand and led me over to the couch.

I snuggled into the nook under his arm and rested my head against his chest, picking up the book he was reading. "*Pride and Prejudice.*" I glanced up at his face surprised in his choice of literature.

"Yes, Mrs. Runyon has a strange sense of humor." He half laughed, half snorted.

"Oh, you got Runyon," I giggled. "I feel sorry for you. She's notorious for being strict and rude. I was so glad that I didn't get stuck with her."

"Thanks," he smirked. "Who did you get?"

"Mrs. Killian. She's fabulous. I love her. We just finished reading *To Kill a Mockingbird.* I loved it. I've seen the movie. Well, we've got it on DVD. It's one of my mom's favorites and I've seen it so many times I've got it memorized. But I was really shocked the book was nothing like the movie."

"I know, but I really love them both."

I flipped over the book and started reading over the paragraph on the back. "I'm surprised you haven't read this before for another course at least."

"No, I have been lucky so far." He sighed deeply and tossed the book onto the coffee table. "I normally love reading, but I cannot get into the way her writing is structured."

"Really? I love her writing. This is one of my favorite books."

"I never do this, but I think this time I will have to rent to the movie." He rolled his eyes.

"No need. I have it. The version with Keira Knightly. I've watched it a million times."

"Great. Can I borrow it?" He tightened his grip.

"Of course, but I do believe you should really finish the book first before you watch it. It honestly is a great book."

"I am sure it is. Maybe I would enjoy it more if I have a beautiful, sexy lady to read it to me." He flashed his mischievous lop-sided grin. "Would you like to volunteer?"

"To read to you?"

"Yes, ma'am."

"Mr. Jackson Chandler, you expect me to spend my time, and neglect my own studies because you don't like her style of writing?" I teased.

"Please." He stuck out his lower lip in a pout.

"I'm sure Taylor would love the job." I gave him a playful shove.

"I'd rather not, thank you very much. Used equipment is really not my style," he quipped.

"Wow . . . I can't believe you said that!" I busted out laughing, completely stunned by his words. "Even though it's true . . . still . . . wow!"

"I'm sorry. That was a horrible thing to say, even if it is true. I just get so tired of her behavior. I hate the way she acts. I swear the girl has no self-esteem whatsoever."

"I know. Don't worry about it. I've said worse about her and she's said much worse about me," I giggled.

"Anyway, will you help me?" he pleaded with those adorable green eyes that I was totally helpless against.

"Of course," I leaned over and kissed him on the cheek. "But first I have some questions for your parents. Are they home?"

"Yes, they are in the study. Excuse me for a moment. I will get them."

My eyes followed him out of the room and lingered even after he had disappeared. His grammar and manners never ceased to amaze me. Strangely enough, I was getting so accustomed to them that it really didn't seem foreign anymore. Stranger still, with the barrier decreasing, slang was sounding so wrong in my ears and it stuck out whenever I heard it, especially at school.

Robert and Emily followed Jackson back into the living room and greeted me with warm smiles. Robert, even on a lazy Saturday afternoon, was wearing slacks, a dress shirt, and a sweater. I smirked to myself thinking of my own father who was home tinkering with God only knows what in his stocking feet, sweatshirt, and flannel pajama bottoms. How different the two of them were.

Emily was wearing a pair of fitted jeans, stylish brown boots, a silk cream colored shirt with a dark brown vest over it with a couple scarfs, one light tan and the other a pale teal, looped elegantly once around her neck and hung slightly uneven down her front. She looked beautiful.

"Hello, dear. How are you doing today?" Emily asked, sitting down on the loveseat with her husband.

"Wonderful, thank you, and you?"

"Relaxing, finally. Everyone headed home this morning, so I started cleaning as soon as they left."

"Yes, it was so nice of you to start vacuuming at 6 a.m.," Jackson smirked.

"I said I was sorry. You should have been up to see them off anyway." She smiled sweetly at her son.

"I'm sorry, but they decided to leave at five in the morning and I was dealing with someone's overactive imagination until four." He gave me a playful nudge.

"Hey, it was not my fault. Blame Sidney. She was the one screaming in the middle of the night, not me."

I playfully shoved him back. "Why did they leave so early?" I turned back towards his parents.

"They wanted to do some Christmas shopping in New York on their way back to Boston," Robert replied.

"That would be fun." I rested back against Jackson.

"Phoebe loves New York and shopping is her favorite past time," Emily offered. "I am glad she has a successful career to go with her expensive taste."

"My sentiments exactly," Robert chimed in. "Her college education was less expensive than her wardrobe."

"You only have yourself to blame for that. You spoiled her rotten. I do not believe I have ever heard you say no to her," Jackson said with a grin.

"What?" Robert attempted to look innocent glancing between his son and his wife. "She *is* my only daughter," he explained, shrugging his shoulders.

I giggled softly while Jackson rolled his eyes and remained silent. Emily took a deep breath and sighed. "Anyway, Jocelyn, Jackson tells us your sister had a rough night. Did she confide in you about what happened?"

"I'm afraid not." Both his parents nodded but said nothing. "The weird thing is, looking at her, well . . . it was like looking in the mirror of my *other* self. I know it sounds strange, but what I can recall . . . the look in her eyes, that terrified uncertainty, was staring back at me again."

"Have you tried in a round-about way of bringing up the subject?" Emily asked, leaning a little forward.

"No. I don't know if it is possible if she could have inherited *EVE* as well."

"It is possible. Your uncle passed it on to you. She could have very well inherited it also. Maybe even Ethan too. Plus, Sidney is the right age for the barrier to start naturally disintegrating," Robert noted.

"But wouldn't there have been signs before the onset of the nightmares?"

"There probably was, you just weren't around her to notice anything unusual. She lives on campus after all and rarely makes it home," Emily offered.

"True," I said in a low voice more to myself than either of them.

"It certainly is possible she was experiencing some of the same symptoms that you did." Jackson looked lost in his own thoughts.

"How would I know? It's not like I can ask her if she is having visions of another time period. Besides, I have never seen her in any of my visions or memories or whatever from my *other* life," I told them.

"I wonder if she did inherit it, but her *other* time period varies from yours," Jackson said without focusing his eyes on me or his parents.

"Can that happen?" I looked from one to the other.

"I am not sure. I suppose." Robert leaned back and rubbed his chin in concentration. "I have not heard of it before, but I would think it could. Especially if she inherited it from a paternal uncle." He took a deep breath and exhaled loudly before getting up and walking over to the hearth. He fumbled around with a tobacco box and picked up a Michelin pipe, packed it absentmindedly and lit it before turning back towards the three of us. "That is precisely what is so aggravating about this *gift*. There are no exacts, no facts, no nothing to explain just what is passed on from one generation to the next. I am sorry, Jocelyn. I wish I could give you a more sufficient explanation."

"So, you are saying it is possible that if she has this *EVE* thing, her *other* time period could be somewhere other than mine or ours?"

Robert shrugged and puffed on his pipe. "I guess, unless Sidney decides to tell you what she is witnessing, there is no way of actually knowing. Unfortunately, with today's psychological standards she would most likely end up on a psych ward if she confided in the wrong person. Then they would pump her full of antipsychotic medications that would affect those neurons in her brain that are overproducing and releasing dopamine during the visions and therefore, shut them down completely, stagnating the barrier in mid breakdown."

"I'm guessing that's bad." Fear for my sister rushed through me. I knew vaguely what antipsychotic medications were and a little about schizophrenia, but my knowledge of dopamine and serotonin neurons was extremely limited.

"Yes . . . very. It's more like taking a caterpillar and holding it in suspension and never allowing it to become the butterfly that it is destined to be. In such an environment, nothing beautiful can flourish and will eventually become a shell of what it is meant to be." Robert turned away from us as the realization of his words fully rested upon me.

"Then we have no choice, we have to talk to her . . . get her to admit what she's seeing," I exclaimed urgently.

"It is not so simple, Jocelyn . . . remember? She would not believe you anyway at this point," Jackson added.

"But we have to do something . . . anything!" I couldn't fathom the thought of something so horrible happening to my sister.

"Do not worry, my dear. We would never let it get to that point. We will intervene long beforehand," Emily assured.

The room went silent for several moments while each of us contemplated what to do. No one knew what to say. The tension in the space between us was unbearable. I leaned against the back of the couch with my arm barely touching Jackson's, but my thoughts were so consumed with Sidney that I hardly noticed his presence.

All I could think about was doing more research on neurotransmitters and their effects on the brain. I vaguely recalled Mr. Rand talking about them in psychology class. I think he said something about their connection with Parkinson's disease which I thought was the under-production of dopamine whereas Schizophrenia was the result of overproduction or vice versa. I couldn't remember. My brain felt fried. Nothing made sense anymore.

"Does that mean that if Sidney doesn't get help adjusting to this before someone tries to put a psychotic label on her, she could struggle the rest of her life?" I looked over at Robert with pleading eyes.

"Like I said before, Jocelyn, most of what we know is speculation. There are no absolutes because anyone who has any credibility has never conducted a study of *It*," he laughed lightly. "And why would they? Who would possibly believe *EVE* to be real?"

"If I wasn't experiencing it, I wouldn't." I shook my head slightly knowing full well that he was right.

"Can you imagine trying to explain this to your friends?" Jackson chuckled half-heartedly. "They would have you committed."

"Yeah . . . ," I sighed. "They would." Our eyes locked for a moment and I knew we were both thinking the same thing. It was an impossible situation and the timing would have to be right.

"So where does that leave us?" My eyes shifted between his parents.

Emily shook her head gently. "I am not sure. It all really depends on Sidney and your relationship with her."

"Excuse me?"

"How comfortable you are with walking her through this experience. You know firsthand how terrifying it can be and what she is going through," Emily said.

"She would never believe me," I laughed. "Seriously, Sid and I are not close, never have been and this . . . well, there's no way," I tried to explain.

"There is some time, a little anyway. I take it she is coming home for Christmas?" Robert asked.

I nodded. "I would imagine so."

"Perhaps we allow this to continue a little longer and by then she may be more receptive to listening and understanding the truth," Emily suggested with a slight shrug.

"Ordinarily I would agree with you, Emily, but I'm afraid that this could severely affect her GPA."

"Trust me, she can recover." Jackson squeezed my hand. "It is not ideal, but she can always retake a class if necessary."

"Oh, my mother would love that . . . especially now!" I smirked, broadening his smile. Even his parents couldn't help but crack a grin.

"Things have a way of working themselves out," Robert added.

*　　*　　*

I spent the rest of the afternoon with Jackson and his family. I helped Emily prepare dinner as she attempted to teach me how to cook. I felt rather foolish when she quickly learned I knew very little in the kitchen. I was positive by the look on her face that she was afraid that her youngest child was going to starve to death with me as his wife. However, true to her nature, Emily was polite, gracious, and patient with me, trying to fix all the little mishaps I managed to consistently create.

After the four of us pitched in and cleaned up the dishes together, Robert and Emily excused themselves and retreated into the study. Jackson and I snuggled down under a blanket on the couch. He started flipping through the channels and settled on *It's a Wonderful Life* that was just beginning.

"Oh, I love this movie," I cooed.

"A classic," he agreed, wrapping his arm tightly around my shoulders and pulling me closer to him.

"It's the perfect way to kick off the Christmas season."

"You realize that we have less than a month before the wedding?" A devilish grin slid across his lips.

"*There* yes, but *here* we have another six months!" I teased.

"You are not seriously going to make me wait until we are married *here*, are you? I know you think I am being old fashioned in wanting to wait until our wedding night, but I don't honestly believe I can make it past our first wedding, let alone the second." His smile broadened.

"That sounds so weird," I laughed.

"For us," he half laughed. "Not really."

"True." I snuggled into his shoulder.

*   *   *

After a quick shower and throwing on a pair of pajama bottoms and a sweatshirt, I flopped down on my bed and grabbed my cell phone. I couldn't get my conversation with Jackson out of my head. As much as I wanted to be with him I knew I was completely unprepared.

"Speak," Jenna answered her phone almost immediately.

"Nice greeting." There was a strange comfort in knowing some things never changed.

"Sorry, I've been waiting for Kyle to call me back."

"Everything okay?"

"Yeah," she paused. "So, what's up?"

"Don't laugh, all right? I need your help with something."

"Why would I laugh?"

I felt so foolish. "Where can I go to get on the pill that my mother will not find out about?"

"Planned Parenthood over by Fifth Third Bank."

"I can't. One of her friends is the doc there."

"What about the Clinic over on Airport Road?"

"Nope." This was a bit ridiculous.

"Well . . . ," I could almost hear the wheels turning in her brain. "We could drive into the city after practice one day this week or next weekend."

"All right, thanks. I just need to go somewhere that my mother doesn't know anyone." Sometimes I really hated her being a physician.

"No problem. We can do some Christmas shopping while we're there if we have time."

"Sounds good. Thanks." I felt a rush of relief.

Jenna's phone beeped in. "Oh, that's gotta be Kyle. Gotta go."

I tossed my phone aside and climbed under my duvet trying to calculate days in my head. I knew I was getting a late start on starting the pill.

I was going to do it sooner but then we separated and without Jackson in my life there was no point. Now, I wasn't going to make the thirty-day deadline before our wedding *there*. So, precautions would still be necessary no matter how much I didn't want our first time . . . my first time with my husband, to be like that.

CHAPTER 4

Sunday, December 1, 1878

THE FAMILIAR COMFORTING SOUNDS of everyone moving about downstairs flooded my ears before my eyes even attempted to open. I tried to block out the visions of my *other* life that persistently shoved its way into my mind. I had little to no knowledge of my *sister* Sidney, but I felt terrible that she was experiencing the horrible night terrors that I went through such a short while ago.

Mimi quietly opened my door and crept across the floor. She leaned slightly over my bed to see if I was awake. I could feel her eyes on me despite mine still being closed tightly. I tried my best not to crack a smile as she assessed my condition.

"Ms. Jocelyn, it's time to get up," she said softly.

I tried my best to remain still, but I failed miserably as a smile slid across my face. "Good morning, Mimi. How are you feeling this morning?"

"I doing betta. I just worried whether this mild fall's gonna hold. I can feel the snow a' coming."

"Do you think we will have a white Christmas?" She was rarely wrong about these things.

"Donchya fret now, Ms. Jocelyn. I sure that you is gonna have a beautiful weddin' with or without the snow." She smiled and pulled the covers off me.

"Mimi, it's cold!" I complained and shuddered, trying to pull my covers back over me, but she was amazingly strong and wouldn't let go.

"Getchya lazy rear outta that bed now. You gonna be late for church." She playfully smacked my leg making me jump up.

"Mimi!" I hollered.

She laughed aloud, instantly sending the painful reminder that soon I would be waking up every morning without her to greet my day.

The mere thought saddened my core. She was the heart of our family and the soul of this house. Her presence made this a house a home.

She picked up the gown she had laid out the night before, my navy-blue velvet one with a cream lace trim. She gathered up my other apparel, setting them neatly beside my gown on my bed while I washed my face and brushed my teeth.

She took her time helping me dress, doing my make-up and hair, and chatted excessively the entire time. It was almost as if she too was dreading that our morning rituals were ending as well.

*   *   *

William was seated at the table alone reading the morning newspaper when I entered the dining room. "Where is everyone?" I inquired, taking a seat across from him.

"Our parents are in the study; they finished breakfast a while ago and Olivia is not feeling so well. Father checked her this morning and said it is just a cold, but she should stay in bed for a couple days."

"I'm sorry. Perhaps I should see her before we leave?"

"You should wait until we return. I believe she is already back asleep," he replied without looking up from his paper.

"All right," I said more to myself than to him.

Jackson showed up before I was even done with my first cup of coffee. He was wearing a dark suit, hat, and overcoat. He looked breathtaking as he took my hand and escorted me out to his carriage.

Reverend Jacobs was as long winded as ever this morning. I sat beside Jackson listening to him drone on about the book of Luke and the parable of the lost sheep. As hard as I tried to concentrate on what he was saying, my mind kept drifting back to Sidney. I couldn't shake the feeling that she needed me.

I could still hear her screams ringing in the back of my mind. I could vaguely recall speaking with Jackson and his parents about them and what they'd said about Sidney's possible other self. It was so overwhelming, and my mind couldn't fully wrap around the concept.

Jackson reached over and took my hand in his. He squeezed it gently. "Are you all right?" he whispered.

"Yes," I lied. Now was not the time to discuss what was haunting me.

"You seem tense."

"I'm fine," I whispered back and tried my best to focus my attention on Reverend Jacob.

But I couldn't. No matter how hard I tried. Sitting here seemed so unimportant. All I wanted to do was get Jackson and his parents alone and find out what really happened with Sidney. I couldn't see it all. Only bits and pieces of it were coming through the barrier in my mind. It was so aggravating. I wanted to scream until I finally got the answers I so desperately needed.

After church services, Robert, Emily, and Jackson's siblings joined our family once again for supper and everyone was in high spirits. There was laughing, teasing, and joking around as everyone talked about the upcoming holiday and wedding. The younger children were running around making a racket, yet no one seemed to notice or be annoyed by it.

The adults gathered around the hearth with coffee and sponge cake after dinner while the little ones were put down for their afternoon naps. A peaceful calm settled over the house and I snuggled in with Jackson. I relaxed and remained still for a moment attempting to savor everything around me.

By early evening, the extended families all retired to their respectable homes and only Jackson, myself, and my parents were left. We chatted endlessly about various songs for the wedding and the reception. My mother had some very specific ideas about the music for my special day.

Jackson and I listened attentively, both of us trying to think of a polite way to express to her that we had our own ideas about what we wanted to hear on our wedding day.

However, we never got the chance to discuss it any further because William ran pounding down the stairs with sheer panic on his face.

"Father . . . Father!" he hollered before he entered the front room. "Please come upstairs. Something is wrong with Olivia!" All heads turned in his directions as he rushed into the room.

Father leapt to his feet and rushed up the stairs with the three of us directly behind him.

Olivia was curled up in the fetal position holding her abdomen with little beads of sweat across her forehead. She was moaning slightly with tears slowing falling onto the pillow. She looked like a small child in pain.

My father leaned over her and gently brushed the hair away from her face. "Olivia dear, can you tell me where it hurts?" he said very softly.

"My baby . . . something is wrong." She physically cringed.

It broke my heart to see her like this. I looked over at Jackson whose face looked as terrified as I felt. I reached over and took a hold of his hand trying to gain some of his strength.

"Can you roll to your back?" Father asked.

William came around and sat down on the other side of Olivia taking her hand in his before placing his other hand on her arm to carefully roll her over. She cried out in pain with the slightest movement and drew her legs up closer to her.

"Jocelyn, Jackson . . . wait for us downstairs," my mother whispered, but neither of us could move.

"Easy, William . . . gently." My father guided William's every move.

My father lightly adjusted Olivia's legs out before her and she yelped out a little in pain. My brother brushed her cheek and kissed her forehead in a vague attempt to comfort his young wife.

My father pressed carefully on Olivia's abdomen causing her to yell out. He moved his hands around, feeling various areas with tender care and expert fingers. He pulled back the covers forcing a gasp of air to escape my lips before I even realized I'd done it.

Both of my parents gave me a disapproving look, but what my father revealed was a large amount of blood pooled between her legs. William's face turned white along with Jackson who swayed slightly before catching himself on the back of the rocking chair.

"Jocelyn, Jackson, William . . . out!" My father said sternly. "Annabelle, I need my bag."

My mother firmly took hold of my arm, pulling me towards the door. Jackson, who was still holding my hand, got dragged along behind me.

"William, come along," Mother requested gently but firmly.

"No, I am staying with my wife," my brother stated firmly in a weak voice.

"Son . . ." Patrick gave him a look that told all of us the seriousness of the situation. "You need to wait downstairs with Jackson and your sister."

William nodded reluctantly and kissed his wife on the forehead. "I will be right outside, my love. Everything is going to be all right. I love you."

William slowly rose from her side with Olivia's eyes following his every move, silently pleading with him to make everything all right again.

My mother closed the door behind us. Jackson and William retreated downstairs while I set up post outside the door waiting for our mother to return with Father's medical bag. Fear had gripped hold of my soul and I couldn't move. My mind was whirling in a thousand directions at once.

How can she lose her baby? I know I'd seen him in the photos. There was proof that William and Olivia had their son and two others after that.

I'd seen the photos in the forbidden album in my other life. Their little boys were adorable. I could still see their beautiful little faces.

I heard Olivia scream out in pain and the sound ripped my heart in two. I felt so helpless. My mother ran past me, threw open the door and slammed it quickly behind her. Her screams also sent William and Jackson running back up the stairs.

Both men came to a sudden halt outside the door beside me. Their faces marred with despair. There was nothing any of us could do.

Time stood still, and impatience was noticeable. Mimi soon joined us along with Sarah and we each took turns pacing about the landing and hall. The screaming had subsided, but muffled cries were sporadic and had us jumping each time they occurred. William soon became inconsolable and reverted back to the small boy being comforted in Mimi's arms as he wept on her shoulder.

Two agonizing hours passed before the door opened again. Our father came out looking haggard and worn. His hair was a mess and wet from perspiration, his face was drawn and pale. We all knew what had happened before the words ever passed over his lips.

"Ms. Olivia is fine. I got the bleeding stopped, but I am afraid she miscarried," he whispered.

A horrible sob escaped from somewhere deep inside William and I rushed into his arms. He held me so tightly he was causing me physical pain. I remained silent and held onto him with all the strength I had left in me. My heart was breaking for both of them.

"I want to see my wife," William blubbered between sobs.

"I just got her to sleep son. Your mother is sitting with her and will let you know when she awakens."

"I can do that." William headed for the door.

"Not now, son, she needs her rest and if she hears your voice, she'll awaken. Let's all go downstairs and have some coffee." He coaxed his son and Jackson gently over to the stairs before he hesitated a moment, grabbing mine and Mimi's arms.

"Jocelyn, Olivia is still awake. I need you to go help your mother. I am afraid that there is quite a mess and your mother will need some help with her. Mimi, Sarah . . . please get some clean sheets, towels, put on some hot water and bring it upstairs just before it boils to wash her well. Also, boil a large pot for the sheets," he said barely loud enough for us to hear him.

My father looked me directly in the eye, noticing the inquisitive look I gave him over his lie to William. "Trust me, your bother does not want to see this." I nodded slightly and turned back towards their room while the others scattered off quietly.

After Olivia was attended to and sleeping soundly with her husband in the chair beside their bed, I joined Jackson on the lounge. My parents had excused themselves to my father's study for which I was grateful since it allowed me some alone time with Jackson.

"I don't understand this." I shook my head in dismay. "None of this makes sense. We saw pictures of them with their son."

"I'm not sure." Jackson thought for a moment. "Did you happen to notice if any of the photographs had dates written on them?"

"No, remember there was nothing written underneath them and I did not dare remove them to see if the dates were written on the back."

"Well obviously the children we saw them with come at a later time."

"I guess. I feel so horrible for the two of them. Olivia is beside herself with grief. She wanted this baby so badly."

"I know, but at least it is a comfort to know that they do have happy healthy children in their future."

We rested for a while, but I could not get the image of Olivia out of my mind. All I wanted to do was drift off into my *other* world where I did not have to endure the sorrow that fell upon our entire household.

CHAPTER 5

Sunday, November 29, 2009

I CLEANED MYSELF UP and threw on a pair of jeans and a sweatshirt. After pulling my hair up in a ponytail and barely applying any make-up, I headed downstairs to find something to eat.

My mom, Sidney, and Landon were in the kitchen when I arrived. My mom took one glance in my direction and walked out the other entrance and headed back up to her room. "Wow . . . do you think she'll ever speak to me again?" I asked my worn-out looking sister.

"Not any time soon," she half laughed. "She's really ticked about Thanksgiving."

"Why? It's not like we were doing anything special for the holiday. She wasn't even cooking for crying out loud," I said.

"It's not so much that. It's more the fact that you two are back together. She's afraid the wedding's back on."

"Great," I muttered, rolling my eyes. "How are you feeling?" I asked casually while pouring myself a cup of coffee.

Landon picked up another donut and his coffee and kissed Sidney on the cheek. "I'll be in the family room." Sidney smiled and nodded as he left the kitchen.

"I'm all right. Weird dream I guess. I'm not really sure what happened." She gave me a weak smile.

"What was it about?" I leaned over the opposite side of the island where she was seated.

"Something stupid." Sidney attempted to shrug it off, but the look in her eyes reminded me all too well of the reflection I'd seen in the mirror in another time.

I smiled sadly, at a complete loss for words. Having been in her shoes before I knew there was nothing I could say that would bring her any solace or make her talk about it. I sipped my coffee trying to think of something else to say just to change the subject.

"Do you guys have any plans for today?"

"I think Landon's going to watch football with the other two delinquents. I'm not sure what time we're going to head back to campus. Why? What are your plans for today?"

"Nothing, do you have anything in mind?"

"Want to go into the city and do some Christmas shopping?" She looked hopeful.

"All right." My smile broadened. "That sounds good."

"Why don't you call Jenna or Caitlyn, see if they want to join us?"

"Okay." Sidney had never hung around with me or my friends. I guess this was her way of avoiding being alone with me. Maybe she was afraid I'd bring up her nightmares again.

"Great, you take care of that and I'll tell the guys we're leaving." She jumped off the barstool and trotted off.

I stood there for a few minutes longer finishing my coffee and debating on whether I should call Jackson or Caitlyn first. Jenna was still in Indianapolis with her family until later this evening. I wanted to speak with Jackson, but I figured I'd better call Caitlyn first simply because I knew it would take her a while to get ready.

*   *   *

It was shortly before one o'clock before the three of us pulled out of the driveway. Caitlyn was talking a mile a minute about her Thanksgiving and all the craziness with her own family.

I think Sidney was thankful because it kept her thoughts off her own terrifying experience or me inquiring any further about it. Instead she stared ahead at the road, smiled, and nodded in all the appropriate places but never joined in the conversation.

Her behavior didn't seem that unusual because she was never that friendly with Caitlyn.

We parked in a large parking garage and wandered through the various shops looking for anything interesting. It was a chilly day with the sun darting in and out of the clouds. I pulled my jacket closer around me and wrapped my scarf once more around my neck. Sidney appeared preoccupied with her thoughts and hardly paid any attention to Caitlyn's overzealous behavior.

She was bouncing around looking at every peculiar trinket that adorned the city windows. I tagged along between them, only concerned with trying to keep the cold wind from ripping through me.

*   *   *

It was six in the evening when we returned home. It was already dark and the temperature was steadily declining. Caitlyn waved good-bye as she pulled her car out of our driveway and headed home. Sidney and I scurried up the walkway and could already hear the voices of the men hollering at the television from the front porch. We looked at each other and laughed before opening the door.

Ethan, Landon, and our dad were all in the family room with a fire blazing in the hearth, empty coke cans and beer bottles covering the tables intermixed with half-eaten bags of chips and pretzels and an almost empty pizza box. None of them noticed our return.

Sidney and I wandered into the kitchen to fix ourselves some hot chocolate. She took a seat at the island while I busied myself getting our drinks.

"Do you think Mom's been in her room all day?" she asked.

"Probably. She's been hiding in there, supposedly dictating patient charts. At least that's what she told Ethan earlier." I took a deep breath, stirring the mix into the hot water. "I don't know. She hasn't really spoken to me since I mentioned BU and marrying Jackson."

"Can you blame her?"

"Sidney . . . don't. I've heard enough already from her, Ethan, and my friends. I really don't want to have the same conversation with you." Our eyes met for a moment.

"All right. I'm just saying, don't be stupid."

"I'm not. And like you really have room to talk . . . I can't believe Mom and Dad let Landon sleep in your room."

"He was sleeping on the couch." I tried not to giggle at how defensive she got. "Seriously . . . he was. He knows sometimes I have nightmares and he wanted to be there in case I had one. It's no big deal." She shrugged it off casually.

"How often are you having them?"

"It's not a big deal, Jocelyn. Drop it!"

"Geez, Sid, calm down. You brought it up."

"Sorry, it's been a long semester. I'll be happy when it's over."

I set the mugs of hot coco on the island and sat down across from her. "Are you taking anything interesting this semester?"

"Finite Math, which I hate and makes no sense whatsoever. I'm not even sure why they call it math." she rolled her eyes with a smile. "Ummmm . . . Behavioral Neuroscience, History of Western Civilization, which would be interesting if my professor wasn't so darn boring. Anthropology. That sounds boring except that I have an amazing professor that makes the class fascinating, and Organic Chemistry."

"Sounds fun. At least you're not taking the boring crap that I'm taking. I'm so sick of high school. I can't wait until I get to college."

"It's okay, I guess. Don't rush high school away, Jocelyn. College is so much harder than you can imagine. I have no life. I'm buried in books and I think I have more coffee running through my veins than blood." A small laugh escaped from somewhere inside her. "I hardly get any sleep anymore, maybe three or four hours if I'm lucky."

"I thought you loved Northwestern."

"I do. It's just a lot more work and harder than I ever imagined it would be."

We sipped our coco in silence for a few minutes listening to the hollering of the men in the other room. Sidney glanced at her watch wrinkling her brow. "It's almost seven. We'd better head back to school or I'm never going to make it to class tomorrow." She smiled weakly.

"I hate to see you leave, Sid. It seems like we're finally getting to know each other." I looked into her tired eyes and grinned.

"Finally . . . I always wanted us to be closer. We just really never had anything in common."

"And we do now?" I laughed.

"No, not really, I suppose. But maybe we're starting to appreciate and accept each other for who we are rather than focusing on our differences."

"I hope so." I took another sip nervously. This sort of dialogue was very out of the ordinary for us. "Are you coming home for Christmas?"

"Most likely. I know Landon wants to spend some time with his family, but I'm not sure I want to. I think I'll come home while he visits his family and then he can join me here later."

"When is your last final?"

"The nineteenth. I should be home shortly after."

"Good, we'll bake some Christmas cookies and make the house more festive."

"Bake cookies?" She narrowed her eyes at me and laughed. "We don't bake cookies, we buy them."

"Oh, come on, it'll be fun." I gave her a playful nudge across the island.

"I'll think about it," she said, rolling her eyes.

"I'm surprised Mom hasn't put up the tree yet. She always does that on the Friday after Thanksgiving."

"Yeah, I know." I looked down at my mug instantly feeling guilty for sucking all the holiday spirit out of the house.

"Hey?" Sidney tapped her fingers on the island. "Don't worry about it, she'll come around."

"I hope so," I muttered, picking up my coco.

*   *   *

Sidney and Landon left before nine o'clock and even though they were only home for a short while, the house felt empty when they'd gone.

I took a long hot shower washing the city smog out of my hair and ridding my bones of the late fall chill. I relaxed under the stream and tried not to think of what was waiting for me when I closed my eyes. I had done my best all day to keep my thoughts focused on Sidney and her night terrors if only to avoid the pain that I could feel in the depths of my soul. The images I had witnessed when Patrick sent Jackson and William downstairs were still very vivid.

I crawled into bed pulling my covers up around me. This big old house was so drafty in cold weather despite the new renovations. I thumbed through my uncle's journal, looking for the place I'd left off when I noticed my bedroom door opening silently.

"Ethan . . . I'm in bed. Leave me alone," I said to the gap.

Jackson poked his head into my bedroom. "It's me," he smiled.

"Jackson!" I whispered. "What are you doing?"

"I wanted to speak to you." He quietly closed the door behind him and sat down on the corner of my bed.

"I have a cell phone."

"I also wanted to see you." There was no way I could be upset when he looked at me that way.

"Please don't tell me you snuck into my house again." I shook my head in dismay.

"No one saw me." He flashed my favorite mischievous lop-sided grin.

"You have any idea what my mother would do if she found you in here?"

"Is she speaking to you now?"

"No, but that's not the point." I gently smacked his arm.

"Then I guess I don't have to worry about her coming in here."

"But my father could."

"He thinks you're asleep. He will not bother you for the rest of the night."

"Are you willing to bet your life on it because he'll kill you if he finds you in here?" I snickered.

"I wanted to see how you were doing with all that happened? Do you remember any of it?"

"What I do remember, I wish I could forget." I looked down at my hands. "I've never seen anything so awful, there was so much blood. I'm glad my father didn't let William see any of that."

"He's a mess."

"I wish there was something I could do for them." I looked back up into Jackson's face. "The whole thing with the photos has been bothering me." I reached under my bed and pulled out the old album and flipped it open. "I took this from the basement after Sidney left. Look . . . here's proof that they have children."

I placed the open album on his lap and pointed to the family picture of William and Olivia with their first son.

"I know, but there is no date written beneath it." He gently slid the photo from its corner tabs that secured its place.

"Careful," I cringed.

Jackson flipped the photo over, "Look, May 18, 1883. That is another four and a half years from where we are now . . . *there* anyway." He handed the picture over.

"I guess Olivia had a hard time either getting pregnant again or carrying a child to term."

"Maybe. Or they were just careful until William finished his degree."

"Perhaps. It seems strange though, doesn't it? Especially after last evening, knowing all that is to happen."

"That is a big drawback to this gift. You see or know things that you cannot share with others whom you care about."

"Sometimes I wish I didn't know so much about our future . . . our children. It's so aggravating to know we have so long before they're here and I want to see them, hold them now. I don't want to wait another ten years."

"Me neither, but just imagine how much fun we are going to have in those ten years. College, graduations, weddings . . . a lot is going to happen in that time and I believe we will have enough to keep us very busy."

"True," I giggled, thinking about how busy planning one wedding was keeping me *here*.

We curled up together and talked for the next couple of hours about all of the things that were happening now on both planes and all the things that still were ahead. The last thing I remember was Jackson talking about our beautiful babies while I rested with my head on his chest, securely wrapped in his arms.

Chapter 6

Wednesday, December 04, 1878

THE SOUND OF THUNDER rumbled through the house followed by a long brilliant flash of lightening, awaking me from a lost slumber. My heart raced from the abrupt noise. I could hear the rain dancing off the house and wind whistling through the barren trees. The drapes around the windows moved softly from the small drafts along the windowsills. The embers glowed from the hearth, casting long, strange shadows along my walls. I pulled my covers up around my chin and snuggled down tight beneath them.

Jackson had disappeared the last couple of days. He was now home from school but buried under a mountain of books and papers preparing to take the bar exam. He had come over briefly on Monday to have supper with my family and then disappeared once more. I believe I saw him more when he was away at school than I was now.

William had stayed home the last couple of days, tending to and comforting Olivia. She had not gotten out of bed since the miscarriage and was consumed with grief. We all spent time with her regularly, but there was nothing any of us could say to console her. William spent his days next to their bed reading to her in attempt to occupy her mind with something else. I was amazed by my brother's compassion for his young wife and touched by the loss that seemed to be overwhelming him.

* * *

Time was dragging on relentlessly. I stared out the window trying to block out the monotone voice of Mr. Grahame droning on about the Revolutionary War. It had finally stopped raining shortly before lunch. The sky had turned a pale gray and was threatening snow. The world outside stood still and silent. It looked cold and lonely as if it wanted to remain untouched until spring.

Mr. Grahame finished up his lecture with a final note that there could possibly be a quiz tomorrow over the material covered in class today. *Great. Exactly what I don't need or care about right now.* I gathered up my things and met Elizabeth by her seat. She smiled warmly at me with a smile that reached all the way to her eyes.

"I cannot wait to get out of here today," she began.

"Excuse me, Ms. Jocelyn," Mr. Grahame spoke up before we could make it out the door. "Could you come here for a moment?"

Elizabeth gave me a questioning look. I shrugged. "It's all right. I will meet you in Choir. I don't want you to be late because of me."

She nodded softly and hurried out with our peers. I took a deep breath and made my way back over to our teacher's desk where he was sorting through a pile of papers.

Mr. Grahame's light brown hair with soft curls was brushed back away from his face. His bluish grey eyes were fixed on the notebook in front of him. He glanced up as I approached with a look of disapproval on his face.

"Mr. Campbell would like to see you in his office immediately." He handed me a slip of paper and went back to his stack of papers without another word.

I walked slowly down the now empty hallway trying to figure out why I was being summoned by the headmaster of our school. I couldn't think of anything that I'd done to warrant an invitation to his office. A cold chill filled the hall. My shoes echoed loudly off the walls between me and the closed administration office in front of me. I took a deep breath and opened the door.

After waiting several minutes, the secretary, Ms. Gladstone, ushered me into the inner sanctuary that in my years at Prep, I'd never seen.

"Ms. Timmons, please have a seat." Mr. Campbell stood as I entered and motioned towards one of the two chairs in front of his master desk.

"Thank you. I received a message from Mr. Grahame that you wanted to see me." I sat down and tried not to fidget.

"Your teachers and I are very concerned about the number of absences you have been accumulating this term," he said, firmly retaking his seat.

"Yes, sir."

"Now I realize that you have kept current on all your assignments and from what I have been told, you are one of, if not the top student in your class."

"Thank you, sir." I sat there uncomfortably not sure what to say to him.

"However, I am concerned that you may not be getting the full benefit of your education because of the number of days you have missed." He folded his hands upon his desk and looked pointedly at me.

"Excuse me, sir. I do not wish to sound disrespectful in any way, but why does that matter?" I questioned.

A look of surprise creased his earlier studious expression. "Why does it matter? Of course, it matters. Your education is extremely important . . . for your present, your future, for shaping the type of lady you become." I hadn't realized a frown had appeared across my face, which he mimicked. "Why the confused look, Ms. Timmons?"

My mind screamed at me to be polite and keep my true feelings concealed for my own sake, but the stronger more forceful voice inside me took over. "Mr. Campbell, you and I both know that my educational prospects are extremely limited. I am fortunate to have been able to continue it to this level. But there is no possibility of my being able to attend a university like my brothers regardless of my desire to do so."

"Ms. Timmons, you must realize that women are now attending universities all over our country and getting higher degrees of education. Why do you believe you cannot? Besides of course, your upcoming marriage to Mr. Chandler."

He paused for a moment, scratching his chin in thought. "I do not recall ever hearing of a married woman attending any university." A slight scowl crossed his face.

"Neither have I and even if I was not getting married later this month, my father would never allow me to continue my education," I explained.

"Are you sure? Have you spoken with your parents about it? Or Mr. Chandler?" His voice dropped an octave.

"Not recently, but my father made it very clear several years ago when he caught me reading one of his medical books that it was improper for a lady to have such knowledge. He took it from me, told me that my role when I grew up was to run the house and take care of my husband and children. Then he told me I was never allowed to touch any of the books in his office and he sent me to my room for the rest of the day." I shook my head slowly with my own disbelief.

"And Mr. Chandler?"

"He is very supportive of my desire to learn, but please do not tell anyone," I asked in a soft voice.

"You have my word. Does he aid you in your studies?"

"Yes, as much as he can. It will be much easier once we are married and have a home of our own . . . a place where I no longer have to hide."

"Ms. Timmons, I am sorry that you believe you have to hide such an amazing gift. You are very intelligent, and you could easily get into any university that you applied to," he said with a sad look.

"Thank you, but I believe that for the sake of my family, peace and acceptance of my place would be best for everyone." If my *other* self wasn't already heading to Boston University those words would never had slid so effortlessly off my tongue.

"All right, Ms. Timmons. However, you do know that your final graduation exam is rapidly approaching." He cleared his throat, shifted in his seat and straightened up in a professional manner once more.

"Since you will not be returning for the spring term, I want you to understand that there will be some material that has not been covered in your classes."

"Yes, I understand."

"You will be taking the same exam as your peers who will have completed the spring semester. Please prepare yourself. I will have a study guide for you on Monday that should give you a better idea of what to expect."

"Thank you."

"You are welcome." He scribbled down a quick note on a piece of paper and handed it to me. "Please give this to Mrs. Eads with my apology for keeping you. Have a nice weekend Ms. Timmons."

"Thank you, Mr. Campbell." I stood.

I hurried out of his room wondering if I had said more than I should have.

*   *   *

Elizabeth and I pulled our caplets tightly around us, trying to keep the wind from breaking us. I wanted to confide in her about what had happened with Olivia, but I knew it wasn't my place to say anything. Instead I made small talk about my meeting with Mr. Campbell and the upcoming final exam. I chattered on like a parrot and she listened attentively, making small comments and assurances where appropriate.

Elizabeth and I said our goodbyes and parted at the gate. I hurried inside and placed my books on the table in the foyer. Eddie came down the hall from the kitchen upon hearing the front door open. "Good afternoon, Ms. Jocelyn." He nodded his head slightly.

"Good day, Eddie." I nodded in return before handing him my hat and caplet. I laid my books on the small table in the foyer and headed into the kitchen.

Cora, Mimi, and Sara were seated around the small table by the back window talking quietly over tea and angel food cake. I paused in the doorway beside the cabinet just out of their line of sight not wanting to disturb them.

"You too young to remember that ugly time an' I glad you is. The war was awful an' tis a bad time in this here city," Mimi said to her daughter.

"I's remember some of it, but not much. I remember the camp. It smelled awful an' was full a filthy rebels," Cora replied.

I listened to them unnoticed for several minutes before I exited the room and walked to the parlor. I sat down at the piano and Beethoven flowed from my fingers. The words from the kitchen lingered in the back of my head. I had no idea what they meant.

* * *

Jonathon and his family arrived for dinner around five o'clock. I heard their voices from the foyer as Mother greeted them. They all gathered in the parlor with my mother and Lizette fussing over the children. I remained at the piano, standing only briefly when they initially entered the room. The ladies took a seat on the lounge. I could hear them discussing Lizette's methods of teaching her little ones the alphabet when my fingers began moving once more across the keys.

"Is Father home yet?" Jonathon sat down on the seat beside me.

"I do not believe so. I have not seen him this afternoon," I answered without pausing the song I was playing.

"Are you excited about almost being done with school?"

"No, not really. I wish I could go to college like you did," I whispered, leaning closer to him.

"That, my dear little sister, would never happen," he chuckled. "We do as we are told and study what we are told. You know that." He looked down at his hands briefly. I knew Jonathon, out of all my brothers, understood that more than anyone.

"Can I talk to you privately for a moment?" I glanced over at the two women still talking happily on the lounge.

"Yes, of course. We can use Father's study."

We stood up and walked out of the room. Neither of the ladies even looked up or seemed to notice our departure.

With office door closed securely behind us, Jonathon and I took a seat in the chairs next to the hearth where Eddie had already built a roaring fire in anticipation of Father's return home. I smiled across at my most quiet and sensitive brother, hoping to make him more comfortable.

Jonathon was stuck in between James and William. A position that would have been difficult for any child considering that James was the athletic and handsome one and William was the charming and carefree brother who never took life seriously. Or at least William was before life finally caught up with him and took a serious bite out of his hindquarters.

"How was work today?" I began slowly.

"It was fine, Jocelyn, but I am sure you did not want to speak with me alone to discuss my patients." He was completing his last year of residency and worked directly under our brother Patrick. He crossed his legs, looking very studious. He reminded me of one of my teachers.

"No, but I did get called to Mr. Campbell's office today." I gave him a brief rendition of my earlier conversation leaving out several key elements like my forwardness and Jackson's feelings regarding my studies.

"I knew you were intelligent, but I had no idea you were first in your class. That is wonderful, Jocelyn. Congratulations!" He leaned forward and patted me on the knee with a broad smile.

"Thank you, I appreciate that. However, it is not the reason I asked to speak with you. You did take American History when you were an undergrad, right?"

"Yes, it was required. Why?"

"When I came home from class today I overhead Sarah, Mimi, and Cora speaking in the kitchen and Mimi said something I did not understand. I was hoping perhaps you would know. She said something regarding a Camp Douglass or Eighty Acres of Hell. I have heard references to that before between Robert and Father and I have never known what it was."

Jonathon sighed audibly. "Father would give me a licking if I spoke to you about Camp Douglass."

"Please, Jonathon? I am not a child anymore. I am tired of being treated like one," I pleaded with him.

"It has nothing to do with treating you like a child. He would be upset with me for speaking to you about it because you are a lady and men do not discuss such topics with ladies," he stated bluntly.

"Do you have any idea how sexist you sound?" My voice raised an octave.

Jonathon's jaw dropped to his lap and his eyes grew huge. "I cannot believe you just said that to me."

"Why? It is true," I glared.

"Jocelyn, how can you be so . . . What kind of people are you exposed to at school? They certainly have been a very bad influence on you," he chastised me like a small child.

"Oh, Jonathon, you sound a lot like Father. Are you going to hold your daughters back the way Father has with my education?" I immediately regretted the words as soon as they slipped through my lips.

"Well then, I can see this conversation is over. Have a good evening, little sister." He emphasized the word 'little' before he stood up and walked out of the room.

"Great," I muttered before leaving the room myself and heading upstairs. I no longer had any appetite for dinner.

CHAPTER 7

Wednesday, December 02, 2009

IN-SCHOOL SUSPENSION was not exactly fun. However, it was well worth it for the opportunity to flatten out Taylor once and for all for her comments and constant pursuit of Jackson. It was not something I was particularity proud of, but that little devil that occasionally sits on my shoulder was grinning from ear to ear.

I'd spent the last couple days in a small room off the side of the main office area alone, doing nothing but schoolwork. On the bright side, I had managed to catch up on the reading I'd been neglecting since the discovery of my uncle's journals. However, being alone for eight hours a day was driving me batty and I hated it. I wasn't even allowed to have lunch with my friends. Still, I was thankful that at least my schoolwork was counted for and I wasn't receiving zeros on a week's worth of assignments and exams like Taylor was.

Basketball practice was grueling. Our first game was the following evening and Coach Smith wanted to make sure we were in top form. I was thrilled when the final whistle blew, and we headed into the locker room.

"I don't know how she expects us to do our best tomorrow, my legs feel like rubber," Hilary complained, leaning against her locker still trying to catch her breath.

"I know, all I want to do is take a hot shower and go to bed," Caitlyn added.

"Wish I could," Jenna, who was changing her clothes, joined in the conversation. "I've got so much freakin' homework I'll be up half the night getting it done."

"Not me. Solitude allows a lot of time to get homework done." I rolled my eyes. "I am all caught up."

"So, all I have to do to get my homework done is punch Taylor? Huh? I can do that!" Caitlyn laughed.

"Must be nice," Jenna grumbled and slammed her locker shut.

"Not really, I am bored to tears sitting in that room alone for hours on end," I complained.

The guys were all waiting for us in the parking lot. It was cold and dreary out with the air full of a misting rain. Jackson and Zak looked as worn out as we did and made very little small talk before climbing into their respective cars and heading home.

*   *   *

I went over to Jackson's for dinner after a quick shower. Emily had made homemade chicken noodle soup with fresh baked bread that simply melted in my mouth. I stuffed myself while they discussed Olivia's miscarriage and how she and William were coping. I added what I could to the conversation, but the topic was so depressing.

"May I ask you an odd question, Jocelyn?" Robert inquired from out of the blue.

"Of course."

"Emily and I were trying to figure something out and we were hoping that perhaps you could clarify it for us," he started. "On Thanksgiving you mentioned something regarding your father, Shane, having another brother."

"Yes, his younger brother, Nicholas."

"Do you know him well?" Emily asked after exchanging a look with Robert.

"No. He and my dad don't speak anymore. I barely remember him at all. I believe my dad has not spoken to him since Uncle Monte's funeral."

"Do you know why they are estranged?" Robert asked.

"Not really. Only that my dad said he's not right in the head. I think he's a professor at Indiana University," I snorted.

"Professor of what?" Jackson joined in the conversation while Robert and Emily's eyes held onto each other, speaking volumes that I did not understand.

"I have no idea. I only know he's there because my mom mentioned it when we visited the IU campus last summer. She asked him if he was going to stop by and see him, but my dad refused and quickly hushed my mother." I looked between Jackson's parents for a second to see if I could pick up on what wasn't being said. "Why are you asking about my uncle Nicholas?"

"Well . . ." Robert hesitantly began. "It seems that maybe he has also inherited *EVE*."

"What?" I almost chocked on a mouthful of bread.

"Monte mentioned something about Nicholas and Shane being estranged, but he told us that we should speak with Nicholas about some work he has been doing regarding *EVE*," Emily said gently.

The realization of what they were thinking fully sunk in. I had not thought about my dad's younger brother in years. It had never occurred to me that my uncle Nicholas *there* was the same one I vaguely remembered *here*. Somehow it just didn't seem possible. "If he has this thing also . . . why hasn't he approached me and said anything to me *there*?"

"We are not sure how much Monte had shared with him and we have never spoken with Nicholas about it," Robert replied.

"So, he knows I have it . . . or that maybe Sidney does also?" I shook my head slowly. "I cannot believe my uncle Nicholas *there* is the one and the same *here*," I said barely loud enough for them to hear me.

"We do not believe he knows you are remembering," Emily added.

I sat in silence trying to let the words sink in fully. A million questions were running through my mind that I wanted to ask my uncle, but I wasn't even positive how to get in touch with him.

* * *

I got home shortly before eight and ran straight upstairs to my computer. I typed in the website for Indiana University and found their search engine. I typed in my uncle's name and it pulled up a picture of him, his credentials, department, and contact information at the university. The face staring back at me on the monitor was indeed the same one that I vaguely recalled from my youth and the visions of my *other* life.

It seemed my uncle Nicholas held a doctorate in history and a bachelor's in Philosophy. *A rather queer combination for the ordinary person.* I pulled up Microsoft Word on my computer and started drafting an email to him. I got as far as the initial salutations and then sat there stumped and staring at the screen. I had no clue how to begin such a letter. *Hello, Uncle Nicholas, this is your niece Jocelyn and I was wondering if you also had the ability to live on two planes of existence like I do. I was told by the Chandlers, who came to Chicago looking for me, that's it's referred to as EVE. If you do happen to have it and would like to discuss it with me, please call me.*

Yeah, that doesn't sound a bit insane.

I sighed heavily and deleted the document. There was no way I could send him a casual email of any sort. I needed to speak with him in person. *But how am I going to get all the way down to Bloomington, Indiana? It's at least a five-hour drive.*

* * *

An hour later I found my dad milling over paperwork in his office.

"Ummm, Dad, mind if I interrupt for a second?" I lingered in the doorway.

"Sure." He looked up as I took a seat in the armchair across from his desk by the hearth. "What's up?"

"I wanted to check something with you. Emily and I were working on the guest list for the wedding and she asked me about our family," I lied, hoping not to draw any suspicion from him.

"Okay." He shuffled some papers around not paying much attention to me.

"Well, I wasn't sure if you wanted me to invite Uncle Nick or not."

His demeanor immediately changed. "No, you most certainly may not invite him!"

"All right, I just wanted to check. I know you didn't want to see him last summer when we were down at IU, but I wasn't sure if you had spoken to him since." I tried to play it off innocently.

"No, nor do I plan to." He shuffled his papers again absentmindedly. "You don't need that crackpot ruining your wedding."

"Crackpot?" I laughed. "I thought he was a professor?"

"He is, but . . ." My dad took a deep breath and exhaled loudly. "Jocelyn, I have not spoken to Nick since Monte passed away unexpectedly. Your uncle said some things at the funeral that well . . . make me believe that he's not exactly playing with a full deck."

"Really? Like what?" I gently urged him to continue.

"It's a long story, Jocelyn and not one you should worry about."

"But what could he have said that was so awful that would cause you not to speak to him for more than a decade?" I pushed.

"He told me after the funeral, when we were alone, that Monte and he had inherited some special gift. Some weird thing, I can't even remember what he called it, but he said that it allowed them to live on two planes of existence and that our brother was in love with a woman named Vivian. She apparently did not have this gift so rather than live only with her part time, he chose to leave our world and is now happily married and living in the late nineteenth century." My dad half laughed and rolled his eyes. "So yes, that is why I call him a crackpot."

I grimaced slightly and nodded my head. "Understandable. So, I won't invite Uncle Nick. Anyone else I need to know about?"

"Nope." He glanced over at his clock. "You'd better focus on your homework right now and worry about the guest list later."

"All right, Dad." I got up and walked over to his chair. I gave him a hug and kissed his cheek. "I'll see you in the morning."

"Sweet dreams," he said before I closed his office door.

I headed back upstairs to call Jackson. I stopped for a moment in front of Ethan's room. His television was blaring, and I could hear him talking on his cell phone to someone. I hated to admit how much I really missed him. He was always someone I'd taken for granted would always be in my life, but now he wouldn't even speak to me.

I flopped down across my bed and picked up my cell phone. I dialed Jackson's number and waited impatiently for the call to connect.

"Hello?" he answered on the third ring.

"Hey, you'll never believe what I just found out!" I rambled on tirelessly everything my dad had just told me.

"Hmmm . . ."

"Hmmm? Is that all you're going to say?"

"What did you expect me to say?" he chuckled.

"I don't know. Something. I can't believe he actually told my dad the truth. What was he expecting him to think?" I asked.

"I am not sure. It is rather unusual," Jackson admitted.

"No wonder they haven't spoken in years."

"I cannot imagine Alexander doing anything that would make me cut him out of my life, even if I did not agree with his views or beliefs."

"I never thought anything could come between Ethan and me either but look at us now. We're not talking."

"Yes, but that is only temporary, and you did not cut him out of your life."

"I want to see him, talk to him in person."

"Isn't he across the hall?" Jackson said in a coy tone.

"Cute. I was talking about my uncle Nicholas. I know where he's at. It's the getting there that's going to be a problem. IU is about five hours away," I explained.

"That's not that far. Let me see what I can do."

"Jackson, what are you up to now?"

"I will let you know in the morning."

"Jackson?" He knew how much I hated it when he pulled this crap.

"I will see you in the morning. I love you."

"I love you too."

I hung up the phone not sure what exactly he had in mind. I set the phone on my nightstand and picked up Uncle Monte's journal hoping I could find something in there that would give me a little insight into what my uncle Nicholas was up to.

CHAPTER 8

Thursday, December 01, 1878

THE RAIN was never ending. It suffocated our world with all the emotions that the entire household was wearing on their sleeves. We remained in mourning for the loss of William and Olivia's child. Sadness hung heavy over all of us and everyone's movements, including the staff, were slower, almost challenging.

The long days at prep seemed torturous as I hated spending the time away from Olivia and Jackson. Classes were the furthest thing from my mind and I had no desire to put any effort into my studies. I felt my time would be better spent comforting Olivia if it was only sitting beside her bed quietly holding her hand.

By the time Elizabeth and I set out for home the temperatures had dropped markedly. The sky had finally opened, allowing soft light flakes to drift down around us. The air was frigid, clean, and crisp. She chatted lightly about Lee and how their relationship was moving along smoothly. She talked about his siblings, his parents and his childhood in Indiana. I listened intently, grateful for the distraction from all the drama in my worlds. I was saddened when we finally reached my house and had to part ways, but she was anxious to get home and complete her schoolwork before Lee stopped by after work.

After putting my things aside, I made my way to the stairs leading to William and Olivia's room. I knocked softly on the door but received no reply. I quietly opened the door, expecting her to be asleep. Instead I found her sitting in the rocker staring blankly out the side window in the direction of the house she had once called home.

"Good afternoon, Olivia. How are you feeling today?" I asked softly.

"I wonder if they know," she said in a low voice without looking in my direction.

I crossed the room and sat down on the end of the bed. "I don't know how they would. No one knows where they moved."

"I would imagine someone knows. I thought about writing my grandmother and asking her. I am sure she knows how to get in touch with them."

"Perhaps you should if it would make you feel better." I couldn't imagine why she would want to after all they had done to her, but I supposed she had her reasons.

"I'm not sure if I am ready to speak with them yet." Olivia shrugged slightly still focused on the house next door.

"Are you all right?"

"Would you mind, Jocelyn, I would like to be alone right now."

"Whatever you want, Olivia. Just remember I'm right down the hall if you need anything."

"Thank you," she whispered before I closed the door behind me.

*   *   *

I joined William and my parents for dinner in the dining room after I had completed my homework. The conversation was light and not over any one subject. William's eyes were dark and heavy, and he looked as poorly as he had in the weeks before his wedding. He remarked once that he would be leaving early in the morning to return to Northwestern. He said he was afraid that he was falling behind in his coursework yet was still unsure about leaving his wife in such a state. Mother promised him repeatedly that we would all take very good care of her.

Once the rest of my family had retired for the evening, I leaned my head against the windowpane in my bedroom taking a moment to collect my thoughts. The overwhelming urge to scream had died out into pure exhaustion. The world seemed to be a cold, cruel, and unfair place.

The soft sound of approaching footsteps broke my train of thought.

"How ya holdin' up, child?" Mimi placed her warm gentle hand on my shoulder.

I peered up into her caring tired eyes and tried to smile. "I'm all right. How is Olivia doing?"

"Finally, asleep."

"Good." I let out a small sigh of relief.

"Yes'm, I's thinks so. She's had a rough time of it. I did get her to drink some chicken broth befo' she drifted off." She sat down on the other end of the bay window.

I nodded my head slowly. "Good. She will need it to regain some strength."

"Yes'm," Mimi gave me a motherly smile.

We sat in silence for a short while. Mimi looked tired and worn out, like the last couple months had weighed heavily on her too.

"I wish I could understand why all of this happened?" I whispered.

Of course, I was referring to the loss of the baby but also this new world that was exploding around me as well.

"I's don't know, child, but everything happens for a reason."

I closed my eyes and tried to fathom what possible event had suddenly occurred to make it necessary to flip my entire world upside down. A part of me was elated with the idea of getting to continue my education and have any career I desired. Still, the flip side of the coin was full of despair at all the new limitations and restrictions being thrust upon me. Having to monitor every word, every action, social cue, was overwhelming. I felt like I was being placed under a microscope and studied. *Perhaps maybe I should be . . . perhaps then I could finally get some answers about this whole EVE thing. Why do I have to be the only one amongst my siblings to inherit such a gift . . . or curse?*

To have the ability to experience life in two lives, in drastically different worlds, remained a concept that felt so surreal to me. *How is it even possible to have one life that is so . . . basic and another that is so challenging and amazing at the same time?* I wondered how many people had the same genetic marker.

CHAPTER 9

Thursday, December 03, 2009

JACKSON WAS ALREADY WAITING for us next to his car when Ethan and I walked out the front door. He was smiling widely, which made me more nervous about what he was up to after our conversation the night before.

"Do you have any plans this weekend?" he asked as we approached.

"No, why?"

"My dad managed to get his hands on four tickets to the Colts game on Sunday for my birthday." Jackson's smile broadened.

"The Colts? They're not playing the Bears this Sunday." Ethan looked oddly at Jackson. It was the first almost polite thing that he had said to him in weeks.

"I know. They are playing Tennessee at the new Lucas Oil Stadium in Indianapolis." Jackson turned his attention back in my direction. "So, would you like to go?"

"Of course," I quickly realized what he had put together for me.

"But you don't even like football!" Ethan said loudly.

"I do so. I go to all your games, don't I?" I glared his way.

"Only because your friends go. You never watch NFL games." His eyes narrowed at me as he opened the back door.

"Maybe you should have thought about that before being such an ass to Jackson. Then maybe he would have asked you instead," I taunted before climbing in the passenger seat and slamming the door.

"You don't even know who their quarterback is," Ethan continued hotly, folding his body into the backseat.

"Peyton Manning. Geez E, even I know that." I turned around and smirked at him.

"There's no way Mom is going to let you go." He returned, satisfied with his quick wit.

"I'm eighteen, remember? I do not need her permission to go anywhere." I turned back around and the three of us remained silent the rest of the drive to school.

Word about our trip to Indy seemed to spread like wildfire throughout our group of friends. During lunch, both Cody and Zak volunteered to take my place and tried several times to change Jackson's mind about taking me to the game. Apparently, this new stadium was some big deal in the NFL and the Colts were great prospects for the Super Bowl. None of which I knew anything about.

Jackson made me suffer all day at school. He wouldn't give me any of the details as to what he and his parents were up to. All he would say is that everything was covered. By the time we made it to Mr. Rand's psychology class at the end of the day, I was ready to strangle him.

Jackson had practice during the small break that we got before our opening game. So, I had no opportunity to drill him on anything. I fidgeted relentlessly, which thankfully Caitlyn attributed to my nerves for the opening game.

"Hey, calm down. This is no different than any other game we've played." She placed her hand on my shoulder in the locker room.

"I can't believe it. This is our last first basketball game in high school." Hilary leaned against her locker. "I can't believe how fast this year is flying by."

"I know, Christmas break is only three weeks away and then 2010," Jenna added, slipping on her jersey.

Their voices faded around me as I went through the motions of changing into my uniform and thought about how different I was with them in comparison to Olivia, Elizabeth, Laurie, and Christine. I couldn't imagine any of them attempting anything remotely close to a sporting activity, nor the girl I was *there*.

"Jocelyn? You okay?" I nodded numbly. "Come on. We've got to get out there." Jenna tugged on my arm.

We trotted out onto the court with the rest of our teammates and performed the same ol' routine we'd done before every game during our high school career. Jenna smiled and waved over at the bleachers causing my gaze to follow. Jackson, Kyle, Cody, and Zak were all sitting together. I smiled at Jackson and scanned to see whether my parents or Ethan had arrived yet. Then my heart sunk a little when I found only my dad sitting beside Jackson's and Jenna's parents without my mom or brother.

We fought hard and barely came out victorious. Being the starting point guard, it took me several plays before I became immersed in the game and forgot about all the drama outside the gym. Luckily, the other team made several sloppy passes, making it very easy for Caitlyn to steal the ball.

*   *   *

Showered and changed, I stood in front of my locker with my friends but could not seem to join in on their enthusiasm for our win. My mind kept wandering back to what my dad had said about his brother's confession. It had destroyed their relationship and splintered our family. I could not help but think of the Uncle Nicolas I recalled from my *other* life and how much I enjoyed his easy-going and jovial temperament. I couldn't help but be curious about the professor at IU. Was this man like the one in my visions? Could he be like the Chandlers and have the same temperament in both eras? Was he well-adjusted to living dual existences? Or was he more like me and struggling with it?

I emerged from the locker room with Jenna to find our little fan club waiting on us.

"You did great, littlen'." My dad said excitedly.

"Dad . . . littlen'?" I rolled my eyes with a playful nudge.

"Sorry," he laughed. "Habit." He turned towards Jenna. "Great game, Jenna."

"Thanks, Dad," she teased.

"You ladies hungry?" Jenna's mother, Melinda, asked.

"Starving," Jenna responded.

"Ditto," I followed.

"Anyone up for a bite at I-Hop?" her dad, Craig, suggested.

"Sounds good," Robert answered and we all nodded. "Great, we will meet you all there."

"Would you like to ride with us?" Jackson leaned towards me.

"Actually, I think I'll keep my dad company if you don't mind." I gave him a quick kiss and took my dad's arm.

"Of course."

*   *   *

The night air had really turned brisk or maybe it was just walking out of the hot gym that made it feel so frigid, but the cold wind tore through my thin sweats. I shivered and huddled closer to my dad. He smiled and put his arm around me as we walked to his car.

"You know, I'm really going to miss this," he said, climbing in the driver's side.

"Me too," I smiled at him before getting in on the passenger side.

"I remember teaching you to play basketball when you were about four and taking you to your first game when you were six. You remember that?" he asked, turning up the heat.

"Yeah . . . I remember. My uniform was navy blue and white and my hair was in braided pig tails," I laughed. "I think you were more nervous than I was."

"That hasn't changed," my dad chuckled.

"It's funny we were all talking before the game about how fast this school year is flying by. You realize Christmas is only three weeks away and half of my senior year is over? It feels like we just started school last week and already my teachers are talking about finals." I shook my head in disbelief.

We pulled down the main street of town and in the back of my mind I could vaguely recall what this place looked like yesteryear. It left me feeling nauseas. I closed my eyes for a moment and leaned my head against the headrest waiting for the feeling to pass. When I reopened my eyes, I turned towards my dad, completely blocking out the world outside the windows.

"Yeah, it goes by quick," he paused for a breath. "And tomorrow you'll wake up and be forty," he laughed.

I smiled over at him. *No, tomorrow I'm gonna wake up in 1878 and be married to Jackson in three weeks!* "Ouch! Don't say that . . . I'm not even twenty yet!" I playfully smacked his arm.

"Robert mentioned that he got some Colts tickets for this weekend for Jackson's birthday." He glanced over at me, eyeing me carefully.

"Yeah, I was going to talk to you about that. Jackson said something about it this morning."

"Emily wants to leave early Saturday morning, so she can do some shopping in Indianapolis. I guess they already booked a double room for you all," he informed me.

"I didn't know anything about that." That information took me completely off guard.

"I know. Robert and Emily told me, and they promised that they would be sharing a room with you both so . . . no hanky panky."

"Dad!" I smacked him playfully on the arm again.

"I'm just saying," he laughed.

We pulled into the parking lot just as everyone else was getting out of their cars. My dad pulled into a space next to the others and turned the engine off. "Look, Jocelyn, I know you're legally an adult and all and that you're planning on marrying Jackson next summer, but you're also still my little girl."

"I know."

"You can go . . . just please call me when you get there and let me know you're okay."

"Thanks, Daddy. I will, I promise." We climbed out of the car and walked towards the others.

"I will say though that the next time you get tickets to the Colts game . . . you'd better remember your future in-law and how much he loves football!" my dad teased Robert upon approaching them.

"What? You got Colts tickets?" Craig asked clearly surprised, and the rest of us laughed.

CHAPTER 10

Saturday, December 03, 1878

THE GROUND WAS COVERED in thick frost dusted with a fine layer of snow that crunched beneath my feet in the early morning sun. I walked across the back grounds out to the carriage house. It was bitterly cold, and I pulled my caplet closer around me. I jiggled the latch and finally it gave way. I walked over to our two horses, Shadow and Storm, and pulled some carrots out of my muff. I held a carrot out in my flat palm and stroked Shadow's gorgeous mane. "How are you feeling today girl?" I said softly, admiring her enormous brown gentle eyes. She gobbled the carrot eagerly as I patted her neck.

"How about you, old boy?" Storm calmly took the carrot from my palm.

I had been neglecting them so much recently. With all the chaos in my life I had not had the time to spend with them that I used to. They were a sweet pair, a brother and sister that my family had bought years before. Both were black, and William and I had chosen the names for them. We used to take them riding when the weather was more favorable. Now the saddles stood covered in dust in the corner of the carriage house.

I chatted absentmindedly to the two of them, feeding them all the carrots I had snuck out of the house. Their eyes followed my every movement around the stables just in case I had some other hidden treats for them. I brushed each of them lovingly and told them about all the craziness of this *EVE* gene. They were an attentive audience that was never judgmental as I ranted and raved about all the changes that I had to adjust to.

When I left them an hour later, I felt much better, more at peace with everything than I had earlier. Even if my rantings fell on deaf ears it was a comfort to get them off my chest. The frost and snow had all but melted away by the time I made my way back up to the house. The sun was waking and leaving a glistening shine upon the dewing grass.

Sarah was taking out a pan of biscuits from the oven and a skillet of sizzling bacon crackled from the stovetop. She placed them on the kitchen table, smiled and nodded my way before rushing over to the stove to attend the bacon.

"Good mornin' Ms. Jocelyn, you up mighty early," Mimi said upon entering the kitchen. "I's just goin' up to your room."

"No need. I got up early and spent some time out in the stables." I picked up a biscuit and immediately dropped it back on the pan. "Ouch!" I stuck my fingers in my mouth.

"Silly child . . . ya saw me jus' take those outta the oven. A' course they's gonna be hot." Sarah shook her head at my stupidity.

No matter how many times we'd been warned or burnt our fingers, none of us children or my father for that matter, could resist trying to steal one of Sarah's fresh buttermilk biscuits.

"I know," I said with my fingers still in my mouth.

"Now ya go on get outta here. I's calls ya when this ready." Mimi nudged me gently out of the kitchen and out of her and Sarah's way.

I drifted off into the parlor and sat down at the piano. Boredom ripped through me as my fingers numbly fell over the keys. Olivia was still in mourning, and it was too early to call upon Elizabeth, and Jackson was taking the bar exam in the city today. I tried to calm my restless thoughts that wanted only to focus on the scattered fragments of my *other* life. They never came in any logical sequence and therefore made little sense to me. I searched my brain trying to figure out what I used to do with idle time before this nightmare began. Nothing came to mind from that carefree era of ignorance.

William appeared about a half hour later looking not much better than before. I attempted to make small talk with him, but he brushed me aside, taking up the morning newspaper and disappearing behind it.

My parents arrived shortly thereafter and the four of us gathered ourselves around the dining room table. Even with the chatter of my parents discussing the bar exam and the latest gossip about town, I couldn't bring myself to share their lightheartedness. It wasn't that I felt sad or angry or upset . . . I couldn't rightly explain my feelings even to myself. I suppose indifferent would have been the most accurate term best to describe my mood.

By noon I made my way down the cobblestone pathway to Elizabeth's house. The sun was shining brightly, giving off a false sense of warmth. The brisk breeze reminded me again that winter was upon us. The bare tree limbs swayed slightly with the wind. The brown grass and hibernating flowerbeds reminded me of happier times that also seemed to have faded into a deep sleep. I could not seem to shake my melancholy mood.

Elizabeth was all smiles as she greeted me in the foyer. Her house was quiet and peaceful, a rarity indeed. We walked into the front room and sat down in front of the hearth. She told me her parents and siblings had gone into town to do some shopping and she was enjoying the time alone by catching up on some reading.

"I'm sorry. I didn't mean to interrupt you." I held my hands out by the fire to warm them.

"Not at all, I am glad you came by. I was going to call on you and Olivia, but I was unsure of whether or not she was receiving visitors." Elizabeth marked the page in her book before setting it aside.

"How did you know about Olivia?" I turned back around.

"Your mother told my mother." *Of course.*

"I'm afraid she is barely speaking to me or anyone else for that matter. She mainly sits in the chair and stares out the window at her old house."

"How sad," her voice trailed off.

"I know. I wish there was something I could do for her."

"I am sure she just needs some time. She has had a lot to adjust to recently and it cannot be easy."

"How is Mr. Lee doing?" I asked, trying to change the subject.

"He is wonderful. He had to go into work for a while today, but he should be over later this afternoon," she sighed with a slight smile on her lips. "How is Mr. Jackson doing?"

"He is taking the bar exam today. It started about an hour ago." I glanced up at the clock on their mantle.

"Did you speak with him this morning?"

"No. I did not want to distract him." I fidgeted my hands in my lap.

"Understandable. I am sure you will see him this evening when he comes home," Elizabeth tried to reassure me.

"I have no idea what time he will return. I am sure he will wait around after the exam for the results." I watched the flames dance around the hearth.

"Yes, probably," she agreed.

*   *   *

The afternoon flew by as we ate some lemon drop cookies, sipped peppermint tea, and discussed our classes, friends, and my upcoming wedding. Anything to keep my mind occupied was a blessing as Elizabeth slowly edged me out of my sullen mood. Shortly before dinnertime, Lee arrived and found the two of us laughing over silly childhood memories.

"You two seem to be enjoying yourselves," he proclaimed as he entered the room.

"Oh, Lee, I am sorry. We did not hear you arrive." Elizabeth got up to greet him.

"Sabina, let me in," I stood up and curtsied slightly to him. "Ms. Jocelyn, how nice to see you again." He took my hand and kissed it lightly. "Are you joining us for diner?"

He sat down beside Elizabeth and took her hand up in his.

"No, not today. I am afraid I must be getting home. I am sure Mr. Jackson has returned by now and is probably looking for me."

Lee gave me a puzzled look until Elizabeth explained that Jackson was taking the bar exam today and we were anxiously awaiting the results.

The sun had departed and been replaced by a brilliant almost full moon. The stars shone brightly lighting my way, but the cold breeze whisking around me made me fully aware of the darkness that enveloped me. Even though it was barely six o'clock, I suddenly wished I had left Elizabeth's earlier when there was still some daylight. Every little sound or rustle made me jump and pick up my pace. By the time I reached my front gate, I was almost jogging and out of breath from fright.

Jackson was waiting for me when I rushed in my front door, anxious for the safe confines of my home.

"Jocelyn, are you all right? What happened to you, darling? You look a fright." He ran over to help me off with my coat and bonnet.

"Nothing." I sat down on the bottom steps to catch my breath. "I'm fine. I just let my overactive imagination get the best of me."

"Are you sure?" He raised an eyebrow and tucked some of the loose curls that had fallen out of their pins, behind my ear.

"Sorry, I must look a mess." I straightened myself up a bit. "How did the exam go?" I wanted desperately to change the subject.

A smile spread across his face giving him a glow of pride. "It was difficult, but I passed."

"Congratulations!" I jumped up and threw my arms around his neck, kissing his lips with enthusiasm. "I knew you would, darling. I'm so proud of you!"

"Thank you," he laughed at me.

"Oh Jackson . . . this is wonderful!" I proclaimed.

"Was there any doubt?"

"Never!"

"I'm so glad it's over." He let out a deep sigh of relief as we walked into the parlor sitting down on the lounge.

"Me too, I have missed you."

"I missed you too. How is Ms. Elizabeth doing?"

"Good. Mr. Lee arrived just before I left."

Jackson nodded. "Have you spoken with Olivia today?"

"No," I replied.

"Why not?"

"She hasn't come out of her room all day. Every time I have tried to speak with her this week, she tells me she wants to be alone," I informed him.

"She is very depressed."

"Yes, but I do not know what else I can do to help her."

"Time is the only thing that is going to help at this point." Jackson took my hands up in his and leaned over whispering, "Have you had anymore visions?"

"Yes." I looked down at our intertwined hands.

"Why the look? Did you see something that bothered you?"

I shook my head. "No, it's not that. I just wish they would make more sense. Nothing appears in sequential order and it can be quite confusing."

"You know if you have any questions my parents and I are here to help you." I looked up into his piercing green eyes.

"Thank you, but most of what I am witnessing is not something I believe you can help me with. You and your family were not around when I was growing up," I explained.

"True, but that does not mean you cannot ask me. I can always ask you *there* and report back." Jackson let out a sound that could have been a laugh.

"I appreciate that. However, it makes me feel helpless to have to constantly rely on you and your family in order to discover the meanings of things. Plus, I feel like this is something I should figure out on my own."

A deep-hearted laugh escaped as he leaned forward a bit. "It's nice to know that some things do not ever change regardless of where you are."

I scrunched up my eyes at him. "And what exactly is that supposed to mean, Mr. Jackson?"

"Your stubbornness," he said as my favorite lop-sided grin slid across his lips.

"Stubbornness? I beg your pardon?" I stood up, but Jackson grabbed my arm.

"Jocelyn don't get upset," he continued laughing.

"Then you had best explain what you mean."

Jackson tried his best to stop laughing but it seemed he couldn't help himself. "I mean your feistiness and zest for life."

My hand went up to my mouth with embarrassed shame. *Feistiness? Zest for life?* Those are not exactly flattering words and I knew my parents would be ashamed if those words were ever used to describe me.

"I'm sorry. I did not mean it to be an insult." Jackson removed my hand and whispered softly. "Do not be embarrassed. Those are two of the many traits that I love about you."

"Seriously? How appalling." I could not believe he was supporting such behavior.

"Don't be so old fashioned. I believe those traits might be more appealing to you if I referred to them as gumption."

"Gumption? That is a polite way of putting it." A smile crept across my face. I leaned over and kissed his cheek playfully. It seemed to be all I could do to keep myself from screaming. I could only hope that he was more in touch with my *other* self and the world attached to it. I hated being so naïve, almost to the point of clueless, about all the things that the Chandlers took for granted. It made me feel stupid and helpless to the point of infuriation.

CHAPTER 11

Saturday, December 05, 2009

WE HIT THE HIGHWAY south from Chicago around eight o'clock. Jackson and I stretched out in the backseat and tried to get comfortable. The four of us talked about their life in Boston, my childhood with both families, and various things for both our upcoming weddings. The time flew by so quickly, I was really surprised when Robert started pointing out landmarks in downtown Indianapolis.

Fifty minutes later we arrived in Bloomington. This small college town was just as I remembered from last summer. The stone pillars, the greenery, the large brick buildings and the students . . . they were everywhere.

"Did you know that IU has the second largest collection of pornography in the world?" Jackson asked with a mischievous grin.

"You're kidding," I laughed with disbelief.

"No, I'm serious. Haven't you ever heard of the Kinsey Institute?"

"Um . . . no," I shook my head.

"Guess who has the largest collection?" Jackson asked.

"Who?" I responded.

"The Vatican," he replied.

"Really?" I couldn't believe it.

"It's true," Robert chimed in. "They have to know what you are not allowed to see."

"Unbelievable," I chuckled.

We parked in a lot off to the side of campus and climbed out to stretch our legs. I looked over everything around me. It was amazing. It was almost as if there was a collegiate atmosphere in the air. A small part of me still longed to attend this university. Just being near it made my heart beat faster. There were students everywhere on the grounds.

Some were studying, some playing football, and some just hanging around socializing. I was so envious of them. This place offered an endless row of countless possibilities just waiting to be imagined.

"Anyone hungry?" Emily asked.

"Starving," Jackson answered, stretching his arms over his head.

I nodded.

We had lunch at a small little mom and pop place that served the best deep-dish pizza I'd ever eaten in my life. I ate until I thought I'd get sick.

"Are we heading over to campus?" I asked Jackson's parents.

"No. I seriously doubt Nicholas would be there on a Saturday. I pulled up his home address the other night. He only lives about ten minutes from here," Robert replied.

"We're just going to show up at his house unannounced?" Jackson asked his dad. "Does he know about us? Or Jocelyn?"

"We do not believe so, but we could not exactly approach him with it either," Emily smiled.

"Why hasn't my uncle Monte spoken to him *there* before we drop a bomb on him *here*?" I looked between the two of them.

"I tried to get in touch with Monte Thursday evening, but Vivian told me that he and Nicholas went to New York for a conference and would not be back for a couple days." Robert shifted in his chair. "I'm not sure how he is going to react seeing us all *here* on this plane."

"Are you ready for this?" Jackson smiled gently in my direction.

"I suppose so," I sighed.

*   *   *

Robert guided the Durango through an older section of town lined with old large Victorian era homes. They were all beautifully kept with decorated lawns covered with mature trees and most with white picket fences. I could see why it appealed to my uncle so. It was like taking a step back into simpler times.

We stopped in front of a huge old white home with dark blue shutters and a porch that wrapped around the house. Butterflies danced in my stomach and my palms began to sweat before I even got the passenger backseat door open. The cool air hitting my face was a welcome relief as I took Jackson's hand. We followed his parents up the cobblestone walkway to the front porch.

My eyes scanned over the area absorbing everything in sight while Robert rang the bell. A few feet from where we stood rested two wooden rocking chairs with a small table placed between them. A short way from them swayed a wooden swing gently in the cool breeze. The sleeping lawn was thick, without a weed in sight. The mulch was placed carefully around the large trees and slumbering flowerbeds.

The front door creaked open causing me to jerk my head back around. There on the other side of the screen stood my dad's younger brother, Nicholas, dressed in khaki slacks, a sweater vest, and long-sleeved, collared shirt. He looked every bit of what I imagined a college professor to be.

"Oh, my Lord!" he gasped. "Robert . . . Emily!" my uncle fumbled to open the screen door between them.

"Hello, Nicholas. Surprise!" Robert grinned.

"My lands, come in, come in," he gushed, holding open the screen door and stepping back a pace.

I squeezed Jackson's hand tighter, walking purposely behind him as we passed through the door hoping my uncle wouldn't immediately see me.

"And Jackson? Boy, this is wonderful!" Jackson shook his hand excitedly. Nicholas leaned a little closer to me causing me to look directly at his face for the first time.

The air rushed from his lungs as the four of us stood there watching the blood drain from his face.

"Whoooh . . . there, Nicholas." Robert grabbed a hold of his arm. "You should sit down for a moment." He guided my uncle to the nearest chair.

"I do not believe it. Jocelyn? Is that you?" His eyes were glued to my face.

I smiled softly. "Yes, it's me, Uncle Nicholas."

"I do not understand this. What are you doing here? And with them?" His eyes drifted over to Jackson's parents.

"Apparently you and Uncle Monte forgot to share a little inherited family secret with me." I smiled over towards my new family.

"I had not realized your barrier was disintegrating already," my uncle muttered, rubbing his chin thoughtfully.

"Monte did. He came and spoke to us about Jocelyn last spring when their engagement was announced. So, we moved to Chicago to find her," Robert explained, taking a seat on the couch across from my uncle. Emily joined him, and Jackson and I hesitantly sat down with them.

"He never said anything to me," my uncle replied in a low voice. "Most likely because Shane and I no longer speak." He looked back up at the four of us.

"I would imagine so," Emily carefully answered.

"How long have you known?" Uncle Nicholas turned his eyes on me.

"They explained everything about *EVE* on Halloween."

"Has the barrier completely diminished?"

"Almost. I am remembering the majority of things, but they are mostly out of order or incomplete. Therefore, a lot of it still doesn't make much sense," I explained.

"I see." He rubbed his chin again. "And how do you feel about all this?"

"Honestly? I don't know. I mean, it's so bizarre and still feels very surreal." It was hard to find the right words since there really weren't any.

"Understandable," he smiled gently at me before shifting his gaze to Jackson parents. "It does me good to see you all here. Robert, you never told me your family had the gift as well."

"We were unaware that you had the gift. Monte never told us about you." Robert put his hand on my uncle's shoulder.

"I am not surprised. He always viewed it more as a curse than a gift. He hated living dual lives and never understood what a truly amazing and unique gift it actually is."

My uncle's point of view did not surprise me in the slightest. No wonder he was not afraid to confide in my dad after Monte's funeral. Still, he must understand how someone who did not live with this gift would have extreme difficulty believing it possible.

"Are you married *here* also, Uncle Nicholas?" I blurted out without thinking.

He laughed and sat back in his chair. "My . . . you are certainly very different *here*, aren't you?" I could feel myself blush. It was not the first time I'd heard those words. "No, I am not married *here*, only *there*. Like my brother, I found the perfect woman for me and there is no one else I could ever imagine loving. But unlike my brother, I see the benefits of existing in two drastically different worlds."

"Benefits? What do you mean?" I asked.

"Take all the technology we have. It gives us an unlimited amount of resources, references, and information that is unavailable in the nineteenth century. There is a wealth of information all at our fingertips that would take years to compile and be almost impossible to uncover *there*. I could never conduct my research during that time period."

"What type of research?" I got a sickening feeling in my stomach.

"On *EVE* of course."

"How do you mean?" Even Robert's voice sounded a tad less steady.

"Not openly," Nicholas smiled coyly. "But I do believe you would be very interested in what I have put together." He moved to the edge of his chair.

"Monte mentioned you were doing some fascinating work, but he failed to offer details." Robert straightened up slightly.

"Will you all please follow me to my study? There are a few things I believe you would find quite interesting." My uncle rose to his feet and we followed him down the corridor.

As I followed them all down the hallway I scanned over his furniture, pictures, and knick-knacks. Almost all of which were antiques and very carefully maintained. It was clear that his home was in desperate need of a woman's touch, but overall it was a very elegant home.

His office, on the other hand, was not nearly as organized as the rest of his house. There were papers scattered about on every surface imaginable, a dual screen PC, and history books of every time and era stuffed into every inch of the numerous bookcases.

My uncle apologized for the mess and hurriedly picked up the stacks of papers and books off the brown leather sofa. "Please have a seat, make yourselves comfortable. I practically live in here when I am not on campus, so it stays an organized mess."

"You have me intrigued, Nicholas. What exactly have you been working on?" Robert asked as the four of us sank into the oversized couch.

I wasn't sure what was going on and had no idea what my uncle could possibly be up to, but he held the undivided attention of both Jackson's parents. Even Jackson sat on the edge of the sofa with seemingly bated breath. I wish I understood a little more about *EVE*, so I too could be as interested in historical research as they were. I was still trying to wrap my brain around the whole concept of a dual existence. To entertain anything beyond that was more than my fragile mind was willing to accept at this moment.

"First off, I began with the basics. I looked through every historical document I could get my hands on. Secondly, I read about every historical philosophy book, article, paper . . . you name it. I dug into everything I could think of and even some illogical things that seemed silly and trivial." Nicholas sat down in his desk chair and I immediately knew what it would feel like to be one of his students. "Finally, I found the common trend that I had been searching for."

"I'm sorry, Nicholas. We are not following you." Robert looked over at his wife and son who wore the same confused expression that rested on my face.

"I am sure you have all heard of Nostradamus, right?" We all nodded. "What about Edgar Cayce, Joseph Smith, or William Branham?"

"The names sound familiar, but I cannot place them. Were they prophets also?" Jackson asked.

"They were proclaimed prophets, either by themselves or by others depending on the source." Nicholas turned and searched through some papers on his desk. "Yes, here it is," he said, turning back around.

"Perhaps you had best start at the beginning, Nicholas," Robert interjected.

"Yes . . . yes, of course. I apologize. It is so exciting to share this with people who can truly appreciate and understand the significance of what it means." My uncle rested back in his chair. "I have never had that before outside of my brother, Monte, and well, as I said before, he views *EVE* more as a curse than anything else. I am quite curious to get each of your reactions on it."

"Well then, you have our undivided attention." I could tell how anxious Robert was to hear more about Nicholas's theory.

"I am sure you are all familiar with Michel de Nostradamus and his *Almanac of Prophecies*, the first of which consists of twelve four-line poems called quatrains." He raised his eyebrows a bit looking us over to see if his words were registering with us. "Anyway, his most well-known work, *The Centuries*, which he began in 1554, contained ten volumes of a hundred quatrains each. Volumes one through four were published in 1555, the following three later that same year and the final three in 1558. Although they were not initially widely distributed, they have consistently been circulated and reprinted for over four hundred years."

"My grandmother had told me that there was speculation among those with the gift of *EVE* that Nostradamus had inherited the gift. She explained that he was not prophesying future events but because his dual lives were set so vastly apart, he cataloged major historical events to track which ones had a major impact on the world and changed the dynamics of life during those time periods," Robert explained.

"Yes, I believe your grandmother may have been correct. Looking at how his work was organized — the writings and the recently discovered drawings, it cannot be happenstance. There are far too many accurate similarities. Plus, the numerous prophets, seers, and such dating back to the first recordings of history — they each fill in specific holes and they all stop at a specific time. Almost as if they could not *see* beyond a certain point in time," my uncle said excitedly. "If you look closely at documents throughout history as far back as ancient times they provide us with significant evidence that the gift of *EVE* has transcended generations."

"I don't understand what you mean. Are you saying that this *EVE* thing has always been around, and no one has ever put the pieces together before?" I asked.

"Exactly," Nicholas smiled. "There are documents dating as far back as ancient Greece beginning with the Delphic Oracle. I am sure you all have heard of the Sphinx, Dionysus, Zeus, and Apollo?" Again, we all nodded. "Well, they were considered all-seeing, all-knowing about future events in ways that mystified everyone around them and the only individuals who also had these magical talents were related to them or direct descendants of them. Each were said to have the ability to uncover and understand the will of the gods by being able to predict the future before it occurred, which in some cases, made them considered as gods themselves."

Robert narrowed his eyes in a thoughtful manner and rubbed his chin.

"Similar documents can be found in every culture in various countries and continents across time from Native Americans, Romans, England, to Greece and on and on. Each had their own ways or devices in which they predicted upcoming events, but most of them used various methods of trances. Our history is literally cluttered with them. There are even more recent ones today that are all over the Internet. Of course, a great many of them regard themselves as spiritual or biblical seers," Nicholas explained.

"And why has no one ever throughout history explained *EVE*?" I questioned.

"Remember when we first explained it all to you? You struggled a great deal with the concept," Emily smiled and placed her hand over mind.

A small laugh escaped from my chest. "I'm still struggling with it."

"Then you can only imagine how absurd this would sound to an outsider. It would land you a long stay in a padded room after the men in white coats come and take you away," Jackson laughed.

"Not to mention the increase in individuals diagnosed with schizophrenia," Robert added.

Nicholas's eyes widened with surprise "Yes — the prevalence rate has increased greatly, not to mention the genetic components. Schizophrenia is passed through families at a higher rate than previously recognized."

"I believe that is more due to the decline in family dynamics and the lack of a family member with the inherited gift to guide them through the adjustment of living dual lives," Robert added thoughtfully.

"Is there a way to differentiate between *EVE* and schizophrenia?" I looked between Robert and Nicholas. "How could someone, I mean how can someone tell the difference between someone who is truly schizophrenic and someone who has *EVE*?"

The room fell into silence. It seemed as if I could actually see the wheels turning in each of their minds as pieces of the puzzle started falling together in sequential order for the first time. I shifted in my seat and tried to grasp the enormity of what I was a part of. This *EVE* thing appeared to be steeped in history and the scope of it was beyond my greatest imagination.

*   *   *

The afternoon passed into evening in a blur. Before I realized it my stomach was growling. I glanced at my watch and was surprised when it read quarter to seven.

The amount of information, hypotheses, conjectures, and theories my uncle laid upon us was overwhelming. Sitting back on the sofa it all seemed very plausible to my young and naïve ears. Strangely, looking at the faces seated beside me, I knew it did to them as well.

How is this all possible? How can it be that no one has pieced this concept together before? Even someone who has inherited EVE . . . just to pass this information on to future generations? Obviously, the children that Jackson and I are destined to have will inherit EVE and I believe the more knowledge we can share with them will make a world of difference to their transition into living a dual existence.

Uncle Nicholas smiled and slapped his knee when the old grandfather clock in the hall began chiming. "Well I declare, it's already seven o'clock. You all must be starving. I know I am. I put a pot roast in the crockpot this morning. It should be sweet and tender by now. Would you all care to join me for dinner? There is plenty."

I nodded without thinking to look at Jackson's parents. Fortunately, the three of them nodded as well.

"That would be wonderful. Thank you." Robert slowly rose from the sofa.

"Sit back down, sir and relax. Jocelyn and I will get everything together." Nicholas rose from his chair and held his hand out for me.

I glanced over at Jackson before slowly standing. He squeezed my hand assuredly with a slight grin. I took my uncle's hand and followed him to the kitchen in the back of the house.

My uncle instructed me on where he kept his utensils, and such then chatted on endlessly while he prepared the food while I set the table. He had a casual air about him and I found him very easy to talk to. He was, in fact, very similar to the man I recalled from my visions *there*. Plus, several of his mannerisms reminded me so much of my dad. It was easy to tell they were brothers despite the number of years they'd been estranged. He questioned me extensively over every detail of my life *here* since Monte's funeral. It was clear to me how much he missed his family and Shane's silence bothered him a great deal.

The dinner was excellent and the conversation superb. We enjoyed a light angel food cake with fresh strawberries grown by Uncle Nicholas himself in his climate-controlled greenhouse out back. Evidently, one of his biggest complaints about this era was all the processed food. My three companions could not have agreed more with him.

When the grandfather clock chimed ten Robert addressed our host. "My goodness, I cannot believe how late it is. I hate to say it, but we really should be going. We still have to drive back to Indianapolis."

"Nonsense, Robert, there is no need to waste money on a hotel when I have all these empty rooms here. You all can get a good night's sleep and drive back in the morning after a good healthy breakfast," Nicholas insisted.

"Thank you so much for the offer Nicholas, but we do not want to impose on you. We realize we stopped by unexpectedly and you have already been hospitable enough. We cannot intrude," Emily smiled gracefully.

"Intrude?" Nicholas leaned back in his chair and laughed wholeheartedly. "Don't be silly, you are family and I enjoy the company."

"Well, if you are sure . . ." Robert hesitated.

"Of course," my uncle answered with enthusiasm.

The men carried in our bags and brought everything up to the second floor. After quick showers and hustling about, Emily retired to the large guest room. Robert, Jackson, and Uncle Nicholas retreated back downstairs while I took my time lingering in the bubbles that filled the old-fashioned tub.

The combination of the hot water and the tantalizing fragranced bubbles were intoxicating. I drifted away from all the information that was laid upon my slender shoulders. I didn't want to think about it, could not let myself think about it or I knew I'd drive myself batty. It all seemed like a not so humorous riddle wrapped up in a concept that felt like the preverbal catch 22. There was simply no room for a plausible explanation that could be shared to make the world understand. *How can I expect my family and friends . . . and the rest of the world to understand this EVE thing when the very comprehension of it continues to elude me?*

CHAPTER 12

Sunday, December 04, 1878

LYING IN BED, I could hear the subtle sounds of the house greeting the day. The clanking of dishes in the kitchen below and the sounds of feet shuffling about brought about feelings of security and love. I closed my eyes and snuggled deeper into the covers trying to focus on the blurred scenes from the night before. I couldn't figure out why the visions were cluttered with images of my uncle Nicholas. He was with Jackson, his parents, and me in a room I did not recognize. I had never seen him anywhere that would give me the impression that Uncle Nicholas had inherited this curse and was in or knew anything about my *other* world. My uncle Monte surely would have told me if he did.

* * *

I knew that it was going to be a long sermon this morning. It seemed it always was when there was something I wanted to discuss with Jackson. I fidgeted with my gloves twisting them repeatedly trying to figure out how all these pieces fit together. I wished I could see things clearly and understand the significance of what things meant. I glanced over at my uncle Nicholas sitting across the aisle with his wife, Lydia, and their sons. On the pew in front of him sat my uncle Monte holding hands with his wife, Vivian. I wanted so badly to drag them both outside and make them explain to me why I was seeing Uncle Nicholas in my *other* world.

Uncle Nicholas, feeling my gaze, turned his head slightly in my direction and our eyes locked. He smiled slightly and nodded with a knowing look in his eyes. I wanted to scream out in utter frustration. Jackson lightly placed his hands over mine and leaned in closer to me.

"Please stop playing with your gloves. It's very distracting." His voice sounded parental.

"Please excuse me, I do not feel well. I need some air." I got up and squeezed past everyone in our row before I made my way out the front door.

I sat down on a bench just off the side of the church entrance. The air was cold, and a light breeze blew through my hair, but I didn't feel anything. My head was spinning and aching at the same time. I rested my head upon my hands and let the tears of frustration run down my fingers.

"It is a bit overwhelming at times I suppose." His voice echoed across the empty yard. Uncle Nicholas smiled warmly and took a seat beside me, wrapping his arm around my shoulder. "I know how hard this is. The time between knowledge and clarity feels like an eternity."

"Why didn't you tell me?" My eyes met with his, pleading for some answers.

"For one, up until yesterday I did not know your barrier was beginning to disintegrate. Secondly, if I had known I still could not have said anything to you for the same reasons Monte, Jackson, and his parents did not. You had to see it for yourself. This is not something that is believable unless it is experienced."

"But I do not understand. How can you and Monte be my uncles in both planes and neither Shane nor Patrick inherited the gift? And what about my brothers . . . or Sidney?"

"Are you sure none of them has the gift?" He raised an eyebrow with a slight smile.

His question both stunned and silenced me. *No . . . I am not sure.*

"You know, just because you, me, Monte, and the Chandlers share a similar time span, that does not mean that your siblings will share yours. They could be on an entirely separate plane from yours."

"Are you serious?" His smiled broadened. "How is that possible?"

"To be honest, I am not sure, but I do know that my father and his sister both inherited the gift and were on different planes from myself as well as each other. My grandmother used to tell us stories when we were kids about futuristic things like telephones, cars, electricity, and indoor plumbing and my father told us tales of King William's War that took place between France and England on the Northern Frontiers in New England and New York from 1689 to 1697. Imagine our surprise when Monte and I learned later after we became aware of *EVE* that our grandmother was born shortly after the turn of the twentieth century and our father was retelling battles to us as they occurred to him in his *other* life."

"This *EVE* spectrum is a great deal more complicated than I ever imagined." My gaze drifted off into the distance staring at nothing. "It is impossible to wrap my brain around this monster," I whispered softly more to myself than to him.

"I suppose that is why I decided to devote my *other* life to uncovering the realm of this . . . monster as you call it." He chuckled softly and leaned back on the bench. "I know it is difficult when the barrier is still partly intact, and I am sure you are tired of hearing that."

"Yes . . . very much so." I let out a deep breath and brushed the last of the tears off my cheeks. "What I do not understand is why you suddenly appeared in my world *there*. I have no memories of you or Uncle Monte *there*."

"You will soon, but you must understand that you will remember his death more than his life. You were very young when he left his life *there*, if I recall correctly, you were about eight years old."

"But where were you?"

"Your father, Shane, and I had a falling out after Monte's funeral. I tried to explain to him the truth of what happened to our brother and why he believed his death *there* was necessary, but I only got out half the story, I am afraid.

Shane thought I was insane and refused to hear any more about it. Since that night he cut me completely out of his life and kept me away from all three of you children." He smiled lovingly over at me. "I cannot tell you how delighted I was to see you *there*."

"Can you please explain something I do not understand?"

"I will if I can."

"Why is it the Chandlers all share both planes but our family is somewhat scattered?"

"From all that I have discovered and pieced together is that when both parents have the genetic trait then their children will reside on the same planes with them. However, if the trait is passed on by only one parent, it seems the children can live on separate planes then their parent, but the siblings can exist on the same plane. Or in rare instances, such as yours, you inherited the gift but have two sets of parents who, as far as we are aware, do not have it. I still have not figured that out because somehow if the individual inherits *EVE* from . . . say an uncle, then their siblings can exist on separate planes." Nicholas ran his hand through his hair.

"So, if my sister *there* — Sidney — inherited *EVE* then she could have another life on a completely separate plane than I."

"It is possible if she does indeed have *EVE*. Robert told me about what happened over Thanksgiving. It sounds like she may, but you should try and find out for sure."

"I am trying, but she is being rather evasive."

The sun had broken through the clouds and was shining brightly upon us yet failed to offer any warmth. I had no idea whether I would remember or not to get in touch with Sidney once I was in the *other* world. Somehow, I thought for sure either the Chandlers or Nicholas would make sure that my *other* self would. We sat on the bench until church services were over.

Jackson walked down the church steps in the sunlight. The light surrounding him looked almost like a halo following him. He smiled brightly in our direction as he walked over to meet us.

Our families and the rest of the congregation emptied out into the churchyard. Everyone was talking pleasantly and enjoying the break from the rain showers.

"Are you feeling all right?" Jackson asked when he approached.

"She is fine, just confused." Nicholas stood and took my hand, helping me to my feet. "I need to rejoin my family. We can talk some more after supper if you like. Your mother was kind enough to invite us over." He leaned down and kissed me on the cheek before he disappeared into the crowd.

"Another memory?" Jackson slid his arm around my waist.

"Yes. I was trying to figure out why I was seeing him in my dreams or whatever you want to call them," I explained.

"We just found out ourselves. It was a complete surprise. We went down to Indiana University in Bloomington yesterday where your uncle is a professor. He has been doing research on *EVE* and gave us a cram session on what he has uncovered. It was very interesting," he explained while we walked a ways away from the others.

"Will you tell me everything after supper?"

"Of course." He put his arm protectively around my shoulder.

*   *   *

Our house was crammed full in celebration of Jackson's twenty-second birthday. Sarah had made a special triple layered chocolate fudge cake, his favorite, for the occasion. The women were bustling about, fussing over the smaller children, trying to get them settled down and away from the cake before supper.

My father and Monte kept Nicholas occupied, even after we finished eating, in a heated political debate. My brothers, Alexander and Robert were also obsessed with the discussion and voices raised from the far corner of the front room as the men carried on. William and Jackson were the only two who had excluded themselves from the conversation. They joined Olivia and me by the piano where I was absentmindedly playing a piece from memory.

The rest of the women enjoyed their coffee while gossiping about things going on in town and things of that nature.

The three of us were thrilled to have Olivia out of her room. She was still not joining us in public or at church, but she had wandered downstairs after we returned home. Everyone was delighted when she entered the dining room and tried to make her as comfortable as possible. She was still pale with red puffy eyes and resembled more of the person William brought home the night they got married. She spoke very little, did not really join in any conversation, but would answer if asked a direct question. I wanted so badly to reassure her that her dreams of becoming a mother were going to come true and that someday soon she would have beautiful children to love and spoil. I was quickly understanding how frustrating various areas of *EVE* were. I hated it.

It was early evening before I got Jackson alone. I felt like I was constantly going back and forth asking for clarity in both my worlds. It was truly aggravating and after a short time I changed the subject. It was more fun just to enjoy spending time alone with him and watch his brilliant green eyes dance when they held mine.

I wrapped my arms around his neck and leaned up to kiss him softly on the front porch just as the sun was setting on the beautiful day. There was a chill in the light breeze and I snuggled closer to him for warmth.

"Happy birthday, darling."

"Thank you," he whispered into my ear.

"I have something for you."

"You did not have to do that. Marrying me is gift enough." His voice was low and soothing.

"But I believe this might look better on your desk at the office." I reached into my side pocket and pulled out an engraved name plate that said, 'Attorney Jackson W. Chandler.' I had ordered it weeks before Jackson took the bar. I was crossing my fingers hoping that it would be delivered in time for his birthday.

"Jocelyn, I love it!"

"I am so glad to hear you say that. I was afraid it was too impersonal, but I wanted to get you something special for your office."

"It is perfect. I will take it to work with me on Monday." Jackson looked at it a moment longer then carefully tucked it into the inside pocket of his jacket.

We walked around the front yard and over to a big wooden swing that hung from the tree by thick ropes. James had hung it there when I was quite young, and William and I had spent hours playing on it.

I sat down on the long board and grabbed a hold of the frayed ropes. I turned around and smiled at Jackson as he stood behind me and pulled the ropes back and up towards himself. He let go and I went soaring through the brisk air. Despite the cold it was a marvelous freeing feeling and I couldn't help but laugh out loud. I could hear his laughter behind me as he pushed me gently each time I returned to him. It had been a long time since I had felt so normal.

CHAPTER 13

Sunday, December 06, 2009

I SILENTLY SNUCK into Jackson's bed while the house was dead silent, and it was still black outside. I straddled over him and leaned down gently, brushing my lips over his. I could feel the shape of his lips change beneath mine as they broadened into a smile. Jackson reached up and wrapped his arms around me, pressing our bodies together. Our desire turned into fire as he rolled me over and lifted himself upon me. I wrapped my arms around him, pulling him closer to me. His lips slid down to my neck and traced over my collarbone as his hand hungrily grasped over my body.

He finally pulled himself back and rolled over beside me. "Jocelyn, what are you doing? Do you know how dangerous it is for you to sneak in here? I could really take advantage of you and it's most unfair of you to tempt me in this way!" The slight smile was still resting on his lips.

"Happy Birthday, darling." I propped myself up on my elbow, still breathing heavily and slightly disappointed that he had squelched the fire.

"You little devil," he laughed.

"I wanted to be the first to wish you a happy birthday."

"And so, you have been . . ." Jackson leaned up and moved towards me. "I cannot imagine a better way to start my day. I can't wait until I can wake up beside you every morning for the rest of my life."

I leaned over and gently brushed my lips over his. His hand reached over and caressed the back of my head, pressing it closer to his. The fire ignited once more with such a strong potency I never wanted it to end.

Jackson rolled back over upon me and my arms embraced him, holding his muscular frame tightly against my body. Our appetite was unquenchable and the thin layer of pajamas between us provided little resistance to our true desires. Our bodies moved in perfect harmony together as our hands explored and our mouths devoured each other.

I could not get enough of him. My body wanted him . . . needed him . . . longed for him. I gave myself fully and completely to him. I was at his mercy, willing and eager to give myself over to this craving, to him . . . once and forever.

But then the small voice in the back of my mind recalled Jackson's words and the importance of them, the words he had said about virtue, honor, and respect and how he would never compromise mine. I knew he wanted me as desperately as I him, but I could not silence his words and what they meant to him. Now, in this moment of heated passion I knew I was taking away something sacred to his very soul.

With great reverence I pushed him away and slid out from under him. "Jackson . . ." I said breathlessly. "We can't do this."

"I know, I'm sorry." His powerful green eyes dropped in personal shame.

I lightly lifted his chin, so his eyes would meet mine. "Tis not you, my love. It was me." I smiled softly. Jackson's eyebrows crinkled.

"You speak in words that belong in another era, my darling. I believe your two worlds are vastly becoming one." I blushed deeply as the realization that the words I had spoken had never crossed my lips before in this world.

"What does this mean?"

"I believe the barrier is coming down quickly between your two worlds," he smiled. "And I trust this would be most agreeable to you."

"Jackson," I whispered as a lone tear slipped from my eye. "I'm afraid that in joining these two worlds I am losing the essence of who I am in the process."

Jackson studied my face for a moment before he replied. "As I have told you before, my love, regardless of what time we are in, you may take full comfort in knowing that you are always my Jocelyn."

*   *   *

After a delicious but healthy breakfast of waffles, scrambled eggs, and ham, we said our good-byes and were on the road before eight o'clock. I hugged and kissed my uncle and promised him that I would come and see him again soon. Emily wanted to make sure we had plenty of time to spend browsing around downtown Indianapolis before the game started.

The air was crisp and clean with a definite feel of winter about it. I leaned my head against the window as I watched the farmhouses scattered amongst browning fields and small businesses blur past us. I hadn't slept well the night before. I never did in unfamiliar surroundings. I had tossed and turned, waking up frequently throughout the wee hours of the morning. The familiar question haunted my mind: *what happens there when I wake up in the middle of the night here and vice versa?*

Jackson reached over and gently slid his hand into mine. "Are you all right? You have been very quiet this morning?"

I nodded my head with a half-smile. "I'm fine, just thinking about yesterday."

"A bit overwhelming." Emily turned towards us from the passenger seat. "I have been living with *EVE* for almost thirty years and I am having trouble absorbing the amount of information Nicholas discussed."

"Do you believe his theories could be correct?" Jackson's eyes drifted from one of his parents to the other.

"Perhaps." Robert rubbed his chin in speculation. "It certainly sounds plausible, but plausibility is not fact. This is not an experiment that could be conducted inside or outside a laboratory. There really is no way of proving or disproving it for that matter. Even though it is hereditary there has never been any DNA markers studied to find the genetic link." His eyes met Jackson's in the rearview mirror.

"What about the genetic markers for schizophrenia? Couldn't those be used?" I inquired.

"Schizophrenia is a real disorder. It would be difficult to use such markers to differentiate between who was really schizophrenic and who had the gift of *EVE*," Robert noted.

"That's what scares me," I added unintentionally.

"What do you mean?" Emily gave me a puzzled look.

"Well, if all he talked about — those famous people in history — is true, I really did not want to know. I realize it may sound silly, but sometimes it's better to believe myths or prophets or medicine men. Legends are better than rationalization. Sometimes it is simpler to believe that some people are special, unique in a way that makes them different from the rest of us." I looked at their faces searching for answers.

"And you do not believe that is what having *EVE* is? Something unique that makes you special?" Robert inquired with one eyebrow raised.

A laugh escaped before I could stop it. "Me? No, I'm not special. I have no ability to predict the future."

"But once the barrier is completely diminished between your two worlds, you will have." Emily gave me a coy smile. "At least *there* you will be able to."

I turned back to the window as her words fully sank it. She was right. *There* I would be able to accurately predict the future, down to amazing detail in some cases. I closed my eyes briefly, pushing those thoughts out of my already overcrowded mind.

*   *   *

We left the car in the Circle Center parking garage and crossed the skywalk into the mall. Emily and I separated from the men, promising them we would meet them at eleven o'clock at *Champps Americana* for lunch.

The mall was just beginning to come alive and Hoosiers milled about getting ready for what was sure to be a very hectic day. The mall was near Lucas Oil Stadium and was guaranteed to be bustling with Colts fans.

We strolled around the multi-level mall enjoying a lively discussion about the upcoming weddings, graduation, college, and the busy Christmas holiday. Emily bought a few items for her family, a new jacket for herself, and we both bought a pair of gorgeous boots at *ALDO's*. I purchased a new pair of jeans for myself and a sweatshirt that I fell in love with. Unfortunately, that was pretty much the end of my birthday money, but I still had the fifty that my dad had slipped me for the trip.

In the small amount of time that had passed since our arrival, people began pouring into the mall at an unbelievable rate. We stopped briefly at the Indiana Pacer's store and browsed the various items representing the city's basketball team. However, the Colt's store was easily three times the size of the Pacer store and carried every imaginable thing a fan could think of to proudly sport the team's logo. Emily and I remarked on the cute baby clothing, license plate covers, and tablecloths in royal blue and white. Still, the most amusing token was the oversized Colts recliner in bright team blue with white lettering and a horseshoe sitting in the front window. Emily picked out a pink Peyton Manning jersey for herself and insisted I select a jersey to wear at the game. I decided on a pink Joseph Addai jersey while Emily picked up little horseshoe earrings for her and me to wear. She also chose a blue Austin Collie jersey for Jackson and a white Anthony Gonzalez one for Robert to surprise them with.

The food court was jam-packed with individuals attempting to pick up something quick in the short time remaining before kickoff as we squeezed our way through the maze to reach the escalator. I couldn't imagine that the city was like this with every home game they held. I knew the Colts were undefeated this season and that Indianapolis was known for its sports venues with their proximity to hotels, shopping, and restaurants throughout downtown, but this was ridiculous.

However, I had never witnessed it firsthand and I now believed the newscasters when they commented on Hoosiers being fanatical about their sports.

After a quick bite to eat and dropping off our packages in the Durango, the four of us headed outside to venture the few blocks to the stadium. It was only a little past noon and the streets of downtown Indianapolis were overrun with Colts fans of every age. Many of them were sporting some fashionable style of Colts apparel. Royal blue, white, and pink jerseys with the number eighteen and Manning adorned on the back could be seen for as far as the eye could see. There was perhaps one Titan fan for every fifty or more Colts fan that filed into the city.

The Lucas Oil Stadium was everything and more that was written on it. It was spectacular. The wide walkways and venues surrounded the heart of the facility, which could be viewed from every seat under its retractable roof. Although I had never been a big spectator of professional football, experiencing a live game changed all of that in one afternoon.

Robert and Jackson laughed outright at the sight of Emily and me as we both got caught up in the spirit of the crowd and spent the majority of the game on our feet cheering for the Colts. They held the Titans at bay and succeeded in victory with a 27-17 win. That day made me a diehard Colts fan.

*   *   *

It was close to nine when we reached our street. I was exhausted and had slept most of our trip home. The enthusiasm of the afternoon after the whirlwind of information that clouded my brain had taken a toll on me and I could not keep my eyes open.

I thanked Emily and Robert several times before Jackson walked me home. The moonlight was bright in the frigid sky and our breath was easily seen on the night air.

"Are you sure you are all right?" Jackson asked, taking me in his arms when we reached my porch.

"Yes, I am sure."

"You seem so distant," he noted.

"I hope you enjoyed your birthday." I mustered up the best smile I could in my tired condition.

"You love to change the subject when the topic is something you do not wish to discuss." He pulled me close and allowed me to rest my head against his chest. Jackson leaned down and kissed the top of my head. "I had a marvelous birthday." I could feel his cheek resting on my head. "And now my love, will you please answer my question truthfully? Are you all right?"

"Yes, I am fine, I promise."

"Fine as in all right or fine as in frustrated insecure neurotic and emotional?" He flashed that lop-sided grin that I loved.

"You are impossible." I playfully smacked his chest. "I believe the excitement of the last forty-eight hours have taken their toll on me and given me much to think about."

"Get some rest, darling. I'll pick you up in the morning." Jackson lifted my face gently to his and kissed me deeply. "Call me if you need me."

"I will." I offered him the best smile I could muster.

"I love you."

"I love you, too."

I watched him from the porch as he slowly walked across the street and disappeared into his own house.

* * *

I snuggled down under the covers after giving my father a full detailed recap of my trip to Indianapolis and marveling about the new stadium, and a long hot shower. I picked up my uncle's journal off my nightstand and began reading where I'd left off before. His words were so vivid that I could easily picture the tragic world he was experiencing. Before I realized it, I was wiping tears off my cheeks.

His attachment and love for his family— his entire family — was like nothing I had ever felt. I could not help but wish that the family dynamics of today were even a tenth of what they were back then. Today, it seemed everyone was out for themselves and family values had, for the most part, fallen by the wayside.

I closed his journal feeling very isolated. I reached under my bed for the photo album of Jackson and I and our little family. I browsed the photos, content in knowing that at least in one of my worlds the words family and devotion meant something.

I slid the album under my pillow, turned off my light and closed my eyes, thrilled in knowing that I was marrying into a family that in both my lives, would always mean everything.

CHAPTER 14

Thursday, December 08, 1878

JACKSON JOINED US almost every evening for dinner. He relished in telling me all about things going on at the office and how different it was to practice law rather than read about it from books. While he still had no clients of his own, he was enjoying sitting second chair to his father while he learned the ropes. He was so eager to learn and prove himself as the prominent attorney that Robert was.

I was surprised when I came home after school and found him in the front room by the hearth speaking with Olivia while she sat staring silently out the window. Occasionally I would hear her utter a reply if only to be polite. I knew he was trying desperately to take her mind off her shattered world and put other thoughts in their place, if only for a short while. I leaned against the doorframe and listened for a moment as Jackson rattled on about a story he'd read in the newspaper recently. Olivia didn't even blink when he finally completed his recount.

"Good afternoon, darling." I smiled from the across the room when he noticed my arrival.

"Hello, sweetheart." A smirk, more than grin, slid across his shapely lips as he stood up and walked towards me. "Please excuse me, Ms. Olivia."

She nodded slightly without turning from the window.

"How long have you been here?" I whispered, leaning up and giving him a welcoming kiss.

"Almost an hour." He wrapped his arms around me and pulled me closer.

"I was hopeful after she emerged from her room last weekend that she was doing better, but all she ever does is stare out the window. I wish I could do something for her."

"Just try to be supportive and understanding. That is really all you can do for her right now."

I rested my head upon his chest and breathed in the intoxicating aroma of his cologne. I tightened my arms around him and couldn't imagine any other place I would rather be.

"You need to gather your caplet and muff, my dear, we have some work to do before supper." Jackson lifted my chin lightly and kissed me softly.

"Where are we going?" I gave him an inquisitive look.

"In case you haven't noticed, our wedding is less than two weeks away and we still have no place to live," he chuckled.

"But I . . . I mean we have not found anything suited for us." We both knew I was procrastinating and pretended I wasn't.

"I am sure we can find a home that would work as a suitable starter we could live in for a while until we can afford to build something more to your taste." His smile broadened, and I immediately felt guilty.

"Am I being that difficult?" I looked deep into his beautiful green eyes.

"Perhaps maybe a little, but that is what I love about you." He kissed me again quickly and added. "Now get your things please, we are losing daylight."

Four homes later the sun was slipping from the sky and we were not an ounce closer to finding a home. We climbed back into the carriage and I wrapped the carriage quilt over my legs. Jackson looked disgruntled and I remained silent. I didn't have the heart to say anything. I didn't have to because he was the one who didn't care for any of the homes. I didn't either, but his displeasure was so evident that my comments would have made it worse.

The gray sky was heavy with clouds and people moved about in the chilly evening bustling home after a long day of work. Jackson's horse pranced at a steady pace while he sighed heavily and headed the carriage back towards my home.

I wanted to say something comforting but everything that entered my mind sounded insincere even to me.

"Look at the bright side, at least we don't have to worry about paying an inspector to check the plumbing or electricity or whether we have to update the appliances," I giggled.

Jackson slowly turned his head towards me with an astonished expression before he suddenly burst out laughing. "Where in the . . . You never cease to amaze me!"

"Well, it is true." I did my best to keep a straight face.

"Yes, I suppose it is." He couldn't seem to control his laughter.

"Do you know how ridiculous this all is?" The laughter I'd been trying to suppress broke free. "Here we are unable to find a home to start our married life together and making such a huge deal about it and when you stop and think, this should be so much easier than trying to do that in the twenty-first century. I mean buying a home *here* should be a breeze in comparison with that headache."

"I love you. You know that, right?" Jackson leaned over and stole a kiss.

"I love you too."

*   *   *

My brother, James, and his wife, Rachel, had stopped over for a visit by the time we returned. We handed our things over to Eddie and joined everyone in the parlor where the room was buzzing with commotion.

"Good evening, Jackson, Jocelyn. Please join us." James was grinning widely.

"Hello, how are you? Where are the children?" I asked, giving my brother a hug and then kissing Rachel on the cheek.

"We left them home with Hannah. It is almost their bedtime and they get so fussy when kept up late," Rachel explained.

Hannah had lived with Rachel's family for most of her life and once she married my brother, Hannah had gone to live with them.

She was probably about ten or fifteen years older than Rachel and was so sweet and wonderful to them and their children. She had a great personality but was not nearly as sassy as Mimi nor could she cook as well as Sarah.

"I understand. It is certainly nice to see you both." I took her hand and we moved over to the lounge to sit down near mother.

The men gathered closer to the hearth as my father opened his humidor and passed out cigars to Jackson and James. It was then that I noticed Olivia was nowhere to be seen. My eyes drifted back over towards the two ladies beside me and they were giddy with excitement.

"Where is Olivia?" I inquired.

"She retired early. She told Mimi she would have dinner in her room," my mother answered.

"Is she feeling all right?" I asked.

"I believe so, physically. Emotionally . . . she is still struggling a great deal." My mother looked guiltily over at Rachel and then back at me. "Which is what makes this so much more difficult."

"Mother? What are you talking about?" I noticed Rachel dropped her eyes to her lap.

"Jocelyn . . . ," Rachel injected. "Your brother and I have some wonderful news." She paused, and I knew what she was going to say before the words came out of her mouth. "I'm pregnant."

"Congratulations!" I jumped up and gave her a hug. "I am so happy for you two!" Then I rushed over and hugged my brother briefly catching him off guard, yet he smiled and embraced me back.

"I am so thrilled to hear you say that," Rachel noted upon my return. "We were so nervous to tell you."

"Why?"

"Because Olivia is having such a difficult time." Rachel looked down at her hands.

"I know she and William will have a hard time adjusting to the news, but I could not be happier for the two of you," I gushed.

"We did not plan this. I know to them that will not matter, it's going to hurt all the same." Her smile quickly faded.

"I am sure William will be happy for you both. I wish I could say the same for Olivia. She is not exactly herself these days. Please, don't take anything she says personally." I gently placed my hands over hers and gave them a gentle squeeze.

"I know she is still hurting and I do not want to be another source of her pain." Rachel looked empathetic.

"Of course, you don't," my mother interceded. "Olivia will come around. Just be patient with her and in time she will come to be as ecstatic as the rest of the family."

"Well, I am not so sure about ecstatic." I grimaced a bit. "But happy will do."

"Yes, happy would be wonderful," Rachel grinned.

Jackson stayed for supper and the household celebrated joyously the anticipated arrival of the new baby. I tried not to think of the possibility that Olivia might overhear our celebration in the dining room as my father drank toast after toast to the newest Timmons's member. I also couldn't help but wonder if any of my nieces or nephews or this new baby was also cursed with the same debilitating ability as I was: *EVE*.

Chapter 15

Thursday, December 10, 2009

I RESTED MY HEAD on my hand, giving up on paying attention to Mr. Rand ramble on about the bystander effect on witness testimony when Jackson poked me in the side. "Wake up." He strained not to smile.

"I am awake. That's the problem," I whispered back.

Any other day I loved psychology class and Mr. Rand was one of my favorite teachers but today I just wanted the bell to ring, and the sound of his lecture was making it hard for me to drift off. We had a big game this evening and I desperately needed a nap. I was spending entirely too much time buried in my uncle's journals and it was seriously cutting into my sleep. Each morning I was waking up exhausted and struggling to stay awake through my classes.

I knew I had to pull it together and find some energy somewhere or Coach Smith was going to wring my neck. She had already yelled at me twice in practice for missing easy shots and not paying attention. If I screwed up in the game, she would surely have me running laps all next week.

Time crept on and I felt myself drifting off into darkness as my head slowly slid down my arm and rested on my desk. Peace . . . and finally silence.

"Jocelyn, wake up!" Jackson gently rubbed my shoulder.

"What?"

"Wake up. Class is over. Didn't you hear the bell?"

"No." I yawned deeply and sat up straight.

Mr. Rand was sitting at his desk shuffling papers. "Are you feeling all right, Jocelyn?"

"I can't seem to get enough sleep. I'm sorry." I gave him a weak smile.

"You should get some Starbucks before the game. We're counting on you tonight," he smiled back.

"That is not a bad idea." Jackson picked up the books off my desk and placed them on top of his in his arms. "Thanks, Mr. Rand."

"Oh, and Jocelyn?" he hollered as we made our way to the door. "Try to stay awake in class from here on out," he winked with a smile.

"I'm sorry, I will," I apologized.

"See you both at the game. Good luck, Jocelyn," he hollered as we exited the room.

We walked out to the parking lot after dropping off our books at our lockers. It's amazing how quick the lot clears out after the final bell. There were only a few scattered cars left when we arrived at his car.

"Starbucks?" he asked, opening my door. Thankfully, his basketball practice was cancelled because their coach, Mr. Minnick, was ill.

"Yeah, we'd better or I'm not going to make it." I smiled and climbed in.

We pulled out of the lot with *Sixx AM* blaring from the stereo speakers and headed towards the more commercial part of the northern suburbs of Chicago. Traffic was picking up as it always did around this time of day.

Starbucks was packed by the time we got there. It appeared that more than half my teammates were in dire need of a pick-me-up also.

"Hey, sleepy. Glad to see you here." Jenna and Kyle met us at the door. "Heard you slept most of the day." She gave me a playful jab in the ribs with her elbow.

"I actually considered bringing you something if you didn't show up after the way you've been practicing this week," Caitlyn remarked as she and Zak joined us.

"Yeah, if you play like that tonight Coach will put your butt in a sling for sure," Hilary said, walking up to us with Cody.

"I know. I know. That's why I'm here," I rolled my eyes at them. They were worse than parents sometimes.

Jackson ordered me a triple espresso and himself a regular while he chatted with the guys about their upcoming game tomorrow evening, so the girls and I escaped into the nearest booth.

"What is with you lately? I thought everything was back on track with you and Jackson." Caitlyn cornered me.

"It is. Everything is great between us. My mind is just all over the place these days." I tried not to snicker aloud at the irony of those words.

"Then what's bothering you?" Jenna inquired.

"You remember a couple weeks ago when my mom made my dad clean out that storage room in the basement? Well, he found some old journals in his brother's things that were apparently a family heirloom from some relative in the nineteenth century written during the Civil War and I've been up reading them. They cover his experiences and I find them fascinating." It was the best I could explain.

"History? How boring." Hilary rolled her eyes.

Jenna made a face in Hilary's direction. "Everything educational is boring to you. I think it would be so cool to find something like that. What do they say?"

Luckily the guys had made their way back over to us and cut me off before I could get started. They squeezed into the booth, squishing us all together. Eight people in a booth designed for maybe six at the most. But the triple espresso was a wonderful intoxicant and exactly what I needed to get my blood flowing smoothly back on this plane so that I could be fully focused on the here and now.

*   *   *

The game was a complete victory for we dominated the court the entire night. We were all in high spirits and pumped full of adrenaline as we hurried back into the locker room. I peeled off my uniform and tossed it into my gym bag alongside my high tops and sweaty socks.

"That was great!" I said, throwing on a pair of old sweatpants and oversized shirt. I couldn't wait to get home and in the shower. I felt so gross.

"It's nice to see you got your game back." Caitlyn teased while changing into her street clothes.

"You realize you were going to get lynched if you didn't?" Jenna remarked.

"Oh really? By who?" I inquired.

"By the three of us!" Hillary answered. "And I believe I'm safe in saying that the rest of the team would have joined us if you'd played anything tonight like you've been playing in practice all week." She gave me the cockiest grin.

"Wow! I feel so loved!" I grabbed my jacket and gym bag. "I will see you ladies later. I'm going to go find someone who loves me unconditionally." I playfully tossed my hair over my shoulder before exiting.

Jackson and my dad were waiting for me near the gym entrance casually talking like they were old friends. I was thrilled to see the two of them getting along so well. The last several weeks had been so horrible with my mother and Ethan wasn't much better. I was grateful that the two most important men in my life were trying to get to know each other.

"Great game, darling," My dad smiled as I approached them.

"I'm glad you came, but you really didn't have to wait. Jackson was going to give me a ride." He lifted my gym bag off my shoulder. "Thanks!"

"I know. I was just talking to Jackson, not so much waiting on you."

"Man, I cannot catch a break tonight." I shook my head as they both stared strangely at me.

"Huh?" My dad looked confused.

"Never mind," I brushed the comment aside.

The three of us walked out to the parking lot still discussing the Colts game from last weekend. My poor ol' dad was so jealous that he hadn't gone it was almost humorous. He was drilling Jackson with four hundred questions about the game and the new stadium. The late evening air had quite a bite and after sweating for the last ninety minutes in the hot stuffy gym I was freezing my rear end off.

"Well you guys had better get going, Jocelyn's teeth are chattering." My dad gave me a brief hug. "You did great tonight, princess." He opened his car door and hollered. "Be careful, I'll see you both back at the house. It was nice talking with you Jackson."

"You too, sir," Jackson opened the passenger door for me.

"Thanks," my dad yelled back before he closed his car door.

"You were amazing tonight," Jackson said as he climbed in on his side. "I don't think you missed one shot."

"Two actually," I smirked.

"And how many did you make?" He started his CRV and headed towards home.

"Twenty-two," I stated proudly.

"You guys won by eighteen points. Yes, you are right those two baskets would have changed the entire outcome of the game."

"Thanks, you're sweet. All I'm saying is it would be nice to have a perfect game."

"No one has a perfect game, Jocelyn. Even the pros miss baskets — some of them a lot! And they make a ton of money doing it." He glanced over, showing me my favorite lop sided grin.

"Yes, I am aware."

"Do you have any plans for this weekend?"

"Why? Are you springing another road trip on me or introducing me to another estranged relative? No wait, that was last weekend!"

"Very funny, I wanted to see if you wanted to study for our biology exam."

"Ah right, I forgot. Yes, we'd better. But I do have to run into the city with Jenna on Saturday morning."

"What for?"

"None of your business." I couldn't very well tell him about my trip to the clinic. It was embarrassing enough as it was. "After all, Christmas is right around the corner."

"Fair enough."

*   *   *

I snuggled under the covers and picked up my uncle's journal. I was already on the second one and they captured me like no other book ever had. I couldn't seem to tear myself away from them no matter how much sleep they were costing me.

September 18, 1862

The last couple days have been dubbed 'the bloodiest battle of the war thus far.' We fought all over Antietam Creek. McClellan is calling it a victory although I cannot understand how something so horrible could be called a victory. We lost almost twelve and a half thousand Union soldiers and I was told the Rebels lost more than ten thousand! Such a horrible senseless loss of life.

We heard this morning that General Lee has taken his troops back across the Potomac River. Does he not realize that if they were to attack us again there would be very little we could do to keep them from advancing into the North?

Still, their retreat was a welcomed blessing. The screams still have not ended. The wounded and dying are a constant reminder of the horrors.

I saw men crumple up in pain or scream out in agony as I shot them. Their blood covered my clothes, my hands. I saw the creek run red with the blood of men from both sides.

The smell of gunpowder and decay still hangs heavy on the air. No matter how the wind blows it cannot cleanse this soiled ground. The vermin run rampant throughout our quarters and none of us are immune to their liking.

One would hope that this squelching heat would have deterred them for it feels like being kept in an oven. There is very little clean water to share and many of the men who survived to fight another day are only left to struggle through on the molded bread and rotten meat for our supplies are few and far between.

My uniform is no more than a mere rag, the buttons gone, and one sleeve is completely missing. My boots have many holes and barely offer any protection for my feet against the elements. Sadly enough, I am better off than most of our men. I cannot recall what it was like to sleep in a real bed with clean linens, clothes or to take an actual bath with real soap.

I think of home every moment my tired brain can rest. I close my eyes and see Vivian with her long blond hair and flowing curls. Her blue eyes sparkle like the stars on a blackened night. I ache to hold her again. I realize now more than ever how much I truly love her. How much my family means to me.

There still has been no word on Nicholas. I pray for his safety, but I fear the worst. Stories have reached our ears about the prisoner camps down South. They say hundreds of men are dying daily from starvation and disease. My only hope is that he is somewhere safe trying to make his way back to us.

I was fortunate late last evening to see my older brother. I was being treated for a mere shrapnel wound in my thigh and stumbled into Patrick, if only for a moment. He appeared haggard and worn, covered in the blood of many of our young boys.

He assured me that his family was well, but he had not been able to see them since our leave last Christmas. He promised we would talk once he got a free moment, yet I imagine it will be some time before I see him again. From the state of our men I pray it shall be days before he and the other physicians even have the chance to assess each of the wounded.

I pray this war would end and we could all go home.

How do people survive such senseless hate?

CHAPTER 16

Friday, December 9, 1878

MR. GRAHAME began his lecture on the causes that led up to the Civil War. I quickly became engrossed in his words. Many were the same words I had heard numerous times, discussed at our dining room table or hotly debated behind closed doors in my father's study. Some of which I was very familiar with but some I was completely ignorant of, like the fact that Jefferson Davis was elected President of the Confederate States before Abraham Lincoln was elected President of the United States.

I had some basic ideas of the war and even though I technically lived through it, I had absolutely no recollection of it whatsoever. Which was a given considering I was born in October 1860. However, through the rapidly diminishing barrier between my two worlds, I was able to recall various writings from my uncle Monte's journals that he had recounted in vivid detail his experiences and daily struggle for survival during his time in the Union Army. He recently became aware that my *other* father, Shane had found, read, and handed the journals over to my *other* self. I knew he was very uncomfortable knowing that I was aware of the depths at which he had bared his soul on the pages of his youth, but he had not mentioned the journals nor the photo albums since Thanksgiving and neither had I.

An hour later, Mr. Grahame concluded his thoughts but not before assigning us another essay to write before our next class. The other students let out a small moan and began to gather their things together to move on to their next class.

I stood up as Elizabeth approached with a weary look. "Would you mind if I came by your house after school to work on my essay?

I am to meet with Mrs. Chandler at five o'clock for a final fitting on my bridesmaid dress."

"Yes, that would be great. Would you like to stay for dinner also? I know Olivia would love to see you too." I was hoping that Elizabeth's presence might coax Olivia into being a little more sociable.

*　　*　　*

I was thankful it was Friday. That gave me two days to work on my essay. Though I wasn't sure when I would find the time to work on it considering Jackson and I were going to be house hunting all weekend. At first it was exciting, now it was something I dreaded.

Elizabeth and I made small talk on our way down the cobblestones towards my house. The sky was threatening to rain down on us as the dark clouds hovered above us. I pulled my caplet tighter around me and wished I had taken my wool coverlet with me this morning.

"Are you getting nervous yet?" Elizabeth asked as we turned the corner.

"Nervous? About what?"

Elizabeth looked at me with a slight smile. "The wedding."

"No, not really." The cold wind tore at my cheeks.

"I would be if I were you."

"I feel like I have been waiting for this for so long. I cannot imagine spending my life with anyone else," I said anxiously.

"I understand exactly how you feel. I believe I am destined to be with Mr. Lee." She blushed despite the cold.

I smiled over at her. "I think that is wonderful."

We passed through the gate and up the walkway. The huge house appeared stagnant and cold against the gray darkening sky. For a moment my mind's eye flashed on the subtle differences in the house before me and the one my *other* self-resided in over 130 years from now. The realization sent a chill down my spine like one the weather never had before.

"Are you all right?" Elizabeth put her hand on my shoulder. I nodded slowly. "You look as if you saw a ghost."

I tried to laugh it off as I opened our front door, but her words were a little too true to be humorous. That had never happened to me to that degree before. The strangest calm came over me as my mind flashed to and fro on the foyer in the same way it had on the exterior of the house. I held onto the banister with one hand to steady myself and handed my things to Eddie with the other. I was thrilled to see Jackson standing in the doorway to our front room.

"Hello, darling. How were classes today?" He gave me a quick kiss on the cheek. "Hello, Ms. Elizabeth. How are you doing?"

"Fine. Why are you not at the office?" I inquired.

"Good afternoon, Mr. Jackson." Elizabeth handed her coverlet to Eddie and carried her schoolbooks into the parlor.

"I am sorry, I hadn't realized you were having company this afternoon." Jackson sat down on the lounge.

"We have an essay due for history and she is meeting with your mother at five o'clock for her final fitting on her bridesmaid's gown," I explained as I joined him.

Elizabeth sat down in the rocker beside the hearth and opened our history book. "Please do not mind me. I promise to stay out of your way." She grinned slightly without looking up.

"No, it is not that," he shifted a little in my direction. "I got a lead on a house that just became available and I left the office early to see if you wanted to look at it before dinner."

"Can we wait until tomorrow?" It felt rude to leave Elizabeth here alone.

"No, the owner will be leaving in the morning for New York on business and does not know when he will be returning," he said.

"Please, take advantage. We cannot have you two being homeless in a couple weeks," a soft voice from the doorway spoke up. "I will be happy to keep Ms. Elizabeth company in your absence." Olivia slowly walked in the room.

"Thank you, I appreciate that." I jumped at the opportunity, not only for us but for Olivia to rejoin her social life a little.

*   *   *

I settled back in the carriage seat and tucked the thick quilt around me. Eddie guided us down the lane as the wind whistled outside the small windows. I leaned my head down on Jackson's shoulder and closed my eyes.

"So, are you going to tell me what upset you so much this afternoon? You looked almost ready to cry when you arrived home today," Jackson broke the silence between us.

"I think the barrier is really starting to fall apart." I went on to explain how my eyes were playing constant tricks on me by flashing back and forth between time periods.

"That sounds strange. I guess I never really experienced that since I lived in two different cities. There was nothing for my mind to do that to." He turned towards the window and stared out into the evening leaving only a calm silence between us.

"Sometimes I sit in class and let my mind wonder off and I see the most amazing things that I never could have imagined in my wildest dreams. What makes it so strange is that it no longer feels foreign anymore. Instead it feels comfortable and familiar." My voice drifted softly through the small enclosed carriage.

"I understand, but Jocelyn, that world, as incredible as it may appear, is still a novelty to your innocent 1878 eyes and I do not want you to lose yourself in it."

"What is that supposed to mean?" I turned towards him, but he was still looking out the window. "Look at me, Jackson."

"That — things like that. Last September you would never have thought of speaking to me in such a manner, but now — you are different. And I am not saying that in a bad way. I absolutely love that you are a strong-willed, independent, career oriented, young lady who knows exactly what she wants in this world, but some of those traits that I love are showing up *here* and people are noticing." He looked solemnly back out the window.

"Who?"

"Your father for one. William for another. Both have mentioned to me independently that you must be experiencing some pre-wedding jitters because you have been behaving so out of character in the last couple months. When Patrick said it in front of my father, my father reassured him that jitters was all it was, but you need to be more careful."

I could not believe my ears. I could not recall anything that I had done in front of either of them that would be construed as out of my normal character. But before I could respond the carriage stopped abruptly and seconds later Eddie opened the side door, offering his hand to me.

The house before me was gorgeous and rested on one of the more bustling lanes that led into the heart of Chicago. The yard was considerably smaller than the vast lawn of our family estate, but the property was still over an acre large. The two-story home loomed before us in full majestic glory. There was no possible way this place was even close to being within our price range.

"What do you think?" Jackson came up behind me and put his arm around my waist.

"I think it's beautiful and something we could possibly afford five years from now, but this is certainly no starter home."

"Why don't we look around before you jump to any conclusions?" He smiled proudly and walked toward the front door.

I followed him up to the large porch that held a couple rockers and small tables. Little pots hung empty from the eaves where beautiful flowers bloomed in other seasons. The white railings and boards looked recently painted and well maintained. The oak front door had two rectangular stained-glass windows and a polished brass knob and knocker. Jackson knocked on the door while I gazed around at the massive view of the surrounding homes of a similar sort.

A gentleman slightly older than my father answered the door. "Mr. Chandler, welcome. Your father said you would be coming by this evening. I apologize for the limited timeframe, but business is growing with each rail laid." He smiled and stepped aside to let us in.

"Good evening, Mr. Tanner. Please allow me to introduce you to my fiancée, Ms. Jocelyn Timmons." I curtsied politely, and Mr. Tanner lightly took my hand and kissed it gently.

"I am very pleased to make your acquaintance, Ms. Timmons." His bushy mustache was tweaked in a fashionable style.

"Thank you, Mr. Tanner. You have a very lovely home." I stood uncomfortably in the oversized foyer.

Mr. Tanner gave us a personally guided tour of his beautiful very modern home. He proudly boasted that not only did the house have indoor plumbing in the kitchen and baths, it also had hot water. The oil light fixtures throughout were a gaudy bright brass, the rugs were multicolored in various styles that matched the colors procured to each individual room. Although I had never been in a brothel in my life, the interior of this home was exactly what I would have imagined one looked like.

Even though the outside appearance and the structural foundation of the home was exactly what both of us desired, the mere cost of having to replace the wallpaper in every single room seemed disheartening. I was suddenly thankful that the house was out of our price range. Yet, Jackson and I followed Mr. Tanner and listened to him boast and brag about the expensive décor that his wife had requested shipped back from Paris. I glanced over at Jackson and I knew we were both thinking the same thing . . . *that explains a lot.*

We finally returned to the foyer where Mr. Tanner handed Jackson a folded piece of parchment. "Here is the list of everything I covered plus some particulars on the home in general. If you have any questions, please feel free to wire me or send me a letter. I wrote all my contact information on that sheet."

"Wonderful, thank you again Mr. Tanner for personally taking the time to show us around your beautiful home. We truly appreciate it." He shook his hand again.

After several more exchanges of pleasantries by all we finally stepped back to the carriage. Jackson wrapped the quilt over me and Eddie began trotting us away from the outlandish palace. Safely away, Jackson and I exchanged a look and both of us burst into unbelievable laughter.

"I am so sorry, I had no idea." He joyfully wiped the tears off his cheeks.

"Was that a brothel or a home?"

"I am not sure. I cannot wait to tell Father. I am sure he had no idea the Tanner Estate held such furnishings. I have never seen so many colors under one roof in all my life," Jackson proclaimed.

"It looks so normal from the street." I took out my handkerchief and dabbed my cheeks. "What does it say on the paper?"

Jackson unfolded the paper and looked it over for a moment. "He wrote down a listing of all the room dimensions, the overall square footage of the house, the property, carriage house, and the modern updates along with the price he is asking."

"How concise. What is his price?"

"Five thousand."

"You must be kidding?" I had no idea what the cost of a house was but that seemed more than a tad out of our reach. "And do you feel that is reasonable?"

"Reasonable? Yes, I would say so. Actually, he could easily get more." Jackson's brow furrowed in thought.

"The cost of redecorating the entire place would surely not be worth it, do you not you agree?" Fear ceased hold of me that he was possibly considering undertaking such a deed. I was up for purchasing a home that I could decorate to my taste with a few changes here and there, but such a massive undertaking was simply beyond my scope of consideration.

"I am not sure. I fear the price is so low because he is an old friend and client of my father," Jackson said as a matter of fact.

"What sort of business does Mr. Tanner do that he can afford for his wife to ship furnishings all the way from France?"

"Railroads. He is part of the group that is expanding the railroads to the west and around the south. He's very wealthy and travels a great deal. This home is one of many that he owns around the country." He rubbed his chin briefly. "I wonder why he is selling it now. It is less than ten years old."

"Perhaps he is building a new one or his business is requiring him elsewhere," I suggested.

"Maybe . . ." He shrugged. "Did you like the structural aspects of the home? Looking beyond the hideous décor?" Jackson turned serious.

"Are you saying you are considering it? We have such a short time before the wedding and not nearly enough to redo the entire home. Not to mention it is entirely too large for just the two of us even if we have help," I reasoned.

"Between our mothers, I am sure the home could be livable by the time we are married." He smiled and placed his hand over mine, which I did not find comforting at all.

"Can we afford such a place?" I had no idea what his salary was at his father's firm. Finances were never discussed between us.

"I believe so."

"But the cost of fixing the walls, purchasing rugs, and furniture to fill the place would simply be more that we could spare." I glanced up at him with speculation.

"Do not worry, I will take care of everything." He kissed me lightly on the cheek as the carriage came to a halt at my front porch.

*   *   *

Jackson and I had missed dinner in the dining room with the rest of the family and Elizabeth by the time we had returned. She was already across the street with Emily for her fitting. Therefore, Jackson and I went to the kitchen to search up some dinner.

Sarah was thoughtful enough to put aside something for us. We both took a seat in the small nook and chatted happily with Mimi and Sarah about the bizarre home we had just encountered. Luckily Jackson never mentioned anything more about undertaking the task of remodeling the ghastly estate.

CHAPTER 17

Friday, December 11, 2009

THE GYM WAS PACKED full of parents, students, and teachers anxiously waiting for our boys to hit the court. The cheerleaders were dancing around on the center court absent one Taylor Perry. Dakota glared in our direction as the six of us made our way over to the bleachers.

"Isn't she sweet?" Jenna laughed and nodded towards Dakota.

"Very," I giggled.

"Knock it off you two," Kyle warned with a grin.

We found a vacant spot about three-fourths the ways up and climbed over a half dozen people to claim the space before anyone else could. Cody and Kyle separated Hilary and Caitlyn from Jenna and me. making it difficult to talk over them. Finally, Coach Minnick announced the team and the boys came running out onto the court to run through their warm-up drills.

As I watched Jackson make an easy lay-up I noticed Ethan's eyes continually scanning over the bleachers. I figured he was probably searching for our parents, yet they were sitting in the third row behind the bench . . . pretty hard to miss.

After the second time Ethan missed his cue to take off for a lay-up, Zak leaned over and said something in his ear that immediately caused Ethan to refocus his attention. I knew that despite being an immature goof off the court, as co-captain of the varsity team with Jackson, the game was of the upmost importance to him and Zak demanded the same of his teammates.

"What's wrong with E?" Jenna leaned over and asked.

I shrugged, having no clue myself. In doing so I glanced over at Jenna and noticed that Kyle was smiling in a way that said he knew exactly what was going on.

"What?" I leaned across Jenna and asked him.

"Over there." Kyle looked down at the lower section on the right.

"Who?" Jenna, clearly as lost as I was, stared in the direction of the overcrowded section below.

"Liang Chi," Kyle moved towards us and whispered.

Both our eyes quickly landed on the petite junior sitting amongst her friends with her eyes following my brother's every move.

"You're kidding," Jenna stared.

"Since when?" I couldn't look away either.

"I don't know," said Kyle, who gave us a look that told us this was clearly not an area discussed between guys.

I watched Liang for several minutes, curious at what my brother saw in her. She was not someone I knew but rather just knew of. I was certain she had a couple classes with Ethan, but I couldn't recall him ever mentioning her other than in passing.

She tossed her long black hair over her shoulder and I realized for the first time how beautiful she really was. She had amazingly dark brown eyes, a gorgeous olive skin tone, and a waist that could bring any woman to tears. And to make matters worse, she was maybe all of five foot three inches tall.

I wasn't sure what to think of her, but as I watched her throughout the game I saw that every time my brother was on the court, the two of them continually stole little looks just as Jackson and I regularly did.

The victory was an easy one for our boys and everyone was bustling about in the hallway after the game waiting for them to emerge from the locker room. I was killing time talking with Hilary about going to the mall on Sunday when Jenna elbowed me in the ribs.

"Who do you think she's waiting on?" She smirked in the direction of Liang and her friends.

"Who?" Hilary looked confused.

"Apparently my brother." I was surprised by the hostile tone of my voice.

"Are they dating?" Caitlyn joined in.

"I'm not sure," I responded, not taking my eyes off the giggling girl who stood several yards from us.

"She's really sweet. She was in my journalism class last spring." Hilary still looked baffled at my obvious displeasure with the girl.

"Wonderful, I'm sure she's precious." I turned back towards Jenna.

"What is wrong with you?" Jenna whispered.

"Nothing, I'm fine."

Jackson and Zak emerged from the locker room followed directly by Ethan.

"Hello, gorgeous." Jackson immediately wrapped me up in his arms and kissed me lightly. "How's my girl?"

"Much better now." I melted into him and rested my head against his chest.

Out of the corner of my eye I saw Ethan standing beside Liang with his arm draped loosely around her waist. He was smiling at her and she was laughing at something he'd said.

"Are we ready to go?" Zak piped up from beside Caitlyn.

"Sure. Where to?" I asked our group.

"Cody's postgame party, I guess," Jackson said as we all made our way out to the parking lot.

Everyone dispersed into their respective vehicles, but I paused next to Jackson's CRV while he stood there holding the passenger door open for me. Across the lot I saw Ethan and Liang climb into the backseat of Kyle's car. Jenna caught my eye and gave me a look that told me this was not her idea.

We pulled out of the parking lot and followed the line of cars to Cody's house. I wasn't exactly in the mood for a party and I really couldn't understand why Ethan's new interest bothered me so much.

I didn't really know anything about her.

"Do you care if we stop and get some coffee?" I turned down the radio a bit.

"Sure." Jackson made the next right turn. "So, what is bothering you?" He was still looking straight ahead. Damn, it bothered me sometimes that he knew me so well.

"Did you know Ethan was interested in Liang Chi?"

"Yes, he has been for a while."

"No one ever told me."

"I just found out tonight when Corbin was teasing him before the game. He certainly did not mention it to me but then again, he and I are not exactly friends any longer." He rolled his eyes.

"Well, join the club. He doesn't like me either," I laughed as we pulled into Starbucks.

*   *   *

We arrived at Cody's shortly after ten. We pushed our way through the front door and wove our way through the crowd until we finally found Hilary in the kitchen. She was fixing herself a plain soda and looking more than a little upset.

"Hey, what's going on?" I asked, approaching her holding Jackson's hand.

"Guess who's here?" she sneered. "And looking for you?"

"Who?"

"Taylor," she replied.

"So?" I shrugged. "Why should I care?"

"Because she's only here to cause trouble," Hilary stated.

"Then perhaps we should just leave." Jackson leaned in closer to me.

"Why should I leave? I have no intention of getting into another fight with her."

"Because you are the better person." Jackson gave me a quick peck on the cheek.

"Well, of course I am. We already know that," I smirked. "Don't worry, I will behave myself," I told them.

"Hey, I am so sorry. Are you mad at me?" Jenna slid in between Hilary and me.

"For aiding and abetting?" I playfully narrowed my eyes at her.

"It wasn't my fault. Kyle offered them a ride. What was I supposed to say?" Jenna shrugged.

"How about no?" I replied.

"That would have looked really sweet on my part." She rolled her eyes at me.

"Why don't you like Liang?" Hilary played with her drink. "She's great."

"It's not that I don't like her. I don't know her. It's just the way Ethan's still being an ass to us and everything he does right now I find annoying."

"You two need to make peace. You've always been so close." Jenna looked down at her hands.

"We will as soon as he grows up and stops acting like a baby." Jenna rolled her eyes at my remark. "Don't be judgmental, you have no idea what it's like living in a house where both your brother and your mother refuse to speak to you and walk out of a room every time you enter it."

"I know. I'm sorry."

"Hey, why so serious? This is supposed to be a party," Hilary piped up in a much louder tone.

I saw Ethan and Liang dancing in the living room with a large group of our peers and instantly felt sick to my stomach. I fought the little devil who sat upon my shoulder that had the urge to storm over there and smack him across the face. After the way he'd been behaving towards Jackson and I, the last thing I wanted him to be was happy.

"I am not feeling very well. Would you mind terribly if we left?" I turned towards Jackson.

"What is up with you?" Caitlyn looked at me funny.

"Pray tell Ms. Jocelyn, do not leave us amiss," Jenna mocked.

"Oh stop, I have a headache." I tried to quickly backpedal.

"Since when?" Hilary piped up.

"Of course," Jackson nodded towards my friends with a coy smile. "Good evening, ladies." I knew he was mocking them right back just as I was positive they thought he was only playing. For a moment I saw in him the Jackson that only danced in my nightly dreams.

"They spend way too much time together. She's starting to sound just like him," I heard Jenna remark as we walked away.

* * *

The moon and stars shone brightly over the night giving everything it touched a luminous glow. Light snowflakes began to glide through the air and fall gracefully upon us. I held onto Jackson's arm and pulled my jacket closer around me.

"Nice little slip up back there," he teased.

"I know. The words fell out before I even realized it." I felt so foolish. "At least they didn't realize it."

"You would be surprised how little people notice something right before their eyes." He unlocked the passenger door and held it open for me.

We pulled out of Cody's neighborhood before Jackson spoke again. "So, why do you not like Liang?"

"I never said I did not like her," I protested. "Why does everyone keep assuming that?"

"Probably because you look at her like a bug you want to squash," he said with his eyes still on the road.

"I do not," I denied, even though we both knew it was true.

"You did this evening."

"It is not her. It's him. Ethan just makes me so mad. I am so sick of the way he's been acting towards you."

"I'm a big boy, I can take it." He kept his eyes forward, but I saw a slight smile slide across his shapely lips.

*   *   *

I flipped on my iPod dock and turned up *Foster the People* before I sat down at my vanity. I pulled the towel off my head and shook out my hair when someone knocked on my bedroom door.

"Yeah," I hollered, picking up my brush.

Ethan casually walked into my room and sat down on the corner of my bed. "What was up with you tonight?"

"Nothing, why?" I continued brushing out my hair looking at him only through the mirror.

"Because you were glaring at me and Liang in the hallway after the game and at Cody's."

"No, I wasn't." But I knew I was. I just hadn't realized he had noticed.

"Whatever," he muttered under his breath. "Liang has done nothing to you and she doesn't deserve you to treat her like that."

I dropped my hairbrush and spun around to face him. "I couldn't care less about Liang. In fact, I don't know why someone like her would want to date you. She's too good for you from what I hear. And as for me treating her badly, I've not ever said a word to her. You on the other hand, treat Jackson like crap and yet you still expect him to give you a ride to school every day."

"I have my reasons for hating him and you know it. Liang isn't trying to ruin my life, Jackson's ruining yours," he spat.

"That's your opinion, not mine," I shouted back.

"That's a fact and you're just too blind and stupid to see it!"

My jaw dropped in stunned silence for a moment. "Then perhaps you can find another way to school from here on out," I said calmly.

"Fine, give me the car keys." He held out his hand.

"I will not. That's my car, not yours."

"If you're riding with Jackson, then I can use the car." He reached for my purse resting on my bed, but I flung myself upon it before he could grab anything more than the strap.

He pulled hard on the strap. "Move your fat butt! I'm taking the keys!"

"You are not . . . let go!" I screamed at the top of my lungs.

"You let go!" Ethan yanked even harder on the purse straps, snapping one side off my purse. He then fell backwards across the floor. "Give me the freakin' keys!" he immediately jumped back to his feet only to be met with a swift kick to the abdomen.

"I can't believe you . . . you broke my purse!" I screamed.

Ethan stumbled back for a moment then launched himself on me trying to dig the purse out from beneath me. Suddenly fists and feet were flying, and loose tongues hurled a constant stream of insults that were enough to send both our parents running into my room.

"Ethan! Jocelyn! Stop that . . . right now!" Mom screamed from the doorway.

Our dad leapt forward, pulling Ethan off me and stood between the two of us. "Enough!" he shouted loud enough that it rang in my ears. "What in the world is going on in here?"

"He tried to get in my purse and broke the strap when I wouldn't give it to him!" I shouted through anger and tears.

"She wouldn't give me the car keys!" Ethan screamed back.

"It's MY CAR!" I spat over my dad's shoulder at Ethan.

"You're not even driving it and I need a way to get to school since you won't let me ride with you and Jackson!"

"WALK!" I screamed.

"Enough!" Dad yelled again.

He turned towards our mother looking for some help, but she just shook her head and walked away, leaving him to deal with us alone. "All right . . . fine," he took a deep breath and looked between the two of us. "Ethan, sit." He pointed down at the floor.

"But?" My brother tried to protest.

"I said sit! And you . . ." he looked directly at me. "Sit down." I slowly sat down on the corner of my bed.

Our dad paced across my floor running his fingers through his hair like he'd finally reached his limit with our antics. Finally, he stopped and looked down at his son. "Ethan, did you try and get in her purse?"

"Well she . . ." he began, but Dad cut him off.

"Did you try to get in your sister's purse?"

"Yes," he replied in a low voice.

"Are you allowed to ever go in your mother's or your sister's purse?" Dad asked, struggling to control his tone.

"No, but . . ."

"Are you?" Dad raised his voice again.

"No," Ethan conceded.

"Fine, then you will pay for her purse."

"But . . ."

"No buts, you will pay for the purse."

"She won't give me the keys to the car!" Ethan raised his voice before he realized it. Dad's face got redder than it already was.

"And why should she?" Dad narrowed his eyes at his son.

"Because I need to drive to school since she won't let me ride with them anymore," Ethan lowered his voice a bit but not much.

"So, you feel you are entitled to drive her car?"

"She's not driving it," Ethan fired back.

"It's her car, not yours!" Ethan's ears turned a bright red telling me he was about to explode. I could see him struggling to control his temper with our dad and tried not to laugh out loud at his pain.

"Then what am I supposed to do?"

"You could try not being an ass to your sister or get a ride with one of your friends." Dad smiled coyly at him. "Or you could always ride the bus."

Ethan stood up. "I'd rather walk." Then left my room.

"That's certainly your choice," Dad hollered after him before turning his attention towards me. "As for you, young lady, what provoked this behavior?"

"He's expecting me to give him rides, be nice to his girlfriend, and do things for him when he's continually being an ass to me and Jackson."

"Language . . ."

"Sorry . . . but I'm sick of it."

He sat down on my bed next to me. He pointed at the red welts on my arms and lightly touched the side of my face. "Looks like he got you pretty good."

"Yeah, but I think I may have given him a couple bruises too." I tried to smile.

He put his arm around my shoulder and gave me a gentle squeeze. "What am I going to do with all of you? I am so tired of everyone in this house fighting all the time."

"I know. Me too," I whispered.

CHAPTER 18

Saturday, December 10, 1878

I WOKE UP and immediately put my hand up to my face. There was a strange tingling, an almost burning sensation on my cheek and the corner of my mouth. I felt like someone had smacked me. A feeling of frustration and anxiety ripped through me.

I climbed out of bed and put on my robe and slippers. I could hear others starting to move about when I opened my door and made my way down the front staircase. I wanted desperately to run across the street and ask Jackson what had happened *there* to elicit such emotions and cause the strange sensation in my face. Still, I hated being so dependent on him for information about my *own* life and thought I could, if I concentrated hard enough without distractions, figure it out for myself.

I sat down at the table and Sarah came in carrying a tray filled with hot cakes, syrup, bacon scrambled eggs, and coffee. The smell was intoxicating, and my stomach began to grumble. Before I could even get my first cup of coffee William came into the dining room carrying the morning paper. He was dressed in his trousers and shirt, absent a tie. His suspenders hung below his waist and his hair was uncombed.

"Good morning, how did you sleep?" I greeted him while sipping my coffee.

He pulled out his chair with a huff and laid the paper beside his plate on the table before pouring himself some coffee. "Fine," he muttered.

"Is Olivia coming down?" I began to wonder if they were fighting and if that was the cause of his foul mood.

"No, she asked Mimi to bring her breakfast upstairs. I do not know what to do to help her." He looked over at me with sad pleading eyes. "Some days I think she is going to be all right and then others . . . I mean we are all mourning the loss of the baby, but there will be others."

"I think this goes much deeper than just losing the baby. She lost her parents and her brothers and her standing because of the baby and now she is probably feeling that losing the baby is payback for her behavior," I said, speculating.

"But that is absurd. Losing the baby is not payback. It is one of those things that happen sometimes. Our mother had a couple of miscarriages also, did she not?" he reasoned while stacking the pancakes on his plate.

"Yes, two I believe."

"There . . . you see, she is being ridiculous." He drowned his plate in maple syrup.

"Please tell me you have not said that to her?"

"No, of course not. I value my life." He smiled between bites. "She is always so sad and there is nothing I can say or do to make any difference."

"I believe time is the only thing that is going to help. Father said physically she is fine, she is just grieving."

"Good morning, my children. How are you both doing today?" Mother walked into the room followed directly by Father.

"Good morning," he greeted while pulling out a chair for his wife.

"Morning," William and I replied in unison.

Our father helped himself to some eggs while Sarah walked around the table pouring my parents a cup of coffee. "So, what is on everyone's agenda today?"

"Studying," William replied between bites.

"I believe Jackson has set up a couple more houses for us to look at this afternoon." I pushed my hardly touched breakfast away from me. "I am beginning to lose all hope in finding something suitable before our wedding."

"Oh, I am sure you both will find a charming little home before then." Mother played with her eggs. "I know you feel frustrated right now, but you mustn't get disheartened."

"I believe you have more faith than I do, Mother." I grinned slightly and took another sip of coffee.

After breakfast I returned to my room where Mimi helped me get ready for my day. She carefully curled my hair after she stuffed me into my corset and dress. The strings were tied so tightly I felt like I could not breathe. We chatted about the gaudy house and touched a little on Olivia's depression.

"Ya no child I's think we shall try something a bit more your status." Mimi began twisting up my hair around her delicate fingers.

"Mimi, what are you doing?"

"You gonna be married in a bit, you gonna have to wear it up from now on. You best get used to it." She nodded her head slightly at me in the mirror, tucking my long waves and curls up to the nape of my neck.

"Ah . . . Mimi, please not just yet. I do not wish to look older than I must."

"Now's, Miss . . ."

"Please, not today. Let me wear it down. Jackson loves my hair so," I pleaded with my eyes at her reflection.

"All right." She smiled and let go of my hair. It cascaded down over my shoulders like a warm blanket of autumn sunshine.

"Thank you," I held her eyes in the mirror.

When she was finished I sat down in my window seat and leaned my head against the cold glass with my eyes closed. I took a deep breath and let it out slowly trying to fully relax my body. I could see myself sitting next to Jenna in a hot stuffy large room.

There were scores of people about hollering and cheering, it was almost deafening. I was watching Ethan and Jackson playing a game that I also played in my life *there*. Yet for some bizarre reason I felt very ill feelings toward Ethan.

I opened my eyes and stared out the window. The Chandler home was barely visible through the morning fog that hovered grossly across the lawns. I turned back towards my bedroom and this harsh eerie feeling fell over me. I could almost see Ethan standing in my doorway, anger marring his attractive brow. I could feel the fury building up within me. We exchanged heated cruel words in a loud tone. Then the unthinkable occurred. We were atop my bed struggling over a pocketbook. We were scratching, punching, and tearing at each other. I had never felt so appalled at my behavior before.

How in the world can I act in such a manner?

Then I realized my father, Shane, was amongst all the excitement, tearing Ethan and I apart. I quickly closed my eyes not wanting to see anymore. The stinging sensation tore through my face once again. My hands instantly covered my face in shame and astonishment.

Have things in my home there truly escalated to violence? Do Ethan and I or my mother, Amy, and I feel such distain towards one another? Such contempt? Such malice?

I rose and paced the room searching for a reason why I allowed myself to be subjected to such torment daily. Surely, I was an adult *there* just I am *here* so what could possibly hold me in such a miserable state. I glanced back at my doorway and I knew the answer . . . Shane. I loved him dearly and he believed in me. His faith in my decision had given me great strength.

*   *   *

Jackson arrived early in the afternoon looking stunning in his blue suit, hat, and overcoat. It was snowing lightly, and little flakes clung loosely to his wool coat. I tied my winter bonnet loosely over my curls. He helped me on with my coat and handed me my muff.

"Are you ready?" He extended his arm for me to take as Eddie opened the front door.

"As ready as I will ever be." I held onto his arm tightly and walked out to the carriage.

He placed the quilt over my legs and settled back into the seat beside me. Eddie climbed up into his seat and took the reins. The carriage gently lunged forward down the lane. I rested my head upon his shoulder. listening to the sounds of the hoofs on the cobblestones beneath us. It was so peaceful and familiar.

"You have been awfully quiet. Is everything all right?" Jackson leaned over and kissed the top of my head.

"Are things really that miserable in my household *there*?" I looked imploringly into his emerald eyes.

"Why do you ask?"

"I believe last evening Ethan and I had a physical altercation. We were arguing and then screaming at one another and the next thing I realized it had become physical." I sat up straight to see his face better.

"I know there has been a great deal of tension in your household."

"Did you not hear me? We had a physical altercation." I could not believe how blasé he was being.

"I heard you."

"And . . . this does not surprise you?"

He shook his head slightly. "No, not really."

I was completely appalled. "What do you mean this does not surprise you?"

"I don't say that to upset you. What I mean is it's not out of the ordinary for the two of you to have the occasional skirmish. Granted, I believe they were more frequent when you both were much younger, but it does still occur occasionally," he tried to explain.

"I cannot believe this!"

"Darling, siblings often squabble with each other. Truly it is no different than how you argue with William."

"We have never had a physical altercation in our lives, not even when we were young." I could not believe he was trying to justify what had happened.

"I know. I understand how horrifying it may sound to you, but I can assure you that your behavior last evening is not out of the ordinary in that time period." Jackson began to look exasperated.

"I had no idea the situation had become so dire. I cannot believe I reside in a home so full of hostility." I leaned my head back against his shoulder.

"I realize that it has not been easy on you and the more the barrier depletes, the more difficult it will be." He ran his fingers lightly through my hair as the carriage came to a halt. "I guess we better get this over with."

"If we must." Eddie opened the door and offered me his hand.

*   *   *

Three hours and five homes later we pulled up to our porch. Jackson's mood had switched to an almost humorous tone. The homes we had toured ranged from one extreme of luxury to borderline rustic. All he could do at this point was laugh. I believe he didn't know what else to do. I, on the other hand, was beginning to believe that we were never going to find a home of our own. At least not until we could afford to build one in the next few years.

The noise was deafening when we opened the front door. My uncles and their families plus my siblings and theirs were all there scrambling throughout the downstairs. Everyone was there for a dinner to celebrate the news of James and Rachel's newest bundle.

The conversation circulated around the baby, our house hunting adventures, and the final preparations for the wedding. Everyone was talking, and no one was doing any listening. The excitement was boiling over as the days were drawing closer. Jackson discussed his positivity in finding a charming starter home while I expressed my uncertainty in doing so.

However, our parents seemed confident that we would find something within the general vicinity that we would be more than satisfied with. Still, since they had not seen the homes we had, I was more than less optimistic.

After dinner when everyone had settled down a bit and broke off into smaller conversations, my uncle Nicholas joined me off to the side of the crowd in the corner of the parlor. I was in a somber mood after such a long day and was trying to figure out how to gracefully sneak upstairs.

"Hiding?" He snuck up behind me.

I jumped a tad. "No, of course not."

"How are you holding up?"

"Honestly, I am not sure." I explained to him the bizarre feelings I experienced when I awoke that morning and how I recalled what had transpired between my brother and me.

"How do you feel about that?" He handed me a cup of coffee from the tray that Sarah was walking around with.

"Thank you. Honestly, it disturbs me a great deal. And to make matters worse, Jackson is acting like the entire experience was no big deal." I waved my hand for emphasis.

"To him I would imagine it wasn't. He has become accustomed to living on both planes for several years now and has seen a great many things on both. By now, I am sure there is little that would surprise him." I knew he was attempting to make me feel better and I loved him for it although it didn't work.

"Is this normal? I mean what is happening to me, what I am feeling?"

"Yes, perfectly normal. I know it can be unsettling at times, even unnerving, but I can promise you that it does get easier." Uncle Nicholas put a fatherly arm around me.

"Please don't take offense, but I am really tired of people saying that." I unintentionally rolled my eyes.

He chucked heartedly. "I am sure you are."

I took a deep breath and let it out slowly. "I'm sorry. I mean no disrespect. This whole concept is . . . confusing at best. And I just do not feel like myself any longer."

"But you are still you. Your world has expanded, is all. You have been blessed with such an amazing gift. Do you realize how fortunate you are? You get to witness the progress of mankind far beyond anything you could ever imagine in this lifetime." He was so passionate in his argument.

"I understand all that and yes, some of it is truly amazing, but I feel as if I do not know where I fit into the larger scheme of things." I tried to express myself the best way I could.

"You fit in the same place as you always have. Like the rest of us you have the best of both worlds. You will get to witness the industrial revolution, see the turn of two centuries, be a part of the technological revolution and experience firsthand the drastic differences between the two worlds. I cannot begin to tell you how truly lucky you are. There are so many people who would be so intrigued to have such a gift." Uncle Nicholas's enthusiasm was almost contagious, but not quite.

"But doesn't it get confusing, trying to keep it all straight?"

"In the beginning, in the stage you are in it can be extremely confusing, even terrifying at times. I remember being in your position and it sounded so condescending when family members would say things like this to me."

"Yes, I know," I chuckled a bit.

Emily walked over and joined us. She looked lovely this evening in her rich coffee brown dress with an ivory lace collar. "Is everything all right?"

"Yes, of course. Jocelyn and I were discussing the fun stages of *EVE*," he explained.

"I see," she sipped her coffee. "I do not believe any of us ever forget those."

"I think what bothers me the most about my other life *there* is the family dynamics. While it appears women have gained a great deal in independence, from what I have seen it appears it was achieved at a great sacrifice to the family. At least that is the way it appears with my own family," I explained.

"Yes, it is true, Amy is very career driven and not exactly a homemaker but not all women *there* are that way. There are still a great many women who manage to work full time and maintain an active and close relationship with their children. Plus, there are those who stay home with their children and are very happy doing so," Emily whispered softly.

"From what I have observed, Amy cannot cook, clean, or really has anything to do with the household or our family. She works all the time and she is more concerned about my education than my happiness," I confessed.

"I know there is a great deal of tension in your home since you and Jackson announced your engagement and that Ethan and Amy are being unkind to you, but I know they both love you very much. I am sure they will come around in time." Emily squeezed my arm gently in reassurance.

"Amy has always been very career oriented. Shane knew that when he married her, but she was a very beautiful and sweet woman when they met. But the long hours and hectic schedules have hardened her in many ways. However, I know she is only worried about you and your future. She has always been a wonderful mother and I am positive she loves you very much," Uncle Nicholas added.

"She sure has an unusual way of demonstrating it." I rolled my eyes with a smile. As much as I did not want to admit it, talking to them did make me feel much better.

Olivia and William had remained upstairs throughout the entire evening. I knew they were both aware of the celebration taking place beneath them. I thought of going upstairs and trying to talk with her, but something held me back. I had no words of comfort for her or for my brother.

CHAPTER 19

Saturday, December 12, 2009

I WOKE UP stiff and score. I stretched, and a small moan escaped from my lips. My tumbling match with Ethan the night before took more of a toll on me than I had initially thought. I climbed out of bed and looked at myself in the vanity mirror. There was a nice knot and bruise under my left eye and I had a bit of a fat lip probably caused by Ethan's elbow or head. It wasn't nearly as bad as the one I'd received from the coffee table but still, it didn't look good.

I quickly threw on a pair of jeans and a sweatshirt. My arms and legs had scattered bruises on them, giving me a very spotted appearance. I brushed out my hair and decided to leave it down, hoping it would help cover the bruises if not my entire face. I felt so ridiculous going to the clinic now. It looked like I was a battered girlfriend trying to get some birth control, so I wouldn't get knocked up by my crazy boyfriend. And no amount of make-up was going to help with the swelling.

*   *   *

Jenna sat in my passenger seat laughing her butt off as I retold what happened last evening between my brother and me.

"I wish I could have seen it."

"It's not funny." I looked over at her out of the corner of my eye.

"Yes, it is. You just don't see it."

"Can we talk about something else please?"

"Fine." I could still see her struggling to stifle her laughter. I turned up the radio and we dropped the subject and sang along, each of us purposely not saying what we were thinking.

*　　*　　*

"Well?" Jenna asked expectantly.

"I got them." I quickly walked out of the clinic with Jenna close behind me.

"That's good, isn't it?" she whispered over my shoulder trying to keep up with me.

"Yes," I pushed the elevator button. "Want to get some coffee?"

"Um . . . sure." She gave me a puzzled look as the door opened and we stepped in.

As the door closed I turned towards her. "I have never felt more uncomfortable in all my life! That was horrible!"

"What?"

"The exam . . . I thought you've had a pap before?"

"No," she shook her head.

"But you and Kyle . . ."

"Condoms."

"Yeah, well we have to use them also, at least for the first month after my next period," I explained.

"They're not so bad," she shrugged as the doors opened on the first floor.

We remained silent as we walked outside and around the corner to some little coffee shop. We ordered our drinks and slid into a booth in the back.

"I was hoping we'd never have to use them. After all, we are getting married."

"Are you saying you two *still* haven't done it yet?" She clearly was surprised.

"No, not yet."

"Why? He's not a virgin, is he?" she whispered leaning towards me.

"No. He's slept with a few girls in college," I slipped before I caught myself.

"College girls? Ouch! Guess you have a right to be so nervous having to compete with them." She made a face before taking a sip of her coffee.

"I hadn't thought about that." I said more to myself than to her. "Damn it . . . great! Now not only am I nervous and scared about my first time, I'm going to suck at it compared to them!" I looked over at her trying not to cry.

"You're not going to suck at it. But yes, the first-time sucks. I'm sorry, but it does." She shrugged.

"Great," I muttered.

"When are you two planning on . . . ?"

"Soon. Probably Christmas break."

"Well, don't worry about it." She tried to smile but didn't pull it off very well. "So, college girls . . . huh?" She sipped her coffee. "That's not all that surprising really."

"What's that supposed to mean?"

"Really, Jocelyn, look at him. He's gorgeous. It's not surprising that he's been out with college girls. You can't tell me that you haven't noticed the way everyone looks at him?" She looked at me over her coffee and raised her eyebrows.

"Yes, I have. It's funny because he doesn't seem to notice it at all."

"Yeah, I guess he and Zak definitely don't have that in common. Zak loves the attention and Jackson seems almost oblivious to it."

We did a little bit of shopping before we headed back to the suburbs. We drove most of the way in silence, just listening to the radio. I couldn't get her comments out of my head. As if losing my virginity wasn't bad enough, all I could think of was how bad my performance would be in comparison to his previous partners. I was positive I was going to be such a letdown to him in that department. I hated the thought of him secretly being unsatisfied with me but there was no way I could ever ask him.

*   *   *

Jenna went home to finish up her own homework, so we could all get together later. The house was silent by the time I returned. I wasn't sure where anyone was, so I hurried up the stairs and closed my bedroom door behind me. I put the three-month supply of sample birth control packs in my nightstand under some loose papers, knowing no one ever touched those drawers but me. It felt silly to sneak around but I really didn't want another confrontation with my mother over Jackson and *really* didn't want to have *that* conversation with my dad either.

My stomach had started grumbling and I realized that it was almost one o'clock and I hadn't eaten anything since breakfast. I grabbed my study material for biology and headed downstairs to find something to eat.

The refrigerator and pantry left little to be desired. I grabbed some bread and peanut butter and started making myself a sandwich when my phone began buzzing.

"Hey sweetie," I noticed Jackson's ID before I answered.

"Hello, where have you been? I noticed your car was missing this morning. Are we still studying?"

"Sure." I quickly began cleaning up my mess. "I'll be over in a few minutes."

"All right, see you soon. I love you."

"You too." I quickly hung up the phone before he could inquire any further and stuffed the sandwich in my mouth.

*   *   *

Jackson answered the door wearing nice fitted jeans and a maroon tee-shirt with a casual dress shirt hanging unbuttoned in various shades of striped grey. His almost black hair was perfectly tousled and curling more than usual as if he needed a trim sometime soon.

"Hello, baby." He smiled and stepped back to let me enter.

"You look nice, baby." I reached up and wrapped my arms around his neck giving him a kiss.

"My sister just sent me this from Boston for my birthday. You like it?"

"Very much so. Phoebe has fabulous taste," I remarked as we made our way to the family room. "Where's your parents?"

"Shopping. They will be back shortly. Have a seat, make yourself at home." He gestured towards the couch. "Would you like something to drink?"

"Sure," I replied, taking a seat and putting my books down on the coffee table.

"Green tea?"

"Perfect, thanks."

He headed off into the kitchen with a giddy lightness to his steps that immediately made me wonder what in the world he was up to. I tried to focus my attention on the first *Lord of the Rings* movie he had playing on the television and made myself comfortable on their oversized stuffed couch.

"Here you are." Jackson returned, placing both drinks down on the table beside my books.

"Thank you."

"Nice shiner." He lightly touched my face.

"Beautiful, isn't it?" I smirked.

He flashed his lopsided grin at me and sat down wrapping his arm around me pulling me closer to him. "So, are you going to confess to your whereabouts this morning?"

"I thought we already decided that you weren't going to ask questions with Christmas right around the corner." I continued to stare at the TV, hoping he wouldn't notice the blush that rushed to my cheeks.

"I would not have asked if you had come home with Jenna and a bunch of packages, but you did not," he said.

"Were you spying on me?" I tried to turn the tables.

"No, my parents were leaving about the same time, so I was at the door talking to my dad when you pulled up," he smirked.

"Some things do fit inside a purse you know?"

"Nice try. Why won't you tell me where you were? Am I going to be upset?" He straightened up to look directly at me.

"No," I stuttered. "It's just embarrassing." I looked back at the movie, wishing he'd just drop the subject although I knew he wouldn't.

"Embarrassing? Why?"

"Because it is, Jackson. Will you please just let it go? There are some things . . ." I didn't know how to finish the sentence.

"What? You've lost me . . ."

In exasperation I turned and faced him. "Fine, you want to know where I was. I asked Jenna to go with me to a clinic in the city where the physicians don't know my mom so that I could get a physical to get on the pill. Happy now?"

"And why is that embarrassing?" He honestly looked confused.

"Because it is . . . that's why"

"We are getting married in a couple weeks. Don't you think this should have been a conversation we already had?" He raised his eyebrows a bit.

"I was going to get on the pill earlier right after Halloween but then we broke up so . . ."

He gave me a tight squeeze. "Not a big deal. We will just use condoms for a while just to be on the safe side."

"And you don't mind?" I had always heard how much guys hated them.

"I have honestly never had sex without one," he shrugged. "I mean, I never thought we would have to use them, but it is all right. As long as I get to be with you, that's all I care about." He leaned down and gave me a reassuring kiss.

"I'm sorry."

"Don't be. So, what did the doctor say?" he inquired.

"About what?"

"Your physical."

"Oh that . . . I'm fine."

"Good, and on a lighter note. I have some great news to share with you."

"Really?" I snuggled back against his chest.

"What are your plans for Christmas break?" A coy smile rested on his shapely lips.

"I thought I was marrying you."

"*Here*, dork!"

"I don't know. Lying around the house in my pajamas all day watching movies and eating junk food," I shrugged.

"How would you like to go to Boston with us?" he asked.

"You mean you're not going to be here for Christmas?" I sat straight up in alarm.

How can he do this? Especially with us getting married on Christmas Eve. I thought it was going to be time for us . . .

"No, my parents are planning on going home for Christmas, so they can spend time with Alex and Phoebe and their families. I figured you knew that."

"No! I thought . . . I mean, I assumed . . ." I stood up and walked over to the hearth. I stared down at the dancing flames feeling foolish for the tears that welled up in my eyes.

Jackson followed. "Hey, none of that." He turned me towards him and wrapped his arms around me. "I was always planning on taking you with us."

"My parents would never let me leave over Christmas," I tried to explain.

"My dad already spoke with your dad this morning and you are coming to Boston with us." He pulled me close to him and kissed the top of my head. "Do you really think I would leave you on our wedding day and honeymoon?"

I rested my head against his chest feeling a rush of relief. Being away from him was like trying to survive without air. I couldn't do it. "I'm sorry."

"Plus, as a wedding gift from my siblings, you and I are going to New York for a few days."

"Seriously?"

"Yes, we will leave the day after school gets out, drive to Boston with my parents, visit everyone for a few days and then you and I will leave the day after Christmas for New York and stay there until January third. Then we will drive back to Boston, spend the night and the four of us will drive home on the fifth."

"And my parents are okay with this?" I looked up into his gorgeous emerald green eyes.

"Well, your dad is, at least about the Boston part. I figured we would not mention New York until after we return and then allude that all of us went." A mischievous grin slid across his lips.

"You little devil." I reached up and pressed my lips upon his.

Fire ignited with a vengeance. I twisted my fingers up in the back of his hair and wrapped my other hand around his waist pulling him towards me. With one hand he cupped the side of my face and the other pressed firmly against my back. Our appetite rose to a heightened level as he guided us back over to the couch. We gently fell backwards upon it with him lying over me. Our hands hungrily explored each other's bodies.

Jackson carefully slipped his hand beneath my sweatshirt, then my tank top. Our mouths devoured each other as I felt his hand slide over my breast and gently caress it. I let out a small moan and tightened my grip on him, letting my other hand roam freely beneath his tee shirt over his sculpted chest and abdomen. I couldn't believe how ripped he was. I couldn't get enough of him. I started tugging on his shirt and got it off him. Jackson leaned up, slowly straddling me as I breathlessly ran my hands over his upper torso under his tee shirt before sliding it up over his head.

His body was amazing. He looked like something out of a movie or magazine. I had to remind myself that he was twenty-two and not a teenager like the other boys in our school. He was a man.

Jackson looked down at me with a sleepy dreamlike expression on his face that heightened every nerve in my body. I traced my hands slowly over his bare chest as our eyes embraced each other. Neither of us said a word nor did we try and deny what we both were feeling or wanted.

He lightly ran his fingers over the middle part of my abdomen that was exposed. Then he slowly placed his hands on my sides under both my shirts and pulled them both off over my head. I rested back on the couch pillow with my hair billowing out around me. He smiled softly down at me making me ever so thankful that I had put on my matching light pink lace bra and panties when I got out of the shower this morning.

"You are so beautiful," he whispered barely loud enough for me to hear him.

Jackson leaned back down over me, one leg standing on the floor and one knee on the couch between my legs. His arms wrapped tightly around me as mine did him. Our lips met in an unquenchable desire for more. My hands were grasping at his body pulling him closer and harder against my own. I could feel his fingers wrapping through my hair, his lips moved down to my breast, my stomach.

Suddenly Jackson leapt to his feet. "Damn it!" He grabbed my shirts and tossed them back at me and quickly picked up his own.

I sat up with a jerk, feeling like someone had just thrown a bucket of cold water over me. I hesitated just a moment then heard what he must have heard: the garage door opening. We barely had our clothes back on and got seated on the couch when we heard the familiar voices of his parents coming through the kitchen garage door.

"Jackson?" Emily's voice rang from the kitchen.

"In here with Jocelyn," he hollered back, picking up our biology books and handing me mine.

"Well, good afternoon, Jocelyn." Emily entered the family room. "Nice to see you today."

"You too. How are you?" I fought through the frog in my throat.

"Just finished the grocery shopping." She made a disgusted face. "Are you two hungry?"

"Starving," Jackson answered, and I nodded.

"All right then, I will start dinner as soon as we get these groceries put away." She smiled sweetly and turned to leave.

"Can I help you with anything?" I offered.

"You should probably start studying for that biology exam . . . after Jackson puts his tee shirt on right side out." I could hear Robert snickering from the kitchen doorway. She headed back towards the kitchen but hollered over her shoulder, "Sorry we interrupted."

Jackson rolled his eyes in the direction of his mother before yanking his shirt back off and righting his tee, but I was flushed red from head to toe.

*   *   *

After dinner and the dishes were done, Jackson and I went back to books. We were knee deep in discussing genotypes when my cell started buzzing telling me that Caitlyn was calling.

"Hey what's up?" she sounded a little too cheery.

"I'm over at Jackson's studying for our biology test on Monday. Why?" I looked over at Jackson who was drawing little doodles on his study guide.

"I just talked to Jenna and Kyle and we were all thinking of doing something. You guys in?"

"Sure, what did you have in mind?"

"Don't laugh, but do you remember that old theatre over in Plainfield? Anyway, they're playing *Grease* tonight and I've never seen it on the big screen. I thought it would be fun."

"You're serious?" Jackson glanced up at me and shrugged his shoulders, telling me he could hear our entire conversation and didn't care either way.

"All right, we're in. What time?"

"My house at eight, movie starts at nine."

"We'll be there." I hung up the phone and tossed it back on the coffee table. "Did you hear all that?" I placed my hand over his to make him stop playing with his pencil.

"Yes, she talks loud enough." He finally put the pencil down and sat back on the couch. "I guess we are going to see *Grease* this evening."

"Yeah, it'll be fun." I gave him a quick kiss on the cheek. "But before we go I need to run home and grab Caitlyn's sweatshirt I borrowed and tell my dad where we're going."

"Mind if I come with you?" He stacked up his study material on the corner of the table then picked mine up. "I will even carry your books for you, Ms. Jocelyn." He slightly bowed.

"Why thank you very much, Mr. Jackson." I curtsied with a mock grin.

*   *   *

I left Jackson in the family room talking with my dad while I ran upstairs to swap my things. I quickly touched up my make-up and ran a brush through my hair. I noticed the bruise on my cheek was still there, but my fat lip was now hardly noticeable. I grabbed a heavier jacket then ran back downstairs.

I heard the two guys still chatting in the family room, so I ducked into the kitchen to grab a Coke to take with me. But when I shut the refrigerator door, I was surprised to see Ethan and Liang walking into the kitchen holding hands.

"Hi Jocelyn, I'm Liang," she said in an all too perky voice.

"Hi," I tried to smile at her and picked up my purse and coat off the island.

"Are you and Jackson going to see *Grease* tonight, too?" she asked, sitting down on one of the bar stools.

I spun around and glared at Ethan who had an evil little smirk on his face. "Cody invited us along," he happily informed me.

"Why don't we all ride together?" Liang piped in. "I mean we're all going to the same place. It seems silly to waste the gas."

"I don't think so," I muttered and glared back at my brother before I leaned over towards her. "And you can do much better than him."

I stepped into the empty dining room and called Caitlyn back. "Hey, what the hell is going on? Cody invited my brother!"

"Yeah, they just arrived, and Hilary told me. She already yelled at Cody about it. He said they were playing X-box when she asked him, and it put him on the spot," she explained.

"Great. He and Liang are here, and she thinks we should all ride together," I mocked Liang's chipper voice.

Despite my sarcasm, Caitlyn giggled. "I'm sorry. What do you want me to do?"

"Nothing." I paused for a moment fuming. "I'll talk to ya later."

I stood in the dark dining room trying to figure out what to do next. The last thing I wanted to do was spend the evening with Ethan. I couldn't have cared less about Liang and her irritatingly perky attitude, but after everything that had occurred between us lately I wasn't going to let him win. If he wanted to hang out with my friends, then I wasn't going to stop him. But I wasn't going to join them either.

I returned to the family room where the new couple had joined Jackson and our dad. They were all talking lively but it was apparent that Ethan was still being curt with my future husband.

"There you are, we were just wondering where you'd gone off to," Dad greeted me. "You guys have fun tonight and enjoy the movie." He stood up expecting to walk the four of us to the front door.

"Sorry, change of plans. We're not going to the movie," I announced, and Jackson gave me a confused look.

"Why not?" Dad asked then glanced back over his shoulder at Ethan.

"I'd prefer not to spend my evening with backstabbers and leeches who like to glob onto other people's friends because they can't make any friends of their own." I knew I was being childish, but I didn't care.

I could see Ethan's ears turning red from across the room. "Cody invited us. He is *my* friend." Poor Liang and Jackson looked like they wished they were anywhere else.

"Funny how you immediately knew I was talking about you. Must be the guilt," I pointed out like a ten-year-old.

"Little Miss Princess, always has to get her way." Ethan rose to his feet.

"That's it . . . enough!" Dad waved his arms between the two of us. "I've had it with you two. You guys didn't act this immature when you were kids! I'm done with this. You two can work it out yourselves." He stormed out of the room and slammed his office door a few seconds later.

The four of us just stood there starring at the empty doorway he'd exited through. All of us were too stunned for several minutes to say anything.

"See what you did?" Ethan finally spoke and gestured towards the doorway.

"Me?" I swung around and confronted him. "How dare you, you little brat! You started all this. You constantly intrude on my life and my friends just to irritate me. If you're not happy with the decisions I've made, fine. I don't care. Just butt out of my life!"

"I don't care if you insist on throwing your life away, but I do think you're an idiot. You're going to get knocked up, quit college, and then get divorced. So, don't get mad at me when you're a washed-up drop-out with a house full of snot nosed brats living on welfare before your twenty-five cause I'm gonna laugh when he leaves your boney ass!" Liang's jaw dropped open along with mine in complete disbelief.

Jackson took several steps towards Ethan and from where I was standing I could see he was struggling to control his temper. Ethan must have seen it too because he took a step back. "You went too far Ethan. Don't ever let me hear you speak to her or any other woman that way ever again. You have no idea how hard this has been on your sister.

What she has been going through living with the never ending mistreatment from you and your mother. It has been killing her and it is killing me watching her suffer through it. And your father's right, enough is enough. I love your sister more than you will ever understand and I will no longer stand by and watch you do everything you can think of to make her life miserable."

"And what are you going to do about it?" Ethan tried to stand his ground. "You gonna take a shot at me?"

"As much as I would love to, no. Only because I respect your sister and your father. But I am going to make your life a living hell if you keep it up. I promise you that." He took another step towards my brother.

Ethan unintentionally took another step backwards and bumped into the couch. "Get out of my house," he said flatly through gritted teeth.

"I will leave when I am ready unless your father requests it beforehand." Jackson turned his back on him and walked back over to me. "So, what do you want to do instead?"

"Let's watch a movie at your house," I suggested, no longer paying any attention to Ethan and Liang.

"All right," he smiled and placed a protective arm around my shoulder.

Jackson and I left without another word to the room's occupants, but I sent my dad and Caitlyn a text telling them where we were going to be.

"I wish you would have hit him," I said once we were out on the porch.

"You're forgetting, I am not allowed to. Your brother is still a minor, I'm not. If your parents wanted to retaliate, I could get arrested and my real age would be revealed. That would not be good for either of us," he said as we walked across the street.

"So, what am I supposed to tell my parents eventually? Are we supposed to hide your real age from them forever?"

"I suppose we have to. It is not like we can explain the entire truth to them." He squeezed my hand gently. "Look how well that worked out for your uncle Nicholas."

"True. So, how did you manage to enroll in high school?" I was curious.

"Being a lawyer, my dad knows how to find the loop-holes in the system. So, he managed to get me a fake birth certificate and social security card. My brother's old college roommate is now an administrator at the high school I graduated from in Boston, so he did my brother a favor and changed the dates on my old transcripts and forwarded them here," Jackson explained.

"Unbelievable." I held his hand as we crossed the street.

"As silly as it sounds, it really wasn't that difficult. But if someone really did some digging, it wouldn't be that hard to find the truth."

"Well then, I guess you'd better behave yourself." I looked up at him and winked.

Jackson and I spent a romantic evening in front of a roaring fire watching old black and white movies. I received several angry texts from Caitlyn, an apology from Hilary, and one from Jenna saying that I was being childish. I didn't care. I was exactly where I wanted to be.

CHAPTER 20

Wednesday, December 14, 1878

I EXCUSED MYSELF from my friends who were talking excessively about what they were getting their boyfriends and family for Christmas and how they were going to spend their time off from classes and such. I walked out the door and down the front steps. The cold air brushed against my cheeks, lifting my hair off my shoulders and sending chills through my body. I pulled my caplet closer around me and walked the short distance to the fence at the entrance of the school. I leaned back against an old oak tree and closed my eyes. I was feeling so overwhelmed that I wasn't sure if I wanted to scream or cry. I honestly felt like doing a little of both.

I had spent the last several days burying myself in my school work and studying for my graduation exam on Friday. It was weighing heavily on my shoulders. I knew I should have started studying for it weeks before, but life always seemed to get in the way. Now that it was upon me, I was in panic mode.

I opened my eyes and glanced around the schoolyard. It was impossible to imagine only having one more school day with my friends. Simply one more day to be a child, an adolescent, carefree and unencumbered by adult responsibilities. I had spent such a large portion of my youth in this building and the surrounding grounds playing games with my friends, talking with my girlfriends, and impatiently waiting to grow up. Now that it was here I was torn between wanting to desperately cling to my adolescence alongside my friends and rushing into my future in Jackson's arms.

I exhaled deeply and watched my breath glide away in the thick air. The trees were bare and looked lonely and lifeless. I wished I could sit down on the steps, but I knew it would be inappropriate for me to do so. I closed my eyes again thinking about how if I was *there* I wouldn't think twice about sitting down on the steps. My two worlds could not be more different. I loved the independence I had *there*, the freedom to express myself, the ability to make my voice heard and to find whatever direction I felt was best for me. Yet still, there was a part of me that hated the insecurity of family *there*, the lack of trust and faith and the callousness that felt overly consuming of most people. I wanted to believe that I was fortunate and that there was a reason for me to have this gift if only for me to ensure that I raised my children with the same love and security as Robert and Emily had.

Of course, if I was *there* I would be wearing something slightly more practical. Something that was a tad bit warmer than the gown, corset, pantalets, and such that I was currently freezing in. At least there was something positive about the future.

Laurie came down the steps and put her hand on my shoulder. "Are you all right?"

"Yes, I just needed some fresh air." I smiled up at her. "This test is a bit intimidating."

"I would imagine so." She wrapped her arms around herself. "I cannot believe how cold it has turned. We will surely have snow by Christmas."

"Most likely," I agreed.

"Would you like to come over to the store and warm up a bit?" she offered.

"That would be wonderful."

We headed off down the path away from the schoolyard. Their family store was only a couple blocks from our school. The gray skies had opened up just enough to let a few light snowflakes drift down. It suddenly made the moment seem more magical than ordinary.

"I am sorry we have not gotten to spend much time together lately. Jackson and I have spent almost all our time house hunting which is the reason I am so far behind studying for this exam." I tried to make small talk.

"I know. Please do not worry about it. I know you have had a lot going on."

"How is everything with you and Mr. Theodore? Have you started the preparations for your wedding next summer?" I glanced over at her.

"We are doing very well," she grinned widely. "Our mothers have started making the arrangements. My mother has already started working on my gown. It is so beautiful. I cannot wait for you to see it." Her voice could hardly contain her excitement as she opened the door to store and the bell overhead chimed loudly.

"Good afternoon," her father, Henry Cain, walked out of the back room. "Oh, Laurie, what are you doing home so early? Are you feeling all right?"

"I am fine Father. Ms. Jocelyn needed some fresh air, so we thought we would walk over here for a moment. She is studying relentlessly for her graduation exam this Friday."

"I see. Hello, Ms. Timmons." He walked around the counter and shook my hand. "It is so nice to see you. How is your family?"

"Very well, thank you."

Laurie and I browsed through the rolls of new fabrics her father just got in. There were some that were stunning. I could only imagine making beautiful spring gowns out of them. I stood there lost in my thoughts, musing over which patterns would look best for the various styles when a loud piercing scream broke my train of thought.

"Henry, come quick! There is a snake in the house!" A female voice screeched from their living quarters.

"What?" Her father took off running towards the back of the store with Laurie and me directly behind him.

We found her mother, Molly, standing in the far corner of the family room with their housekeeper, Grace. Both their faces were white with fear. "Quinton, get away from there! I will not tell you again." Mrs. Cain shouted at her youngest son who was perhaps maybe four or five years old.

Quinton was crouched down on the floor in front of the burner stove. "Ah . . . but Momma," he complained but failed to relocate.

"What is all the screaming about? You nearly gave me a heart attack." Mr. Cain scanned the room, seeming to notice nothing out of the ordinary.

"There is a snake in the house, Henry. Over there!" An exasperated Mrs. Cain pointed to where her son was looking. "It has wrapped itself around the base of the stove." The burner stove sat in the corner of the room on a bricked enclave that reached up to the ceiling and was adorned with a beautiful mantle.

"For lands sake." Mr. Cain knelt near his son and stood back up quickly while moving his son out of harm's way. "I reckon' it came in because of the cold weather."

"I don't care why it's in our home. I just want it out," Mrs. Cain said nervously.

"Is it poisonous?" Laurie asked in a weak voice from beside me in the doorway.

"I'm not sure. I cannot tell what kind it is." Mr. Cain rubbed his chin thoughtfully for a moment. "Ladies," he turned back towards the two of us, "would you please run over to Mr. Donaldson's shop and ask him to come here straight away?"

"Yes, Father."

I followed Laurie back through the store and across the street to Dimitri's father's business. He was a carpenter by trade and made the most beautiful furniture in Northern Chicago. The snow had picked up a little and was now sticking to the ground.

We found George Donaldson easy enough and Laurie quickly explained the situation. He immediately grabbed his rifle and rushed off towards the store with us trailing behind. Returning to school did not occur to either of us.

When we rejoined the others back in the family room at Laurie's as the two men were discussing the best way to coax the snake back out. Mr. Donaldson kneeled a good distance from the stove. "I cannot rightly say what kind of snake that is. I cannot get a clear view of its markings, but I believe we should err on the side of caution and assume it is poisonous."

"How do you think we should proceed?" Mr. Cain watched his friend carefully.

"Well, perhaps I can hit the side of it to make it move."

"You want to fire that rifle in my house?" Mrs. Cain spoke up with surprise.

Mr. Cain took several steps back. "I would not recommend that. The bullet will ricochet off the bricks and hit one of us."

"Than what do you suggest, Henry?" Mr. Donaldson stood back up.

"Do you think we can reach it with the fireplace poker? We could jab at it. See if that won't get it to move," Mr. Cain replied.

"I do not believe the poker would be long enough. We would still be within striking range of it." Mr. Donaldson rubbed his hands together absentmindedly. "No, we need something else." The room fell silent as the women looked from one gentleman to the other.

"All right, George, take the shot," Mr. Cain said, caving in. "But first, all you ladies and Quinton go back into the store."

"But . . ." Mrs. Cain began but was quickly hushed by her husband.

"Please, dear."

The five of us stood close together just inside the passageway that separated the store from the house. We could hear the low voices of the two men, but it was impossible to make out what they were saying.

Then in the still quiet the blast of the rifle sent a deafening shutter through each of us. It was shortly followed by a barrage of profanity that I had never heard before and the scuffling of boots.

"Grace, take Quinton over to Ms. Patty's immediately," Mrs. Cain ordered, pushing them gently towards the entrance of the store. I glanced over at Laurie knowing we were thinking the same thing . . . any second her mother was going to order us back to school. But she didn't. Instead she simply turned to us and grabbed a hold of each of our hands. "Careful, ladies," she advised as the three of us inched our way towards the doorway and peeked inside the family room.

The once elegant room had transformed into a battleground. Mr. Cain and Mr. Donaldson were hop-skipping around the room like their shoes were on fire. Mr. Cain was swinging the fireplace poker while Mr. Donaldson swung the butt of the rifle down repeatedly trying to hit the wounded snake that was flipping wildly about the room leaving splatters of blood in its wake. For a creature with no legs it sure had the agility to move rapidly. If the situation had not been so serious, the scene would have been almost comical.

"Hold on." Laurie let go of our hands and turned back into the storeroom. She returned within seconds carrying a gardening shovel. "Father here take this."

Mr. Cain scuffled over and traded his daughter the poker for the shovel. He then scurried over and opened the only door in the room that led to the outside. "This way George, we've got to get it outside."

"I'm trying," Mr. Donaldson shouted back with a wild swing as the snake slithered between the loveseat and the ottoman.

Mr. Cain came down hard on the tail quarter of the snake, cutting it almost through and sending a spray of blood across the rug onto the furniture.

"Oh, for crying out loud, Henry!" Mrs. Cain shouted in my ear at her husband.

He shot an angry look at his wife over his shoulder and continued his dance with Mr. Donaldson trying to maneuver the snake towards the door. It lasted another ten minutes of shouting, screaming, and several phrases of profanity. However, the two men managed to coax the snake out the doorway where Mr. Cain flipped it off the porch and onto the lawn. He jumped down the steps and in one fatal blow sent the blade of the garden shovel straight through the snake several inches behind its head.

Everyone breathed a sigh of relief that it was finally over. The beautifully decorated family room was left in shambles and covered sporadically with blood. Mrs. Cain surveyed the damage and wiped the tears off her cheeks. "Don't worry, Momma, we will have this cleaned up in no time. No one will ever be able to tell the snake was ever here." Laurie placed her hand gently on her mother's arm.

"Of course, we will," I chirped in, having rediscovered my voice.

The two men went to work straightening up things outside and disposing of the remains while Laurie and I disappeared into the storeroom to get the cleaning supplies. "Well, I can say that an afternoon with you and your family is anything but dull," I remarked, taking a bucket and brush off the shelf.

Laurie giggled. "We always like to keep life interesting."

*   *   *

We never made it back to school that afternoon. Instead we spent it scrubbing every inch of the family room until there was no evidence that anything had happened. As it turned out, a trivial afternoon of strange occurrences was exactly what I needed to take my mind off all the other trials in my life.

I walked home in the late afternoon past all the shops that cluttered the business end of our little corner of the world. I slowed down as I reached the park and gazed over at the now silent white gazebo covered in a light layer of snow dust.

A cold chill ran through me as I recalled how it had transformed over the years. I saw myself lying on the grass in the rain begging Jackson to leave for Boston. My heart ached as I could still see the sorrowful look in his emerald green eyes and how the rain clung to his black curls.

CHAPTER 21

Wednesday, December 16, 2009

BURIED UNDER the pressure of final exams, I hardly had time to notice that every evening when I returned home from practice, Liang was at my house studying for her finals with Ethan. He and I continued to ignore one another, much the same as my mother and I were. The tension in our household was building like a powder keg that could blow at any moment.

The school was buzzing with complaints about finals, but even more so about our upcoming Christmas dance on Friday night after the basketball game. Our last game before break was this evening and I was trying to figure out how I was going to study for my two finals tomorrow after being exhausted from the game. This was one of the few times that I regretted not adding a study hall to my schedule this semester.

The cafeteria was louder than usual with people discussing the dance, complaining about finals and what they were going to do over break. I sat down at our usual table and looked down at the disgusting meatloaf the school tried to pass off as food. I ate my peaches instead and listened to Jenna talk about her dress for the dance.

"I can't wait for you to see it," she bragged. "My mom and I picked it up Sunday at the mall. It's teal with a black lace overlay, strapless, and a black bow at my waist in the back. It's so gorgeous."

"What are you wearing?" Caitlyn looked over at me.

"I'm not sure. I was thinking of raiding Sidney's closet. I know she left many of her clothes behind when she went to school," I shrugged.

"Oh, Zachary, what are you wearing?" Cody did his best female imitation voice.

"My, my . . . there are so many choices I just don't know. Blue, I think, is blue my color?" Zak replied in a high-pitched voice with a cocky grin.

"Oh definitely, but really I think Jackson should wear green. It really brings out the color in your eyes," Cody mocked in Jackson's direction.

"Thanks, Cody. I am flattered and a little nervous that you noticed." Jackson pretended to be uncomfortable and scooted his chair a tad bit away from Cody towards me, making everyone laugh.

*   *   *

The four of us climbed up on the bus shortly after the final bell. Our last game before break was over in Graysville, about twenty plus miles away. I settled in a seat towards the back of the bus with Jenna beside me and Hilary and Caitlyn in the seat in front of us. I reached into my backpack and pulled out my phone and headphones ready to listen to some tunes and relax before the game.

"So, what is going on with you and Liang?" Hilary leaned over the seat as the bus pulled out of the school parking lot.

"Yeah, what gives? It was pretty crappy of you to stand us all up on Saturday night just because Cody had no choice but to invite Ethan and Liang," Caitlyn added.

"I have nothing against Liang. Although I do believe she has really bad taste in men." I tried to laugh it off, but they weren't going to let the subject drop.

"I know it's a bummer that your little brother is only a year behind you in school and that some of your friends overlap because of sports, but this is our senior year. Get over whatever it is that you two are fighting about because it is ruining things for everybody," Jenna added.

My eyes moved from one of them to the other. I could not believe they were turning this around on me. "You three are unbelievable, you know that? My house has turned into a war zone.

My mother hasn't spoken to me in over a month and Ethan dumps all over me every chance he gets. Now you three are giving me grief. Seriously?" I turned away from them and stared out the window.

"Come on, Jocelyn, don't be that way," Hilary began, but Caitlyn cut her off.

"Hey, we're not trying to start an argument or anything and you know how much we all like Jackson. He's a great guy and he treats you well, but you have to understand, the whole idea of the two of you getting married at this age is a little difficult for all of us. You know we love you and for that reason we are all being supportive whether we agree or not."

"And I appreciate that, I really do. But none of you know what it's like to have your own mother tell you she's not going to help you plan your wedding let alone attend it." I continued to look out the window.

"Are you sure you don't want to wait a little longer, like a year or so?" Hilary asked in a low voice.

"I don't understand the rush," Jenna piped in. "I just feel like there is something more that you're not telling us."

I continued looking out at the rain outside my window, so they couldn't see the lie in my eyes. I hated lying to them, but it wasn't like they would ever understand the truth. "I am not hiding anything." I turned back to the three of them. "I love Jackson. I cannot tell you how much he means to me. He makes me happy. We connect on a level that I cannot explain, nor should I have to." I quickly put in my earphones before any of them could say another word as I fought back the strong desire to smack their heads together.

There was an awkward silence in the locker room as we got ready the game. The three of them kept exchanging glances of unspoken whatever that I was not privy to and I couldn't have cared less. My only concern was getting home and studying for my finals. I should have been trying to focus my attention on the upcoming game, but I was in too bad of a mood to care about that either.

It had completely slipped my mind how therapeutic playing basketball was for me. No matter how upset I was everything turned around as soon as the buzzer sounded, and Jenna inbounded the ball to me. I melted into a world where problems didn't exist, and everything made sense. It no longer mattered what my friends thought or anyone else, I was happy.

*   *   *

After our first loss of the season my teammates boarded the bus like a bunch of school girls who just got dumped by their first boyfriend. It was a close game and we had fought hard. I hated losing and our loss did nothing to improve my earlier mood. I put in my earphones before I left the locker room just, so I could avoid another ambush from the three stooges. I sat down in the seat and leaned my head against the window before Jenna sat down next to me. She left me alone as did Hilary and Caitlyn in front of us. The three of them continued complaining about how unfair the referee was and the other team's tiny gym and how it all contributed to our loss. I turned up my music a little more and closed my eyes, enjoying the cold window against the side of my face. It had been a long day and I was anxious to go home.

Chapter 22

Friday, December 16, 1878

MIMI CAME IN before seven and jostled me awake. "Good mornin' Ms. Jocelyn. Rise n' shine," she placed my breakfast tray on my nightstand. "I brought ya some breakfast. I's afraid you might be a bit uneasy 'bout your test."

"Good morning, Mimi. I really don't think I can eat anything this morning." My stomach was in knots.

"I knew you say that. That's why I only brought you some toast an' poached eggs with some hot tea."

"Thank you so much, Mimi. You are a life saver." I climbed out of bed and put on my robe.

I sat down on the corner of the bed and munched on the toast while Mimi picked out my gown for the day. I watched her lay everything out on my bed and I slowly sipped my tea. My stomach still would not settle down. I got up and splashed some cold water on my face and brushed my teeth. I finally started to wake up a bit. What I really needed was a lot of coffee.

"Mimi, could you please get me some coffee?"

"Do you thinks that's a good idea?" She raised her eyebrows a bit.

"I believe it is necessary." I sat down on my vanity stool and rested my head down on the table.

"All right, I be right back." I closed my eyes and seriously considered crawling back into bed and forgetting the whole thing. I felt so utterly unprepared for this exam.

*   *   *

Almost five hours later I left the school alone. All my friends still had a couple hours left before their last class was over and their holiday break began.

I considered waiting around for them, but it was too cold outside. I walked down the front steps, absorbing the cold air around me. I closed the front gate behind me and took one last look at the school. It was impossible for me to believe that I never had to step into that building again. It had been my life for almost as long as I could remember. My childhood days were officially behind me.

I walked down the cobblestone walkway slowly, thinking of all the times that Christina, Laurie, Olivia, Elizabeth, and even Maryanne and I played games, worked on schoolwork, and giggled over boys. It was silly to think of such times, but I could not help myself. Those days were over now and never to return again. I never would have guessed until now that I would want them back.

I waited so long for them to be over with. I guess it's true that you never realize what you have until it disappears before you.

William, Olivia, and Jackson were waiting for me in the front room when I arrived home. I walked in quietly without Eddie even noticing my arrival. I placed my bag on the foyer table and draped my coat over the stair rail. The three of them were laughing about something William had said and I hated to interrupt them. Instead I followed the delicious aroma drifting from the kitchen.

Sarah was taking a fresh loaf of bread out of the oven. Nothing in the world could compare with the intoxicating aroma of fresh baked bread. I inhaled deeply and smiled when I felt Sarah turn her gaze in my direction. "How was your test?"

"It was fine. I will not get the results back until next week. Mr. Campbell said he would send me a letter with the results." I tore a small corner off the bread, which was followed quickly by a slap from Sarah across the top of my hand. "But it smells so good . . . please?"

"It's fo' dinner. Now scram." She gently scooted me towards the kitchen door.

"Fine, fine . . . I'm going." I smiled at her over my shoulder as she stood there shaking her head at me with the same smirk she'd been giving me for years when she playfully chastised me.

I paused in the foyer outside the front room and glanced in at my family again. They all looked so happy. It was almost as it used to be . . . back before our lives had been turned upside down earlier this fall. William turned his head slightly and noticed me standing in the doorway.

"Are you going to linger out there or are you going to be a little sociable and come in?" William's voice sounded more like his old playful self.

"I prefer to remain unsociable, thank you very much." I grinned and joined the others.

"Hello, darling, how was your exam?" Jackson stood up and kissed me on the cheek.

"Over . . . finally." I took a seat beside him on the lounge.

"So, was it horrible?" Olivia asked.

"Yes. I am not sure if I passed or not. There was so much material that I was not sure of," I complained.

"Says the smartest one in our class," Olivia mocked.

"I am sure you did very well." Jackson put a reassuring arm around me.

"Are you staying for dinner?" I wanted to shift the subject off school.

"Actually, little sister, we were thinking of going out to dinner this evening to celebrate your graduation." William fidgeted with his hands.

Olivia quickly placed hers over his to make him stop.

"I do not even know if I passed yet so there is nothing to celebrate."

"You passed," the three countered in unison.

"Plus, I already sent Eddie over to Mr. Miller's office inviting him and Ms. Elizabeth to join us. They will be here at five o'clock," Jackson added.

*   *   *

The six of us sat down at a restaurant in mid-town Chicago. It felt like my first real glimpse of what my now present life as an adult entailed. As much as I hated letting go of everything I loved about my youth I finally realized moving forward was not something I needed to fear. Rather I anxiously embraced it with both arms.

After the waiter took our order we sipped our red wine and enjoyed the ambiance of the elegant restaurant. It was the same place where Jackson and I had shared dinner with my parents on my birthday.

"I love this place," I remarked.

"I remembered how nice it was the last time we were here and thought it would be nice to eat here again," Jackson said.

Lee tapped the side of his wine glass, silencing our table. "I would like to make a toast to Ms. Jocelyn for successfully completing her studies and also to her and Mr. Jackson on beginning the next phase of their lives together. May all your days be happy and blessed."

"Thank you," Jackson and I said in union.

"Are all the final preparations completed?" Elizabeth asked.

Before I could even answer Olivia spoke up. "Yes, I believe so. Mrs. Timmons and I have been extremely busy. Sarah went over the final menu with us this morning."

I shook my head a little and laughed. "Then I guess so."

"I'm sorry," Olivia flushed a bit. "That was directed at you."

"Please, don't apologize. You have been a Godsend to me. I am perfectly fine with you handling all the final details. I am sorry I have not been of more help to you."

"I thought that with the house hunting and exam you have been very preoccupied." She looked a little embarrassed.

The gentlemen quickly fell into office talk and the three of us discussed all the things Olivia had handled for me. I had no idea how much she had done in my stead.

I was thrilled with the fact that she knew me so well that she had made all the same decisions I would have. Olivia informed me what our wedding dinner consisted of all the way down to the appetizers. It seemed there was nothing left for me to worry about and for that I was very grateful to her.

CHAPTER 23

Friday, December 18, 2009

I SET DOWN my pencil and couldn't decide if I wanted to cry in relief now that my last final was completed or out of pure exhaustion. It had been such a long week all I wanted to do was go home and take a nap. I really didn't care about the dance, nor did I want to go. Especially since things still weren't on the best of terms with my three comrades.

I rested my head on my desk and waited patiently for my peers to finish their exams. There was still thirty minutes left and thus far only two other students were done. I closed my eyes, grateful for the peace and quiet. The only sounds were the scribbling of pencils and the occasional eraser with a frustrated sigh.

My mind drifted to Boston and our departure in the morning. Despite having never been there I imagined the grand old city filled with historical buildings and exciting escapades. I thought of the large universities it housed and what it would be like taking a final exam in one of them. How thrilling it must be to be a part of such an enthralling atmosphere. I could not wait to be a college student myself.

"Pencils down. Pass your exams forward please," Mr. Rand announced from the front of the room. "That means you too, Mr. Bennett." All eyes turned towards Keith who was scrambling to fill out the last couple questions. "If you don't know it by now, you don't know it at all." Our teacher smiled graciously.

Sounds of shuffled papers drifted about the room with a rash of low murmurs of every sort. "For those of you who have passed the first semester final, I will see you back in January. However, if by chance you have not you will be notified by the twentieth by email.

You will have the option of picking up another elective or taking a study hall during this hour. Either way, before you leave I wanted to wish you all a very Merry Christmas and a fabulous New Year." Mr. Rand straightened the exams and walked back over to his desk.

The final bell rang, and everyone jumped from their desks, eager to begin their Christmas breaks. I grabbed my backpack and waited for Jackson to gather his things.

*   *   *

"Why the cocky grin?" I asked Jackson as we pulled out of the student parking lot.

"You know I had to purposely miss an occasional question on his exams." The grin remained but he stared ahead at the road.

"Why would you do that?"

"You are forgetting, Ms. Jocelyn, I graduated last spring with a BS in psychology. Mr. Rand's rudimentary AP Psych class is terribly simple in comparison to the college courses in psychology I took at BU."

"Yes, I suppose it is."

I, on the other hand, had found Mr. Rand's class quite challenging and somewhat difficult to decipher although I was not about to say so. For the first time I began to really have doubts about whether I was ready to attend BU or not.

*   *   *

Jenna was waiting impatiently for me on the sidewalk between our houses when we pulled into Jackson's driveway. She was talking with Kyle and bouncing up and down in the cold afternoon air. I could see their breath as the two of them jogged across the street towards us.

"It's about freakin' time!" Jenna pounced as soon as I opened my door.

"Sorry, everyone was trying to get out of the parking lot at once. It took us a minute." I shook my head and rolled my eyes.

"We've been freezing out here." She shifted her weight back and forth.

"You could've waited inside at your house or his." I looked over at Kyle who was standing on the other side of the CRV talking to Jackson.

"Whatever, I thought you guys were right behind us. Anyway, let's go!" She tugged my arm. I barely grabbed my backpack and shut his door before she was dragging me down the driveway over to my house.

"We'll see you at the game," she hollered over her shoulder to the two men staring after us.

Hilary and Caitlyn showed up right before six o'clock to take us to the game. They were both still being very guarded in the way they spoke to me and it seemed that the distance between us was growing by the minute. I felt like we were all starting to keep secrets from each other as we slowly pulled away from one another and began searching for some sort of identity all our own.

The game was agonizing. It was so close. The two teams stayed within a couple points of each other throughout all four quarters and it was quite frustrating to watch. The gym was filled with parents and students screaming for their team, but I could not seem to catch the festive mood of it all. I tried cheering, but I just couldn't muster up the enthusiasm to match everyone else. I was very proud of both Jackson and Zak and even Ethan; they all played a great game, but my mind was already on its way to Boston.

*   *   *

Jenna came over right after she had showered still with the towel on her head. I had just gotten out of the shower myself and barely got my robe on when I heard her knocking on the bathroom door. "Come on, we're going to be late, slow poke!"

I hurried back to my room with my hair still wrapped in a towel also and turned on some music and began working on my make-up for the dance.

"What are you getting Kyle for Christmas?" I asked, applying my foundation.

"I'm not sure. I'm going shopping this weekend with Hilary and Caitlyn. I have no idea what I'm getting him."

"I know the feeling. I haven't a clue what to get Jackson," I complained.

"I can't believe you're leaving the entire break. This sucks!" She made a face at me in the mirror. "It seems your entire world revolves around Jackson."

"Like yours doesn't revolve around Kyle?" I rolled my eyes at her reflection.

"Even so, I feel like I never see you anymore. We all do."

"How can you say that? I see you every day. And what about all that time when I was the odd man out? You had Kyle, Hilary was with Cody, and more often than not, Caitlyn was with Zak, and I was alone. I never complained to any of you about all those times you guys did stuff as couples and I was left out. Now that I have someone in my life, you all act as if I've done something wrong." I quickly applied the powder and walked away from the vanity.

Jenna turned around and faced me. "It's not that. It's just that you guys have gotten so serious. You're engaged, Jocelyn. It worries me that you're actually going to go through with it."

Her words were like a slap in the face. "What do you mean . . . go through with it? Of course, I'm going to go through with it. I love him. I want to marry him. And I am so sick and tired of everyone bitching about it. If you can't be supportive then keep your mouth shut. You don't have to partake in my wedding. Hell, my own mother and brother aren't going, why should my best friend be any different?" I glared.

"That is not what I meant, and you know it." She got up and stood beside me at my closet. "I only want to make sure you have thought this through. I'm worried about you."

"Do not bother yourself. I am quite capable of looking after myself, thank you very much."

"It's that!" she exclaimed.

"What?"

"The way you talk. You're even talking like Jackson, very proper and all."

"Oh, for Heaven's sake . . . really? Grammar? You're going to complain about an improvement in my grammar. If that is the worst thing that you can comment on that I have picked up from my future husband than you sound more ridiculous than the arguments my family have made."

"It makes you sound snobby."

"Are you saying Jackson is snobby?" I wanted to scream at her but decided not to give her the satisfaction.

"No, but . . ."

"Let's just get ready for the dance before we have a wicked argument." I returned to the vanity to finish my make-up.

Jenna and I hardly spoke another word while we readied ourselves. I hated the strain that my upcoming nuptials had placed on our friendship. It appeared that at almost every turn I was facing an adversary of some sort against our relationship. I wanted desperately for the school year to end so I could finally be married to Jackson and we could leave for our new life in Boston and finally be rid of all this harshness.

The boys arrived at nine o'clock. Ethan and Liang were already in the living room with my parents. My mother was taking pictures of them in front of the Christmas tree. Liang looked very beautiful in her dark green gown. Her long black hair was pulled up with just a few curls hanging loosely to accent her face.

Ethan was wearing a black suit but typical of his personality rather than wearing traditional dress shoes, he wore his new pair of black Converse. They were all smiles, that is, until we entered the room.

The tension was so thick it could have been spliced with a knife. The only smile that remained was that on my dad's face. "My goodness ladies, you look absolutely beautiful. Please come in. I would like to get some pictures of you all before you leave." But my mom angrily shoved the camera at him before hastily leaving the room through the kitchen, so she wouldn't have to walk past us. Seconds later we all heard her heavy footsteps on the stairs followed by the slamming of my parents' bedroom door.

"I'm sorry," my dad looked at the four of us apologetically. Ethan took Liang's hand and exited the room the same way our mother had and then disappeared out the front door without so much as a word to anyone. I heard my dad let out a deep breath and force a smile. "So, can I take a couple pictures?"

"Of course," Jackson replied, trying to ignore what had just transpired.

*   *   *

The smaller gym was decorated with multi-colored Christmas lights and streamers. It was a gaudy display that resembled the work of some ill-talented high school students on the entertainment committee. The Christmas tree in the corner was the only artfully decorated piece in the room. On the opposite side of the gym were tables with punch, cookies, and holiday cupcakes.

The place was crowded and stuffy as the Christmas formal was open to all students unlike the prom held later in the spring. Students of all grades were jammed together, and the noise was deafening. I stood between Jackson and Jenna, looking over the crowd, thinking how much I wanted to be anywhere other than here, except perhaps my own home.

"Are you all right?" Jackson inquired.

"Yes, it's a little stuffy in here," I casually remarked. I didn't want him to know how dreadful this evening was.

"Look. There's Caitlyn. Oh, I love her dress," Jenna proclaimed, dragging Kyle and me with her. I grabbed Jackson's hand and tugged him along.

Caitlyn was standing off to the side of the crowd looking bored in her short navy-blue dress. Her hair hung loosely around her bare shoulders. She spotted us as we approached and greeted us with a smile that reached up to her eyes. "Finally, I was beginning to think you guys weren't coming."

"I told you we were going to have dinner first," Jenna explained. "Where's Zak?"

"Getting us some punch. It's absolutely stifling in here. I can't breathe." She was fanning herself with a paper plate.

"Would you like to dance?" Jackson whispered.

I nodded, and he led me away from our friends.

"Are you sure you want to be here?" The music had slowed down and he wrapped him arms around me. I draped mine over his neck and rested my head on his chest.

"Not really, but we can't just leave Jenna and Kyle stranded."

"I am sure they can ride home with your brother and Liang," he said snidely.

"Probably, but who is going to ask them?" I giggled with sarcasm. "It doesn't matter anyway. I don't want to go home right now, or ever for that matter. I hate being in that place. It's like walking around on eggshells waiting for a bomb to drop."

"I am so sorry, my love. I feel like this is all my fault."

"Don't say that. You are the best thing in my life and I cannot imagine living without you." I looked up into his shinning emerald eyes. "I wish we could leave for Boston right now."

"We will be leaving in a few more hours my love."

"No, that's not what I meant. I wish we were already married, starting BU and didn't have to worry about this place ever again."

"Family is very important, darling. I hope you do not choose to dismiss them so easily."

"It is not I who has dismissed them, they have dismissed me." It hurt to admit.

"Not your father. Do not do that to him, he loves you so much," Jackson said in a comforting tone.

"You know Jenna is getting almost as bad as my mother and Ethan. We had an argument this evening about you. I'm just so sick of all the fighting and tension. I don't know how I am going to make it to graduation." I held him even closer to me as if I could feel the security of his love surrounding me.

*   *   *

It was a little after eleven when we parted ways with Jenna and Kyle in Jackson's driveway. They wished us a safe and happy trip, but it was cold and distant, lacking all the warmth of our former friendship. Kyle, at least, was genuine in his well wishes before they crossed the street and headed towards Jenna's house.

"See what I mean?" I asked as we walked up the path to his front door.

"Yes, I do." Jackson opened the front door and stepped aside for me to pass. "I'm so sorry that it has turned out this way."

Jackson made us some hot coco and joined me in the family room. I was warming myself by the hearth and admiring their beautifully decorated Christmas tree. He set our mugs down on the coffee table and wrapped his arms around my waist. "Feeling better?"

"Yes."

"Good, I am glad." He leaned down and kissed me softly.

"Where are your parents? The house is so quiet." I hadn't realized it was until that moment.

"I would imagine they went to bed hours ago. They always like to get a full night's sleep before heading to Boston. It is such a long ride." He kissed me softly again.

"Have I told you how beautiful you look this evening? I love this gown on you."

"Thank you. It belongs to my sister. She left it behind when she went to college. I wanted to get something new, but it is not like I can ask my mom these days to go shopping with me." I tried to laugh but it didn't come across well. "Thankfully, Sidney has fabulous taste in clothes." I ran my hands over the soft silk black material. It was a simple dress that accented my figure very nicely. It had spaghetti straps and came down a few inches above my knees. There was nothing glamorous about it, which is what made it so perfect for me.

"You do know that my mother would be more than happy to take you. I believe she really misses shopping with Phoebe. The two of them practically lived at the mall."

"Thanks, I just may do that sometime." I smiled up into his emerald eyes.

We stood there for several minutes without speaking. The only light in the room was from the burning embers and the soft white Christmas tree lights. It was so romantic. I could not possibly think of anything that could make this moment better.

Jackson leaned down and kissed me deeply then paused a moment and kissed my forehead lightly. "You know, Jocelyn, there is still one more thing we need to take care of before we leave for Boston." My favorite lop-sided grin slid across his lips as he bent down on one knee holding my hands in his. "Ms. Jocelyn Timmons, I cannot believe that I was so fortunate to find you in one of my lives but knowing that I have the honor to love you in both my lives makes me the happiest, luckiest, and most proud man in this world. I love you Jocelyn and I would be honored it you would be my bride."

"Yes . . . yes, of course!"

Jackson reached into the inside pocket of his jacket and pulled out a little black velvet box. Inside was an amazing white gold diamond ring. It was not too flashy, but there was nothing simple about it.

"This belonged to my grandmother. She and my grandfather were married for sixty-seven years. So, I thought it would be perfect for you. I hope you like it," he said nervously.

"I love it. It's so beautiful." He carefully slid it on my ring finger.

"I love you," he whispered, standing before me.

"I love you, too," I whispered back and wrapped my arms around him. I kissed him passionately as he lifted me into his arms and carried me over to the couch. He sat down with me on his lap. I ran my fingers through his hair and got swept away by the desire between us. I knew I could never tire of him.

"I really have to go home." I reluctantly pulled my lips from his. "I'm still not done packing and we're leaving in a few hours." A smile was plastered across my face.

"All right," he whispered as his finger gently traced the side of my face and I melted under his touch.

CHAPTER 24

Saturday, December 17, 1878

I JOINED MY MOTHER and Olivia in the carriage shortly before one in the afternoon. It was brisk out with a little more than a dusting of snow over the grounds. It would have been picturesque but for the bright sunlight that was glaring off the snow, making it difficult to see. We were due at Elizabeth's home at one o'clock for a small bridal shower she had insisted upon giving me.

I rested my head back against the seat and closed my eyes. I vaguely heard my mother rattling on to Olivia about something or other. I completely blocked them out and let my mind drift away. I could see Jackson proposing in front of the hearth next to the Christmas tree. I was wearing a beautiful black gown. Something I was surprised to discover. I was beginning to believe that my *other* self never wore dresses. Jackson looked so handsome in his modern suit. I heard myself say 'yes' and saw him placing a gorgeous ring on my finger. Then he lifted me up and carried me over to the couch, setting me down upon his lap. I could feel myself giddy with happiness.

"Jocelyn? Hello?" Olivia reached across the carriage and tapped me on the knee. "Are you feeling all right?"

"What?" I opened my eyes trying to refocus them. "Oh, sorry. I must have dozed off for a moment."

"Are you still having those night terrors sweetheart?" Concern flooded my mother's voice.

"Not recently," I shook my head. I couldn't exactly tell her I was experiencing them while I was wide awake and relaxed.

"Good, I believe every bride gets a little nervous as her wedding day approaches." She smiled lovingly.

I nodded in return and looked out the window. It was easier to remain silent and agree with her than to tell her my nervousness had absolutely nothing to do with my upcoming nuptials. Then again, with only seven days until the wedding, it was hard to tell at this point.

*   *   *

Laurie, Christina, and several of our other classmates along with their mothers were already there when we arrived. Emily, Phoebe, and Veronica were talking in the parlor with Mrs. Donaldson and Mrs. Cain. It looked like an oversized henhouse with everyone talking all at once, catching up on all the recent gossip that they hadn't gotten to share since the weather had turned cold and was keeping most of them inside.

Elizabeth's mother, Ester Maddox, was the most gracious hostess. She and her youngest daughter, Elisa, carried around silver trays with perfectly arranged finger sandwiches and shortbread cookies. Their housekeeper, Sabina, kept everyone's teacups full and busied herself trying to make Elisa behave like a proper little hostess.

"Your little sister is so cute," I remarked, sitting down beside Elizabeth.

"Mother wanted her to leave with my dad and brothers this afternoon over to Christina's, but she insisted on staying for the party. Mother finally relented, saying she could if she did not get in the way and helped Sabina."

"How old is she now?"

"Elisa is almost eight," Elizabeth said.

"That is hard to believe. I remember when she was born," I laughed.

"Yes, she was quite the surprise. I really thought my parents were done having children after the terror twins." She shook her head while rolling her eyes.

The terror twins were what Elizabeth called her two younger brothers, Edwin and Elijah. They were sixteen and fourteen years old, respectively, and always into some sort of mischief.

Her older brother, Easton, was very quiet and reserved like her.

"And here I thought they stopped having children because they ran out of E names," I teased.

"I know, it is awful. I cannot believe they did that. If it is not bad enough that both of their names started with an E, they had to do it with all their children." Elizabeth's father's name was Elmer, same as her grandfather.

"It is not that bad. Although granted, it is a bit unusual." She rolled her eyes again at me but at least she grinned with it.

Shortly thereafter, Ester put a rocking chair at the top of a circle where I was expected to open the mound of gifts everyone had brought. I felt very uncomfortable as everyone's attention shifted in my direction. I carefully made my way through the pile of beautiful things ranging from kitchenware to bedding. I was pleasantly surprised with their generosity and overwhelmed with the number of things I had not even considered I was going to need in our new home. Suddenly the terror set in on how unprepared I was to venture into this next part of my life.

*   *   *

Eddie and the Maddox's houseman, Peter, carried in all the gifts from the party and piled them in the corner of Jonathon's old bedroom that was now used for guests. Peter was kind enough to follow us home with their carriage since ours could not carry all the packages.

My father and Jackson were surprised by the number of gifts we received for our new home. They made several comments as the three of them stood in the foyer and watched the packages being carried upstairs. However, they had no interest in being shown the actual gifts when I offered to show them. My mother smiled graciously at me before remarking, "Do not be silly, my dear, men do not bother themselves with such things as bridal shower gifts."

"I know, Mother. I was only trying to be polite." I looked at Jackson and grinned. He smiled back with his lop-sided grin that I loved so much.

"Did the party go well?" Jackson came over and placed his arm around me.

"Yes, Mrs. Maddox and Ms. Elizabeth did a beautiful job. I had a wonderful time."

"Yes, yes, we all did. Even little Elisa behaved herself like a little lady," my mother added.

"I do not know about the rest of you, but I am starving. Can we eat dinner now?" Patrick asked impatiently.

"Of course, dear."

CHAPTER 25

Saturday, December 19, 2009

I ROLLED out of bed bone tired at four thirty in the morning. It was the only time I could recall being happy when the alarm went off so early after such a short night of sleep. I looked down at my left hand and marveled again at the beauty of the ring Jackson had placed there. I stretched and yawned but could not stop smiling. I quickly showered, dressed, and placed my luggage next to the front door. I had about thirty minutes before I had to be over at the Chandlers. I entered the kitchen and found my dad sitting there reading the morning paper and sipping his coffee.

"Good morning." He set the paper down beside him.

"What are you doing up so early?" I inquired, pouring myself a cup before sitting down beside him.

"Did you really think I was going to let you leave for two weeks without saying good-bye?"

"I hoped not." I added the sugar and creamer and willed myself not to get emotional.

"I am really sorry about last night."

"Why? You didn't do anything."

"I was hoping she would come around by now. Hell, she's hardly speaking to me these days. I don't know what to do anymore." He shook his head slightly. "This place feels more like a war zone than a home."

"Yeah, I know," I said quietly.

"Promise me you will be careful. I know you're not a child anymore, but you'll always be my child and I worry about you." He reached over and placed his hand over mine.

"I will Daddy, I promise. And thank you for letting me go. It means a lot to me. Besides, I think you may have a merrier Christmas without me here," I chuckled, trying to lift his spirits.

"I doubt that." He sighed and drummed his fingers on the table for a minute. "I remember when you kids were little, how excited you all would get this time of year. You guys would write letters to Santa and constantly play under the Christmas tree. You used to disappear for hours just lying under the tree staring up at the lights." He sighed heavily lost in his own memories. "I remember the Christmas morning when you were three, you went creeping down the stairs about five a.m. Ethan and Sidney were still sound asleep, but your mother and I heard you get up. We had barely reached our bedroom door when the paperboy opened the screen door to drop off the morning paper and let it slam shut. You flew back up the stairs light a bolt of lightning screaming in tears that it was Santa Claus and that he wasn't going to leave you anything because you were awake. You leaped right into my arms completely hysterical. It took me almost a half hour to get you to calm down and only when I took you downstairs and showed you that Santa had already been here and left, did you finally stop crying."

"Huh," I giggled. "I don't remember that at all."

"No, I guess you were too little, but I'll never forget it. You were so cute in your footed pajamas and pigtails."

"Is Sidney coming home soon?" I changed the subject before I started tearing up.

"Yeah, I talked to her last night. She'll be here Sunday evening and I guess Landon is coming on the twenty-sixth. He wanted her to spend Christmas at his place, but she said she wanted to come home."

"I wish I could see her." I really wanted to talk with her and see if she was still having those night terrors.

"I know. I'm glad you two seem to be getting along better."

"Yeah, I enjoyed her over Thanksgiving break. Do you think she'll come home over Spring Break?" I played absentmindedly with my mug.

"Who knows?" he shrugged. "I never know what's going on with her these days."

I glanced down at my watch. "Well, I'd best get going. I don't want to make them wait on me." I got up and put my mug in the sink.

My dad walked me over to the door. "Are you sure you don't want me to carry your bags over there for you?"

"Nah, it's okay. I got it." I reached up and wrapped my arms around his neck. "I'm gonna miss you, Daddy."

"I'm going to miss you too, pumpkin. Be careful and have a great Christmas. I love you." He hugged me tightly. "Call me when you get there." He reluctantly let me go.

"I will, I promise. I love you, too, Daddy. Merry Christmas."

* * *

Thankfully, the weather was mild for December and the roads were clear. Robert and Emily were talking quietly in the front seats and Jackson fell back asleep beside me in the back. I leaned my head against a small travel pillow and curled myself up in a fleece blanket. It didn't take long before I drifted back off to wonderland.

The sun was beginning to peek over the horizon when I finally opened by eyes again. Emily was dozing up front and Jackson slept soundly beside me in the backseat. I reached into my bag and pulled out the first *Vampire Academy* novel that I'd borrowed from Caitlyn. I quickly became engrossed in the book and finally understood what she had found so alluring about Dimitri, the love interest in the book. I made it into the sixth chapter before Jackson woke up. He sat up and rubbed the sleep out of his eyes.

"How can you read in the car? I would be getting sick by the second sentence," he said.

"I don't know. It's never bothered me." He took my book from me and looked at the cover.

"Did you just start this?"

"Yeah, why?"

"You read fast." He handed the book back to me. "Where are we?" He leaned between the two front seats and I went back to my book.

Robert pulled into a Denny's for breakfast shortly before nine. It felt good to stretch my legs and move around a bit. I hadn't even realized how hungry I was until I started in on my French toast and hash browns.

"Is your sister coming home for the holidays?" Emily asked, stirring more sugar and cream into her coffee.

"Yes, my dad said she'll be home tomorrow. I wish I could see her and talk to her. I don't even know if she's still having those nightmares," I said.

"You can always call home on Christmas day," Robert remarked.

"I planned to. I wanted to at least wish my dad a Merry Christmas and talk to Sidney, but I'm not sure it would be the right time to bring it up," I explained.

"You can always make it seem casual, like you're just inquiring how she's doing. Something like, Merry Christmas, ask her about school, her finals, and then throw in the question about her night terrors," Jackson offered.

"And that's supposed to sound casual?" I laughed. "I'm sure she won't pick up on that."

"You know what I mean. Don't blurt it out, keep it as conversational as possible," Jackson added.

"I know what you're saying. And I will ask." I smiled over at him.

The four of us made some small talk for the rest of our breakfast, but mainly we ate. My mind was filled with thoughts of Sidney as I wondered once again if she had inherited *EVE* as well. And if so, where was she in my *other* life? Was it really possible that she was on a plane that varied from my own? I had no idea. There were just so many things about *EVE* I still did not understand. And if I was struggling with it, how in the world was I going to be of any help to Sidney if she should happen to have it as well?

When we were done, I looked at the clock and noticed we'd made it back on the road in less than forty-five minutes. Thoughts of Sydney gave way to thoughts of Boston.

I have never been a big fan of road trips and by noon I remembered very clearly why. I was so grateful to Caitlyn for the book and was afraid that I would have it finished before we got halfway to Boston. I kept shifting around in my seat trying to get comfortable, but nothing seemed to work. Jackson had his eyes closed, listening to music on his phone with his feet stretched through the console between the front seats. Although he appeared comfortable it was obvious that he was bored out of his mind. It was going to be an extremely long day.

*　　*　　*

Emily pulled the Durango into the driveway of their Boston home about ten thirty in the evening. There were a couple lights on downstairs as well as the porch light that added a homey feel to the old Victorian home.

"Timers," Jackson answered my unasked question before I could even inquire. "We have the lights on timers. Phoebe and Alex take turns taking care of the place since we've been in Chicago."

"Do they live nearby?" I asked, stepping out and stretching my legs. The cold air was a welcomed relief to my lungs.

"Yes, a couple miles from here," Robert responded.

"That's nice." I helped unload the bags while Emily unlocked the house.

I stepped back a bit and looked over the huge old house. I finally understood what Jackson and his family had been talking about how individuals with *EVE* like to live in surroundings that make them feel more like home. While this house was probably twenty or thirty years newer than their home in Chicago it still fit within the yesteryear genre of simpler times.

Emily showed me around the house and put my things in Phoebe's old bedroom. It was cozy with a soft queen size bed, an antique desk. and dresser. There were artifacts from her high school and college days left behind and posters of her favorite musicians adorned the walls.

It was easy to see that Phoebe was more feminine than I and clearly loved her clothes and accessories. There were pictures of her in her school cheerleading uniforms, silly photos of her and her friends, and several from the proms she had attended.

After a long hot shower, I was completely exhausted. All I wanted was to sink down under the covers and drift off to sleep. Although I had been stuck in a vehicle all day I felt like I had run a marathon. Nothing like sitting in a car all day bored out of my skull to suck the life right out of me. I had barely crawled into bed and flipped off the bedside lamp when Jackson knocked on the open door.

"Tired?" He looked worn out as well. He walked over and sat down on the bed.

"Very. How are you feeling?" I sat up and leaned against his shoulder.

"Exhausted." He stroked my hair for a few minutes in silence. "I am so glad you are here."

"So am I. I feel so comfortable with your family. But I wish I was sleeping in your room, not Phoebe's." I looked up into his beautiful green eyes that were lit up by the soft glow of moonlight.

"I know, but my mother would have a coronary if you did. You know that."

"Yeah, I know."

"I will be right across the hall if you need me."

"Don't tempt me."

CHAPTER 26

Sunday, December 18, 1878

I SAT DOWN at the dining room table with William and Olivia and started buttering a piece of toast from the bread basket. I was already dressed and ready for church services and for once was running a little ahead of schedule. William was buried behind the morning paper as usual, so Olivia and I began discussing something she had heard from Mrs. Donaldson at the party yesterday . . . that her son, Dimitri, had started courting Ms. Evelyn Brice. She was a year younger than us and neither of us knew her very well. She was mostly a quiet young girl with blond wavy hair and light blue eyes. Funny enough, she was the exact opposite of Maryanne in every possible way. Which we both speculated was her main appeal to Dimitri.

"I never would have put the two of them together, but I think it is wonderful that he is taking an interest in someone new," I remarked as someone I had never seen before entered the dining room and placed a plate with eggs and bacon down on the table in front of me. I looked over at Olivia with the question in my eyes, but she simply shrugged. "Excuse me, I do not need to be rude, but who are you?"

The young black lady looked so embarrassed as if she wanted to crawl under the table and disappear. "I sorry, miss, my name's Tamesha."

Just then Sarah came bustling into the room wiping her hands on a dishrag. "Ah, good mornin' Ms. Jocelyn. I ain't heard you come down. This here's Tamesha. Mrs. Timmons hired er to be yur new cook once you an Mr. Jackson is married. I's training her this week."

"Well, it is very nice to meet you, Tamesha. You are in good hands. Sarah is an amazing cook and we love her dearly."

The young woman just smiled and slowly backed out of the dining room as my parents finally entered.

"Good morning ladies, William." My father pulled out a chair for mother.

"I see you met Tamesha." Mother took her seat while our father walked to the other end of the table and took his own. "I believe you and Jackson will be very happy with her."

"Mother, you never told me you had hired someone already."

"I told you not to worry, I would take care of staffing your home." She smiled sweetly and added creamer to her coffee.

"But I figured I would have some say in it. Besides, we do not even have a home yet to staff."

"You will, my dear. Plus, Tamesha comes highly recommended. She and her husband, Davonte, worked for Mr. and Mrs. Seaton. You remember them, the elderly couple several streets over? Anyway, I ran into their daughter-in-law last week and she told me that Mr. Seaton had finally moved in with them. Mrs. Seaton passed away two months ago and since then they have been trying to talk him into it. Of course, he did not want to impose on his children, but his health has been very poor. So, she said she was keeping an ear open if anyone was looking for some help. Tamesha was born into their household and Davonte joined them when he and Tamesha were married fifteen years ago. So, I hired them both for you. They are in their early thirties. She is a marvelous cook and he has experience tending the stables and other household repairs. They are a very charming couple and they only have one child. Her name is Betsy and she is eight. She is a delightful young girl who is very talented with the sewing and is learning how to cook. I do not believe she will be any trouble at all. Plus, she will be wonderful help with your babies."

"But, Mother, I have never met them," I tried to interject.

"That is why they will be shadowing here until the wedding. So, you and Jackson can get to know them. Plus, I also hired you another housekeeper."

"I thought you were going to let us take Cora with us."

"I am, but you and Jackson will be starting a family right away, so you will need a minimum of two housekeepers, a cook, and stableman."

"Who is this other woman you hired?"

"She is also from the Seaton household. Her name is Bertina. She is only twenty-two years old and she is Tamesha's little sister. She is working with both Mimi and Cora this week."

"All right." I wasn't sure what else to say so I turned back to my breakfast.

"I do not understand why you are so hesitant, dear. Emily and I both interviewed all three of them last Friday and even met Betsy. We both felt that they would be a perfect match . . . personality wise with you and Jackson." My mother looked truly hurt and I immediately felt horrible.

"I am sorry, Mother. I am sure they are. I am only worried about finding a home. We are running out of time," I tried to explain.

"I am sure Jackson will take care of everything," Father piped in. "You do not need to worry about such things."

"Yes, Father." I placed my napkin upon the table. "Please excuse me, Jackson will be here in a few minutes." Olivia grinned sympathetically as I walked out of the room.

*   *   *

"Did you know that our mothers have already hired our staff?" I asked Jackson on our way home from church.

"My mother mentioned it to me last evening."

"I guess they are shadowing our staff this week. I met our cook, Tamesha. Her husband . . . oh, I cannot recall his name now, but he is going to take care of the stables and repairs. They also have an eight-year-old daughter named Betsy who Mother says will be wonderful for our children," I snickered. "Too bad she will be in her late teens before they are born."

"There was one more also, right?"

"Yes, Tamesha's younger sister, Bertina, I think."

"Mother said they are from the Seaton estate. If that is the case, they will need no training from us. Mr. Seaton was a tyrant to his servants as well as his family. I am sure they are all happy to be out of that environment," Jackson said.

"I vaguely remember seeing the Seaton's years ago."

"I do not believe either of them ventured out much in the last few years. I heard they were both declining rapidly in the last several years or so." Jackson steered the horses past our road. "There is a house Father wanted us to look at if you do not mind."

"How could I mind? We need to decide on something." I snuggled in closer to him.

* * *

Jackson sighed heavily as we walked off the porch of the tiny two-bedroom cottage. "I cannot believe my father sent us over here to look at this place. It is not even large enough to house the staff they hired for us." He chuckled in a non-humorous way.

"Perhaps he did not know how small it was," I offered as he helped me into the carriage.

"This is getting ridiculous, you do realize that?" The tension and frustration were written all over his beautiful face.

I decided it was best not to answer him. We rode home in silence.

CHAPTER 27

Sunday, December 20, 2009

I WAS THE FIRST to awaken the next morning. The house was eerily quiet as I wandered downstairs. The early morning light was struggling to break through the clouds and I could barely navigate my way around the unfamiliar surroundings. I was starving but I didn't want to impose on them by searching their kitchen cabinets. Besides, I doubted there was any food in the house anyway. I knew his parents had gone to bed shortly after I did. I suddenly began to wish I knew my way around the area. Just so I could get something to eat and some coffee. Instead I got my book and took a seat next to the Christmas tree, which I was sure Phoebe had put up in anticipation of our arrival and read until someone else decided to get up.

About nine thirty Jackson strolled down the stairs. By then I was lying comfortably on the couch making myself completely at home and engrossed in my book.

"Good morning," Jackson leaned down and kissed me softly. "How did you sleep?"

"Very well."

"Are you hungry? I am starving, and I will bet there is nothing to eat in this house." He sat down on the edge of the couch beside me. "Want to go find something to eat?"

"Sure, I could eat." I didn't want to admit to him how hungry I was or that I was dying for some coffee.

"All right, get your purse and I will leave a note for my parents."

He didn't have to tell me twice. Jackson took off towards the kitchen while I quietly ran back upstairs and put the book on the bed. I grabbed my coat and purse and rushed back down to him.

*   *   *

Jackson pulled into the parking lot of a little café a few miles from their house. It was quite charming and had probably been there forever. We took a seat in a booth and began looking over the menus when the waitress brought over a couple of mugs and a pot of steaming coffee.

"Are you ready to order?" the petite blond waitress asked.

"Yes, I will have the spinach and mushroom omelet, hash browns, and a glass of orange juice." Jackson smiled and handed her the menu.

"And for you?" She looked down at me

"I'll have the same. Thank you." I handed her my menu.

"All right," she scribbled on her pad and walked away.

I added sugar and creamer to my coffee and played with the spoon while stirring it. "So, what are our big plans for today?"

"I thought I would take you over to BU and show you around campus."

"Seriously?" I almost jumped out of my seat.

"I figured you might want to see where you will be going to school next fall." He slid his hand across the table and laid it over mine. "That ring looks really good on you."

"Thank you; I think so. I love it!" I took a sip of my coffee. "I don't know why but I was so nervous yesterday that my dad was going to see it."

"But he already knows we are engaged." Jackson looked confused.

"I just feel bad that our engagement is causing him so many problems with Ethan and my mom."

"Things will work themselves out," he assured me.

"Glad you are still an optimist." I sighed heavily. I no longer held any optimism where my mom and Ethan were concerned.

*   *   *

We parked the Durango in one of the student parking lots. There were only two other cars in the entire lot. I wrapped my scarf a little tighter around my neck and buttoned up my coat. The wind was bitter cold and cut right through me.

"This is it." Jackson waved his outstretched arms. "What do you think?"

"It's huge!" I slowly looked all around me completely in awe of it all. "I had no idea it was so big."

"I thought you looked it up online," he said, giving me a strange look.

"I did, but it looks a lot smaller on a computer screen," I laughed.

"Yes, I would imagine so." He walked over and put his arm around me. "Come on, I'll show you around. Pretty soon you will get used to it and it will not seem so big at all and you will wonder how you ever felt intimidated by it."

We walked across the quad. There was a mixture of old and new buildings throughout the enormous campus. I loved the architecture, especially on the old buildings. They had so much character like nothing we had around our suburban part of Chicago. Most of the walkways were concrete but still, some of them were brick-lined and very beautiful. They reminded me a lot of the cobblestone walkway that lined the street in front of our homes in my *other* life. Somehow that little glimpse of the past made me feel less scared of this place.

"Did you know that the Boston Public Library is the oldest library in the country?" Jackson said as we browsed through the campus book store.

"Really?"

"Yes, and Alexander Graham Bell invented the telephone here in a BU lab in 1875." He gave me a cocky grin.

"What are you? Some sort of encyclopedia of useless information?" I gave him a playful shove.

"I spent four years here. I guess I picked up some trivial knowledge here and there," he laughed. "There is always something going on either on or off campus. There are tons of museums, theaters, concerts, sporting events, and historical sites. You are going to absolutely love it."

"I know I will." I took his hand in mine. "As long as we are together, I could be happy anywhere." I leaned up and kissed him quickly.

*   *   *

By the time we arrived back at the house, Phoebe, Carson, and Wallace had joined his parents. Phoebe and Emily were in the kitchen putting groceries away when we walked in.

"Jackson Wyatt?" Emily's voice rang out. "Please come here."

We hurried into the kitchen as Phoebe passed by us. "You're in trouble," she whispered to Jackson in a low voice.

"Jackson, I understand that you want to show Jocelyn around, but could you at least be considerate enough to think about us? You left your father and me here with no vehicle and no groceries. I had to call your sister over to take me to the store." She paused at the island holding a roast.

"I apologize. I was not thinking." He looked slightly embarrassed to be chastised by his mother in front of me.

"I'm sorry, Emily." I didn't know what to say. I had never really seen her upset before.

Luckily Wallace scurried into the kitchen and broke the tension. He wrapped his little arms around his grandmother's leg and she happily picked him up promptly kissed his chubby little cheek. Jackson seized the opportunity and disappeared back out of the kitchen, leaving me alone with her.

*   *   *

Phoebe and Emily began cooking supper. I offered to help but they only let me cut up the potatoes. The three of us talked about BU and the different majors I was considering. Phoebe recalled her days there and how much she had loved it. She said the coursework was grueling, but she had loved being a cheerleader there and being involved in various campus activities. She reminded me more and more of Sidney. I couldn't help but think that the two of them would probably become the best of friends once they met at our wedding next summer.

A short while later Alex and Leslie showed up with their children. Lucinda was six and Charlie was almost four years old. They were so adorable and immediately began running around playing with little Wallace. Cindy Lou, as her family liked to call her because her favorite storybook was *How the Grinch Stole Christmas*, was a very precocious young girl much like the character she enjoyed from the story. Her blond pigtails adorned bright red ribbons that matched the jumper she was wearing and her white tights with red polka dots. She favored Leslie a great deal. Charlie, on the other hand, resembled Alex more than his mother. Like Alex, his hair was the same color as Emily's although they got their stature from Robert.

All of us gathered around the oversized dining room table for dinner. I sat between Jackson and Phoebe and enjoyed the playful dynamics of his family. They easily teased each other, laughed, and purposely tormented one another. It reminded me a great deal of how my family used to behave before our engagement was announced. I watched them throughout the meal and said very little, suddenly missing the family I'd left in Chicago.

CHAPTER 28

Thursday, December 22, 1878

TWO DAYS until the wedding. The words rang through my ears before I even opened my eyes. I was almost in sheer panic mode as we still had yet to find a place to live after the ceremony. Even though I knew we could either stay here or at the Chandler estate, it was something that neither of us wanted to do.

Mimi opened my door and carried in my breakfast tray. "Rise n' shine, Ms. Jocelyn."

"Good morning, Mimi. How are you this morning?" I propped myself up on the pillows.

"I's feeling well. I so excited, two more days till the wedding."

"And we still have yet to find a home," I sighed heavily.

"Don't-cha fret, you will." She set the tray down in front of me.

"Thank you very much, Mimi, but I was planning on eating downstairs. Why the special treatment?"

"I's only got two more days to spoils you." She smiled and sat down on the edge of my bed. "I's gonna miss you something awful, Ms. Jocelyn."

"I'm going to miss you too, Mimi. I cannot imagine not having you with me every day and you being the first person I see every morning." I reached over and hugged her tightly. "Oh Mimi, why can't I take you with me? Is there no way Mother would let you go and Cora could stay here?" I whined like a small child.

"Now, child, that'll never work. I's can't leave my Eddie. He needs me too."

"Of course, Eddie could come too. Tamesha and her husband could stay here in your place." But Mimi shook her head slowly.

"Ya'll be all right. Now's eat up. Your food's getting cold."

*   *   *

Mother was already bustling about making everyone crazy. She was supervising Cora and Missy on where to put each ornament on the Christmas tree although they had been doing it for years. Poor Bertina was putting the stockings and the garland up on the mantel. I could hear my mother correcting her over and over again about the order of the stockings. She liked them a specific way from Father at one end, her, then her eldest child, their spouse, and so on with the children listed by age from oldest to youngest. There was no way Bertina could possibly get something like that right in the short amount of time she had been here.

I walked over and gently took the stocking she was holding out of her hands. "Honestly, Mother, you should have let Missy or Cora put up the stockings." I gave her a sour grin. Bertina looked like she was about to cry.

"Oh yes, I am sorry. What was I thinking?" She shook her head slightly. "Bertina, would you please set the garland and bows on the stair railing. Jocelyn, please finish the stockings."

Bertina took the rolls of garland and mountain of red velvet bows out into the foyer and began working diligently. "Mother, what time are you going over to decorate the church?"

"I thought we would head over there around two. Emily and Phoebe wanted to go with us and she is working on the finishing touches on the gowns." She pointed her hand to where she wanted each ornament Missy was placing on the tree.

I paused for a moment when I realized that Olivia and Jackson now had their own stockings added to ours. "When did you make these?"

She turned and noticed what I was holding in my hand. "Mimi made those. I have been so busy with your wedding it never occurred to me. Luckily, she remembered. She brought them down last evening. She did a beautiful job on them."

"Yes, she did," I traced my fingers gently over them before hanging them up on the mantel next to William's and my stockings.

I was completely exhausted by the time evening set in. Mother and Emily had everyone jumping around doing ten things at once. Even being the bride did not lessen my subjection to their harsh orders. By the time they had agreed they had tortured us enough for one day I wasn't even sure I liked either of them anymore.

I crawled beneath the warm coverlets and rolled over to face the hearth. The fire was roaring, and I watched the shadows dancing across my walls. It was a familiar habit that I'd done since childhood. For some strange reason it had always made me feel safe and secure. It was home, my room, my life. And now the time was closing in on saying goodbye to it all.

The feeling left me both excited and sad. Things had changed so much in the last couple weeks my head was still reeling. I was doing my best to wrap my mind around *EVE* and tried to think like the Chandlers and my uncle did, that this gift was truly a gift . . . the best of both worlds. I closed my eyes and tried to imagine what it was going to be like to go to Boston University. The part of me that had always dreamt of furthering my education was ecstatic. I could not wait to walk the campus grounds, attend classes, and explore the sciences.

It all seemed so unbelievable to me. I couldn't imagine what my father would think about me going all the way to Boston to attend the university. He would have a nervous breakdown at the mere mention of it considering I wasn't even allowed to touch the books in his study. I smiled to myself at just the thought of what my mother would think of it. She would surely faint thinking of her daughter doing something she considered so improper for a young lady. I could almost hear her voice in my head telling me that I shouldn't even entertain such inappropriate thoughts.

I snuggled up with the pillow next to me and thought about the children that Jackson and I would have ten years from now. A tear escaped from the corner of my eye and landed on the pillow.

I hated the thought of having to wait so long to begin our family. I was so jealous of Rachel for being pregnant now. I truly was happy for her and my brother and excited about having another niece or nephew, but I was envious also. I could still see the photos in that album and the little faces of my angels: Gavin, Ethan, and my sweet little Alyssa. They haunted me. And I knew they were going to haunt me for years to come.

I tightened my grip on the pillow and felt very alone.

CHAPTER 29

Thursday, December 24, 2009

JACKSON WALKED UP behind me and rested his head on my shoulder. I stared at our reflection in the mirror, thinking how happy I was to be here with him and his family. I was having the best time with Phoebe and Emily. They were both patiently teaching me how to cook, taking me shopping, and Jackson had even taught me how to ice skate. This was by far the best Christmas break I had ever had.

"Jocelyn?" he whispered in my ear. "Will you marry me?" I could feel his lips brushing against my neck setting fire to every neuron in my body.

I looked at his serious expression in the mirror. "Yes," I turned to kiss him fiercely.

"Today?" He stopped to look deeply into my eyes.

"Are you serious?"

"Very much so."

"But what about our wedding in June?"

"That is for them. This would be for us." I stood there completely at a loss for words. "One of my father's friends is a judge and he has agreed to marry us this evening. This way we would have the same anniversary in both our lives: Christmas Eve. We would not have to tell anyone back in Chicago. This would be for us. That way you would be my wife on both planes."

"My goodness, you're serious, aren't you?" I took a small step back and bumped into the dresser.

"Yes." The lopsided grin that I loved slid across his shapely lips as he took me back into his arms. "I love you more than I could ever put properly into words. I would be honored if you would become my wife this evening." He leaned over and kissed me tenderly.

"But I don't have a dress . . . my family, our friends?" I stumbled.

"We can have our big wedding in June just as we planned. As for your gown, I am sure Phoebe has something that would be suitable." Jackson's eyes held my own.

"And your family already knows about this?" I hesitated a moment before the full picture truly emerged in my mind. "Wait a second . . . you all planned, this didn't you? That's why I am here and the trip to New York is supposed to be our honeymoon, isn't it?"

"Yes, I wanted it to be a surprise."

"Well, you succeeded. I am surprised, that's for sure." My thoughts were whirling all over the place, and I could not think straight. All I could think about was escaping the horrors that had become my home and my life in Chicago and beginning my new life with the man I loved more than anything else in this world.

"And?"

"And I say yes!" I threw my arms around his neck.

Phoebe, Emily, and I spent the next three hours hidden away in Phoebe and Carson's bedroom. Her walk-in closet was the size of a storage locker. When Jackson had said that she had a slight obsession with clothes, shoes, and accessories, he wasn't kidding. It was like being caught up in one of Sidney's dreams. I had never seen anything like it outside of Carrie's closet in the *Sex and the City* movie.

I spent the first two hours mainly feeling foolish in my bra and panties trying on various gowns that Phoebe had worn on previous New Year's Eves, Christmas parties, and elegant business dinners. She was slightly taller than I so all of the full-length gowns looked ridiculous on me. There was no way I could wear them without at least five-inch heels and I was having great difficulty not falling in three-inch ones.

The three of us finally agreed on a silk winter white gown that clung gracefully to my body. The open back draped loosely down to the small of my back. The front hung the same way atop my breasts yet enhanced them in a very fashionable way. The spaghetti straps were so delicate I was almost sure that I was going to break them.

They crisscrossed across my back to the sides of the thin silk material. The gown hung just below mid-calf on me and had a slit in the side that reached all the way up to my right hip. It was so soft and delicate and felt very foreign to me. It was more Sidney's style than my casual jeans and sweatshirt garb, but I knew Jackson was going to love it. Thankfully, I wouldn't have to worry about wearing it outside.

Phoebe handed me her matching three-inch heels with the thin ankle straps. They made my legs look so long and shapely. I felt more like I was getting ready for the prom than getting married. I was so nervous. My stomach was in knots and my hands were shaking so badly I had to take a deep breath and close my eyes for a moment just to get the buckles fastened on my heels.

By four o'clock Emily said she was going downstairs to help Leslie get dinner started. I couldn't help but wonder what she and Carson must be thinking considering this impromptu wedding and my absentee family, especially after my family's behavior on Thanksgiving. They probably had the worst impression of them possible. It was with that realization that it finally occurred to me that I was getting married without any of my friends or family present. I desperately wanted nothing more than my dad at that moment and for him to be the one to give me away instead of Robert. I turned my back to Phoebe and hastily brushed a tear off my cheek.

"Jocelyn, are you all right?"

"Sure, just getting a little nervous." It wasn't exactly a lie.

"I know my little brother sprung this on you out of the blue." She shook her head. "I told him he should have spoken to you about this earlier."

"I know it may sound childish to say, but I wish my dad could be here." The tears slowly slid down my face.

"I know these last few months have been difficult with your mother and brother. Jackson explained to us what was going on. I'm sorry that they are taking this so hard." She wrapped her arms around me and let me cry on her shoulder.

"I wish they could be happy for me. If they would at least try and understood how much we love each other, how happy he makes me . . ." I blubbered.

"They will . . . in time," Phoebe did her best to comfort me. "Now, we must get busy or we are going to run out of time and we cannot have the bride with red swollen eyes, so dry your tears."

I sat down at the vanity mirror in her oversized bathroom. She had nearly as big a collection of cosmetics as her mother. Phoebe pulled my hair up away from my face and began working on my make-up. Like her mother, she had the knack of beauty and style with an untethered grace that was seldom seen in our current time.

I watched her carefully, thinking I could never match her skill at applying make-up so perfectly. When she was finished she unclipped my hair and let it fall loosely around my shoulders. "I think we should leave your hair down since we are going for casual. I am just going to add a few curls around your face."

I took a deep breath and smiled at her reflection. In the back of my mind I could almost see Mimi's face instead of Phoebe's looking back at me. It was the strangest sort of déjà vu I had ever experienced. I shuddered briefly trying to clear my mind. "Whatever you think is fine with me."

Standing back from me Phoebe examined her masterpiece. "I think you are ready." She held my hands out in her own. "You look absolutely gorgeous."

There was a knock at the door. "May I come in?" Emily cracked the door a bit.

"Of course," Phoebe answered.

She walked in wearing a beautiful satin and lace sage dress with long sleeves and skirt. Her hair was pinned up, eloquently showing off her slender neck. She was wearing a red Christmas apron on over it to protect her dress in the kitchen.

"Oh, Jocelyn, you look so beautiful." She hugged me loosely so as not to mess up our dresses.

"Thank you, so do you." Emily walked over and sat down on the corner of her daughter's bed while Phoebe slipped back into her closet to change clothes herself.

"Please, have a seat dear." She patted the spot beside her. I came over and carefully sat down trying not to wrinkle my gown. She took my hands in hers. "Jocelyn, I know this is not how you envisioned your wedding and you do not have to go through with this if you truly do not wish to."

"I know it may not be ideal. Of course, I would love it if my family were here. Well, I should say that I wish my dad and Sidney were here." I tried to smile. "Maybe not my mother and Ethan. I think they would ruin it for me. Besides, I think this way may be better. At least I will have wonderful memories of a drama free wedding day because I'm certain that I will not have that for our wedding in June. I know my family will do something to make it unpleasant."

"I truly hope not. I know things at your house are not exactly comfortable as of late, but you must hold on to the belief that they will come around by June." She squeezed my hands tenderly in hers.

"Well, I'm not going to hold my breath. I know how stubborn they can be. If they ever speak to me again it will not be until I successfully complete graduate school without any children." I shook my head in disbelief.

"Certainly, you cannot believe that."

"I don't believe it, I know it." I attempted to laugh it off, but Emily just gave me a sad look.

Phoebe came out of the closet wearing a stunning red dress that enhanced her shapely figure. She spun around before us with one hand on her hip. "So, how do I look?"

"Amazing." I suddenly felt very drab in comparison.

"I know it may be a tad to 'night out on the town' for a wedding but it was the only thing I had left that was Christmas that was not black. I refuse to wear black at your wedding, it's bad luck." She sat down beside her mother.

"You look very nice my dear." Emily stood up and walked over to the door. "Robert will be waiting for you at the top of the stairs in about ten minutes Jocelyn."

"Thank you, Emily." She closed the door behind her.

"Are you ready?" Phoebe turned towards me.

"I have my something old and borrowed." I held up my wrist showing off the tennis bracelet her mother had lent me and gesturing to my entire ensemble.

"And I have your something new and blue." She rushed over to her dresser opening the top drawer and pulling out a small oblong box. "I bought this for your wedding in June when I saw it several weeks ago at a lingerie shop. Now I'm really glad I did." She came back over, sat down, and handed me the box.

Inside it was a baby blue garter trimmed in white lace. "Oh, Phoebe, It's perfect. Thank you." I stood up and she helped me slip it onto my right leg. I spun around and looked at myself again in the mirror. The garter was barely detectable but just knowing it was there made me feel even sexier.

"One last thing." She handed me a white gold band with three small diamonds inlaid in it. It was very beautiful and classy. "You will need this."

"Where did you get this?"

"Jackson gave it to me downstairs."

"Did he show you mine?" Curiosity was killing me.

"Of course," she smiled coyly.

"And . . ."

"And you shall see it shortly." She leaned over and kissed me on the cheek.

There was a soft knock on the door, interrupting her torment. Phoebe opened it and much to my disbelief there stood my uncle Nicholas wearing a black suit. He looked incredibly handsome.

"Surprise." He walked over and stood in front of me placing his hands on my arms. "You look absolutely gorgeous, dear. Jackson is a lucky man." He gave me a fatherly hug and kissed me lightly on the cheek.

"Thank you, Uncle Nicholas. What are you doing here? How did you know?" Phoebe smiled and slipped out the door.

"I got a call last week from Robert telling me what Jackson had planned. So, whether you agreed to get married this evening or not, either way I get to spend the first Christmas with you since you were just a child. How could I say no to that?" he explained.

"I am so glad you're here." I could feel the tears welling up in the back of my eyes and I forced myself not to cry. "This means so much to me."

"Me too." Again, I was struck by how much he and my dad resembled one another. "Ready?"

"Very."

I took his arm and we descended the stairs carefully. I was terrified I was going to fall in these heels and held his arm tighter than I intended to, but he never seemed to notice or was just too polite to say anything. At the bottom of the stairs we turned and entered the living room where everyone was gathered.

There were no special flowers, no wedding march playing in the background although someone had turned on Bing Crosby signing Christmas carols softly. There was no aisle to walk down, no bridesmaids or groomsmen, just Jackson and someone I assumed to be their judge friend waiting for us in front of the fireplace by the Christmas tree.

The lights in the living room were low and the Christmas tree lights glowed brightly along with several candles and the fire roaring in the hearth. Jackson was wearing a black suit with a red silk handkerchief in his front breast pocket. His brother, Robert, Carson, and Leslie had also changed into their Christmas dress attire.

Uncle Nicholas leaned over and kissed me once again on the cheek then took my hand and placed it in Jackson's.

"You look so beautiful," Jackson whispered with my favorite lopsided grin.

The man standing to the side of the Christmas tree in a dark grey suit had salt and peppered hair, was clean-shaven with kind looking clear blue gray eyes. He was almost as tall as Jackson and held an air of strength about him that made him a strong presence in any room. He cleared his throat and began in a very deep voice, "I am honored to have been asked by my old friend Robert to perform the ceremony for his son and his lovely bride on Christmas Eve. I have known Robert since our college days at Harvard, stood up with him when he married his beautiful wife and was there when each of his wonderful children were born. Therefore, this day also has a special meaning for me as well." He paused for a moment. "Jackson Wyatt Chandler, do you take Jocelyn Alyssa Timmons to have and to hold, in sickness and in health, to love, honor, and cherish and forsaking all others keep thee only unto her until death divides you?"

"I do," Jackson's voice was barely audible.

"Jocelyn Alyssa Timmons, do you take Jackson Wyatt Chandler to have and to hold, in sickness and in health, to love, honor, and cherish and forsaking all others keep thee only unto him until death divides you?"

"I do," I whispered.

"Very well, now I understand that the bride and groom have written their own vows to one another." Sheer panic rose through my chest. No one had mentioned anything to me about having to write any vows. I had nothing prepared, no clue what to say . . . my legs went numb and I tightened my grasp on Jackson's hands.

Jackson swallowed hard like he was trying to swallow a jawbreaker then cleared his throat. "Jocelyn, you are the love of my life. I know there are those who believe we are too young to understand what love is and what it takes to make a successful marriage.

But I know that as long as I have you beside me, there is nothing in this world we cannot conquer. I look forward to each new day with you beside me. I love you." I noticed a single tear slid down his cheek as he squeezed my hand in his and placed the band on my ring finger next to the engagement ring he had just given me. It was clear the two were a set by how well they complimented one another.

"Jackson," I whispered through the frog in my throat. "You have taught me the meaning of love and the great lengths that one would go through for the one they love. I am so honored to have your heart. I will protect and cherish it every day of my life. I love you with every fiber of my being, every ounce of my soul and more with each passing day. I never dreamt of finding someone who not only I could love so much but would also be my very best friend. I love you." I nervously placed the band on his ring finger.

"By the power vested in me by the great state of Massachusetts I pronounce you husband and wife. You may kiss your bride," The judge stated heartedly.

Jackson wrapped his arms around me tightly and kissed me so passionately it took my breath away. I could still hear the judge's words echoing in my ears: husband and wife. Jackson was my husband. Truly and honestly my husband! I was married! The reality of it made my entire body go numb. I could barely hear everyone applauding behind us.

Jackson finally released me. I stood dazed while he shook hands with the Judge and didn't even realize my body was moving as I shook his hand also as he congratulated the both of us. My new family and Uncle Nicholas gathered around. Everyone exchanged hugs and kisses and happy words of congratulations and welcomes to the family.

It was all very surreal and then someone starting snapping pictures and I saw flashes across my vision. My head began to spin. I reached out to grab Jackson's arm to steady myself. I was suddenly very hot and felt like I was about to faint. I willed myself to focus on Jackson.

I refused to spoil this moment by fainting. It would ruin this perfect day.

After the initial hype had settled down, I was finally introduced to the man who married us, Judge Michael Stewart. He was a boisterous man with a hearty laugh. He and his wife, Sharon, a robust woman who I initially hadn't even realized was there, stayed long enough to make a toast and take several photos with us before they announced that they must get to their son's house for Christmas Eve dinner. He quickly led Jackson and me along with Phoebe and Alex to the dining room to sign the actual marriage license. Jackson and I signed along the dotted line and his siblings signed as our witnesses. It was done.

A half hour later we were all seated around the dining room table eating ham, mashed potatoes, yams, sweet corn, green bean casserole, and yeast rolls. A floral centerpiece surrounding a crystal candleholder blazed amongst all the dishes. The china dishes shone alongside the sparkling silverware and rested upon a satin white tablecloth that completed the picturesque meal.

After dinner I changed back into the jeans and sweater I had worn over earlier in the day. I hung Phoebe's gown back up in her closet and looked at it for another moment.

"Please, take it with you," a voice came from the entryway of the closet.

"What?" I turned and saw Phoebe leaning in the doorway. "No, I can't, but thank you so much for letting me wear it."

Phoebe lifted the dress off the rod and handed it to me. "Every bride should have her wedding gown. Please, I want you to have it." She then handed me the box containing the shoes. "Don't forget these." I embraced her tightly.

"How can I ever thank you enough?"

"You make my brother very happy, that is enough."

Downstairs I joined the others in the foyer fully expecting my uncle Nicholas, Robert, and Emily to be putting their coats on and getting ready to leave also but they were standing together at the foot of the stairs talking with Jackson.

"Anything wrong?" I asked joining them.

"Not at all, we were just telling Jackson that we have decided to spend the night here, so we can spend Christmas morning with Wallace and you two will have the whole house to yourselves." Emily hugged me tightly.

"You don't have to do that." I let go of her. "I feel bad, like we're kicking you out of your own home."

"Nonsense, you two need some time alone. We will be fine here," Robert piped in.

Jackson helped me on with my coat. "Thank you very much, Father."

I walked over and hugged Uncle Nicholas tightly. "Thank you so much for coming. I cannot tell you what it means to me. I love you."

"Thank you allowing me to be a part of your special day. I love you too. Don't worry, I will be here when you return tomorrow." He kissed me lightly again on the cheek. "Congratulations, I am so happy for you two."

We kissed and hugged everyone goodbye, thanked them repeatedly for everything and made our way through the snow to the Durango.

"Well, Mrs. Chandler how do you feel?" Jackson asked, pulling out of their driveway.

"Dazed. I mean, this is unreal. We got married today!" I put my feet up on the dash and slumped down in the seat.

"Yes, we did. Are you happy?" He glanced over at me.

"I don't think I've ever been this happy. This has been the best day of my life. I love you so much."

"I love you too."

* * *

Jackson pulled into his parents' drive and shut the car off. "Wait right there; do not move." He jumped out and ran around to the passenger door. "Mrs. Chandler?" He held out his hand, which I took and climbed down. Standing before him in the cold, I kissed his shapely lips. Then he reached down and scooped me up into his arms.

"Jackson . . . the ice." I wrapped my arms around his neck fearing we'd both fall.

"Trust me?" He gave me a devilish grin.

"You, yes. The ice, no!" I laughed as he slid our way to the front door and struggled to get the door unlocked.

He flung the door open and carried me across the threshold, kissing me. Once inside, he kicked the door closed and carried me up the stairs to his bedroom. There was no slipping into something sexy, lighting candles, or anything else. We fell together down on his bed locked in unquenchable desire.

Our hands were grasping, pulling and tugging on each other's clothes trying to remove them. Jackson pulled the zipper down on my sweatshirt too quickly and snagged it on my bra ripping the lace a bit.

"Darn it," he stopped and leaned up. "I think . . . oh, I just ruined your bra. Sorry." He smiled, and I started giggling.

"That's okay. I believe I tore two buttons on your shirt."

He rolled off me and started laughing. "This is not exactly the romantic wedding night I had planned." Jackson leaned up on his elbow. "I wanted everything to be perfect." He brushed a bit of my hair away from my face. "For our first time to be perfect."

I rolled towards him. "Don't you see? It is." But he shook his head. "I am with you, my husband, and I love you." I traced my fingers down his cheek then over his lips. He kissed them.

"I love you," he said. I ran my fingers through the back of his hair and pulled him down gently to me.

Jackson slowly rolled back on top me. His lips moved down to my neck caressing it softly while my fingers tangled in his black wavy hair. The smell of his skin was intoxicating. He kissed my shoulder, then my collarbone. He expertly unhooked the clasp on the front of my bra. Jackson lifted me up with ease kissing me slowly and deeply. He slipped my bra off and tossed it aside along with his own shirt. Our bodies pressed warmly together, our hands exploring freely. We lay down beside one another locked in ravenous hunger.

Chapter 30

Friday, December 23, 1878

I BLUSHED DEEPLY as the images of Jackson and I lying in bed together as husband and wife blazed across my mind. The passion between us, the desire, the longing, the lust . . . had all been fulfilled. Never had I felt so incredibly satisfied and happy in all my life.

"Good mornin' Ms. Jocelyn." Mimi pulled back the drapes across my windows flooding my room with the morning light. "You lookin a tad pink this mornin'. Are you feelin' all right?"

Embarrassed, I quickly climbed out of bed. "I am fine. Just a little warm from the heavy covers and the fire," I lied.

"Eddie's kept the fires a roaring all night. Tis gotten mighty cold and snow's a blowing heavy." She helped me on with my robe.

"Has Mother awakened yet?" I walked over to the basin and washed my face and brushed my teeth.

"Yes'm, she's in the dining room,'" She picked up my silver brush and ran it through my hair.

"I thought she would be up early. I know she wanted to make sure all the last-minute details were attended to before tomorrow."

"Yes'm, she's been up since six this mornin.'" I wasn't surprised in the least.

*   *   *

I wrapped myself in my caplet, placed my woolen bonnet over my hair, and stepped out into the winter wonderland that had shown up overnight. The cold air blasted me in the face and burned my cheeks. The sun gleamed brightly off the snow. I had to squint my eyes just to navigate my way down the porch steps and through the walkway over to the Chandler household.

Barnaby opened the door and helped me off with my winter covers. Jackson strolled down the stairs in gray slacks and vest with a neatly pressed white shirt underneath. His pocket watch dangled gracefully across his midsection.

"Good morning, my love. How are you feeling today?" He embraced me warmly.

"Wonderful," I blushed, recalling the images that ran through my mind when I had awakened. "Can we talk privately?"

"Of course." He took my hand and led me into his father's study. He closed the door behind us and turned back to me with a knowing smile.

Being alone with him I felt my stomach jump. "We got married last night."

"Yes, we did." He took me in his arms tightly and pressed his lips against mine.

"We . . ." I couldn't bring myself to say the words out loud.

"We did." His smile broadened.

I felt the heat rise in my cheeks. "It was . . ." I choked.

"The most amazing night of my life," Jackson finished my sentence.

"Mine too." I rested my head against his chest.

"I love you." He leaned down and kissed the top of my head.

"I love you too. Do you think it will be like that *here*?" I whispered.

"I believe it will be just as perfect *here* as it was *there*." His hand ran lightly over my hair.

"But we will have to be so careful."

"We will be." A slight smile slid over his shapely lips.

"Are you sure? I don't want everything we have so carefully planned to fall apart because I get pregnant." I could feel the blood rushing to my face.

"I promise you we will take every precaution we can."

"It really was wonderful." I rested my head against his chest.

"And it will be *here* for us as well."

*   *   *

My mother and Emily had the entire household in an uproar according to our fathers. When Jackson and I came out of Robert's study, we found them hiding over at Jackson's along with my brothers, Alex, and Silas. They were gathered around the dining room table playing cards and discussing politics.

"Mother is looking for you," William informed me as soon as we entered the room.

"Does she know where I am?"

"She knows you are with Jackson," Jonathon added.

"There is no way I am going over there. You remember how insane she was for my birthday party. I cannot imagine what she is like right now."

"A pure nightmare," I heard Patrick II mutter under his breath causing my other brothers to snicker.

"Patrick . . ." Father turned his attention over to me. "She is trying to make everything perfect for your wedding."

"And that is why you are hiding over here also, Father?"

"Oh, you could not pay me to go back over there," he smirked and laid down another card. "You will be lucky if I show up in time to walk you down the aisle."

"I understand that," Robert added.

"Cowards," I laughed and walked out of the dining room.

It was almost eight o'clock in the evening before I mustered enough courage to return home. Jackson and I walked into complete chaos. My mother rounded on us almost as soon as we walked in the door. She appeared frazzled, with several long strands of hair escaping from her normally elegant bun at the nape of her neck. Her sleeves were rolled up and the apron protecting her dress was smudged with a little bit of everything.

"Jocelyn Alyssa, where have you been? I have been looking for you all day!" She scolded me like I was six years old.

"My apologies, Mrs. Timmons, we were house hunting."

"Oh, all right. Well, Jocelyn, say good night to Jackson. You have to get your gown and things ready for tomorrow and you must get a good night's sleep."

"Yes, Mother." I turned towards Jackson. "I suppose I had better comply before she has a total nervous breakdown," I whispered.

"I think you may be too late." He leaned towards my ear and whispered back. "Besides after tomorrow, we never have to do this again."

"What do you mean?"

"Say goodnight and go our separate ways. After tomorrow we will never have to spend another night alone." Jackson wrapped his arms around me and held me tight.

"Now if we only had a place to sleep in," I couldn't help but laugh.

"We will, I promise. I booked us a room at the Rosewood Bed and Breakfast in the city for tomorrow night and we will figure out what to do from there. I suppose we could stay with my parents until spring and then we will build us a home."

"If that is what you believe is best then it is fine with me." I really didn't want to stay here since William and Olivia were already living with my parents. Still, I wasn't exactly thrilled about staying at the Chandler estate either. But I wasn't about to share that with Jackson. Considering our options, it was clearly the wisest choice.

"I will make it up to you. I am so sorry it worked out this way. I know this is not how either of us wanted to begin our married life." He cupped my face in his hands and stared deeply into my eyes.

"I do not care where we live as long as I am with you."

Jackson wrapped his arms around me, kissing me deeply and pulling me closer to him.

"That is enough of that. Jackson you need to go home. Jocelyn has things to do." Emily walked into the foyer from the kitchen.

Both of us chuckled a bit. "All right, Mother." He rolled his eyes playfully. "I will see you tomorrow at six o'clock. Sweet dreams, my love." He gave me another quick kiss under the scornful watch of his mother. "I love you."

"I love you, too."

CHAPTER 31

Friday, December 25, 2009

I COULD FEEL Jackson's arm wrapped around me and his body spooned next to mine. I didn't want to open my eyes, didn't want to breathe, didn't want the moment to end. Then I felt him stirring and followed by his hot breath on my neck.

"Merry Christmas, Mrs. Chandler," he said in a low voice.

"Merry Christmas, husband." He kissed me lightly on the cheek.

"Did you sleep well?"

"Yes. I love waking up in your arms."

"Ditto." His lips brushed across shoulder.

I rolled over and faced him. "I don't ever want to go home. How am I supposed to go back into that house, sleep alone in my bed, and pretend that you're not my husband, that we aren't married?"

"Then don't."

"What?"

"Tell them the truth. We are legally married. Why not just tell them the truth?" Jackson rolled onto his back and stared up at the ceiling. "It would get you out of that house and away from all that torment."

"Are you serious?"

"And if I said yes?"

"Jackson, this would kill my father. I can't do that to him." I couldn't believe he was suggesting such a thing.

"Shane has always been very supportive of our relationship and it's not like he does not see what is going on under his own roof. He is very aware of how difficult things are," Jackson reasoned.

"Being supportive of your daughter because you do not wish to jeopardize your relationship with her is a lot different than being happy that she ran off and got married without your knowledge," I tried to explain.

"But if we talked to him together, explained . . ."

"Explained what? That since we were already getting married on Christmas Eve in 1878 we wanted to have the same anniversary in 2009 or that we didn't want to have sex until we were married and couldn't wait six more months. Which do you think he would be more inclined to understand?" I giggled at my own absurdity.

"Since you put it that way, why don't we explain to him that your living conditions have become unbearable and this way you would be right across the street and he could see you whenever he wishes, but you would not be subjected to the harsh treatment of your brother and mother." Jackson traced his fingers softly over my lips.

"Do you really believe he would not be furious with us?" I raised an eyebrow at him.

"I would expect him to be upset. However, I do believe that he would be sympathetic because of your living conditions. He loves you. He doesn't want to see you so unhappy."

"I know, but I'm just not sure what I should do," I sighed heavily. "But right now, I've gotta use the ladies room."

I climbed out of bed wrapped in a sheet and went into the bathroom closing the door behind me. I cleaned myself up a bit and brushed my teeth all the while Jackson's words played over and over in my mind.

Can I really tell Dad what I've done? Will he truly understand and be happy for us or at least, not hate us? I wasn't nearly as sure as he was.

Still wrapped in the sheet I opened the bathroom door. Jackson was sitting on his bed, his hair all tousled with only a pair of blue boxer briefs on. The sight of his sculptured muscular body took my breath away. I still could not get used to the idea that he was my husband.

How in the world did I ever get so lucky?

"Excuse me for a moment." Jackson stood up and went into the bathroom as I crawled back into bed. I tossed the heavy comforter across my legs and looked around his room. It was not a whole lot different than the one he had back in Chicago. It was obvious that he had taken only those items that would not contradict the age he was posing as with him. The artifacts that showed his true age were still here.

I crawled back out of bed and walked over to his dresser. His college degree from BU hung proudly on the wall beside it. His bookcase held dozens and dozens of various paperbacks and old college textbooks. His graduation cap with the tassel still attached was propped up in the corner on one side and his high school diploma on the other. There were various little graduation trinkets with the year proudly displayed and other little mementos. Beside the bookcase was a corkboard that held many sports awards from his former high school days, team photos, pictures of old friends, concert stubs, and all the silly things that are important enough to display. Then a prom picture caught my eye. Jackson was dressed in a black tux with a hot pink rose pinned to his jacket. He wore a black fedora and looked gorgeous. The girl beside him had long blond hair, an hourglass figure, bright blue eyes. and a short strapless black gown on. She was beyond anything I could ever hope to be. Jackson had his arm around her waist. She was turned towards him with her hand resting loosely on his chest showing off her hot pink rose wrist corsage. There were several other pictures of them with other classmates standing in front of a limo all smiling and getting ready to leave for the prom.

"That's Brittany. She was my high school girlfriend." Jackson slid up behind me and wrapped his arms tightly around my waist. He leaned down and kissed my neck.

"She's gorgeous." I kept looking at the picture of the two of them.

"I'm sorry her picture is still up. It was there when I left for BU and I guess I just never bothered to remove it. After graduation we spent all our time trying to gather information about you and then we moved to Chicago."

He reached over my shoulder to remove the picture. "Guess I should remove it."

I placed my hand over his. "I'm not worried about some girl you dated over four years ago. It's fine. Leave it be." He dropped his hand back around me. "For now, anyway." I turned and kissed him fiercely.

We stumbled back over to the bed and fell on it. We giggled and continued kissing. The sunlight was streaming in through the windows. I suddenly became very aware of the fact that the only time Jackson had seen me naked was in the dark and that was suddenly about to change. The intensity of our kisses increased, and all self-conscious thoughts fell by the wayside and nothing mattered but being with him.

*   *   *

It was almost one in the afternoon before we managed to make our way to the shower. Neither of us could stop smiling or giggling or being playfully stupid. We played and kissed and made love in the shower until long after the hot water was gone. I was freezing, and my skin was covered in goosebumps, but I didn't care. I couldn't get enough of him.

With every intention of getting ready to go over to Phoebe's for our first Christmas together, we failed miserably and instead without drying off we found ourselves back in his bed. The entire world outside his room drifted away and nothing existed but the two of us.

After we'd both finally gotten dressed to make our way over to Phoebe's I picked up the phone to call my house. Even with everything going on, I still missed my family dearly and it truly bothered me that my dad and Sidney were not here to witness my wedding. I paced around the living room waiting for my dad to pick up his cell.

"Hello, pumpkin, Merry Christmas," his voice sounded cheery.

"Merry Christmas, Daddy. How are you?"

"I'm fine. I miss you though. It doesn't seem like Christmas without you here."

"I know. I miss you too. It's weird for me too, being here for Christmas. But Boston is beautiful. Jackson showed me around the University. I love it," I told him.

"Good, I'm glad. You sound happy," he remarked.

"I am. I'm having a great time. Jackson's family is so sweet. They've been taking really good care of me, so you have nothing to worry about."

"I wasn't worried," he informed me. "But someone wants to talk to you. She's standing here huffing at me." He laughed. "I love you, pumpkin. Have a great time and be careful. I'll see you soon."

"Okay Dad, I will. I love you too."

"Hold on, here's Sidney." I heard the muffled sounds of him passing the phone to my sister.

"Merry Christmas, Pigeon." Sidney's voice rang in my ears.

"Pigeon? Why are you calling me Pigeon?" I asked.

"Pigeon's take flight. Isn't that what you did? Take flight to Boston to your little love nest away from Mom and Ethan?" she teased.

"Well, Merry Christmas to you too. And no, I didn't exactly take flight. The Chandlers invited me to spend Christmas with them and I accepted. Anything's better than sitting around being ignored by them for the entire break," I explained.

"I know. I talked a little to Mom and she's adamant about your wedding. She even gave me grief about my relationship with Landon. Now I'm not so sure about him showing up tomorrow."

"I'm sorry. It's my fault she's giving you grief, but at least she's still talking to you. That's one step ahead of me." I tried to make light of it.

"You know how she can be."

"So, how are you? How were your finals?" I attempted to change the subject.

"Fine. I'm glad they're over. Hopefully, the spring semester will be better," she said.

"Are you still having nightmares?" I asked as casually as I could.

"Some," her tone changed. "They're just weird dreams, is all. I think my imagination is working on overtime." She laughed awkwardly. "Either that or I've watched one too many Jane Austen movies."

Jane Austen movies?

"I don't get it? What do you mean, Jane Austen movies?" I gently nudged her to elaborate.

"Oh, it's nothing really. It's just weird. It's like being in that time period. I don't know why. For some reason it's where my brain likes to wander." Her voice sounded almost scared.

"That is strange." I tried to remain calm. This was the first clue I had perhaps of where Sidney was traveling if she did in fact inherit *EVE*.

"I know, right? It figures," she laughed. "Leave it to me to dream about the Romanticism period. Talk about bizarre."

"What are they like?" I treaded carefully.

"They're no big deal, Jocelyn." She paused for a moment. "So how is Mr. Wonderful? Still walking on water?"

"Seriously, Sidney? You of all people are going to go there?"

"I'm just teasing. When are you coming home?"

"After New Year's. When are you heading back to school?" I asked.

"Around the same time. I was hoping I'd get to see you. Maybe you can come up for a weekend or something after you get back." I was surprised and delighted by her offer.

"That'd be great. I'd love to."

"Well, I'd better get going. Give me a call when you get home. And have a great Christmas." Her voice was light and happy again.

"I will, I promise. Take care, Sidney."

"Always. Bye."

"Bye."

I looked down at the phone in my hand running over the conversation with Sidney once more. It was strange to say the least. I wasn't exactly sure what to make of it.

The Romanticism era? Is that where she's wandering off to every night? And what time period was that? For the life of me I couldn't remember. Early eighteenth century? Late nineteenth century? I had no idea. But just the fact that she told me that much was huge. Plus, it gave us something to go on. I couldn't wait to tell the rest of my new family and Uncle Nicholas about it.

*   *   *

"I was wondering if you two were going to make it." Phoebe greeted us when we turned up at her house at five o'clock.

"We're sorry, we got distracted," Jackson apologized while we took off our coats.

Phoebe glanced between the two of us standing there with our arms around one another and smiled. "I bet."

His parents wished us a Merry Christmas and ushered us into the living room where the rest of the family was gathered. Unlike my own home on Christmas, there was no television blaring in the background, only the soft sounds of *Mitch Miller* singing Christmas carols. His family and my uncle Nicholas were formally dressed in direct contrast to how mine lounged around in pajamas the entire day. The smell of turkey and stuffing filled the house. The adults were sipping red wine from elegant crystal. I stifled a smile thinking of how I was positive that at this moment my dad was sitting in his recliner wearing pajama bottoms and a sweatshirt drinking a cold beer.

Jackson and I sat down on the floor beside the tree where the evening before we had gotten married. Everyone was in great spirits and shared stories from Christmas pasts, childhood memories, and opened presents. I sat silently leaning against my husband, thoroughly enjoying the atmosphere. It was the polar opposite from the structure of my own home life and resembled more of the life I was becoming increasingly aware of in my *other* world.

By late evening, after the dishes were done and the little ones were sound asleep, the nine of us talked about our trip to New York in the morning. It was so peaceful and homey sitting in the living room around the blazing fire and the lights of the Christmas tree. Jackson and I cuddled up together on the floor beside the hearth. I told everyone about my conversation earlier with Sidney. We all agreed it was a good start, but it still was not enough to go on to know whether she had in fact inherited *EVE*. However, I noticed that Uncle Nicholas was unusually quiet. When I asked him, he simply remarked that he was tired. But still, I couldn't help but wonder if it was something more.

CHAPTER 32

Saturday, December 24, 1878

THE SNOW WAS FALLING in large fluffy flakes across the ashen sky. I climbed from my bed and stepped over to my bay window, pulling the drapes aside. The entire world was covered in a thick blanket of snow. It was so peaceful and beautiful. But even that did nothing to squash the watermelon sitting in my abdomen. I tried to swallow but couldn't. My throat was dry and rough as the full magnitude settled over me. I kept reassuring myself that I could get through this day. After all, I had already done this once before.

"Good morn,' Ms. Jocelyn, today's the big day." Mimi strolled happily through my door.

I gave her the best smile I could muster. "Yes," I squeaked.

Mimi laughed wholeheartedly. "Every bride feels like you do on her weddin' day."

"I think I'm going to be sick." I jumped up and ran over to the basin, losing everything I had eaten the day before.

She placed the sterling silver tray with my breakfast down upon the night table. "Tis just your nerves." She came over and carefully pulled my hair away from my face.

"I never thought I would be nervous. I have been waiting for this day for as long as I can remember." I sat down at the vanity and took a deep breath.

"Your bath is drawn, child, please eat somethin' before ya get a headache." Mimi gently squeezed my shoulder.

"Ah Mimi, I cannot eat. My stomach is in knots." I got up and began pacing across the foot of my bed. "Has Ms. Emily brought my dress over yet?"

"No, but tis early." My eyes fell to the clock resting on the mantle. Nine thirty. The wedding wasn't to begin until six o'clock.

"What was I thinking with a Christmas wedding? Christmas Eve of all things." I paused to wring my hands a bit.

Mimi picked my robe off the foot of my bed and held it out for me. "Time to get in the tub."

"Yes, Mimi." I slipped out of my nightgown and wrapped the robe around me.

*   *   *

I soaked in the hot water trying to relax and swallow the chicken bone that I felt for sure was stuck in my throat. Mimi finally forced some toast with strawberry jam down me after much urging and threats to call my mother in. I barely got it down with the help of some very strong coffee.

After my hair was washed and set, I lay down across my bed. It was almost noon and the downstairs were bustling with activity. I was dying to check things out for myself, but my mother had appeared a short time before and reiterated her speech from the night before. That I was to spend the day confined to my room since Jackson was milling about and I was not to see him before the ceremony. Instead, she insisted I take a nap so that I would be refreshed for the long eventful evening ahead.

Yet the hours passed so slowly, and sleep would not find me. I stared at the hearth and watched the flames dance about while I listened closely to the noise drifting up from below. My body was so nervous and anxious. My restless spirit fought to stay awake. My mind drifted back and forth between my two lives. I noticed the silver pocket watch resting in its dark blue box on my nightstand. I reached out and picked it up, thinking about how terrified and intrigued I was of it only a short while ago. It was hard to believe that this small gift had ignited such a change in my life and opened a whole new world. I gently placed it back in its case and settled back down under the duvet. I closed my eyes and tried to let the sounds below me drift away.

*   *   *

It was almost four in the afternoon when Olivia sat down beside me on my bed and gently woke me from my dreams. She looked so incredibly beautiful.

"Wake up, sleepyhead. It is time to get you married." A sly smile slid across her lips.

I pulled myself into a seated position. My mother, Mimi, Elizabeth, and Emily were arranging garments across my bed. Mimi stepped forward and helped me on with my robe. I took a seat at the vanity and at once hands were all about me pulling and twisting my hair in various fashions. Out of the corner of my eye I noticed a rather large garment case resting beside my dresser. I was sure that Emily and Mimi snuck that into my room earlier in the day.

Olivia and Elizabeth had on similar forest green taffeta gowns trimmed in matching green velvet. Bows rested atop their inlaid bustles and rippled in slight ruffles down the back of their full skirts. Emily had clearly outdone herself once again with her creative talents. Both wore their hair pulled back in chignons with traces of curls left loose to highlight their faces.

"How are you feeling?" Mother smiled down at me while Emily curled my hair.

I grinned back at her in the mirror. "All right," I squeaked, finding it hard to breathe even without my corset on yet.

She placed her hand on my shoulder. "I know you will be fine. Just remember to breathe."

"I believe Jackson is more nervous than you are." Emily laughed lightly. "I will be surprised if he remembers which way to put his pants on. When I left earlier he was tearing around the entire downstairs trying to find his vest for almost thirty minutes before he realized he was already wearing it."

"I's recall all your brothers was like that before they married." Mimi's full chuckle filled the room. "They's quite a site, they was."

"Yes, yes they were," Mother agreed, trying to pin back some fallen curls from her own hair.

*   *   *

Emily helped me drape her full-length ivory coverlet over my shoulders and gently placed the hood over my hair. She handed me the mink muff that matched it perfectly and wiped a tear off her cheek. Only she and Mimi had been allowed to see me in her gown before the wedding ceremony. We had wanted it to be a surprise. I didn't have the heart to tell her that Jackson already knew about the dress.

"You are a gorgeous bride my dear. My son is a very lucky man." She embraced me gently so as not to wrinkle any part of me.

"I am the lucky one. Thank you for raising such a man. I promise to take good care of him." I kissed her cheek.

"I know you will, my dear." She stepped back and straightened her gown. "Now, we best get going. Everyone has already left, and your father is downstairs waiting for you."

She hurried down the stairs and I heard her talking to Phoebe for a moment. Then the front door closed behind them.

My footsteps echoed on the stairs in the vacant house. The silence was deafening, void of the servant's footsteps and voices. It was a rare occasion to find the house in such a state. I stopped in the foyer and did one last turnabout absorbing all the little silly things I had taken for granted. My hand rested on the banister while my eyes drifted towards the top of the stairs.

I could picture the images of two small children climbing upon the railings and sliding swiftly down only to be met by a scolding Mimi at the foot of the stairs. I smiled to myself, remembering how much fun William and I had trying to get a rise out of her.

She would scold us again and again, but we never listened. She was sure one of us was going to break our necks sliding down the banister. I took a deep breath and sighed audibly.

I would miss this home so much and I could not help but wonder where I was going to find myself waking up in the morning.

My father opened the front door with great haste. "My goodness, Jocelyn. I swear you are going to be late for your own wedding. Come along, child. We should have been at the church ten minutes ago."

"Yes, Father, I am coming." I crossed over the foyer to the threshold for the last time as a single woman, closing the door behind me and leaving my childhood forever. I carefully walked down the steps towards my future as Mrs. Jackson Chandler.

The evening air was brisk, and I could see my breath as my father helped me into the carriage. He draped the heavy quilt over my lap before he seated himself across from me. Eddie took the reins and the carriage lunged forward. I shivered in the cold and leaned back against the seat.

"I cannot believe this day arrived so soon. I confess I have been dreading it since your birth." My father leaned forward and placed his hand over my muff. "While I am quite pleased with your choice, I still feel the sorrow of waking up in the morning and finding your room empty. A part of me wishes to keep you my little girl forever. But alas, I know I must let you go since you found it necessary to grow up on me."

"I know, Father, a part of me wishes I could stay eight years old forever. Willow Pines has been the only home I have ever known."

"I know you will be very happy and very well taken care of. Jackson is a good man." He smiled lovingly.

The carriage pulled up in front of the church more rapidly than I could ever recall before. Every muscle in my body tensed and I struggled greatly to breathe beneath my corset and stays. Eddie opened the door and offered me his hand. He held a slight smile across his face that was quite rare for a man of his calm gentle nature.

I took his hand and willed myself to step down from the carriage. My whole body was numb, and I felt like I was drowning in both excitement and fright. My foot did not register the ground beneath it as my knees went out from under me.

Father lunged quickly from the carriage along with Eddie and grabbed me before I collapsed completely to the frozen ground.

"Jocelyn!" Father's voice rang hollow in my ears as four arms wrapped around me.

"I'm . . . I'm . . ." I stumbled with words. "I am all right." I steadied myself holding onto the two of them. "I got a little light-headed."

"Are you sure?" Father studied me not with the eyes of a physician but those of a concerned father.

"Yes, I am sure." I offered him a weak smile. "Are you ready?"

"Are you?"

I nodded and took his arm. Eddie reached into the carriage and took out my bouquet of white lilies and violets and handed them to me before walking up the church steps. He paused with his hand on the doorknob waiting for us to approach. I looked up for a moment at the skies above. The stars had just arrived and began sparkling in the cloudless night. My father followed by gaze just as a lone star streaked between the trees.

"Make a wish, my dear."

"You make one Father, mine is about to come true."

He kissed me gently on the cheek, and I squeezed his arm and we began walking up the steps together.

Eddie opened the doors as we reached the top. The wedding march began to drift swiftly through the hall and everyone stood, turning towards us. Eddie helped me quickly remove my cover and took his place beside the door holding my things for me. It seemed he had the best spot in the house. He could see everything from where he stood.

I placed my hand on my father's arm and took the first step forward. I squeezed his arm a little tighter as we slowly approached, and I saw Jackson standing up at the alter smiling brightly at me. I noticed his hands were shaking slightly and he looked a shade paler than normal. Emily wasn't kidding when she said he was nervous.

He looked so incredibly handsome. His dark grey suit fit him perfectly and showed off his broad chest and brilliant green eyes. William and Alexander stood beside him both with slight smiles across their faces. On the other side of the aisle stood Olivia and Elizabeth, each holding their lilies and watching me try not to stumble towards them.

The faces of everyone I had ever known were staring back at us. My mother and Emily were crying softly as was Rachel, Lizette. and Phoebe. I blinked away from them and turned my eyes back to Jackson. As far as I was concerned, we were the only two people there. I kept repeating . . . *one step at a time, once I reach Jackson everything will be fine.*

Pastor Jacobs motioned for everyone to be seated when we finally reached the altar. He opened up with a prayer before my father kissed me one last time and placed my hands in Jackson's. Yet, before he took his seat beside Mother, he placed his hand on Jackson's arm and whispered something in his ear that I couldn't hear. Jackson grinned slightly and nodded in return.

I handed Olivia my bouquet and faced Jackson, each of my hands holding his. My eyes embraced his while Pastor Jacobs rambled on for what felt like an eternity. My body still felt numb and the whole ceremony passed by in a blurred haze. We each recited our parts perfectly and finally said our "I do's." Jackson slipped a beautiful white gold band with several small diamonds encased in it on my ring finger with the biggest smile I had ever seen across his shapely lips. I blushed brightly and took his ring, a simple white gold band, from Olivia and slid it on his finger with trembling hands. I gazed back up at his gorgeous face and heard the minister say, "You may kiss your bride."

Jackson wrapped his arms about me and kissed me deeply. Fire raced through every fiber of my being and I embraced him back. Reluctantly, he pulled away with a cheesy grin.

"Ladies and gentlemen, I would like to introduce for the very first time, Mr. and Mrs. Jackson Chandler," Pastor Jacobs announced loudly.

Everyone in the church stood up and applauded. It was then that I noticed standing in the back of the church was not only Eddie but Mimi, Sarah, Cora, and our entire newly hired house staff. I was so happy to see them all there.

Jackson and I stepped down from the altar and made our way through the crowd that gathered quickly around us. Several minutes later the cold air hit our faces like razor blades after being so long inside the hot stuffy church.

He helped me climb into his awaiting carriage and stuffed my dress in around me. "We did it! Can you believe it? We actually did it, Mrs. Chandler!" He beamed and climbed in beside me.

"I love the sound of that." He leaned over and pulled me closer to him as Barnaby launched the carriage forward. Jackson wrapped me in his arms and kissed me passionately.

"Mrs. Chandler," he whispered softly in my ear and brushed his lips over my neck. I felt goose bumps run over my entire body and not from the frigid night air.

"I love you." I brought my mouth to his and devoured it.

"I love you," he replied breathlessly.

I could not get enough of him. I loved the way his lips molded to mine, hot and firm yet soft and caressing all at the same time. His arms wrapped around me with a gentle force compelling me to do anything he wanted. One of my hands held onto the back of his jacket tightly while the other slid gracefully through the back of his hair, each pulling him into me, crushing me against the back and side of the carriage. I wanted him so badly. I couldn't have cared less about going to the reception, taking pictures and cutting the cake. All I wanted, all I would ever want, was right here in my arms. Nothing else in the world existed but the two of us.

Barnaby halted the carriage at the porch steps of my parents' home and cleared his throat loudly. Jackson and I relented and released each other from our passionate spell. "Guess we have to make an appearance," he said sadly.

"I wish we didn't."

"Me too." Yet, Barnaby opened the door and offered me his hand to help me out of the carriage.

"Congratulations, Mrs. Chandler."

"Thank you, Barnaby." I stepped down and waited for Jackson.

"I's took a turn or two through the park on our way here, Mr. Chandler. I wanted to give everyone time to return from the church." He winked at Jackson who grinned and nodded in return.

"Thank you, Barnaby. Please come in and share a piece of cake with us."

"Thank you, Mr. Chandler."

Jackson took my hand and led me up the steps as Barnaby held open the front door. We were greeted by an outcry of cheers and greetings. Everyone surrounded us conveying their congratulations and best wishes. My mother pushed her way through the crowd of family and friends.

"Pictures first . . . pictures first." She grabbed my arm and tugged us through the commotion into the front room by the hearth. I glanced back towards Jackson with a slight smile on my face. I knew each of us was thinking the same thought . . . these are the photos that I had discovered in the old album in 2009.

By the time the pictures were over I was seeing spots from the numerous flashes going off in our faces. I tried to close my eyes but that only made things much worse. I held loosely onto Jackson's arm to steady myself. He guided me towards the dining room where Sarah and Mimi had put out an amazing buffet of food with a tiered caked in the center that was easily twice the size as the one she had made for my birthday.

With the entire house in commotion, the cutting of the cake and everyone smothering us for the next several hours, we never got five minutes alone. I could hardly breathe in my gown and I was quickly growing tired with the whole fiasco of it all. I only wanted to be alone with my new husband.

I had been dreaming of this night for years and now that we were officially married, I could not get a word to him.

*   *   *

The house had begun to clear around ten o'clock. Jackson and I settled down on the lounge to breathe for a moment. I leaned my head against his shoulder and closed my eyes. All I wanted to do was go to sleep. I began to wonder if I would even have the strength to be conscious long enough to have the night I'd been dreaming of for as long as I could remember.

Robert stood and walked over to the hearth with Emily and raised his glass. "I would like to formally toast Jocelyn and Jackson. I wish you two all the happiness in the world." Everyone took a drink believing that was the end of his toast but instead Robert continued. "Now it is typically the tradition that the parents of both the bride and groom give them a special wedding gift to enhance their new lives together. However, in this case it has been very difficult to come up with something since you are having so much difficulty finding a suitable new home. Well, we put our heads together and I believe we have come up with a solution that will make you both very pleased." My parents were seated beside one another holding hands with a smile across their faces that told me they were in on it as well.

Our siblings and their families lined the walls in a fashion that made me feel uncomfortable. My eyes scanned over the room, carefully looking for some sort of facial expression that would give me a hint as to what was coming next. There was nothing.

Robert continued, "Emily and I purchased a home for the two of you."

Immediately my heart sank to my feet. Jackson and I had searched every available home within a ten-mile radius and could not find one suitable home that we could agree upon. I had finally accepted that we would stay with his parents and start building a new home in the spring.

"Now, Jocelyn, wipe that look off your face. Do you think I would allow him to proceed with this without having some say so in it?" Emily laughed. I hadn't realized I physically cringed when he dropped the news.

"Sorry," I said softly.

"What she meant to say," Jackson glanced my way before looking back at his father, "is that we looked at all the homes in the area and did not find anything, that we felt, portrayed our personality." I could tell he chose his words very carefully.

"But somehow you managed to miss one particular house," my mother smiled coyly.

Robert reached into the inside pocket and handed Jackson a cream enveloped tied with a green ribbon.

"What is this?" Jackson took it with slight hesitation.

"Open it." Emily shifted impatiently.

Our eyes locked for a moment before he slowly untied the ribbon and pulled out the contents. It was a single silver key. "Okay. It's a key." Jackson looked confused as he stated the obvious.

Everyone around us broke out in a low giggle as if the two of us were ignorant and did not get the punch line.

"It is a key to your new house." William came up behind us and slapped him lightly on the shoulder.

"All right, but where is it?" I locked eyes with my mother, knowing she'd crack under the pressure. But for once, she didn't. She and my father continued their stoic stance.

"Our wedding present to you both is a new house." Emily could hardly contain herself.

"And our gift was the furnishings," my mother piped up. "It is all ready for you to move right in."

I was speechless. My whole body went numb and I felt lightheaded. There were no words to express the shock and gratitude I was feeling. I placed my hand over my new husband's. He sat stone faced, stunned and at a loss for words.

"My goodness, I cannot believe this. Thank you all so very much," I managed to squeak out.

"Emily and I with the help of these other ladies," she nodded towards my extended family, "picked out the new furniture, wallpaper, and accessories for your new place. It was quite the ordeal keeping it all a secret from you both. But we had to include them because we wanted to make sure that we picked a décor that matched your taste."

Jackson turned the key over and over between his fingers nervously. "Silly question, but where is this house located?" He scanned over the faces around him.

"Haven't you figured it out by now, little brother?" Alex teased him only to be met with a glare from Jackson. I knew he was as tired as me, and I don't believe that either of us was in the mood to play games. "All right," Alex glanced over at his father who nodded in return. "Your new home is next door."

"Are you serious?" My eyes immediately landed on Olivia.

"I cannot believe you did not figure it out before. All those times you saw me watching the house being renovated from the window, I thought for sure you knew." She grinned widely as she got up and walked over to us.

"Are you all right with this?" I whispered.

"Are you kidding, it was my idea." Very few things shocked me these days, but her words completely floored me. She leaned down and hugged me tightly. "I know you two will have a wonderful life there. Besides, this way I still get to see you every day."

"True. Thank you so much."

"Well now, I am sure you both would like to see your new home. I believe Bertina and Cora have everything ready for you." My mother rose and placed her hand gently on my arm.

*   *   *

Jackson carried me over the threshold of our new home and put me down in the foyer. "I apologize for not carrying you upstairs except I do not know which bedroom ours is," he chuckled.

"If it is all right with you, I would like to look around the house first and see what they have done."

"Of course," Jackson agreed.

Cora walked around the corner. "Good evenin', I thought I heard you." She embraced us both. "Congrats."

"Thank you," we replied in unison.

"Would you mind showing us around the house? I am afraid we are a little lost." I felt so foolish. This house had practically been my second home as a child, in both my lives.

"O' course."

We explored our new home with Cora in the lead. Tamesha, Davonte, Betsy, and Bertina were in the kitchen relaxing around the small informal table drinking tea and enjoying a piece of wedding cake from my parents' home. The four of them jumped to their feet when we walked in the room.

"I sorry, sir." Davonte immediately hung his head and the other three followed.

I looked over at Jackson confused. "Please, sit down and relax. It has been a long day," Jackson smiled. The four of them nervously sat back down. "Well, I guess now is as good a time as any to talk to all of you." He cleared his throat and leaned against the counter. Cora and I stood off to the side of him not sure what he was going to say.

"I know that the four of you have lived with the Seaton's for many years and that he was a very demanding, strict, and unpleasant sort of man. Cora, on the other hand, is the daughter of Mimi and Eddie and was born into the Timmons's household. Therefore, she has been with Mrs. Chandler since birth."

He glanced over at the two of us. "I believe Cora is about ten years older than my wife. Is that right?" We both nodded but remained silent.

"Anyway, I know our mothers Mrs. Timmons and Mrs. Chandler went over your job descriptions with you when you were hired. If you have any questions, please do not hesitate to ask Cora, myself, or my wife. This is your home now and we want you all to feel comfortable here. If there is anything that you need, please tell us. We are a great deal relaxed than your previous employer. Any questions?" Jackson searched their faces for some sort of recognition. He received none. They all just stared blankly back at him.

"Well then, are your living quarters suitable to your liking?" The four nodded without meeting his eye. "Is there anything you need?" he questioned.

"No, sir," They answered in unison.

"Very well, have a good night. Sleep well." He took my hand and Cora led the way out of the room.

"I beg ya, pardon sir, but I think it may take some time before they feel comfortable here. They seem very skittish with me," Cora explained walking into the parlor.

"What a lovely room!" I remarked spinning around slowly taking it all in. "I cannot believe it. This is exactly what I would have chosen had I been given the chance."

"I am so pleased you like it, my dear."

Cora continued the tour giving us a glimpse of everything from the cellar to their quarters on the third floor. The ladies in our lives had done an astounding job in transforming the old Adams's estate into something entirely new. It resembled nothing of its former self . . . thankfully.

Cora saved our bedroom for last. She opened the door and stood aside. "Now the master's quarters." Jackson scooped me up and carried me into the bedroom laughing. She closed the door behind us and disappeared.

"Can you believe this? I cannot fathom the amount of work and money our families must have put into this place." Jackson set me down on the corner of our new oversized canopy bed.

"I must admit, I was very worried when I first learned what they had done. After all that had happened here with Mr. and Mrs. Adams I thought I could not bear to live in this home."

"I had the same thoughts, my dear. Luckily, there is no proof they ever resided in this place." He casually strolled about the room, taking it all in.

Our bedroom furniture, like all the others in the house, was a brilliant cherry wood. There were two large armoires in the room, matching bedside tables on either side of the large canopy bed with cornflower blue drapes. A large dresser, a vanity with a taupe coverlet and all my accessories were waiting for me beside a full-length mirror. The walls were painted taupe to match the duvet with its decorative cornflower blue design throughout. It was such an elegant room so tastefully decorated.

As I looked around one thing stood out above everything else. On the mantel above the roaring fire rested the glass vase from my old bedroom. My wedding bouquet of white lilies and violets were artfully arranged as a centerpiece in the room. I knew no one else but Mimi would have thought to do such a thing and it made me smile to myself.

"Are you happy, Mrs. Chandler?" Jackson came over and sat down beside me.

"Yes, very much so."

He leaned over and took me in his arms. "I have been waiting all day to be alone with you."

"Me too," I whispered and kissed him fiercely falling back on our new bed.

CHAPTER 33

Saturday, December 26, 2009

JACKSON AND I delayed our departure by a day, so we could drop my uncle Nicholas off at the airport that afternoon with promises that we would see each other again soon. He was such a sweet man, a little quirky but had a true heart of gold. I thanked him repeatedly for coming to my wedding and for giving me away. We exchanged cell numbers and email addresses before he left. I told him that I would try to come see him on spring break and that I would keep him updated on things with Sidney.

It was harder to say good-bye to him than I initially thought it would be. I really enjoyed the time I got to spend with him and he patiently answered the million and one questions I had. Plus, he was my one genetic link to my *other* life in this one and that gave us a truly special bond. I realized this as I hugged him tightly and gave him a kiss on the cheek. Jackson and I watched him until he disappeared through the security check-point. I wiped the tears off my cheeks and took Jackson's hand as we walked away.

*   *   *

Jackson gave me a tour of his little section of the world. The life he had before he realized I was on this plane with him. He showed me the elementary school he went to, the intermediate school, and the high school he graduated from.

He parked in one of the high school's many lots. We got out and walked around the grounds. He pointed out the tennis courts and confessed that he and his siblings as well as his parents all played.

And I confessed that I had never played outside of gym class. We walked over to the football fields and strolled around the track while he gave me a detailed account of his four years of football on this field.

It was so strange for me to think of him having this entire life that I was never a part of.

He slipped his hand into mine as we crossed the field and climbed the bleachers to the top. I stood leaning on the railing looking out over the vast grounds, the trees, and the houses off in the distance. The wind was a little stronger at this height and it whipped around us. causing Jackson to pull me a little closer to him.

Next, Jackson took me by this little café that was close to his high school where apparently, he and his classmates hung-out. It was a charming little place that truly looked like something out of the fifties with counter service, spinning bar stools, old art décor, padded booths, and even a jukebox in the far corner. He raved about the fountain cherry and vanilla cokes and the hand-dipped milkshakes.

We slid into a booth, ordered bacon cheeseburgers, fries, and chocolate shakes. Even after we ordered our food, I was looking over the menu that was printed to appear as if it was made in the fifties. I was so engrossed in taking in the ambiance of the place that I hadn't seen the three guys that walked up to our booth until they spoke.

"Hey, Jackson, how ya doing?" a tall man with dirty blond hair and broad shoulders said.

"Hey Dylan, what's going on?" Jackson stood up and greeted his friends.

"Not much. I'm working at Coswell Marketing firm in New York. I just came home for Christmas because my mom insisted." He rolled his eyes with a smile.

"Congratulations." He looked over at me as if he was just remembering I was sitting there. "Oh, I'm sorry. Guys, I'd like to introduce you to my wife, Jocelyn. Jocelyn, this is Dylan, Jerimiah, and Chris. We all graduated from high school together."

I stood up and shook each of their hands. "It's very nice to meet you all."

"Wait a minute," Jerimiah looked over at Jackson. "Did you say wife? When the hell did this happen? And why weren't we invited?"

"Won't you guys join us?" I scooted over allowing Dylan and Chris to slip in beside me while Jerimiah sat down beside Jackson just as the waitress brought our food. The three guys placed their orders quickly before the waitress had a chance to walk away.

Chris, a man with strawberry blonde hair, blue eyes, and a charming smile reached over and stole a fry off Jackson's plate. "So, congratulations, man. I can't believe you got married. That's great."

"I still can't believe we weren't invited." Jerimiah playfully complained. He had brown hair, brown eyes, and was the short, stocky one of the group.

"Sorry, it was a very small ceremony with only family two days ago. We didn't want all the fanfare of having a big wedding," Jackson informed them.

"Just family. No friends?" Chris asked.

"Yeah, that's right." Jackson looked uncomfortable.

"Did you two meet at BU?" Dylan inquired.

"No, in Chicago. I'm taking a year off before I start law school. My dad got transferred there and I thought it would be fun to spend some time in Chicago before hitting the books," Jackson said.

"I'm guessing you enjoyed Chicago." Dylan glanced over at me.

"You could say that," Jackson laughed.

"So, how long are you in town for?" Jerimiah asked.

"We're leaving for New York tomorrow on our honeymoon," Jackson said.

"Well, this sucks." Jerimiah nudged Jackson. "We didn't get to throw you a bachelor party."

"That's right, man. You know we're going to have to rectify that," Dylan laughed.

"Not anytime soon, I'm afraid. After we get back from New York, we're heading back to Chicago the next day." Jackson shrugged.

"You suck!" Jerimiah gave him a playful shove just as the waitress reappeared with their food.

The five of us sat in silence for several minutes enjoying our food. It was so weird being around Jackson's friend and immersed in his world. I had become so accustomed to him being in my world that I really hadn't ever witnessed his. But the more I saw, the more I was intrigued about his life in Boston.

"Did you guys play football also?" I asked between bites.

"Football, basketball, outrageous parties, and study hall pranks on the teacher. The four of us also won the scavenger hunt on senior night." Chris laughed. "I still can't believe your dad covered our asses on that one." The other three joined in the laughter.

"What did you guys do?" It was so hard for me to imagine Jackson doing anything foolish or ridiculous. It was so out of character for the man I knew.

"Well, ya see, our school has this long-standing tradition of senior night pranks, girls versus the guys. Each year there's a different sort of theme if you will. So, our senior year the theme was signs," Dylan explained.

"Signs?" I was confused.

"Yeah, signs. As in who can collect the most," Chris added.

"I still don't understand." I looked between the four of them.

"It was a contest to see who could steal the most signs. Anyway, we all set out in our buddy Jim's truck. He had this old beater that we all used to go off-roading in. Well, we all piled in the cab with our other friends, Bobby and Chad, in the bed. So, with a couple coolers filled with ice cold beers, we headed out along some back roads outside of town, some pretty curvy roads that have some fairly sharp curves and of course, being so far out in the middle of nowhere, there are no street lights. So, we dug out all the road signs between two small towns, then stole a few realtor signs, a couple mailboxes, and several street signs. When we got back to the school we lined our trophies along the side of the building. We kicked the girls' asses. We had stolen twice as many signs as they did. And then we backed up several trucks up to the school and spray-painted Seniors 06' on the side of the school," Dylan said with obvious pride.

"Oh, my god!" My jaw dropped, and I stared over at Jackson. I could not believe he ever did anything like that.

"But that was just half of it. The following Monday morning when we arrived at school there were two local police cars and one state police car parked up by the entrance. Apparently, we had done thousands of dollars of damage by removing the road signs, caused two separate accidents by drivers who weren't familiar with the roads, and committed a federal offense by stealing the mailboxes," Jerimiah added.

"We were all a little nervous when all the seniors were called down individually and questioned. And of course, our group of friends was known to have been responsible for pulling pranks," Jackson chuckled.

"But it was all speculation. They never proved it was us who snuck into the teacher's lounge and put the chocolate ex-lax in the coffeemaker," Chris grinned.

"Wait . . . what?" I interrupted completely astonished.

"You know, the coffeemaker in the teacher's lounge? In our school they always had an industrial size coffeemaker since almost all the teachers live on coffee. So, Jackson snuck in there during our third period study hall and took one of those chocolate ex-lax bars, broke it into pieces, and hid it in the fresh coffee grounds and brewed a fresh pot." Jerimiah kept laughing and I could hardly make out what he was saying.

"I guess our little prank gave about a dozen teachers screaming diarrhea." Dylan laughed so hard he grabbed a napkin to wipe the tears from his eyes.

"You did that?" My eyes turned towards Jackson.

"It sounds terrible, but god it was funny." Jackson was laughing right along with them.

"Best homecoming prank ever," Chris added.

"So, what happened with the police? Did you guys get caught?" I asked.

"Everyone who was involved, guys and girls, all agreed that we were at my house hanging out and watching a movie. When they questioned each of us our stories all matched. And since it was my house we were supposedly at, they called my dad at the office." Jackson took a sip of his chocolate milkshake and continued. "Well of course, I thought we were doomed since my dad knew full well I was out running around with the guys. I sat there almost sweating in the chair with these officers staring down at me waiting for me to get busted. But when our principle, Mr. Wright, called my dad, my dad claimed all of us were hanging at our house. It was priceless watching Mr. Wright's face drop and turn red because my dad was a well-respected attorney and no one, including the police, were about to call him a liar." Jackson shrugged like it was no big deal and took another bite of his burger.

"I can't believe you did that." I shook my head, absolutely stunned by this new side of Jackson that was completely foreign to me.

"Did you ever tell her about the roosters?" Dylan asked Jackson.

Jackson shook his head.

"Roosters?" I looked between the four guys.

"On the last day of school before Christmas break, the four of us snuck out during lunch period to Jim's truck where we had four roosters in this crate. We snuck them into the school and let them loose. Two upstairs and two downstairs," Jerimiah chuckled. "The teachers had a hell of a time trying to catch them. And god, they shit all over the hallways."

"Weren't you worried about the cameras?" I inquired.

"Our school didn't have cameras back then. They installed them the year after we graduated," Chris informed me.

"I can't imagine why," Dylan laughed.

We spent another hour with Jackson's friends. I sat there and listened to them retelling stories of all the silly antics they did throughout their youth. It was an eye-opening experience. I never would have thought Jackson could do such things.

It was the exact opposite of the man I knew in Chicago. Even when Cody, Zak, and my brother were up to something devious, Jackson never participated in it.

I really enjoyed getting to know these guys. I had such a good time and could see they were more than a little mischievous when they got together. By the time we left we had made plans to get together with them when we came back to Boston next summer.

When we climbed in the Durango on our way home I leaned over to Jackson and kissed him on the cheek. He smiled back and pulled out into the early evening traffic.

"What was that for?" he asked.

"For not being as perfect as I thought you were."

"I'm not perfect," he chuckled. "Far from it actually."

"It was really nice to meet your friends from school and hear about the things you used to do. It's like you were a totally different person from the man I know in Boston."

"How so?" Jackson glanced over at me while waiting for the light to turn.

"Well, you're just so serious in Chicago." I was trying to find the right words. "It's like, there you're this straight and proper young man who never misbehaves. Yes, I know it sounds silly but it's weird. It's like here, you did all the young and silly things our friends are doing there. You know what I mean."

"I was a teenager when I did all that. I guess back then it seemed like a fun thing to do just to see if we could get away with it. Now, if I behaved like that there and got caught, it would cause me and my parents a world of trouble since I'm lying about my age and carrying false documents," he explained.

"What about your driver's license? Is that fake too?" I was curious.

"No. I carry my real license. So, I guess I would be in trouble if someone insisted on seeing it there." He smiled and pulled into the driveway.

"I just can't get over how wild you were in high school. It seems so out of character for you, Bae," I said, before climbing out of the car.

"Not really. I was young and stupid just like every other teenager." He came around the front of the Durango and pulled me close to him. "I had a great time in high school with my friends. But I must admit, it is sort of fun going to high school with you." He leaned down and gave me a kiss.

"Well, just for the record, our school is loaded with cameras. There's no way you could pull stunts like that there," I teased.

"I guess Zack, Cody, and I will have to be a little cleverer when we pull our senior prank this spring." He flashed a devious smile at me.

"Oh, good Lord . . ." I rolled my eyes at him and opened the front door.

CHAPTER 34

Sunday, December 25, 1878

WAKING UP on Christmas morning in our own home felt more like a dream than reality even as the sunlight broke through the drapes and found my face on my pillow. I rolled over to hide away from it only to come face to face with my new husband smiling softly at me.

"Merry Christmas, Mrs. Chandler."

"Merry Christmas, my love. Did you sleep well?"

"Very well and you?"

"Wonderful." He leaned over and kissed me gently. "I cannot recall having ever had a better night of sleep."

"Me neither." Jackson rolled on top of me, kissing me deeply. I wrapped my arms around him, feeling the fire soar between us once again.

*   *   *

An hour later Jackson climbed out of bed and washed up before he dressed in his dark blue suit. I lay there silently watching him closely. I had never observed his morning routine before and found it rather fascinating. He brushed his teeth carefully before he stood in front on my vanity mirror and brushed his wavy dark brown hair. A smile spread across the shapely lips of his reflection when he noticed I was watching him.

"Are you going to stay in bed all day, my dear? I believe your family is expecting us for Christmas dinner in about an hour." He walked back over and sat down beside me.

"I would rather stay here with you."

"I would too, but alas we cannot," he grinned, got up, and walked over to the door. "So, get up or we will be late." Then he was gone.

I leaned back for a moment against the mountain of pillows rethinking everything that had happened last night and this morning. It had been perfect in every way. I closed my eyes thinking about how different and yet alike Jackson was in our two lives. He seemed a little more like the man I recalled from 2009 when we were alone, but somehow that man felt so conservative in comparison with all the other men that flooded my high school days of that time. It was all so odd.

I heard a low knock on the door and half expected Mimi to be on the other side of it. "Mrs. Chandler, ya bath is ready." Cora barely opened the door.

"Thank you, Cora. I will be there directly." I climbed out of bed and grabbed my robe.

*   *   *

Christmas festivities were grander than usual. The smaller children were running around playing with the many new toys Santa Claus had brought them. Their excitement was contagious. It was easy to remember when it used to be my brothers and me in their shoes. There was a large part of me that hated the idea of waiting another ten years before Jackson and I could have a child of our own. Now that we were married I wanted one immediately although I knew it wasn't possible. However, that certainly did not stop my mother from bringing the topic into conversation right after dinner when the gentlemen were in the other room smoking cigars and drinking brandy.

"All I am saying is that I hope by next Christmas you and Jackson will have given us a new grandbaby." She at least had enough tact to wait until Olivia had retired for the evening citing a headache.

"Now do not rush them, Annabelle." Emily smiled over in my direction. "Give them some time to adjust to being married first."

"As long as they do not wait too long." My mother sipped her coffee.

"Mother," Lizette began, "do not pressure them. They have not even been married twenty-four hours yet."

"All right, all right." My mother waved her hand as if dismissing the topic. "On a happier note, Mrs. Maddox told me at the reception that Mr. Miller spoke with her husband about Ms. Elizabeth's hand. She said Mr. Miller was going to propose to Elizabeth today."

I nearly spit my coffee back into my mug but choked on it instead. "Oh, my goodness, are you serious?"

"Yes, that is what she told me."

I couldn't help it, I squealed like a small child. "How wonderful! I cannot believe this. I am so happy for her. Oh, I wish I could go over there and congratulate her."

"You can speak with her tomorrow." My mother poured herself a little more coffee from the sterling silver pot that rested on the matching tray before us.

"She must be ecstatic," I beamed. It was quickly shaping into a busy summer with Laurie's wedding and now possibly Elizabeth's as well.

CHAPTER 35

Sunday, December 27, 2009

JACKSON AND I headed out right after we finished breakfast. I was so excited to see New York City. I had always dreamed of seeing it and had never had the opportunity before. The drive seemed like nothing in comparison with our journey out here. Plus, there were so many things to see, even from the roadside. It was a beautiful day with clear skies. The sun was shining and there were only a few scattered fluffy clouds.

"How are you feeling?" Jackson asked, reaching over and taking my hand.

I tore my eyes away from my side window and looked over at him smiling. "Like this is all a dream. Like any minute I'm going to wake up back in my room and none of what transpired in the last week had ever happened."

Jackson chuckled a bit. "Sorry, it did. You are my wife. We are married and headed to New York City to enjoy our honeymoon."

"I know, but it still feels so surreal."

We checked into the Marriott shortly after one o'clock. The bellboy carried our bags up to the honeymoon suite. I felt so nervous and excited I could hardly contain myself as the elevator hummed its way to the top floor. Jackson finally placed his hands on my shoulders to stop me from rocking back and forth.

"I'm sorry, I hate elevators," I whispered, hoping the bellhop wouldn't hear me.

"Really?" he gave me a quizzical look.

"Yes, very much so."

"Since when?"

"For as long as I can remember. I hate enclosed spaces. They scare the life out of me." I glanced up at the numbers, waiting impatiently.

"I'm sorry, you should have told me. We could have taken the stairs."

"I may be in shape but even I am not that ambitious." I smirked up at him. "Don't worry, I am fine."

The view from our room was breathtaking, from what I could see a safe distance from the window. I wasn't about to admit to Jackson that I was deathly afraid of heights after confessing my fear of elevators. After the bellhop had placed our luggage in the bedroom and Jackson tipped him I stood in the middle of the living room area and absorbed the splendor of it all. I had only seen hotel rooms like this one in movies, never in real life. This was more than I could imagine for a honeymoon suite.

"This room is so beautiful. Everything about it, the view, the furniture . . . everything." I spun around taking it all in while Jackson laughed at me. "Not to be rude, but how can we possibly afford something like this?" I could not even fathom what this place must cost.

"Don't worry about it. It is a wedding gift from my siblings." He walked over and took me in his arms. "I am glad you like it."

"Are you kidding? I love it." I gave him a gentle kiss and rested my head down on his chest.

"Want to get cleaned up and go exploring?"

"Definitely." That was exactly what I wanted to do.

*   *   *

New York City was everything I had imagined it to be and more. It was chilly out but not cold and thankfully, there was no rain in the forecast. I threw on skinny jeans and a maroon shirt. Then a woolen blend black and cream checked knee-length coat with a black cap and the new black boots I had gotten for my birthday.

The wind howled around us between the tall buildings, forcing me to wrap my black fleece scarf tighter around me and dig my gloves out of my pockets.

Jackson was wearing jeans and his bomber jacket with his olive-green scarf. He was a striking sight to behold. I noticed several women turn to look at him when we passed by. I couldn't help smiling to myself and thinking, *he's my husband*. I reached over and took his hand in mine.

We toured all the attractions that all the tourists hit: Times Square, Rockefeller Center, the monument at the World Trade Centers, and everything in between. It was late afternoon before either of us realized that we had not eaten since we had left Boston early that morning. We finally settled into a small café as the sun was beginning to set.

The place was a dive and probably hadn't been updated since it opened. The checkered floors were, once upon a time, black and white. The fake red leather coverings on the bar stools were cracked and, in some places, ripped open. The place looked as if it couldn't possibly have passed any health code regulation.

But Alex had told Jackson that it had some of the best hamburgers in the city and insisted that we try it while we were there. We settled into a booth in the back and had the best greasy cheeseburger and hot chocolate I'd ever tasted in my life.

"Are you enjoying yourself, Mrs. Chandler?" Jackson asked over his fountain cherry coke.

"Very much so. You?"

"Yes."

"I wish we didn't have to go back to Chicago." I picked up a fry and absentmindedly played with it.

"I know, but we have to. You must finish high school. It's only another six months."

"Six months," I said softly, smearing the ketchup around my plate with the fry. "Sounds like an eternity."

"What do you want?" He reached over and placed his hand on mine to stop my fidgeting.

"I don't want to hide our marriage." I dropped the fry and looked up at him. "I honestly couldn't care less about having a wedding in June. In fact, I don't want to have it. It's pointless and a waste of money. All I want is to live with my husband."

"Are you ready to go home and tell your parents that we got married on Christmas Eve? Are you ready to tell your friends? Do you really believe you could live with the fallout?" He raised his eyebrows debatably.

"If it means that we get to live together then yes, I am."

"Are you serious?"

"Yes," I said with determination.

"We still have time to think about this before we head home. We should think about it for a few days and then decide what is best. There is no need to make a decision tonight."

"I am not going to change my mind," I told him.

"All right, but I just want you to consider how your dad is going to feel."

"I know he will be upset and hurt. I expect that. Still, he lives in that house the same as I do, and he knows how difficult it has become. He knows how miserable I am and that my mother and Ethan are doing everything to make it worse," I reasoned.

"I know, but are you ready to tell your friends? I am sure Jenna will be thrilled." He chuckled a bit.

"Honestly, I couldn't care less about what any of them think. Jenna never asked me what I thought when she hooked up with Kyle and he was practically our brother. I thought it was sick and twisted but I never opened my mouth. And Caitlyn has no room to talk, her relationship with Zak has been on and off again for years because he acts like a moron often. Plus, Hilary and Cody . . . well, there's nothing I can pick on about them," I laughed. "Except maybe that their relationship is too boring to be interesting."

"Wow, Mrs. Chandler. You really should learn to express yourself." He slurped his drink with a coy look on his face.

"Well for the last several years I have listened to them complain and brag and been supportive of their relationships whether I agreed with them or not, and when I need them, all three turned judgmental. You should hear some of their lame arguments like, I am beginning to sound like you." I mimicked Jenna's voice. "Seriously? Like having good grammatical skills is such a terrible asset. I swear to hear them talk about your proper grammar it's like you're an alcoholic drug-addict who got me hooked on heroin."

"I do not think they can be that bad," he laughed. "You are exaggerating just a bit."

"If I am, it's not by much."

It was completely dark outside by the time we left the café and headed back to the hotel. I held onto Jackson's arm and tried to act like I wasn't scared out of my mind. It made me extremely nervous to walk around downtown Chicago after dark and I knew my way around that city well. I did my best to act casual, but in my nervousness, I chatted excessively about nothing all the way back.

*   *   *

We shared a bottle of champagne and a long bubble bath in the oversized tub. Jackson had moved the champagne bucket filled with ice next to the tub and lit numerous candles around it while I was watching television. He disappeared into the bathroom a short time before and I was hoping the questionable diner we'd eaten at hadn't made him sick. I was pleasantly surprised when he finally showed me what he was up to.

I lowered myself into the mountain of bubbles filling the heat of the hot water absorb deeply into my chilled skin. "This is fabulous, thank you."

"I wanted to surprise you." He climbed in across from me and handed me a champagne glass.

"I thought you were getting sick," I laughed, and he blushed.

"Thankfully, no I was not."

"Good to hear it."

"Do you have any idea how beautiful you look in this light?"

"Not nearly as gorgeous as you." I sipped my bubbly.

"I cannot imagine sharing my life . . . either of my lives," he smiled, "with anyone other than you. You have made me the happiest man alive."

"I am so happy you came looking for me."

"Me too. I know things may appear odd to everyone in your life *here* and it is impossible to explain the truth to them. For that, I am sorry. But I am not sorry for making you my wife."

"I know my friends and family will never understand us. I know they believe we are insane, too young and that all of this happened too fast, but I do not care. I feel as if I have lived a lifetime within these last few months with all that has happened and I have learned, I realize that I have a long way to go before I can be as comfortable with *EVE* as you and your family are, but already the things I have seen has utterly amazed me."

"I am so happy you are transitioning so well."

"That is only because of you and your family. You all have been so wonderful and understanding. There is no way I could have made it through this without you." I reached out and took his hand in mine.

"It truly is an amazing gift."

"Yes, it is. Considering what I have seen already, it blows me away. I cannot wait until the barrier is completely down and I have full awareness of both time periods. I know you may have to muzzle me for the next several years or so after what happened with Phoebe *there*," I laughed, and he splashed me a little. "But it would be well worth it to know everything." I splashed him back.

"You say that now, but just wait until something there frustrates you to the point of tears and you cannot do anything about it because what would solve your problem has not been invented yet."

"Give me a for instance."

"Let me think." He finished off his glass and refilled it. "All right, for example, two years ago friends of ours, Clayton and Melanie, went out for a picnic by the lake with their two little girls. One of the girls got her pantaloons caught on something beneath the water. By the time Clayton got her to the shore, she was not breathing. Melanie and the other girl went for help, but the nearest house was over a mile away. Their daughter was already gone by the time your father, Patrick, got there."

"I remember that. It was awful."

"In that case, knowing CPR or having access to a hospital, ambulance or a cell phone could have been the difference between life and death," he explained.

"But those instances are rare are they not?" I took another sip and lowered myself deeper into the water.

"It depends on the situation; mare a case by case basis, but I do know we have all experienced it at one time or another."

"Okay, I see your point," I conceded. "Nevertheless, I am still excited about it."

"As you should be. And I promise I will be there to help you in every way I possibly can." Jackson floated over and kissed me deeply. He lifted my glass from my hand and set it on the side of the tub with his own. A devilish grin slid across his face. "Now if you have no further questions, I would like to enjoy this bubble bath with my beautiful wife."

Chapter 36

Sunday, January 1, 1879

JACKSON AND I awoke early for church services. Cora came in after Jackson had gotten dressed and headed downstairs for breakfast. I was starting to get used to our morning routine and how she fixed my hair. I was now wearing it pulled up at the nap of my neck and I hated it even though Cora did such a beautiful job with it. I had always loved my hair down and wasn't sure if I would ever get accustomed to wearing it up. Luckily, she did leave a few stray curls loose to accent my facial features.

She tied my stays much tighter than Mimi ever did, probably because she was younger and much stronger, but I could hardly breathe. My ribs ached, and it was impossible for me to inhale deeply by the time she slipped my dark green velvet gown over my head.

Davonte drove us to Sunday services in our new carriage with our two new young stallions that were a gift from all my brothers. They were a beautiful pair, coal black and named Cheyenne and Jasper. We were hopeful that in the next few years they would give us a beautiful foal.

We arrived several minutes early and were greeted by all our neighbors and friends who had not seen us since our wedding. Jackson and I had been keeping mostly to ourselves since Christmas and this was our first public appearance as a married couple. I had forgotten how big of a deal it was to everyone. We shook hands, hugged, smiled, and struggled to make our way towards the front to join Lee and Elizabeth.

After another long sermon from Pastor Jacobs welcoming in the New Year and warning us all to bid our tidings, I finally got the opportunity to speak to Elizabeth. Jackson knew I was anxious to do so, so he casually directed Lee a small distance from us, giving her and me the chance to speak alone without being overheard in case my mother or hers was mistaken.

"Well, Mrs. Chandler, how is married life?" she asked.

"Wonderful. I have never been so happy. Jackson is such an amazing man. I feel like the luckiest woman in the world," I said proudly.

"Make that the second luckiest." She thrust her hand forward for me to see the beautiful ring adorning her left ring finger. "Lee asked me to marry him on Christmas," she beamed.

"Oh Elizabeth, it is so elegant. I love it!" I admired it fully before hugging her. "I am so happy for you. When is the big day?"

"We were thinking about the end of next summer, most likely August or September. I want to be sure we have enough time to plan everything." She smiled over in Lee's direction.

"Well, I think it is wonderful. You two must come over this evening for coffee. In fact, we should invite Olivia, William, Laurie, Theodore, Christina, Thomas, Dimitri and Evelyn over as well. We shall make a small little engagement celebration for you."

"Are you sure that is not too much trouble? I know you two have barely settled into your new home."

"Of course not, we would love to do it. Besides it will give our new cook, Tamesha, a chance to show off. I am sure she gets bored cooking for us two when she is so used to such lavish parties at her former employers," I assured her.

"All right then, what time would you like us there?"

"Is four thirty too early?"

"It is perfect. Let me just tell Lee."

She made her way towards her fiancé as my husband crossed through the crowd back to me. I explained to him what Elizabeth had told me and how I wanted to have our group of friends come by late that afternoon for coffee and treats. He thought it was a wonderful idea and we spent the next thirty minutes inviting everyone on our list.

Jackson and I stopped by our house for a moment on our way to Sunday dinner with our families to let Tamesha know we would be expecting guests later that afternoon. She and Bertina seemed excited that I gave her free reign over what they could serve.

*   *   *

Laurie and Theodore were the first to arrive, followed closely by Christina and Thomas. We had barely gotten seated in the parlor when Dimitri and Evelyn got there. I had to admit they looked sweet together and complimented each other's personalities well. William and Olivia were next to arrive and then finally Lee with Elizabeth.

Bertina and Betsy came in once everyone was there with silver trays of coffee, wafers, and cheese and little white mini cakes with chocolate frosting. Bertina was trying to teach Betsy how to serve guests and she was quite the darling little sight to behold. She mumbled and fumbled about trying to remember every little thing her aunt had told her.

Jackson and I stood together in front of the hearth. The heat from the blazing fire was almost too much. Davonte had done well at keeping the cold air from reaching our little party.

Jackson greeted everyone. "I would like to thank everyone for coming on such short notice, but my beautiful wife and I wanted to formally congratulate Mr. Lee and Ms. Elizabeth on their upcoming nuptials." Jackson raised his cup towards the happy couple." I wish you two all the happiness that I have been so blessed to share with Jocelyn. Congratulations!"

"Congratulations!" Sprang out in chorus from everyone in the room.

"Thank you all so much. I must admit I was a little leery when I first moved here from Indianapolis. Never in my wildest dreams did I ever imagine I would find what I was always looking for . . . a wonderful, beautiful, and intelligent lady and a group of amazing friends who have made me feel truly at home. I am indeed very blessed." Lee tipped his mug to the room.

We spent the rest of the evening reminiscing about the days gone by with our youth. We filled Lee's ear with all the trials and tribulations that had fallen upon our group in the rowdier, more carefree days that had disappeared with time. Jackson and William, who were slightly older than the other boys, apparently had done some antics that neither Olivia nor I had known about. Still, neither of us was surprised by what we heard. I had heard my parents mutter numerous times over the years that 'what one of them did not think of, the other one did.'

The house cleared out around nine o'clock. All of the young ladies, save Olivia, had to return to school tomorrow as did the young men except of course Jackson and Lee. While William did not have classes until Tuesday, he did have to get some sleep, so he could travel back to campus in the morning after breakfast. The food was delicious, the company divine. All in all, our first time playing host and hostess, I would have to say was very successful.

CHAPTER 37

Sunday, January 3, 2010

OUR HONEYMOON in New York City flew by with the blink of an eye. I savored every possible moment with Jackson as we toured the busy city. It was beautifully decorated for Christmas and everyone seemed in such a festive mood. We completed our honeymoon on New Year's Eve with our last evening in Times Square with thousands of strangers freezing and screaming in the New Year. The next morning, we checked out of our lovely hotel and drove back across the river, heading towards Boston. I had silently wished we could stay in that city forever, just the two of us. I hated to consider what was awaiting me back in Chicago and I selfishly wanted to keep Jackson all to myself.

*   *   *

Jackson's siblings and their families all came over for supper and to say good-bye on our last evening in Boston. Phoebe, Emily, and Leslie made a phenomenal dinner including an amazing turtle cheesecake for desert. I offered to help a couple of times, but each of them gave me different excuses to get me out of the kitchen. I tried to tell myself that it was a bonding thing between the three of them and nothing to do with my lack of cooking experience, but of course I knew it was. So, I spent the time instead in the living room playing with the kids and listening to the gentlemen discuss various aspects of the news.

I hated to see them all leave at the end of the evening. They were all sweet and Phoebe and I were developing a wonderful friendship. Plus, it was so nice not to have to worry about what everyone thought of Jackson and my relationship for a change.

No one in his family judged us, not even Leslie or Carson. We didn't have to hide or pretend or put on a show for them the way we did around my family and friends. A part of me really dreaded going back to Chicago.

CHAPTER 38

Monday, January 2, 1879

JACKSON LEFT FOR WORK directly after breakfast leaving me alone in the house with our servants for the first time. I went over the daily household chore list and menu with Cora before wandering off into the study. I browsed over the titles of Jackson's books in his growing library, most of which were law books and held no interest to me. I settled for Shakespeare's *Julius Caesar* and sat down in Jackson's comfy chair by the hearth.

Two acts into the play I was bored out of my skull. The constant back and forth between two of the main characters, Brutus and Cassius, was mind numbing. Shakespeare's work was always somewhat challenging to read, and this morning I was struggling greatly with it. I gave up and put the book aside. I was half tempted to go next door and ask my mother what she did with the long hours of the day before she had children when she was newly married but thought better of it. I did not want to open myself up for another conversation about having children right away.

The clock on the mantle told me it was only ten o'clock. There was still a good eight hours yet before Jackson would return home and all my friends were still at school but Olivia. I paced the study hoping beyond all hope that she would drop over for some coffee or tea. I peeked out the curtains of the side window that faced my old house and saw nothing at all. The place looked unusually still. Now I understood how Emily became a writer.

I went to the foyer and grabbed my winter coat and bonnet off the rack by the door. The bitter wind took my breath away and tore at my exposed face as soon as I opened the front door.

I pulled my scarf higher around me until only my eyes could be seen and fought my way down the snow-covered walkway and over to the Chandler Estate.

"Good mornin, Mrs. Chandler," Barnaby greeted me before I even reached the front porch. "Tis mighty cold, ya shouldn't be out in this here weather." He quickly closed the door behind me and helped me off with my winter gear.

"Thank you, Barnaby. I had no idea it was so awful outside. Is Mrs. Chandler at home?"

"Yes'm, she's in the study. You go an' warm yourself by the fire while I fetch her." He nodded towards the parlor before he took off in the direction of Robert and Emily's study.

I was so cold I practically crawled into the fireplace to warm myself back up. My stockings were still dry, but the hem of my gown was completely saturated.

"Good morning, Jocelyn. What brings you out on a morning such as this?" Emily's voice startled me. "Let me guess, my son has gone off to work and you are bored to tears?" She gave me a knowing look and took a seat in the rocker opposite me.

"To be honest, yes," I confessed.

"Would you like some coffee?"

"Please."

She called for coffee and their cook, Francis, promptly entered with a silver tray, teapot, cups and saucers. She set them down on the small table and poured our coffee and handed me one.

"Thank you, Francis. That will be all." Francis disappeared back into the kitchen.

Emily and I sat in silence for several minutes sipping our coffee. It tasted wonderful and I could feel the heat from the liquid soaring through my body. My toes and fingers began to slowly come back to life. I looked over and noticed that Emily was rocking slowing and keeping her eyes on me.

"Feeling better?" she inquired in her soft voice.

"Yes, much. Thank you. I am sorry for my intrusion on your morning."

"Not at all. I thought perhaps you might come around after Jackson returned to the office."

"Am I that transparent?" I chuckled.

"Nonsense, I know because I was in your shoes once too. I know how lonely and long the days can become." She leaned forward and dropped her voice an octave. "Especially when you are more accustomed to a much livelier lifestyle in other places." She sat back in her rocker and smiled gently.

"I do not know how you and Phoebe do this day in and day out."

"We all find little things to keep us occupied. I write and sew. Before Wallace was born Phoebe baked a great deal, sewed some, and read a lot. You only need to find something you feel passionate about, something to keep you busy. Things will become easier once your friends finish school and they become married too. That alone will keep you more than busy with social engagements and you will soon be wishing for these days of peace and quiet again."

"I doubt that." I tried not to giggle. "It would be so different if Jackson and I could start a family. I truly wish we could."

"I know, and you will — in time. Your circumstances are unique, but I know that someday the two of you are going to have a beautiful little family all your own," she assured me. I didn't dare tell her what Jackson and I already knew because somehow, I was sure she already knew it as well.

"Can I ask you a personal question, Mother?"

"Of course." She sipped her coffee and continued to rock absentmindedly.

"What is your secret? By that I mean, how do you and Mr. Chandler maintain such a successful marriage? The two of you make it look so easy, and after thirty years together you are still very much in love with each other."

I fidgeted stirring my coffee for a moment. "I have seen images of my *other* parents and they really do not appear to like each other let alone be in love. Jackson told me that their relationship is not that uncommon for that time period and that in fact, yours and Robert's is. How is that possible?"

"Unfortunately, Jackson is correct in his assessment of Amy and Shane's relationship. However, I do not know them very well, so I cannot tell you specifics."

"I remember discussing it with Sidney the last time we were together, and she said that they no longer have anything in common or spend any time together," I stated casually.

"She would know better than I. However, I know things tend to be much different for couples in *our* positions. We share such an amazing and intense gift with our spouses that no one else could possibly relate. That alone does make you much closer. Personally, I believe the key to a successful marriage is being able to not only keep your own identity in the relationship but also sharing the little everyday things with one another. Things such as cooking together in the evening while chatting about your days, doing the grocery shopping together, eating meals together at the dining room table, and attending the children's activities as a family creates the memories that last even after the children are grown. However, it is just as important to keep a sense of yourself separate from your family as well."

"How do you mean?"

"Well, I have a successful career as an author and Robert is a successful attorney in both his lives. We enjoy our individual careers and identity, but we do them together. When I write during the evening hours, I do so in our shared study and Robert works on his briefs. We enjoy working within proximity of each other but on our own projects. We also take long walks together in the evenings where he tells me about his cases and I run over various characters, story twists and settings with him. Robert is my best sounding board for all my novels. I cannot imagine trying to create without his feedback."

"I had never realized." My voice was barely above a whisper.

"It is true. Robert is my most trusted advisor, my confidant, my beloved companion. I have spent over thirty years of my life being married to him and I cannot fathom waking up without him beside me. You will discover, Jocelyn, with the passing of time, your love for your husband will grow stronger than you ever deemed possible. In time you will know his thoughts as he will yours. You will finish each other's sentences and have entire conversations with a single look across a room. It is a powerful bond, stronger than any I have ever known with one exception . . . that being between a mother and a child."

"I believe my parents *here* share such a relationship, but I have serious doubts about my parents *there*. From what I can recall my dad is a kind-hearted man who loves his family dearly. My mother, on the other hand, is not nearly as kind. I believe she loves her children, but that love is very conditional upon them or rather us, leading the type of life she desires. She seems to care very little about her husband," I stated as a matter of fact.

"As I mentioned earlier, I know very little of Amy. I do know she is a very career driven woman with extremely high expectations for her children. Her social standing and how the outside world perceive her harmonious family is everything to her. You, my dear, have caused her a great deal of stress in all those categories."

"No wonder she despises me so." I looked down at my coffee that had now gone cold.

"No darling, she does not despise you. Not at all. I believe she is jealous that you may be able to find the life that she so desires. She knows how much you love Jackson and her biggest fear is that you have the strength to have it all," Emily said in a motherly tone.

"I had always thought that a parent wanted their children to be successful, but to also remain true to themselves and their dreams."

"Sadly, that is not always so. A great many things have changed within the last one hundred and thirty years and women have changed along with them. Some, not for the better. I wish things were different for you *there*. I truly do." Emily placed her cup back on the tray. "I believe it is time for lunch. Would you care to join me?"

"Yes, thank you. I would love to."

*   *   *

Emily's words haunted me long after the comforting lullaby of Jackson's deep sleep breathing had begun. I worried a great deal about how my family and friends *there* were going to react when they discovered our marriage and how it would impact my relationship with them. I tried to recall every instance I had previously seen of Amy and Shane to get a better idea of what their life was like together. Nothing in my memories gave me much peace about them. They seemed not to like each other and fought a great deal.

I draped my arm across Jackson's body and rested my head upon his chest. I closed my eyes and listened to the steady rhythm of his heartbeat. I wanted desperately to believe what Emily had said about people with our gift being more closely bonded than most other couples. I hated to think that the family dynamics demonstrated by most in the twenty-first century could someday invade the bond that we share.

CHAPTER 39

Monday, January 4, 2010

WE SET OUT EARLY for the incredibly long and boring drive back to Chicago. I had been dreading this drive ever since we initially pulled into the Chandler's driveway in Boston. And so much had happened in the last two weeks it felt like we had been gone a year. In such a short time I had gotten married, went on my honeymoon in New York City, visited the museums, and spent New Year's Eve in Times Square with thousands of strangers freezing our rears off. Now it was all over and we were headed back to reality at 75 mph. Back to school, homework, friends, basketball practice and games, and the chilling silence from my brother and mom.

We stopped at an IHOP somewhere in Ohio around noon for some lunch. The wind was whipping around us as we fought against it to make our way across the parking lot to the restaurant. I grabbed ahold of Jackson's arm and snuggled tightly against him trying to keep warm. The wind felt like it was tearing the skin off my bones.

We sat down in a booth in the back of the diner and immediately ordered some coffee while we scanned over the menu. After placing our orders, Emily reached across the table and placed her hand over mine.

"So, Jocelyn, have you decided what you are going to do when you get home?" she asked.

I took a deep breath and looked over at Jackson before answering. "Yes, I think I am going to tell my dad the truth."

"We are going to tell him," Jackson stated.

"Babe, I know you want to be there, but I believe it will go much smoother if I talk to him alone." I smiled gently. "I am just happy that I don't have to tell my mother." I tried to laugh it off but didn't manage it.

"How do you think he will handle it?" Emily asked, ignoring the statement about Mom.

"I am not really sure."

"But he knows how difficult things have been for you ever since we announced our engagement. Surely he must see what Amy and Ethan are doing?" Jackson pointed out.

"I know he does but still, I am not sure eloping was exactly what he had in mind to solve the problem." I tried to imagine the look on his face when I broke the news and the image it brought forth sent chills through my body.

"You realize you can wait to tell him if you want," Emily offered.

"At least until he files his tax return anyways," Robert spoke up while pouring another cup of coffee from the pot the waitress had left on the table.

"Excuse me?" I didn't understand what Robert meant.

Robert looked over at Jackson and raised his eyebrows. "Oh crap, I completely forgot about that." Jackson slapped his hand down on the table.

"Explain, please." I looked between the three of them as recognition settled on Emily's face.

"You and Jackson got married before the end of 2009. Therefore, your parents cannot claim you on their income tax return," Robert explained.

"Well, that's that. I guess I don't have an option then. I have to tell him," I said less than enthusiastically.

*   *   *

I tried my best to fall asleep, but it would not seem to find me. The hum of the tires, however, managed to lull Jackson and Emily off to sleep shortly after we got back on the highway. I leaned my head against the cold backseat window and ran different scenarios through my mind about how in the world I was going to break the news of our marriage to my dad.

In every single one I kept picturing Mom's head exploding and my dad's face beet red as he screamed at me for hours on end.

*   *   *

We turned down our street and every muscle in my body tightened up into a knot. I felt sick to my stomach. I reached over and grabbed Jackson's hand. "I really do not want to do this," I whispered.

"We have some time. Nothing says you have to do it tonight," he whispered back.

"No, I have to. If I wait and tell him later then they will be even more upset at me for keeping it from him." That much I was sure of.

"I still believe I should go with you."

"Thank you, but I feel this is something I should do alone. I do not know how he is going to react and I do not want him to take his anger out on you."

Emily pulled into the drive and shut the Durango off. Robert and Jackson jumped out and stretched then started unloading the luggage. "Jocelyn, what do you want us to do with your bags?" Robert asked when Emily and I joined them.

"Why don't we take it inside just in case? That way she will have some clothes here if things go poorly with her parents," Emily offered, keeping her voice solemn. She gave me a weak smile and placed her hand lightly on my shoulder, giving it a gentle squeeze telling me she was just as worried about this conversation as I was.

"Well, I guess I should go talk to my dad." I stood there hesitating.

"Are you sure you do not want me to go with you?" Jackson offered again.

"Yes, I'm sure. I'll be back shortly." I leaned up and kissed him briefly.

The three of them watched me walk slowly across the street like I was a prisoner on death row walking to the electric chair, which is exactly what I felt like.

The night air was cold and damp, but it did nothing to cool me down. I was burning up with fear and fighting my best to keep down the hamburger and fries I'd eaten a couple hours before. I reached the front porch and inhaled deeply. I let it out slowly before turning the knob on the front door.

I was greeted by the sounds of Monday night football before I even got the door closed behind me. I knew my dad was in the family room enjoying the game. I only hoped Ethan wasn't in there with him.

"Hello, I'm home," I hollered from the foyer.

"Hey, sweetheart, in here," my dad replied. No one else responded to my announcement.

I casually walked into the family room where my dad was sitting in the recliner watching the game alone. I immediately went to him and gave him a hug and kiss. "Hi Daddy, I missed you."

"I missed you too. It's been so quiet around here since you left. How was your trip?" He wrapped his arms around me and hugged me tightly.

"It was fabulous. I had the best time." I went over and sat down on the sofa. "How was your Christmas and New Year's?"

"Quiet, you just missed Sid and Landon. They left about an hour ago," he said.

"Aww . . . I wish I could have seen her. How is she doing?"

"Fine, gearing up for another semester. I think she and Landon are getting serious. They seem very happy together," he shrugged. "He seems like a nice enough young man."

"I think so. Did anyone miss me while I was gone?"

"I did," he smiled over at me.

"I am guessing Mom and Ethan weren't too torn up about me being gone for the last couple weeks."

My dad tore his eyes away from the game and looked over at me with sadness in his eyes. "Well, they haven't mentioned you."

"Sweet," I rolled my eyes. I should have known better. It really didn't even surprise me either but still a small part of me was disappointed.

"You know how stubborn they can be," he mumbled and took another drink of his beer.

"I guess it's nice to know some things never change."

"They'll come around . . . eventually." He turned his attention back to the television.

"Where are they?" I wanted to check in case one of them came down while I was breaking the news and made things ten times worse.

"Ethan is over at Corbin's and your moms at the hospital. It seems one of her patients decided he didn't want to take his nap this afternoon and decided to put crayons in his ears to get out of it."

"Really?" I giggled.

"Yeah, some five-year-old boy. Now your mom's stuck in surgery."

"Surgery? How far did he get them in there? Did he puncture his eardrum?" I asked.

"I don't know," Dad answered like he was already bored with the topic.

"Dad, can I talk to you for a minute?"

"What about?"

"My trip."

"Sure honey," he answered but continued to watch the game. "Go ahead."

"Daddy, I need you to listen. This is pretty important," I began.

"I am," but his eyes remained on the game.

"You know how difficult things have been around here the last few months between Mom and Ethan and me?" I swallowed hard trying to force the words to come out.

"Yes, and your point?" he asked with his eyes still on the television.

"Well, it's been very hard for me to be around them when they both won't even be in the same room with me."

"I know, but I'm sure they will come around," he said for the millionth time.

"I don't believe they will anytime soon. So . . ." I couldn't get the words to come out.

"What did you do?" His eyes suddenly turned towards me.

"I married Jackson on Christmas Eve," I blurted out.

My dad's face went blank. For a minute I thought perhaps he was having a stroke. Then he reached for the remote and flipped off the television without uttering a word. He calmly set the remote back on the end table before rising slowly out of his chair. "You did what?" he roared at the top of his lungs. "Of all the stupid asinine things I have ever seen you do, this one tops them all. How could you?"

"Daddy, would you just calm down and listen to me?" I pleaded.

"I cannot believe . . . ," he muttered, storming out of the room. I realized quickly that he was getting his shoes in the foyer and I jumped to my feet knowing exactly where he was headed.

"Daddy, please! Don't do this!" I begged, grabbing hold of his sweatshirt as he was trying to get out the door. With his strength and size, he merely pulled me along with him.

I trotted alongside him begging him not to do this all the way to the Chandler's front porch. My father didn't even bother to knock on their door. Instead he threw open the door like he was ready to kill someone. Our immediate vision was empty of anyone, so he trailed off into their living room, family room and then rounded around into the kitchen where Jackson was fixing himself a snack.

"You!" My dad screamed, yanking Jackson off the barstool.

"Mister . . ." Jackson began but was abruptly cut off as my father punched him square in the jaw.

"Daddy, NO!" I screamed and ran to Jackson's side. He was sitting on the floor rubbing his jaw.

"How dare you . . ." Dad began just as Emily and Robert came bursting through the kitchen entryway. "And you two. I trusted you with my daughter and this is what you allow to happen behind my back? How could you?" he roared.

"Shane, please . . ." Robert started only to have my father interrupt him.

"Don't you 'Shane please' me, you have a daughter of your own. How could you do this?" His face was every shade of red possible. I had never seen him so angry in all my life.

"I would want my daughter to be happy," Robert stated as a matter of fact.

"How would you feel if your daughter was in high school when she ran off and got married?"

"Shane, I understand how you must feel," Emily said in a gentle soft voice.

"Do not tell me you understand how I feel. You have no idea what I feel. You move in across the street and within weeks my daughter who has always been a straight A student, dreamed of going to college and grad school, always had strong goals in life, suddenly becomes engaged. Now while I'm not happy about it I kept my mouth shut and tried to make the best of it even though my own wife hasn't spoken to me since. But I tried. I tried to keep the peace. I tried to stand up for my daughter. I kept telling myself that she would eventually come to her senses and see how silly it is to get married at eighteen or get married and wind up divorced before she is even legal to drink. Then she would really need my support and not for me to throw it up into her face that I told her so." He turned to look directly at me and his voice dropped. "Never in this scenario did I ever imagine you being married before you graduated high school."

"I know, Daddy," I whispered with tears of shame running down my face.

"You can clear out your room and all your things tomorrow while your mother and I are at work. Have it done before we get home," my dad lowered his voice and looked defeated.

"Daddy . . . ," I begged.

"I don't want to see or speak with you for a while." He turned to leave.

I scrambled off the floor and followed him to the front door. "Daddy, please don't leave like this. Can't we talk this through? Please!"

He paused for a moment. "I always dreamed I would someday walk you down the aisle, see you graduate from college and spoil your children, and you took that all away from me. How could you do something so thoughtless?" he asked in a very weak voice.

"You still can, and you will, Daddy, but I had to get out of that house. Do you know what it has been like for me living in such a hostile environment? It has been a true nightmare. We were getting married in a few months anyway," I tried to explain.

"You would be a high school graduate by then too. Are you pregnant?"

"No, I am not pregnant! How could you even ask me that?" I stood there stunned.

"Because it is the only excuse I can come up with that justifies you doing something so incredibly stupid." He ran his fingers through his hair with frustration.

"I am an adult. Will you stop treating me like I am still a child?" I asked in a low voice.

"You are *my* child, Jocelyn Alyssa. Good Lord, you are not even old enough to drink at your wedding reception."

"I am old enough to join the military, get drafted to somewhere in the Middle East, and die for my country, but I cannot legally have a beer. Yeah, you are right, that really makes sense."

"This is not the time for your smart mouth. I have had enough for today. I am going home. I have to work in the morning," my dad said softly.

"You can't leave like this. We still have to talk about this." It killed me to think of him walking out the door and never speaking to me again and the last thing I said to him was some smart-ass remark. "Please." I touched his forearm lightly.

He took a deep breath and looked down at the floor for the longest minute. Then he finally looked up and wrapped his arms around me tightly. "I just need some time. I love you, baby girl." He kissed my cheek and walked through the front door closing it softly behind him.

I stood there in the foyer staring at the closed door with tears still running down my face. The house around me was silent. For a brief second, I considered chasing after him, but I knew it was best to let him work this through in his own way. I turned around slowly to find Jackson standing in the entryway to the family room. His face was forlorn and there was a large red mark on the side of his jaw. He opened his arms to me and I rushed into them burying my head against his chest.

"I am so sorry, my love," Jackson whispered softly into my hair.

"I hate hurting him. He looked so disappointed in me."

"He loves you very much and he always will." He stroked my hair.

"It's been a long day. I think I just want to take a long shower and go to bed."

"All right."

He took my hand and led me up the stairs. My suitcase was lying open on his bed. "I am afraid I need to clear out a few drawers in my dresser and make some room in the closet for your things."

"Okay," I muttered, picking out some panties and nightclothes.

"There are clean towels and a new loofah in the linen closet." He crossed over to his adjoining bath and flipped on the light. "Is there anything else I can get you?"

"No, thank you. I think I am going to soak in a bubble bath for a while. I will meet you back downstairs. Please apologize to your parents . . . once again, for my father's intrusion."

I placed my clothes and toothbrush on the counter before beginning my bubble bath. I poured some Japanese Cherry Blossom bubble bath from Bath & Body Works that I had received from Phoebe as a stocking stuffer into the hot water.

I turned around and got a good look at Jackson's face in the bright bathroom light. The mark was much more prominent than I had realized. "Oh, sweetheart, your face." I reached up and traced my fingers along the side of his gorgeous face. "I am so sorry."

Jackson turned towards the mirror and smiled at the blackening side of his face. "Your father has a hell of a punch. That's going to make Ethan proud when we return to school on Wednesday."

I sat down on the edge of the tub and ran my fingers through the hot water. "Do we really have to go back? I really don't want to."

"You cannot start BU in the fall unless you graduate." Jackson leaned against the counter and watched me play absentmindedly with the bubbles.

"Can we not just move back to your home in Boston and I can graduate from the same high school you did?"

"Would you really not want to graduate with all your friends that you have known since kindergarten?" He raised a quizzical brow at me.

"Do you honestly believe I will have any after Wednesday? All of them are against us and have been very vocal about it."

"Just like your father, they love you and only want what is best for you."

"I am not nearly as optimistic as you are. I have known these people a lot longer than you have, and I know what they can handle. This, unfortunately, is not one of them." That much I was sure of.

"But I have never seen you run away from a fight." He stood up and slipped off his shirt. "Do you mind if I join you?"

"Of course not." I watched him step out of his jeans. He stood there in nothing but his boxer briefs smiling coyly at me. His gorgeous toned body never ceased to leave me breathless. I still could not believe he was my husband. "And I am not running away from a fight. I am only being realistic."

Jackson came over and leaned down beside me at the tub taking my hands in his. "If moving to Boston is something you truly want then we will do it. But I think you should give them a chance first. Try it out. See how the next couple of weeks go before you decide what you really want. Maybe they will surprise you."

I smiled weakly and kissed him softly. "I hope so."

CHAPTER 40

Tuesday, January 3, 1879

JACKSON CAME HOME right at supper time. Tamesha prepared a lovely meal and Davonte had the hearth in the dining room toasty with a roaring fire. I recounted my day with Olivia to him but did not believe he heard a word I said. He seemed to be greatly distressed by something that was consuming his thoughts.

"After lunch I met with my father about a stomachache I have been having all week. He gave me a quick exam and told me I was due in late September or early November," I said, trying to prove he was not listening to me whatsoever. "Sweetheart . . . is that not wonderful news? We are expecting," I proclaimed proudly trying not to giggle.

"That is wonderful, my love, I hope you will be very happy," Jackson responded dully. He fidgeted with his dinner for a few more minutes before recognition set in and he looked by up at me. "Wait . . . what did you just say?"

I could not help myself but start laughing. "Nothing important my love, just proving a point that your mind is elsewhere."

"Are you pregnant?" Confusion was written plainly across his beautiful face.

"No, of course not," I shook my head with a smile. "But it is nice to know you were listening to me."

"I am sorry my dear. I had a really bad day at the office and it does not seem that it is going to get any better any time soon." He went on to recount his busy day as he acclimated himself with various aspects of a new case that was just assigned by Judge Reynolds. His father was sitting first chair and he second.

Jackson felt ill at ease with this defendant and had tried to persuade his father against actively participating in the defense. Apparently the two men had met with him at the county jail and the defendant bragged about having committed his crime. Jackson would not tell me what it was only that it was horrific in nature and the man deserved to die for it.

After dinner he retired to his office and poured over his briefs. He remained quiet for the remainder of the evening. By nine thirty I was worn out and struggling to keep my eyes open. I debated whether I should disturb him and decided I should probably leave him alone.

I went to bed by myself and wondered how many more nights like this I would have to endure before this trial was over.

CHAPTER 41

Tuesday, January 5, 2010

I WOKE UP to the smell of bacon flooding my senses. I could hear Emily and Robert moving around in the kitchen and the sound of their quiet laughter filled me with a sense of calmness. I rolled over and saw Jackson's sleeping face on the pillow beside me. He looked so peaceful and beautiful. As if sensing my gaze, he opened his eyes slowly.

"Good morning, my love. How are you feeling?"

"Okay, how are you?"

"I do not believe I will ever tire of waking up to your beautiful face." He smiled and rolled over upon me kissing me zealously.

Over breakfast the four of us discussed school, moving my things over, and the confrontation with my dad. His parents agreed with Jackson that we should both go back to school tomorrow and see how things go for the next couple weeks before we decided to return to Boston for me to complete high school. I apologized several times for my dad's intrusion and they were all very understanding even though Jackson had a large bruise on the side of his face and a hint of a black eye.

I did finally convince Jackson to let me go over to my house alone in the morning to see if everyone was gone first before they all joined me. I knew both my parents were supposed to be at work but considering the circumstances I wasn't sure if they would have taken the day off to talk things over with us. Ethan, I knew, could also be a problem if he was lurking around. I was positive he had heard of our marriage by now and was probably dying to have it out with me.

I really didn't want to put Jackson, let alone his parents, in the middle of all that. I promised I would text him once I got there and tell him what was going on.

I opened the front door to be met with complete silence. I hoped it was empty as well. I wanted to get my things and get back over to the Chandler's before any more drama erupted. I closed the door behind me and crept quietly up the stairs to my room. I breathed a sigh of relief that no one was around. I took out my phone to text Jackson that the coast was clear for him to come on over when Ethan poked his head in my room startling me and causing me to drop my cell phone.

"Are you really married?" I nodded and picked up my phone. "Do you have any idea how mad Mom and Dad are right now?"

"Ethan, I just came over to pack up my room. I don't want to fight with you." I walked over to my door wanting to close it with him on the other side.

"That's easy for you to say. You're not the one who had to listen to world war three that broke out here last night because of your stupid stunt." He pushed hard against my door blocking me from closing it then stepped into my room.

"My life is none of your business. Now will you please get out of my room?"

"No and you can't make me. You don't live here anymore!"

"Whatever . . . just leave me alone." I turned away from him and went over to my closet. I started pulling out my clothes and laying them across my bed when I heard the front door open and close. I thought for a second it was Jackson, but I didn't think he would just walk in without me texting him an all clear.

Multiple footsteps pounded up the stairs as a watermelon size knot of fear grew in my stomach. I was positive it had to be my parents and I really didn't want a confrontation with either of them. But then Jenna, Caitlyn, and Hillary came bursting in my room.

"Is it true?" Jenna didn't even bother saying hello.

I looked from the three of them over to Ethan who stood there with a satisfied grin on his face. "I texted them," he stated proudly.

"Thanks," I muttered sarcastically.

"What? Was it supposed to be some big secret?" he taunted.

"Not at all," I said with pride.

"Is it true?" Jenna nearly shouted with her hands on her hips.

"And hello to you three. How was your break?" I smiled coyly at them.

"Stop playing games. Are you married or not?" Jenna asked hotly.

"Yes, I am."

"Seriously?" Hillary looked stunned.

"You guys knew we were going to do it this summer anyway, but with things being so difficult around here we decided to just move it up a couple months. Don't act so surprised."

"We never thought you'd actually go through with it. We thought for sure you'd come to your senses by summer." Jenna looked stunned and sat down on the corner of my bed.

"Sweet. Thanks a lot." I rolled my eyes at them and returned to my closet.

"Doesn't this all seem a bit ridiculous to you?" Hillary took a step closer to me. "You've only known him for three months . . . and you married him!"

"It's complicated." I glanced back at her.

"Then explain it to us. We've got all day," Jenna rudely responded.

I turned around again to face my three friends and Ethan. "You know something, if I thought I could I would but with the attitudes you all have, I honestly do not believe you would even be open to hearing it."

"Whatever, I knew you wouldn't tell us. You've been acting so strangely ever since you met him. I don't know what's going on, but I know something isn't right," Jenna glared up at me.

"You can believe whatever you like. I really don't care. So, if you're done bothering me, feel free to leave. I have a lot of packing to do before my parents get home." I continued piling my clothes on top of my bed.

"I knew this was pointless." Hillary shook her head and turned towards Jenna and Caitlyn. "Come on, I don't want to spend the last day of break here with her."

"Agreed," Jenna stood up and she and Hillary walked towards my door when she noticed Caitlyn hadn't moved. "Caitlyn, come on."

"I think I'll stick around and help Jocelyn pack her things." She waved them off and walked over to my closet.

"Suit yourself." Jenna narrowed her eyes a bit as she and Hillary left. Ethan followed them out and closed the door behind them seeming rather satisfied with himself.

"I am so sorry, Jocelyn. I just want you to know that not all of us feel the way they do." She was putting my shoes into a large duffle bag.

"Thanks, I appreciate that."

"Zak and I are both very happy for you and Jackson." She paused for a minute and stood facing me. "I know how hard things have been around here with Ethan and your mom. I cannot imagine my mother treating me that way regardless of the circumstances. It would break my heart. Zak and I know why you two eloped and why you want to move in with the Chandlers."

I walked over and sat down on my bed and patted the empty space beside me. Caitlyn sat down and asked. "You're not pregnant, are you?"

"No, I am not pregnant, and we did not exactly elope."

"You didn't?"

"No, we didn't." I went on to explain to her the details of our wedding ceremony, our trip to BU and our honeymoon in New York. I told her everything except about Uncle Nicholas being there just in case that small detail somehow reached Ethan's ears, which would then reach my father's. I knew his estranged brother being at my wedding when he was not would be unforgiveable.

Caitlyn listened attentively and when I was finished, she hugged me tightly. "How romantic. I'm so jealous. I wish I could have been there."

"I wish you could have been too."

She finally let me go. "Well, let's get you packed. I'm sure you don't want to be here when your parents get home."

"Not particularly," I laughed.

Caitlyn, Jackson, his parents, and I spent the next couple of hours moving my things across the street. It didn't take too long and I was thrilled that Ethan decided to remain in his room once he discovered Robert and Emily helping me move. I guess he was braver confronting Jackson when he was alone. Caitlyn was even sweet enough to hug Jackson and congratulate him on our marriage.

When the final suitcase was closed and the last of the duffle bags was zipped shut, the four of them carried the last of my things across the street. I stood alone in my room that was now void of all the little things that had made it mine for the last eighteen years. My clothes and things were packed; the vanity was cleared as were all the drawers, closet, nightstands and walls. There was nothing left here that proved this room had ever been occupied by me. These walls had been my sanctuary, my haven; my respite from the world outside and now it was all a memory. As I closed my bedroom door for the last time, I brushed a tear off my cheek and silently said good-bye to the girl I had once been.

APPENDIX

2009

The Timmons

- Shane Douglas, VP Compliance of Chicago General
- Amy Marie, Pediatrician at Chicago General
- Sidney Harper, Sophomore at Northwestern University
- Jocelyn Alyssa, Senior in high school
- Ethan Jude, Junior in high school

The Chandlers

- Robert Abraham, Corporate Attorney
- Emily Jade, Novelist
- Alexander Nolan, Divorce Attorney in Boston
- Leslie, Alexander's wife
- Lucinda, Alexander & Leslie's six-year-old daughter
- Charlie, Alexander & Leslie's four-year-old son
- Phoebe Rochelle, Criminal Attorney in Boston
- Carson Adler, Phoebe's husband
- Wallace, Phoebe and Carson's one-year-old son
- Jackson Wyatt, Senior in high school/Studying law at Boston University

The Burks

- Craig, Jenna's father
- Melinda, Jenna's mother
- Jenna, Jocelyn's best friend/Dating Kyle/Volleyball, Basketball player

The Clausens

- Brett, Kyle's father
- Sonya, Kyle's mother
- Kyle, Jenna's boyfriend/Senior in high school
- Brandon, Kyle's brother/Freshman in high school

Friends

- Caitlyn Buchanan, Zac's girlfriend/Volleyball, Basketball, Softball player/Senior
- Zak Engling, Caitlyn's boyfriend/Quarterback, Point Guard/Senior
- Hilary Wade, Cody's girlfriend/Volleyball, Basketball player/Senior
- Cody Porter, Hilary's boyfriend/Wide receiver, small forward/Senior
- Mariah Jones, Ethan's ex-girlfriend/Junior
- Corbin Stewart, Hailey's boyfriend, Ethan's best friend/Junior
- Hailey Collins, Corbin's girlfriend/Junior
- Taylor Perry, Jocelyn's nemesis/Cheerleader/Senior
- Dakota Anderson, Taylor's sidekick/Cheerleader/Senior

Coaches/Teachers

- Coach Smith, Volleyball & Girls Basketball Coach/Teaches English Lit 9
- Coach Shelburne, Football Coach/Teaches computer programing
- Coach Minnick, Boys Basketball Coach/ Teaches algebra
- Coach Kane, Girls Softball Coach/Teaches PE
- Mr. Rand, Teaches AP psychology
- Mrs. Neal-Beliveau, Teaches AP biology
- Mrs. Killian, Teaches Jocelyn's English Lit 12
- Mrs. Runyon, Teaches Jackson's English Lit 12
- Mr. Dunn, Teaches chemistry

- Mrs. Ulbright, Teaches history
- Principal Julia Cosgrove

1878

The Timmons

- Patrick Michael, Physician
- Annabelle Nichole, Married to Patrick/Jocelyn's mother
- Patrick Michael II, Physician
- Katherine, Patrick II's wife
- Jonathon Niles, Physician
- Lizette, Jonathon's wife
- Isaac, Jonathon & Lizette's nine-year-old son
- Louisa, Jonathon & Lizette's eight-year-old daughter
- Derek, Jonathon & Lizette's four-year-old son
- James Henry, Attorney
- Rachael, James' wife
- Abbigail, James & Rachael's five-year-old daughter
- Aiden, James & Rachael's three-year-old son
- Hannah, Housekeeper/Nanny
- William Arthur, Married to Olivia Adams/First year at Northwestern University
- Jocelyn Alyssa, Engaged to Jackson Chandler
- The Timmons' Household
- Eddie, Stableman/Married to Mimi/Cora's dad
- Mimi, Manages the household/Married to Eddie/Cora's mom
- Cora, Housekeeper/Daughter of Eddie and Mimi
- Sarah, Cook
- Missy, Housekeeper

The Chandlers

- Robert Abraham, Attorney
- Emily Jade, Married to Robert/Jackson's mother
- Alexander Nolan, Attorney
- Veronica, Alexander's wife
- Casper, Alexander & Veronica's six-year-old son
- Wyatt, Alexander & Veronica's five-year-old son
- Kyra, Alexander & Veronica's three-year-old daughter
- Phoebe Rochelle
- Silas Monroe, Phoebe's husband/School teacher
- Wallace, Phoebe & Silas' one-year-old son
- Katie, The Monroe's housekeeper/Nanny
- Jackson Wyatt, Law School at Northwestern University

The Chandler Household

- Barnaby, Stableman/Married to Carly
- Susan, Housekeeper
- Carly, Cook/Married to Barnaby
- Norma, Housekeeper

The Adams

- Benjamin, Banker/Married to Harriett
- Harriett, Married to Benjamin
- Olivia, Jocelyn's best friend/Married to William
- Kincade, Olivia's seven-year-old brother
- Oscar, Olivia's four-year-old brother
- Grady, The Adams' stableman

The Cain's

- Henry, Owns the mercantile
- Molly, Married to Henry
- Laurie, Friend of Jocelyn's/Theodore's girlfriend
- Quintin, Laurie's five-year-old brother
- Gracie, The Cain's housekeeper

The Maddox's

- Elmer, Elizabeth's father
- Ester, Elizabeth's mother
- Easton, Elizabeth's twenty-year-old brother
- Elizabeth, Jocelyn's friend/Lee's girlfriend
- Edwin, Elizabeth's sixteen-year-old brother
- Elijah, Elizabeth's fourteen-year-old brother
- Elisa, Elizabeth's eight-year-old sister
- Sabina, The Maddox's housekeeper

The Donaldson's

- George, Carpenter/Married to Corrine
- Corrine, Married to George
- Josiah, Dimitri's twenty-five-year-old brother
- Dimitri, formerly engaged to Maryanne
- Calliope, Dimitri's sixteen-year-old sister
- Ingrid, Dimitri's fourteen-year-old sister

Friends

- Christina Bowden, Jocelyn's friend/Thomas' girlfriend
- Thomas Reynolds, Christina's boyfriend
- Theodore Norris, Laurie's boyfriend
- Maryanne Kendrick, Formerly engaged to Dimitri/Jocelyn's nemesis
- Sean Preston, Dimitri's best friend/Died of pneumonia in Spring 2009/Formerly engaged to Olivia Adams
- Lee Miller, Elizabeth Maddox's boyfriend/Architect
- Mr. Grahame, History teacher

Review of
Illumination
EVE Series, Book 4

CHAPTER 1

Saturday, March 27, 2010

I SAT AT the desk by our bedroom window and stared at my childhood home across the street. The huge Civil War built estate loomed across the vast lawn in the mid-morning sky. I watched the porch swing swaying slightly in the breeze on the wrap-around porch and the rockers moving gently. There was a light drizzle clinging to the chilly air. The house looked hollow and unfriendly. I imagined my dad, Shane, in his pajama bottoms and sweatshirt sitting in his recliner watching some documentary on the History Channel. My mother, Amy, was most likely in her office dictating patient charts and my younger brother, Ethan, was probably scavenging through the kitchen looking for something to snack on. It was just another typical Saturday morning in the Timmons's household with one exception . . . me.

"Good morning, I brought you some coffee." A female voice breached the silence from the doorway behind me.

"Thank you. When did you arrive?" I got up and hugged my sister-in-law Phoebe.

"This morning. My parents picked me up about an hour ago at the airport." She handed me the mug and sat down on the corner of the bed I shared with Jackson. She lightly patted the empty space beside her. "Sit down."

I filled the vacancy next to her and took a long sip letting the warm liquid course through me. "I was not aware you were visiting us this weekend."

"It was a last-minute decision actually. After talking to my mother last evening, I decided to come visit for the weekend." She smiled softly. "Everyone is very worried about you."

"I am fine." Phoebe raised a questionable eyebrow. "Seriously, I am." I rolled my eyes at the floor and took another sip of coffee.

"It does not sound like it to me."

"Did you bring Wally with you?" I inquired with vain hopes of changing the subject.

"No, I left him home with Carson. They can survive a weekend without me."

"Oh, I was hoping he was with you. I miss him." Wally was Phoebe's son who was just shy of his second birthday. I simply adored him and had not had the opportunity to see him since Christmas.

"You will see him over Easter," Phoebe sighed exasperatedly. "I understand that the relationship with your family has deteriorated since your wedding over Christmas Break."

"Deteriorated? Unfortunately, there was no relationship to deteriorate with my mother or Ethan for that matter. We stopped all communication at Thanksgiving. And things with my dad are improving somewhat. He did wave to me yesterday when Jackson and I were leaving for school and he was off to work." I tried to sound more optimistic than I felt.

"Jocelyn, I know the last six months have been challenging for you. I honestly cannot imagine how difficult it must be to learn about *EVE*, be a newlywed, estranged from your family, and most of your friends all while trying to complete your senior year of high school with the highest possible scores."

I fumbled over a couple of ill-gotten words then remained silent. There was no use fighting anything she had said. It was all true and we both knew it.

"Jackson told our mother that you cried all the way to school and that many nights when you believe him to be asleep, you cry."

I continued to stare down at my coffee mug. "He had no right to reveal something so personal. And if he had, he should have confided in me, not his mother." I got up and walked out of the room ending our conversation.

*   *   *

I pulled my jacket and scarf out of the foyer closet and walked out the front door without saying a word to anyone. I felt so angry that Jackson had betrayed me. *How dare he confide in his mother about his concerns! I am his wife. He has no right to speak to anyone about me behind my back.*

I stuffed my hands in my pockets as my feet reached the sidewalk. I didn't even bother to look back to see if anyone noticed my departure. I didn't care if they did or didn't. I followed the sidewalk down to the sports park. Thankfully it had cleared up and the sun was fighting to break through the clouds. It was still fairly chilly out but everywhere I looked there were signs that nature was awakening after her long winter sleep.

I crossed over the soccer fields where the grass was still saturated from the periodic snows and rains so typical of our springs in Chicago. I walked aimlessly around the path to the playground by the baseball diamonds. I sat down on one of the swings and kicked off the ground. I pumped harder with my arms and soared into the sky leaving all my troubles on the ground below me.

"I figured this was where you were headed," his voice startled me from behind. "You always loved the swings." My dad sat down in the swing next to mine. "I saw you leave a little while ago and thought I would take advantage of the chance to speak to you alone."

I dragged my feet to bring myself to a halt beside him. "I am glad you did." I wasn't sure what to say to him. We had not spoken in almost three months.

"I wasn't sure you would be too happy to speak with me." He swayed a bit in the swing. "I am not proud of my recent behavior. I know this hasn't been easy on any of us, but I want us to be a family again. I hate knowing that you are right across the street and I feel like I can't speak to you."

"Daddy, you can speak to me any time you want to. Nothing has changed between us. I love you!" I leaned over and wrapped my arms around his neck spilling my tears all over his shoulder. "I have missed you so much," I cried.

"I missed you too." He hugged me back. "Are you doing all right?"

I sat back in my swing and brushed the tears off my cheeks with a smile. "I am doing much better now."

"How is married life treating you?" he inquired.

"Wonderful. He makes me very happy."

"I'm happy to hear that. How about your friends? Ethan told me that they have been giving you a lot of grief about your marriage." My dad looked sympathetic.

"He would know. He has caused a lot of it," I told him.

"I figured as much. I have tried to talk with him."

"Oh, don't worry about it. He's not the worst of them. Jenna puts Ethan to shame. She has been truly horrible, and Hilary is not much better. Thankfully, basketball season is finally over. I never thought I would be happy to see the end of it, but I was. I decided that I am not going to play softball this year because of them."

"Why would you let them take that away from you? You love softball, and this is your last year to play. Who cares what they think?"

"They ruined basketball season for me and I really don't want them to ruin softball for me also." I ran my sneakers over the mulch under the swing.

"So, don't let them. I have never known you to give up a fight, especially over something you love." He half laughed. "You're married, aren't you?"

"Yes," I accidently snorted and side-stepped the jibe. "But Caitlyn has been wonderful. So, has Zak. Most people are except for the ones who were supposed to be my friends."

"I'm sorry, but you still should not let them dictate what you do," he said, trying to reason with me.

"I don't know what I am going to do. Try-outs are a couple weeks away and I have not decided on anything yet."

The sun warmed up the gentle breeze that brushed the clouds lightly across the sky just enough to take the morning chill out of the air. We laughed and talked on the swings for the next couple of hours. It felt like a load of worries had been lifted off my shoulders. My heart soared like a child again. It was so easy and natural to fall back into being Daddy's little girl again.

By noon I was sorry I had skipped breakfast. My stomach was growling relentlessly. Finally, I couldn't ignore it any longer.

"Hey, Dad, would you like to join me for lunch? I know Jackson would be thrilled to see you and his sister is visiting from Boston for the weekend. I would love for you to finally meet her. She is so amazing." I took my father's hand and led him back down the pathway towards home.

"I do admit that it is a little strange having a married daughter who is still in high school," my dad confessed, swinging our hands like we did when I was little.

"I know," I weakly admitted.

"You should hear some of the names your mother has come up with for Jackson." He chuckled and rolled his eyes.

"Should I even ask?" I hated to even imagine.

"Well, for the first month after you married him, she called him 'the home wrecker.' One of the nurses at the hospital told me, Patty . . . you remember her, right? Anyway, I said something to your mom that evening, which as you can imagine, went over very well, but at least she doesn't call him that anymore." I laughed; I couldn't help it. He shoved me playfully.

"Now she refers to him as 'Jocelyn's first husband.'"

"Cute. It sounds like her," I giggled despite myself.

"I know and I'm sorry, but you know how she can be." He squeezed my hand tenderly.

"I am familiar with her work," I muttered under my breath.

We strolled up the walkway of the house that I now considered my home. The landscaping was awakening with tiny little buds beginning to break free of the soil and reach for the sky. The topiary was a lush green and the crimson was practically dripping off the burning bushes. It stood in perfect accent with the red bricks of the Chandler estate that was greatly complimented by the black iron fences. The year may have been 2010, but the estate was definitely from yesteryear.

"Are you sure they won't mind me simply dropping in uninvited?" My dad paused on the porch. "We haven't actually spoken since you returned from Boston and the last time I was here I punched your husband." He chuckled despite his best efforts not to.

"Of course. They will be fine with it. They are not the kind of people who hold a grudge." I grasped his hand and opened the front door.

"There you are! Thank goodness you are all right. I was . . ." Jackson came to a halt in the foyer when he noticed my dad standing behind me. "Sir." He extended a hand to my father.

"Hello, Jackson." My dad shook his hand. "How have you been, son?"

"Good sir, very good. And you?" Jackson smiled but glanced at me with a questioning look in his eyes.

"I went for a walk to get some air and he found me on the swings."

"I was cleaning the garage and saw her leave. She looked upset, so I knew where she was headed." He placed his hand on my shoulder. "It's where she always hides when something is bothering her." My dad gave me a knowing smile.

"Well, please come on in." Jackson led the way into the family room.

My dad and I took a seat on the couch and my new husband sat down on the loveseat across from us. Jackson smiled uncomfortably. "Can I get you a cup of coffee?"

"Thank you," Dad nodded.

"Would you like some also, Jocelyn?" Jackson offered as he stood up.

"Please. Would you like some help?" He shook his head with a grin.

"I thought I heard voices in here." Emily's voice rang out as she and Phoebe entered the room.

"Oh, hello." My dad stood up and shook hands with Emily. "It's nice to see you again."

"You also." Emily looked elegant in her beige slacks, silk tank, and violet half jacket. "I would like you to meet my daughter, Phoebe." The two shook hands.

"It's nice to finally meet you. I've heard a lot of good things about you. I'm Jocelyn's father, Shane." My dad smiled at her.

"Thank you. It's nice to meet you as well." Phoebe smiled gracefully. I could only imagine what she must have been thinking about my dad after all that has transpired in the last several months.

Jackson excused himself while his mother and sister took his place on the loveseat. Phoebe had all the professionalism only an attorney could muster in an uncomfortable situation. She crossed her legs nonchalantly looking anything but casual in her stylish cream-colored jeans, light brown calf boots, soft teal sweater, and gray plaid scarf. Her long thick brown curls were swept and pinned loosely over one shoulder.

"I'm sorry it took me so long to come over." My dad leaned forward a little. "I know it has been entirely past due."

"I know this whole situation has been a little difficult on your family and I apologize for that," Emily said politely.

"I realize my wife and son have made things worse for the two of them and for that I am sorry. As for me," he took my hand and smiled, "my feelings were hurt because ever since you were born I have dreaded the day I'd have to give you up. But I always thought I would be the one to give you away."

"I am sorry, Daddy. It all happened so fast and I wanted you there. You were the only thing missing." I leaned over and hugged him tightly.

Jackson reentered the room with his father, Robert, carrying a tray with a kettle of freshly brewed coffee, saucers and cups, sugar and cream and a plate of finger sandwiches. "Is everything all right?" he asked, setting the tray on the coffee table.

"Yes, everything is wonderful." I released my father and wiped a few stray tears off my cheeks.

*   *   *

Jackson was propped up on some pillows reviewing his notes for a government test we had on Monday when I climbed into bed beside him. I took the papers out of his hand and tossed them on the floor. "I will have none of that in my bed." I crawled onto his lap and straddled him. I leaned down and kissed him playfully.

"You seem to be feeling much better," he stated with a sly grin and wrapped his arms around me waist.

"I am. It felt so good to talk with him again." I kissed him again.

"It does me good to see you acting like your old self. I'm glad you two finally managed to talk things out." He reached over and turned out the lights. I giggled as he kissed me intensely and rolled over on top me.

Author Bio

A. L. Waddington grew up in a small town in Indiana and always had a vivid and overactive imagination. She loves music, playing sports, and can be quite mischievous at times. She has been known to play practical jokes on occasion and is a firm believer in the theory of organized chaos. She has a slight addiction to coffee and when she's not hidden behind her laptop or buried in a book, she can be found exploring the Southwest region of the country and trying to lose that last stubborn ten pounds. She has a master's in military psychology and resides in Arizona with her husband, Eric, their girls, four puppies, and a bearded dragon.

MORE GREAT READS FROM SCARLETT INK PUBLISHING

THE EVE SERIES

Essence, Book 1

Jocelyn Timmons does not believe she is anything special. She's about to find out how wrong she is. Our minds often wander, but can our souls?

Enlightened, Book 2

Can Jocelyn Timmons have it all or will she lose the love of her life instead? Time stands still cause time can't heal.